THE FRONTIERS SAGA
PART 2: ROGUE CASTES
EPISODE 12

A PRICE TOO HIGH
RYK BROWN

CHAPTER ONE

It had not been long since the Aurora had jumped away, leaving the Gunyoki behind to protect the Orswellan system. They'd received word of the Aurora's successful defeat of the Dusahn battle group, shortly after their departure. The fact that four battleships had been destroyed and a dreadnought turned back was difficult to believe on its own. That it had happened more than three hundred light years away, when the Aurora had been here, with them, just over an hour ago, was nearly impossible to fathom.

Under Vol's orders, his weapons and sensors officer was taking a much-needed nap. They had all been sitting in their cockpits for nearly two hours. Normally, that would be considered a short hop for a Gunyoki crew since, over the last month, they had been flying ten-hour patrols nearly every day. Unfortunately, the adrenalin from battle had worn off rather quickly, leaving them all exhausted.

"*You awake?*" Jenna Hayashi asked from nearby Tekka Five.

"Unfortunately," Vol replied, keeping his voice low to avoid waking Isa. "Why aren't you resting?"

"*The way Delan snores?*"

Vol smiled. "I had forgotten."

"*How could you?*" Jenna joked. "*Pretty amazing, isn't it?*"

"His snoring?"

"*The Aurora,*" she corrected. "*Jumping so far, so easily, fighting battles on two fronts within minutes of each other, and defeating four battleships... It boggles the mind.*"

"It is simply technology," Vol assured her, "or, rather, the adept use of it."

"Maybe," Jenna replied, *"but when I think about it, I can't help feeling as if this alliance can accomplish anything."*

"A basic tenet of the Gunyoki code," Vol began.

"I know, many are the okah, few are the yagi."

"It never ceases to amaze me how little regard your generation has for the ways of the Gunyoki."

"It's not that we have no regard," Jenna insisted. *"It's just that times have changed. The ships we fly today are far more advanced than those of your day."*

"It is true, the sixth-generation Gunyoki require far less effort and far less concentration to operate. However, that does not mean that such ways are misplaced. Imagine what you might do with such discipline."

"I'll try to remember that, sir," Jenna promised. *"Might I ask a question?"*

"Of course."

"Are the Orswellan cruisers supposed to be changing course?"

Vol looked over at his tactical display. "No, they are not." He pressed a button on his side console, signaling his weapons officer. "Isa, wake up."

"Huh?" Isa blinked several times, looking around. "What is it?"

"Why are the Orswellan cruisers changing course?"

"What?" Isa studied his sensor display, making adjustments and gathering data on the targets. "They've raised shields, as well," Isa reported. "Uh, they're accelerating."

"I thought their crews abandoned ship?" Jenna asked.

2

"They did," Isa confirmed. "Hey, Delan, are you picking up any life signs?"

"*Negative,*" Delan replied from the back seat of Tekka Five. "*Not on any of them.*"

"*They are heavily automated, right?*" Jenna asked.

"Yes, but..." Vol stopped mid-sentence, unsure.

"But what?" Isa wondered.

"I would not think them able to institute such maneuvers without orders from their crews," Vol explained.

"Uh, they're changing course toward Orswella," Isa reported, "and they're *still* accelerating."

"*This can't be good,*" Jenna decided.

"Prepare to launch a comm-drone," Vol instructed.

* * *

"Jump flash," Kaylah reported from the Aurora's bridge. "Comm-drone."

"Incoming message," Naralena announced from the comm-station at the back of the bridge. "It's from the Falcon. They report the Dusahn dreadnought has jumped another ten light years."

"They didn't even wait for a full charge so they could jump twenty," Jessica commented from the tactical station.

"Maybe they wanted to get as far away from us as fast as possible," Josh suggested. "I mean, we did just kick their asses."

"He's got a point," Jessica said, smiling.

"I assume the dreadnought is still on course for Takara?" Nathan inquired.

"Affirmative," Naralena confirmed. "The Falcon reports they have not changed course. However, they have accelerated back to their standard jump speed."

"Mister Hayes may be correct," Nathan decided.

3

"At this point, they must at least *suspect* that our jump range has changed."

"Or that it was always a lot further than we let on," Jessica added.

This time it was Nathan who smiled. "Yeah, I'd want to get as far away from us as possible, too."

"Another jump flash, Captain," Kaylah interrupted, "and another comm-drone."

Nathan turned to Naralena, awaiting the impending message.

"It's from Tekka One," Naralena announced. "They report that three of the four cruisers have changed course toward Orswella. They have raised their shields and are accelerating."

"Captain," Kaylah said, "those cruisers have antimatter reactors. Only one each, and not as large as those on the Dusahn battleship, but if even *one* of them reaches the planet..."

"What level of damage are we talking about?" Nathan asked, fearing he already knew the answer.

"It depends," Kaylah replied. "If they crash into land, the damage will be severe. Everything within a thousand kilometers will cease to exist, and that's a thousand kilometers in *all* directions, even *toward* the planet's core."

"*That* is a big hole," Josh commented.

"And that's the good scenario," Kaylah continued. "Orswella has some *really* deep oceans. If they crash into one of them and sink all the way to the bottom before their reactors go critical, they could crack open one of the planet's main subsurface lava flows."

"But then, the *people* would survive," Josh said.

Kaylah looked at him, surprised by his ignorance. "Something like that could alter the planet's orbit, screw up its rotation, and send ejecta into low orbit that could be falling back down for decades."

"Did Tekka One transmit target data?" Nathan asked.

"Yes, sir," Naralena replied. "I'm transferring it to Commander Yosef's station."

Kaylah examined the data on her display, running a myriad of calculations. "Assuming they maintain the current rate of acceleration all the way to Orswella, their impact will be directly into the middle of its population center."

"That can't be a coincidence," Nathan decided.

"Oh, my God," Commander Andreola exclaimed, having been silent thus far. "It's another Dusahn booty trap."

"That's *booby* trap," Jessica corrected.

"They're using our *own ships* to punish us," the commander continued, "and it's all my fault."

"Comms, send orders to Tekka One," Nathan instructed. "Destroy all Orswellan ships."

"Aye, sir."

"Captain, without crews to support, our ships will be free to channel *all* available energy to shields," Commander Andreola surmised. "They will be all the harder to destroy."

"How much harder?" Nathan asked.

"By at least fifty percent."

"Man, the Dusahn really did not trust your people, did they," Nathan decided.

"For good reason," the commander replied.

"Captain," Kaylah interrupted, "I'm not sure the Gunyoki *can* take them out in time."

"Jess, is that dreadnought still within single-jump range of Rogen?" Nathan wondered.

"Yes, but barely," Jessica replied. "We have no

way of knowing how much jump energy they have at the moment, though; not without moving the Falcon in a *lot* closer."

"Captain, you have to do something," Commander Andreola insisted.

"We've barely got enough energy to reach Orswella," Nathan told him. "If we jump now, and that dreadnought comes about and jumps to the Rogen system, there will be *two* worlds destroyed instead of one. Damn. If I didn't know better, I'd think they *planned* it this way."

"Captain, my people..."

"The Gunyoki are probably opening fire on your ships as we speak," Nathan interrupted. "Give them a chance."

"Maybe the Glendanon will get there in time," Jessica suggested.

"They're still six hours away," Nathan told her.

* * *

"Whoa!" Vol exclaimed as his shields suddenly lit up from incoming weapons fire. "Just how automated *are* these ships?"

"Why did they even have crews?" Isa added as he routed power to the shields being impacted.

"*This is going to make things more difficult,*" Vol's wingman declared as he followed his leader into the fray.

"Isa, drop a comm-buoy with instructions to all units. Concentrate on the lead ship's midship dorsal shields. High-low, opposite angles, random Alpha Four, odds and evens, in pairs, ten-second engagements, five-second intervals."

"That's awfully tight for forty-eight ships," Isa warned while he typed in the instructions for the comm-buoy.

"That will give each ship a few minutes' rest between engagements," Vol said as their Gunyoki fighter streaked over the top of the lead cruiser, pounding it as they passed. "With any luck, we can all keep our shields strong enough to take out all three ships."

"Comm-buoy away," Isa reported.

Vol pressed the jump button on his flight control stick, instantly escaping the barrage. "Clock?"

"Already started," Isa assured him.

Vol pressed a button on his console, switching his time display to the engagement clock that all the fighters would be using to synchronize their attack runs.

"Why doesn't the Aurora just jump back and take them out?" Isa asked as Vol took their fighter into a long, sweeping turn.

"I'm certain Captain Scott has good reason," Vol replied. "Besides, protection of Orswella is our responsibility. Drop a comm-drone to inform the Aurora that the cruisers' point-defenses are also automated."

"Right away," Isa replied.

Vol pulled his fighter out of the turn, rolling out onto the perfect heading to reengage the lead cruiser, and then glanced up at the clock to time his next attack.

* * *

"Tekka One reports Orswellan cruisers' point-defenses are also automated and have engaged them," Naralena reported. "They are focusing their attack on the lead ship."

"I'm not sure that's the best strategy," Jessica commented. "Those cruisers aren't bunched up.

When the lead one goes, it's not going to take out the other two."

"I think he's just trying to take them out one at a time," Nathan said.

"That's not going to work, either," Kaylah warned. "They can probably take out one, perhaps two, of the cruisers, but there's no way they can take out all three, and it only takes one to destroy the planet."

Nathan thought for a moment. "Comms, send a message to the Falcon. Tell them to discreetly reveal their presence to that dreadnought."

"Aye, sir," Naralena acknowledged.

"Captain?" Jessica queried, feeling the need to question Nathan in Cameron's absence.

"They're not short-jumping in order to put more distance between us and them," Nathan replied. "It doesn't matter if they jump two ten-light-year jumps or a single twenty-light-year jump; it's still the same distance. They're short-jumping to keep their options open."

"You think they plan to jump past us and attack the Rogen system," Jessica surmised.

"To be honest, I don't know," Nathan admitted, "but I'm pretty sure they're up to something."

"So, you're letting them know we're watching them so they *don't* try anything?"

"Something like that."

"What if *they* signaled those cruisers to attack?" Jessica suggested. "They could be trying to force *us* to react."

"That's also a possibility," Nathan admitted, "but I'm betting the cruisers are acting under pre-programmed standing orders, and that dreadnought knows it. They jumped short so when we jump back to Orswella to deal with the cruisers, they can jump back to Rogen and attack."

* * *

"They've got every gun from all three ships targeting us!" Isa exclaimed as Vol jumped their Gunyoki fighter away from the engagement zone. "That's not each ship automatically protecting itself. That's all three ships working together. That's some awfully good automation, I'd say."

"I know," was all Vol was able to say as he brought his ship into a turn toward his next jump point.

"That's three passes with forty-eight ships," Isa continued. "At forty-eight shots per pass, that's *five hundred seventy-six* impacts on the *same damned shield*, and it's *still* at forty percent!"

"It is just a matter of time," Vol insisted.

"Time is not going to do it, Vol," Isa argued. "That's what I'm trying to tell you. Six minutes between passes may seem like an eternity, but it's not enough to keep up with the drain we're experiencing with our *own* shields. We're taking two steps forward and three steps back with each pass. It's only a matter of time until *we* start losing ships."

"Once we defeat the first cruiser, the number of guns on us as we pass will be diminished by a third," Vol replied as he jumped their ship to the next turn point.

"At which point we'll be at least even, yes, but that doesn't increase the rate at which we destroy those cruisers."

"Then we will shorten our cycles and attack with greater frequency."

"Vol, there just isn't enough time," Isa argued. "Even if that works, at least *one* of those cruisers is going to get through. For the sake of all those

9

people, we need to swallow our Gunyoki pride and call for help. We *need* the Aurora."

"That is the math?"

"That is the math," Isa confirmed.

"How much time until impact?"

"Forty-seven minutes until the lead ship impacts the surface."

Vol sighed. "Two, One, I am out of comm-drones. I need you to send word to the Aurora. Inform them that we are unable to destroy the cruisers before they reach the planet. If they are unable to assist, we need to warn the population."

"To what end?" Isa wondered. "There's no time to evacuate them."

"They can at least make peace with their God," Vol said.

There was silence for several seconds.

"*Launching comm-drone,*" his wingman finally acknowledged from Tekka Two.

* * *

"Update from Tekka One," Naralena reported from the Aurora's comm-station. "Commander Kaguchi reports they will be unable to destroy all three ships in time. At least one, possibly two, of the Orswellan cruisers will reach the planet."

"How long?" Nathan asked.

"He estimates forty-seven minutes," Naralena replied, "and the time stamp on the message shows it is two minutes old."

"We have to help them," Kaylah urged.

"I know," Nathan replied calmly.

"What if we send some more Gunyoki or a few Orochi?" Jessica suggested.

"There's no time," Nathan reminded her. "We're

the only ship in the *galaxy* that can jump that far in a *single* jump."

"Captain, is there nothing you can do for my world?" Commander Andreola pleaded.

"I'm not going to let any of your cruisers reach your world, Commander," Nathan promised. "I just have to find a way to do so without putting two other worlds at risk." Nathan tapped his comm-set. "Prechitt, Scott."

"*Go ahead, sir,*" the commander replied over comm-sets.

"How soon can you get your Nighthawks back up?"

"*Seven are refueled and ready now. The other three sustained damage and were lucky to have made it back. What's the mission?*"

"We need to jump back to Orswella, but that dreadnought is still within jump range of Rogen. I need to leave some muscle behind as insurance."

"*I'm flattered, Captain, but we can't take down that dreadnought by ourselves.*"

"What about with the help of two Strikers, twelve Orochi, and fifty Gunyoki?" Nathan asked. "Oh, and the Weatherly, as well."

"*That would certainly help,*" the commander replied, "*assuming we are able to get enough of their shields down.*"

"I'm betting they're not going to jump back; that they're running home with their tail between their legs, but I'd feel better if you could take your working birds back to Rakuen for the time being."

"*We'll be off the deck in five minutes,*" the commander promised.

"Thank you, Commander," Nathan replied, looking to Jessica.

Ryk Brown

"It may sound like a lot, but it's still doubtful they can take that dreadnought down without us," Jessica warned.

"Their forward shields are already down," Nathan reminded her. "That's a start."

"Not much of one," she replied.

"They're running home, I'm certain of it." Nathan turned to face forward again. "Josh, turn us toward Orswella. Loki, plot a jump and stand by."

* * *

Vol pressed the jump button on his flight control stick, but when his fighter came out of the jump, the visual was not what he expected. The lead cruiser was breaking apart, secondary explosions deep within its hull splitting it into multiple sections, and debris spinning away from the doomed vessel. "Finally!" he exclaimed.

"The second cruiser is at two seven, eleven up, three hundred thousand kilometers," Isa reported. "We might have enough time to stop it, but..."

"I don't want to hear it," Vol said, cutting him short as he turned toward the next target. "Drop a comm-buoy, target the second cruiser, forward port shields, left-right, sharp angles, switcheroo, eights and fours, random Zeta Four, plus two."

"Got it," Isa replied.

Vol rolled his fighter out of its turn, adjusted his jump range, and jumped again, coming out only a few hundred meters away from the front of the second cruiser, head-to-head and closing fast. He pressed and held his firing button, sending bolts of plasma energy from the mighty cannons on the front of his port and starboard engine nacelles.

Its guns already pointing forward, the automated Orswellan cruiser opened up on them, lighting up

12

their shields with each impact, their ship bouncing wildly from the blows. So frequent were the impacts, he did not bother looking out his forward window since the flashes only obscured his vision.

His attack lasted only seconds, pitching up and jumping away just before the much larger cruiser blocked his jump line.

"That pass cost us half our shield strength," Isa warned. "We're not going to be able to make many more of those."

"I know," Vol replied as he began his turn.

* * *

Vol's fighter rocked violently as its port shields failed, and several blasts from the cruiser's point-defense cannons impacted its armored hull.

"Port shields are gone!" Isa announced, stating the obvious.

Vol immediately rolled their fighter over, putting their starboard shields toward the third cruiser, which was attempting to defend its partner.

"We've gotta jump," Isa urged.

Vol ignored him, holding his course as he continued to pummel the second cruiser with his own plasma cannons.

"Vol!"

Vol glanced up at his attack timer as it reached eight seconds and pressed the jump button on his flight control stick, instantly transitioning to his escape point. "How bad?"

"Port shields are gone," Isa replied. "We've lost two emitters on the aft quarter."

"Can you isolate them and give us just the forward half of the port shield?" Vol asked as he initiated his turn.

"Yes, but it will be iffy, at best."

"It will have to do."

"Vol, the second cruiser's shields are still over fifty percent, and we've only got fifteen minutes to impact."

"What's your point?"

"We won't survive another head-on pass, but we can draw some of their cannons off the others."

"You mean, attack the third cruiser?"

"If we attack from their stern port quarter, we should be able to get quite a few shots off before they can bring their defenses around. And there won't be anywhere near as many guns on us..."

"...Because the second cruiser won't defend the third while *it* is under attack."

"And the third cruiser will *stop* defending the second one while *it* is under attack," Isa added.

"A simple and elegant solution," Vol admitted. "I am embarrassed I didn't think of it myself."

"That's why there are two seats in this ship," Isa replied.

"You may regret your suggestion," Vol warned as he came out of his turn and pressed the jump button again. Suddenly, the third Orswellan cruiser appeared before him, filling up his forward window. He pressed his firing button, sending streams of red-orange plasma bolts toward the cruiser, lighting up its shields. But the target's shields held, as expected.

Vol continued firing, taking advantage of the few seconds of unchallenged attack their change of tactics had bought them, but that's all it was. The cruiser's top and bottom aft cannons came around quickly, abandoning their defense of the second cruiser in favor of its own defense.

Again, Vol's forward shields lit up with the incoming energy impacts. He yawed his ship to port just enough to protect his weaker port forward shield, while adjusting the angle of his engine nacelles to keep his main cannons on the target. As they passed over the top of the target, he pitched down, again keeping his cannons trained on the enemy ship as he fired continuously. The cruiser's bottom turret was forced to disengage, but the forward topside turret was able to take its place. Vol could no longer maintain a lock with both cannons and was forced to jump away to protect his ship. "I don't suppose we did any damage to them?"

"Maybe a one-percent drop in their aft port shields," Isa replied. "But at least we've kept three guns off everyone else."

"Then, we'd better get back to it," Vol decided as he pulled their ship into a tight, one-hundred-and-eighty-degree turn.

"We can only survive a half dozen passes at the most," Isa reminded him.

"I know."

"I'm just saying..."

"You don't need to," Vol interrupted. "I am well aware that we are fighting a losing battle, but there are several million people on Orswella, and we cannot just sit by and watch them die."

"Even if we die trying?" Isa wondered.

"Even if we die trying," Vol confirmed.

"What about Rakuen?" Isa asked. "We're supposed to defend *them*, aren't we?"

"You mean the Rogen *system*," Vol corrected.

"You know what I mean," Isa insisted.

"We are part of an alliance, now," Vol reminded his friend. "We fight for more than just our *own* people." Vol rolled his ship out of its turn, lining up on their next attack vector. "Trust me, my friend, I have no desire to die, but if I must, I prefer it to be for good reason. Protecting millions is good enough for me."

"Me, as well," Isa assured him.

Vol dialed in the distance for his next jump and then pressed the jump button. Again, his forward window was filled with the third Orswellan cruiser, only a few hundred meters ahead of them and growing larger with each passing millisecond.

Vol opened fire again, sending streams of red-orange plasma into the target's shields, causing them to flash brilliantly with each impact. This time, the enemy's guns were already pointed in their general direction and opened fire within a few seconds of their arrival.

The ship jolted, its back end kicking to the right, causing Vol to slam into the left side of his canopy. Alarms began going off, and red warning lights lit up across his console.

"We just lost our port nacelle!" Isa reported. "The port forward shield couldn't take it!"

"I'm losing lateral control," Vol stated as he struggled to control the ship. Another blast slammed into them, cutting through their port side, just behind their empty missile pod.

"We're hit!" Isa barked as the critical systems alarm began blaring.

"I've lost all maneuvering!" Vol replied. "Drop a mayday marker!"

"Dropping marker!"

"Stand by to eject!" Vol added.

"Marker away!" Isa announced as he reached down for the ejection handle between his legs. "Ready!"

"Eject!" Vol ordered.

There was a rapid series of explosions, and the

canopy flew away from their tumbling fighter. A second later, the cockpit filled with smoke, and Vol's back became warm. He glanced at his console and saw that Isa had ejected, then reached down and pulled his own ejection handle.

Vol felt a sudden slap in the underside of his seat as the ejection thruster blasted him clear of the tumbling Gunyoki fighter. "Isa!" he yelled over comms. "Can you hear me?"

There was nothing but silence.

"ISA!"

The interior of his helmet lit up, filled with yellow and white flashes. Debris streaked silently past him on all sides. He tried to look down but could not get visual confirmation of what he already knew to be true.

"*Tekka One! Tekka One Four! I have your marker! Say your status!*"

"I am uninjured," Vol replied, "but Isa is not answering my hails!"

"*I've got you on sens...*"

Another flash of yellow and white light washed over him. "TOMIDA!"

The ejection thruster stopped, and Vol found himself beginning to rotate slowly on at least two axes. As he came around, he spotted both cruisers, still headed for the planet. In minutes, they would reach the surface, and all life on Orswella would be wiped out.

Vol watched in silence as a Gunyoki fighter jumped in, fired on the lead cruiser, and then jumped out eight seconds later. Four seconds after that, another fighter appeared from an entirely different angle. It, too, fired upon the lead cruiser for eight seconds before jumping away.

From his new vantage point, it seemed an exercise in futility. Tiny little Gunyoki, like toray bugs attacking a vella hog, hoping to kill the beast with a million stings. Possible, but unlikely, at best.

After a few minutes, he tired of the view and, instead, shifted his eyes to the doomed world below. It was smaller than Rakuen, with not even half as much water, but from space, it appeared beautiful in its own right. He wondered how its appearance would change once the cruisers struck it and took a large portion of it away with its antimatter reactors. Ironic that he would now have to witness that which he had been trying to prevent: the death of an entire society and, perhaps, an entire world.

Another brilliant flash appeared, this time from behind him, and this time a different color: bluish white.

A shadow came over him. Vol looked up as a familiar shape passed overhead. No other ship had those curvy lines, almost like that of a beautiful woman.

He watched as the Aurora opened fire on the third cruiser with everything it had: plasma torpedoes, plasma cannons, rail guns, and point-defense weapons. The barrage was terrifying. The trailing cruiser tried to defend itself, but to no avail. Within a few seconds, its aft shields fell to the immense energy being thrown into them, and the back of the cruiser was defenseless.

All of the Aurora's weapons suddenly ceased fire; all of them *except* her forward plasma torpedo cannons. A single wave of four torpedoes, firing in rapid succession, tore open the cruiser's stern, breaching her main drive, as well as her antimatter reactor. The Aurora disappeared in another blue-white flash of light just as the cruiser's antimatter reactor lost containment, consuming what was left of the vessel in a brilliant white ball of light that dissipated within seconds.

Vol wondered how he had been lucky enough to be out of the blast range of the cruiser's antimatter event. Despite surviving the blast, he was certain that he had been bathed in some sort of deadly radiation that would greatly shorten his life, if not kill him in minutes.

Another blue-white flash of light. This time, in the distance and to the right of the remaining cruiser. Again, the Aurora opened fire, pounding the target with everything it had. Again, the target's shields were overwhelmed, and the mighty Aurora's plasma torpedoes tore it apart. The Aurora disappeared, yet again, just as the last Orswellan cruiser was consumed by its own antimatter event.

It was worth it, Vol thought to himself.

* * *

General Telles stood at the edge of the makeshift landing zone as the Ranni shuttle touched down. The side hatch opened, and Captain Scott stepped out, followed by Lieutenant Commander Nash, Commander Andreola, and his daughter.

"Welcome to Orswella, Captain," General Telles greeted.

"How are things?" Nathan asked.

"We believe we have rounded up the majority of the Dusahn combatants," the general said as the group walked toward the building, "but we suspect that many of them may have abandoned their weapons and gone covert."

"How are you going to deal with them?" Nathan wondered as they entered the building.

"For now, we are conducting in-depth surface scans looking for energy signatures that would indicate weapons, but there are many weapons that are undetectable. At some point, we will need to conduct a city-wide search."

"You'll need more than a hundred men," Nathan surmised.

"Far more," the general agreed. "In the meantime, the best we can do is to protect critical infrastructure and assist the people of Orswella in rebuilding their security forces."

"The Orswellan constabulary was never armed," Commander Andreola told the general. "It was never necessary, since the citizenry possesses no weapons."

"The guard had weapons, though," Jessica said.

"Yes, but those were taken from us when the Dusahn took over," the commander explained.

"Can the original officers be reinstated?" Nathan wondered.

"Most would be past their prime by now," the commander warned, "and they would likely fear being targeted by covert Dusahn agents."

"For now, I have instituted martial law, but my men are spread terribly thin," the general said. "We could use something other than cargo shuttles to move teams around more quickly. They require larger landing zones."

"We can give you the Diggers," Nathan told him. "They are still a bit large, but they are armed and definitely smaller than a cargo shuttle."

"Anything would help," General Telles admitted.

"Commander Prechitt was wondering why you haven't availed yourself of the Corinari who have been training with your men," Jessica stated.

"I plan to," General Telles promised, "but for the

time being, it is safer for my men to function without them."

"Why?" Nathan wondered. "At the very least, they could help with the searches."

"No offense to the Corinari, but their very presence will hinder operations at this point. They are fine soldiers, but they lack the willpower and self-discipline to do some of the morally distasteful things that often must be done. For the Ghatazhak to be effective, we must be allowed to *be* Ghatazhak."

"So, you're saying babysitting the Corinari will slow you down," Nathan surmised.

"I am trying very hard *not* to say that," the general corrected.

"Well, once things settle down, I think the Corinari can serve as an effective police force until such time as the Orswellans are able to police themselves," Nathan said.

"That could take some time," General Telles warned. "From what I have gathered, there are currently no political leaders on Orswella."

Nathan looked at Commander Andreola. "Is this true?"

"It is," the commander confirmed. "Orswella's entire political structure was dismantled, and all our politicians were jailed and eventually executed."

"On what charges?" Jessica wondered.

"The Dusahn never offered any explanation," Commander Andreola stated. "Many theorized that they feared them, but I believe they did so to make *us* fear *them*, which, incidentally, *worked*."

"Having a former leader around would speed things up considerably," Nathan commented.

"It will be difficult to find someone willing to put their family at risk," Commander Andreola warned.

General Telles stopped at the door. "Inside are the captains of the cruisers. Perhaps one of them would be willing to lead their people."

"Let's find out," Nathan said, gesturing toward the door.

General Telles opened the door, allowing the others to enter before him.

"Captain Scott," one of the men greeted, standing.

Nathan immediately recognized him. "Captain Yofferst," he replied, offering his hand.

"Marlon," Commander Andreola greeted. "It is good to see you again."

"You, as well, Stethan."

"It is a pleasure to meet you in person, Captain," Nathan said. "I trust your crews were safely evacuated?"

"Yes, from all ships," Captain Yofferst assured him. "Your Ghatazhak were kind enough to ensure that we were *rounded up* safely."

"My apologies, Captain, but it cannot be helped. We must make certain that there are no Dusahn operatives among your ranks."

"I can promise you that no man under my command is Dusahn. Some may have been born under Dusahn rule, but they are *all* Orswellan, born and bred. I am certain my fellow captains can say the same."

"It should be simple enough to verify this via simple DNA tests," Nathan said, "but that will take some time."

"During which your men are stuck guarding mine," Captain Yofferst pointed out. "Perhaps it would be more efficient for them to return to their families until testing can be completed."

"It is necessary to keep them under scrutiny until

we can be certain of their identities," General Telles insisted.

"Every man in the Guard has been fitted with a tracking chip. You can track us all using the Dusahn's own systems."

"We are aware of this," Nathan replied.

"They safely removed mine prior to my mission, here," Commander Andreola told Captain Yofferst.

"General?" Nathan asked, looking to Telles.

"I will need to learn more about this tracking system and verify its capabilities," the general replied. "However, if adequate, it would free up at least two full squads, as well as remove the logistics of feeding and caring for the Orswellan crews."

"I'll get some med-techs down to begin drawing tissue samples for testing," Nathan promised. "Where is this tracking system located?"

"The Dusahn turned all of our constabulary stations into troop stations," Commander Andreola explained. "There are tracking systems in all of them."

"I'm afraid most of them have been destroyed," General Telles commented.

"The master system is in the capitol building," Captain Yofferst said. "It may be possible to connect it to the city's surveillance systems. Perhaps that would suffice?"

"I'll have my people take a look at it," Nathan told him. "In the meantime, I was hoping one of you might volunteer to serve as leader of your people, at least in a temporary capacity. It would be better for all concerned to turn control of your world back over to you as soon as possible."

"I will speak with my fellow captains," Captain Yofferst assured him.

"I'd like to remain with them," Commander Andreola told Nathan. "There is much I can tell them about the Karuzari Alliance. I believe I can be of great help in that regard."

"Good idea," Nathan agreed.

"I only ask that you allow my daughter to return to her residence. I assure you she is no threat."

"I think that can be arranged," Nathan agreed.

"I can see that she gets back to her place safely," Jessica offered. "I've been there before."

"Very well," Nathan agreed. "General?" Nathan added as he headed out the door. He exited the room and took several steps further down the corridor before speaking. "I know you don't like the idea of letting them go, but we need to start off on the right foot with these people. It's going to be difficult enough for them with your scary-looking troops policing the streets with an iron fist."

"I am not opposed to the idea of allowing the Orswellan crews to return to their families, but not until *after* genetic samples have been taken. The commander's tracking chip was easy enough to remove, after all."

"Agreed." Nathan tapped his comm-set. "Aurora, Scott."

"*Aurora, go ahead, sir,*" Naralena replied.

"Patch me through to Doctor Khanna."

"*One moment.*"

"Mind if I take a squad with me, sir?" Jessica asked General Telles.

"A wise precaution," General Telles agreed.

"*Doctor Khanna here.*"

"Doctor, how long would it take to test a tissue sample to determine whether someone is Dusahn or Orswellan?"

"The Dusahn are a mixture of several human subgroups," Doctor Khanna explained, *"so, proving that someone is Dusahn is impossible, at least not without a broad sampling of the current Dusahn gene pool. However, if we can first collect a few dozen samples of Orswellan DNA, we should be able to identify Orswellan ancestry."*

"How accurate will that be?" Nathan asked.

"The more samples of known Orswellan DNA we can collect, the more accurate we can be. With a few dozen samplings, maybe eighty percent accuracy."

"And how long will it take to process each sample?" Nathan wondered.

"Minutes," she replied. *"Doctor Chen sent back a marvelous, portable DNA tester that Doctor Symyri provided."*

"Very well; prepare teams to collect and process the samples of about fifteen hundred people and have them report to the Diggers on the main hangar deck."

"Aye, sir."

"Aurora, Scott."

"Yes, Captain," Naralena replied.

"Doctor Khanna is assembling personnel to report to our location. Use both Diggers to bring them down and tell the Digger crews to pack for a long-term mission on Orswella. They will be attached to the Ghatazhak."

"Aye, sir."

"That should do it," Nathan told General Telles. "The Glendanon will be arriving soon and can provide you with all the support you need. One Gunyoki squadron will also remain in the system, using the Glendanon as their base of operations."

"That will be very helpful," the general agreed.

"In the meantime, I strongly suggest you utilize Commander Andreola as the liaison between yourself and the Orswellan people."

"I agree; the commander appears well suited for the task."

Nathan sighed. "I have to admit; this all went a lot better than I expected."

"There is still much that can go wrong," the general said.

"Don't remind me," Nathan replied as he headed for the exit.

* * *

Tham immediately checked his tactical display the moment he came out of his final jump in the long series that brought his squadron from Rakuen to Orswella. "Dota One, Maigo One," he called over comms. "You awake, Tariq?"

"*Yeah, I'm awake,*" Tariq replied.

"Where's everyone at?"

"*You didn't hear?*"

"We've been in a series jump for the last eight hours," Tham reminded him. "I assume you guys took the system?"

"*We did,*" Tariq confirmed, "*but it cost us.*"

Tham's mood suddenly soured. "How many?"

"*Eleven ships, eighteen souls.*"

Tham scanned the ID tags on all the Gunyoki fighters showing on his display. "Vol?"

"*He's alive,*" Tariq replied. "*Injured, but alive.*"

"We'll take the watch for you, my friend. Take your people home."

"*Gladly, just as soon as everyone is refueled.*"

"Anything we should know?" Tham asked.

"*Only one,*" Tariq replied. "*Keep your guard up at all times.*"

"You think they'll come back?"

"*I have no idea,*" Tariq admitted, "*but if they do, you'll have no warning.*"

"If they do return, we'll make them pay, my friend."

* * *

Commander Kellen watched as the two Contra ships touched down in the park in front of the Orswellan capitol building. "Those are, without a doubt, the most unattractive vessels I have ever laid eyes upon."

"I would offer an argument, but..."

General Telles exchanged glances with his second, Commander Kellen, and then headed toward the two ships as their engines spooled down.

"Sort of reminds me of my first barracks nanny," Commander Kellen decided. "Robust and purpose built."

"The only thing that would make them better is if there were ten of them," the general said.

The forward ramp on the nearest ship deployed, and the crew came walking out.

"Captain," General Telles greeted.

"General," the captain replied, pausing to salute his senior. "I'm Angus Hosick, this is my copilot Lieutenant Erskin, and my gunners, Sergeant Dunson and Corporal Trott."

"Quite the ship," General Telles said with one eyebrow raised and a smirk on his face.

"She's not much to look at," Captain Hosick admitted in his thick Corinairan brogue. "But she can get the job done and take a beating while doing it."

"What are her armaments?" Commander Kellen wondered.

"She's got a mark two plasma torpedo cannon on each side that can launch both fore and aft," Captain Hosick began. "Two manned mark ones with twin-barreled turrets, both on top, one just behind the cockpit where the escape hatch used to be, and one at the back of the cargo bay. Plus, we also added an automated anti-personnel mini-rail gun turret that pops out of the underside of the nose; great for hot LZs. And, of course, countermeasure pods in the back."

General Telles nodded his approval. "What about her hull? Is it shielded?"

"No shields," the captain replied. "Her grav-lift systems would screw them up. They're *really* beefy. She used to be a cargo ship, after all. But her hull *is* heavily armored, so, as long as we don't take a direct hit with a missile, we should be okay. What's the mission, if I might ask?"

"Quick response, troop relocation, patrols," General Telles replied.

"So, an air taxi," the captain surmised.

"Basically, yes. We're trying to protect a few million Orswellans from an unknown number of potential, covert Dusahn agents, with only one hundred men. Our hope is to use your ships to move squads from place to place in rapid fashion and to quickly respond to any threats."

"How hostile is the population?" the leader of the second crew asked as they joined the group. "Busby Orrock," the second captain introduced himself. "This is Lieutenant Westwood, Sergeant Kinney, and Corporal Pattie."

"Gentlemen," the general greeted.

"So far, the population seems happy to be rid of the Dusahn," Commander Kellen said. "However, we have learned from the locals that there are many Orswellans who *were* loyal to the Dusahn. Whether or not they will pose a problem has yet to be determined."

"At the very least, we do not anticipate any truly *hot* LZs," General Telles added.

"Good to know," Captain Orrock said.

"The hours will be long," General Telles warned. "Because there are only two ships, downtime may be difficult."

"We're Corinari, General," Captain Hosick replied. "We may not have seen action in years, but once a Corinari, forever a Corinari."

"Understood, Captain," General Telles replied. "Welcome to Orswella."

* * *

"How is he doing?" Nathan asked Doctor Khanna.

"He was exposed to a considerable amount of gamma radiation. Nanite therapy will take care of it, but he'll be out of commission for a while. To be honest, at his age, I'm surprised he is doing this well."

"If he is anything like Master Koku, it will take more than an antimatter event to take him out of action."

"Well, he may be permanently out of action, at least as a pilot," Doctor Khanna explained. "He has suffered some retinal damage that the nanites may not be able to repair."

Nathan sighed. "Does he know?"

"Yes."

"Can I see him?"

"Of course. One of his pilots is in there with him now."

"Thank you."

Nathan pulled back the curtain to find Tariq standing next to Vol's bed.

"Captain," Vol greeted.

"I just came to see how you were doing."

"I have seen better days, but your physician is taking good care of me. I cannot say that I care for your nanites, though. My insides feel...*itchy*."

"You get used to it," Nathan assured him.

"I should be going," Tariq said. "We have a long journey ahead of us."

"Are you sure you don't want us to give you a lift?" Nathan wondered.

"Thank you, no," Tariq replied. "Those of us who are still able would prefer to return to Rakuen under our own power."

"Understandable," Nathan agreed. "Safe journey."

"To you, as well," Tariq replied. "I will see you back home," he told Vol.

Vol nodded, watching him exit.

"Does he know?" Nathan wondered.

"That my vision has been impaired? I saw no reason to tell him."

"And if you are unable to return to the cockpit?"

"That day would have come, regardless," Vol insisted. "Soon, the Gunyoki's numbers will grow, and I will no longer be able to command them from the cockpit. Perhaps it is best that my vision does not fully recover. It would have been difficult to leave the cockpit for any other reason."

"You remind me of Master Koku," Nathan said.

"I'll take that as a compliment," Vol replied, nodding. "I trust all is well on Orswella?"

"It's getting there," Nathan assured him. "I am sorry that it took us so long to get back."

"There is no need to apologize, Captain. I am

certain you did what you felt was best for all. You have stepped into an entirely new realm. Protecting two systems, three hundred light years apart, while trying to defeat an enemy an equal distance away would seem an impossibility to anyone else."

"It does require a different set of logistics, that's for certain," Nathan replied.

"Considering you just defended one system against all odds while liberating another, I would say that you have done Master Koku proud."

Nathan smiled. "I should be going, as well. We are fully charged again, and it's time we got you home."

"Thank you, Captain," Vol replied.

"No, thank *you*, Commander; you and all your Gunyoki who have given their lives to protect others."

"There is no better way to die," Vol insisted.

Nathan nodded his agreement, then turned and left.

* * *

"You look like hell," Cameron commented as she met Nathan in the corridor outside of the Aurora's command briefing room.

"It's been a long day," Nathan replied with a sigh.

"From what I've heard, you pulled off a miracle."

"More like a series of fortunate events."

"You'll have to tell me all about it after the briefing," Cameron insisted.

"The only thing I'm doing after the briefing is taking a nap."

"After that, then."

"Deal," Nathan agreed, heading into the briefing room.

"Captain on deck!" the guard announced.

"As you were," Nathan insisted before anyone could stand. "Congratulations on a job well done, everyone," he began as he and Cameron took their seats. "Never in a million years did I think we could take out four battleships *and* turn around a *dreadnought*."

"I'm pretty sure the Nighthawks had a lot to do with it," Jessica commented.

"No doubt," Nathan agreed, "which leads me to our first topic. Abby, is there any way we can use the grav-lift technology to give our jump missiles the ability to penetrate shields?"

Abby took a deep breath, letting it out slowly. "We're not even certain *why* they're able to penetrate shields. Theoretically, they *shouldn't* be able to."

"Are you saying it isn't possible?"

"No, but until we know *why*, it's unlikely we'll be able to do much of anything."

"Then, *that's* your priority," Nathan told her. "Figure out *why* the Nighthawks can jump through the Dusahn's shields."

"Yes, sir."

"Why can't we just continue to use the Nighthawks?" Cameron wondered.

"First, they're not ours to use," Nathan explained, "and second, Nighthawks have pilots, missiles don't."

"Understood," Cameron replied.

"Deliza, how hard would it be to equip the Gunyoki with grav-lift systems?" Nathan asked, shifting to the next topic.

"We'll have to figure out how to make space for them, but it shouldn't be *too* difficult from an engineering standpoint. However, the grav-lift systems are controlled by computer algorithms that balance the force exerted by the emitters. Without them, the pilot would not be able to keep the ship level."

"Then, you need to add a control module, as well," Nathan surmised.

"*And* figure out how to integrate it into the Gunyoki's current flight control systems, which, as you know, are quite different from those in a Nighthawk."

"Or any other ship I've ever flown," Nathan agreed. "Give it your best shot. The lack of ability to operate in the atmosphere, or land on the surface, presents both logistical challenges *and* tactical limitations, both of which would be resolved with grav-lift systems."

"We'll do our best, Captain."

"Thank you," Nathan replied, turning to look at Vladimir. "Commander, how long will it take you to install a second long-range jump array?"

"We can begin upgrading the secondary power distribution grid immediately, but we don't have any more emitters at the moment. We don't even have spares," Vladimir explained.

"It will take about a week to fabricate another full set of emitters," Abby added.

"It will take *three* weeks just to upgrade the secondary grid," Vladimir warned, "then *another* week to install the emitters."

"Two weeks, then," Nathan surmised.

"No, *four* weeks," Vladimir corrected.

Nathan looked at him. "Two weeks."

"Yes, sir," Vladimir replied. "Two weeks."

"Lieutenant Commander, what's the current position of the dreadnought?" Nathan asked.

"The dreadnought made its third jump two hours ago," Lieutenant Commander Shinoda replied. "They are still on course for Takara and are now forty light years from the Rogen system, so two max-range

33

jumps. If they decide to turn back now, it will take them six hours to get here, more if they want to arrive with enough jump juice for combat. It's safe to say they are out of quick-strike range."

"The dreadnought, yes, but their gunships and octos could reach us in minutes," Cameron pointed out.

"That dreadnought is the only one I'm worried about," Nathan admitted.

"Do you still want the Strikers and Nighthawks tailing them?" Cameron asked.

"Negative," Nathan replied. "Let's bring them home and give them some downtime."

"I'd advise we keep the Falcon on station," Lieutenant Commander Shinoda suggested, "at least until the next jump."

"Agreed," Nathan replied.

The intercom beeped, interrupting the briefing.

"*Captain, Comms, flash traffic,*" Naralena announced over the intercom.

"Captain, what is it?" Nathan asked.

"*Message from Doctor Chen...*"

Nathan's expression changed in a heartbeat.

"*Your sister is awake, Captain.*"

A wave of relief washed over him. "Did she say anything else?" he asked after a pause.

"*Only that you should come as soon as possible.*"

"Understood," Nathan replied, turning off the intercom.

Everyone in the room could see that their captain had been knocked off his game.

"That's wonderful news," Cameron said.

Nathan looked over at her, frazzled. "I have to go."

"It's eighteen hours to Sanctuary by shuttle," Jessica reminded him.

"Captain, perhaps you should use the Aurora to get there," Abby suggested.

"What?" Nathan asked, confused.

"We need more long jumps to finish calibrating the array," Abby explained. "Might as well make them *useful* jumps."

"The Aurora isn't cleared for entry into Sanctuary space," Jessica pointed out.

"We can jump in just outside of their defense perimeter," Cameron suggested, "then you can shuttle in. The entire trip would take half an hour."

"How far is Sanctuary from Orswella?" Nathan wondered.

"Just over four hundred light years," Cameron replied. "Rogen, Sanctuary, and Orswella form a triangle of sorts, with the leg between Sanctuary and Orswella being the longest. If we wait until we have a full charge before jumping to Sanctuary, it would be about ninety minutes until we'd have enough charge to jump back to either Rogen or Orswella."

"How long until we have a full charge?" Nathan asked.

"Three more hours," Vladimir replied.

"By that time, the dreadnought will have made their next jump," Lieutenant Commander Shinoda added.

Nathan looked around at his officers, overwhelmed by their desire to get him to his sister's side.

"Let us do this for you," Cameron urged.

Nathan nodded. "As soon as we're fully charged," he told Cameron, "and thank you... *All* of you."

CHAPTER TWO

Nathan's eyes popped open at the sound of the intercom's alert beep. Oddly enough, he had no recollection of what he might have been dreaming about. Ever since his memory had been restored, his dreams had been exceptionally vivid, but today... nothing.

He reached over to the nightstand, fumbling for the intercom button in the dark. "Yes," he muttered after finally finding the button.

"*Apologies, Captain,*" Naralena began. "*You left orders to wake you once the jump drive was fully charged.*"

"Of course," Nathan replied. "I'll be there shortly." He sighed, then swung his legs off the side of his bed, sat up, and switched the lights on. A glance at the clock revealed that he had only slept for two hours...in *two days*.

After a groan, he was on his feet, headed for the exit, picking up his uniform jacket as he passed through the living room.

Once through the door and into the corridor, Nathan donned his jacket and ran his hands through his hair in a feeble attempt to tame it.

"Captain on the bridge," the guard at the entrance to the bridge announced as Nathan passed.

Cameron rose from the command chair, turning toward the captain. "Have a nice nap?"

"*Blissful,*" Nathan replied sarcastically. "Update on the dreadnought?"

"The dreadnought has made its fourth jump and is still on course for Takara," Jessica reported from the tactical station. "They are now sixty light years from the Rogen system, and three hundred and sixty-eight light years from Orswella. So, we can safely jump to Sanctuary and still be able to respond in plenty of time, should they turn back."

"Very well," Nathan said, taking his seat. "Mister Sheehan, I assume you have calculated the jump?"

"About ten times, yes," Loki assured him.

"Ten times?"

"It's a long jump."

"Yes, it is. Mister Hayes, take us out of orbit, and put us on course and speed for the jump to Sanctuary."

"Breaking orbit," Josh replied, entering the new course into the ship's helm.

"How's the jump drive looking?" Nathan asked, turning toward Abby at the starboard auxiliary console.

"All systems appear normal," Abby assured him. "The jump to Sanctuary is only two hundred and eighty-seven light years," she added, "not even half our estimated maximum jump distance. You have nothing to worry about."

"Then, why are you here?" Nathan wondered.

"I'd like to gather as much performance data as possible *before* we start production of the next batch of emitters."

"On course and speed for the jump to Sanctuary," Josh reported.

"Very well," Nathan replied. "Let's give Doctor Sorenson some data, shall we?"

"Jumping to Sanctuary," Loki replied as he initiated the jump. "Jump in three......two...... one......jumping."

A blue-white flash of light washed over the bridge.

For a moment, Nathan felt as if the stars on the main view screen had shifted ever so slightly.

"Jump complete," Loki reported. "We are now two light years from Sanctuary."

"Very well," Nathan replied, rising from his chair. "Lieutenant Commander, shall we?" he asked as he headed aft.

"Contact," Kaylah reported, "at the extreme edge of our sensor range...and we've just been scanned."

"ID?" Nathan asked, stopping in his tracks.

"It's small...it just jumped."

"Toward us?" Cameron wondered.

"Negative," Kaylah replied. "It was on a perpendicular course. If anything, it jumped *past* us."

"If it had been jumping toward us, we'd know it," Cameron stated.

"Raise shields," Nathan ordered, uncertainty in his tone.

"Raising shields," Jessica replied as she activated the Aurora's shields, as well as her point-defenses. "I'm activating point-defenses, as well."

"I'm pretty sure it was just a drone," Kaylah assured him. "It was *way* too small to... New contacts! Missiles! Eight of them inbound! Ten seconds!"

"General quarters!" Nathan ordered, heading back to his command chair.

"Point-defenses!" Cameron ordered, stepping over next to Jessica at the tactical station.

"General quarters, aye," Naralena acknowledged.

The trim lighting around the bridge suddenly changed to red as the general quarter's klaxons sounded throughout the ship.

"Five seconds!" Kaylah updated.

"Escape jump!" Nathan added.

"Changing course!" Josh reported.

"Four..."

"Point-defenses engaged!" Jessica announced.

"Three..."

"Two down...three...four..."

"Two..."

"Escape jump ready!"

"One..."

"Jump!"

Nathan braced himself as blue-white light swept across the bridge.

"Jump complete!" Loki reported with a sigh of relief.

"Position?" Nathan asked.

"We jumped five light minutes along a course only a few degrees off our original heading," Loki reported.

"So, we're *closer* to Sanctuary," Nathan surmised.

"New contact!" Kaylah announced. "Another drone, same as before. We're being scanned."

"Helm, turn to one five seven, up twenty relative, on my mark," Nathan ordered. "Stand by to jump four light hours."

"Drone has jumped!" Kaylah warned.

"Mark!" Nathan barked.

"Turning to one five seven, up twenty," Josh acknowledged.

"Ship is at general quarters," Naralena reported.

"What the hell is going on?" Cameron wondered.

"On course one five seven, up twenty," Josh announced.

"More missiles!" Kaylah warned. "Eight again! Ten seconds!"

"Jump is ready," Loki reported.

"Jump!" Nathan ordered.

Ryk Brown

"Jumping in three..." Loki began.

"Five seconds," Kaylah updated.

"As soon as we come out of the jump..."

"Two..."

"...Turn to zero five two, down forty..." Nathan continued.

"One..."

"And jump seven light hours," Nathan instructed.

"Jumping!"

Again, the flash of the jump washed across the bridge.

"Turning to zero five two, down forty," Josh acknowledged.

"Preparing to jump seven light hours," Loki added.

"New contact!"

"Let me guess, another drone," Nathan surmised.

"Affirmative!" Kaylah confirmed. "We're being scanned."

"Jump!" Nathan ordered.

"I haven't finished my turn," Josh warned.

"Jump now!" Nathan insisted.

"Snap jump!" Loki acknowledged.

Another wave of blue-white light swept across the bridge.

"Two light years!" Nathan ordered. "Jump when ready! Helm! Hard to port and pitch down."

"Jump is ready!" Loki reported.

"Another drone!" Kaylah warned.

"Jump us in the turn!" Nathan ordered. "Now, now, now!"

"Jumping!"

Yet again, the jump flash filled the Aurora's bridge.

"Jump complete," Loki reported. "Next jump?"

"Position?"

"Three point eight five light years outside of the Sanctuary system," Loki reported. "Half a light year from our original approach course and headed *away*."

"Kaylah?" Nathan asked.

"Nothing yet," she replied.

"Helm, turn to zero two four, up fifty. As soon as you finish your turn, jump us ahead one light year."

"Turning to zero two four, up fifty," Josh acknowledged.

"Dialing up a single-light-year jump," Loki added.

"Still no contacts?" Nathan asked.

"Negative, sir," Kaylah replied.

Nathan breathed a sigh of relief, settling back into his command chair.

"Somebody want to tell me what the hell just happened?" Cameron demanded.

"I think someone upgraded their defense systems," Nathan replied.

"And expanded their 'shoot first' perimeter," Jessica added.

"That was *Sanctuary* firing at us?" Cameron realized.

"It would appear so," Nathan confirmed.

"Turn complete," Josh reported.

"Jumping ahead one light year," Loki added.

"How did we not know about this?" Cameron wondered. "Don't they have a mailing list, or something?"

"I don't know," Nathan said as he rose from his command chair. "But I intend to find out," he added as he headed aft. "Keep the ship out of their 'shoot first' perimeter. Move further out if needed."

"If we move, how are you going to find us?" Cameron asked.

"Use the transponder-equipped comm-drone that we use to communicate with our people on Sanctuary," Nathan suggested. "They don't seem to be shooting *those* down...*yet.*"

Cameron watched as Nathan and Jessica left the bridge. "Not exactly the welcome I'd expected."

* * *

"Turn complete," Lieutenant Teison reported from the Falcon's pilot's seat. "Ready for the zag?"

"Zag jump is ready," Ensign Lassen replied.

"Why are we even doing this?" Sergeant Nama wondered. "We already tipped our hand."

"That was two jumps ago," the lieutenant reminded him.

"Yeah, but they've got to know we're still monitoring them."

"Probably, but if we don't keep *acting* like we're trying to be covert, then they'll *know* we allowed ourselves to be detected on purpose."

"Still don't think it matters."

"Do you have something better to do?" the lieutenant wondered.

"Yeah, sleep," the sergeant replied.

"Zag jump point coming up," Ensign Lassen warned.

The lieutenant turned his attention back to his flight displays.

"We should just drop a passive sensor buoy on them, and back off and take a nap," the sergeant complained.

"Jumping," the lieutenant announced as he jumped the ship back across the dreadnought's flight path, passing behind them from the target's right to left. "Jump complete."

"Scanning."

"You know, I'm with Riko," Ensign Lassen stated as he began preparing for the next jump. "I'm more than ready for some rack time."

"We all are," the lieutenant agreed. "One of the Strikers should be here to relieve us soon."

"Uh, LT?" the sergeant called from the sensor station behind the flight deck.

"What, you need to pee again, Sarge?"

"Where are the gunships?"

"Aren't they flanking the dreadnought?" the lieutenant replied.

"They *were*, but now they're gone."

"How many of them?"

"All of them," the sergeant replied.

"They were just there," Ensign Lassen insisted.

"And now they're not," Sergeant Nama replied.

"I'm changing course to fall back," the lieutenant decided. "We need to look at their old light, to see if we can determine when those gunships left and which way they were headed."

"We've only got a light minute of lag time," Sergeant Nama said. "That's an awfully tight window to time a covert departure jump."

"Not if they've been watching *us* the entire time," the lieutenant surmised.

Sergeant Nama sighed. "I guess a nap is out of the question."

* * *

"Have you considered the possibility that we're no longer *welcome* on Sanctuary?" Jessica asked as they prepared the shuttle for departure.

"We were *way* outside the two-light-year perimeter," Nathan insisted. "There's no reason they should be firing on ships *that* far out."

"Maybe they're not used to ships as large as the Aurora?" Jessica suggested.

"Flight, Shuttle Four, ready for departure, starboard side," Nathan reported over comms. "That's possible, but they don't have the *right* to fire on a ship so far outside their own heliopause, even if it is on a course for their system."

"Shuttle Four, Flight. Clear for immediate starboard departure. Safe journey."

"Shuttle Four, departing," Nathan reported as he activated the departure function of the shuttle's auto-flight system.

The modified Ranni shuttle rose slowly off the Aurora's starboard flight deck and began to move forward, accelerating at a comfortable rate. As it cleared the forward opening of the starboard flight deck, its rate of acceleration increased sharply.

"Something has changed on Sanctuary, and *you're* going to find out what that is," Nathan continued as the shuttle sped past the nose of the Aurora.

"Me?"

"Yes, you," Nathan replied as their shuttle cleared the Aurora's nose, and he initiated a gentle turn to port. "I'm going to be busy, remember?"

"Let's just hope they don't try to shoot us down, as well," Jessica said.

"Cam sent a comm-drone to Sanctuary informing them of the Aurora's position and intent, and that we were on our way," Nathan explained. "That should do it."

"Unless they're mad at us, for some reason," Jessica countered. "Have you considered the possibility that Miri *isn't* really awake and that the message was meant to *lure* us here?"

Nathan looked over at her, one eyebrow raised. "How do you live that way?"

"What way?"

"Always suspicious of everyone."

"How do you not?" Jessica asked.

"I'm suspicious when it's warranted," Nathan insisted. "You see that?" he added, pointing at the jump system display.

"An escape jump?" Jessica realized. "Then, you're *not* hopeless."

"Someone long ago said, 'Trust but verify,'" Nathan told her. "I prefer, 'Trust, but be prepared for deceit.'"

"So, 'Hope for the best, but prepare for the worst?'"

"Something like that," Nathan replied. "Are you ready?"

"Transponder is active," she replied.

"Here we go," Nathan announced as he pressed the jump button. The blue-white jump flash washed over the Ranni shuttle's cramped cockpit, and the conglomeration of modules clinging to what little remained of the asteroid known as Sanctuary appeared a few kilometers ahead of them.

"Sanctuary, Alliance Shuttle," Nathan called over comms.

"*Alliance Shuttle, Sanctuary Approach. Identify your occupants and intentions,*" a rather stern voice demanded.

"Alliance Shuttle, two occupants. Captain Nathan Scott and Lieutenant Commander Jessica Nash," Nathan replied. "Care to explain why you attacked my ship when we were well outside your defense perimeter?"

After a pause, the controller responded. "*Alliance Shuttle, you are cleared to bay one five seven. Set your auto-flight systems to accept remote automated approach."*

"Alliance shuttle, setting auto-flight to accept remote automated approach," Nathan acknowledged, setting his auto-flight system appropriately. A moment later, the auto-flight system indicated it was under the control of Sanctuary's automated approach control systems, and the shuttle began a slight turn to port, pitching down to pass under the station.

"I guess that question was above her pay grade," Jessica commented.

* * *

"Jump complete," Robert's copilot announced. "We are now at the rendezvous point."

"Any contacts, Kas?" Robert asked over his comm-set.

"*Negative.*"

"Keep an eye out."

"*Always,*" his sensor officer replied.

Robert looked concerned. "They were supposed to be here, waiting for us."

"We're about a minute early," Sasha reminded him.

"They've been out here for more than twenty hours, now," Robert said.

"We've flown missions more than three times that long."

"We've got bunks, a galley, and a head," Robert replied. "They've been using pee tubes in their pressure suits the entire time."

"Yeah, it does help to be able to use a normal toilet," Sasha agreed. "Maybe we should jump forward and take a peek at the target ourselves, just to be sure?"

"If they don't show up in a few minutes, we just might," Robert agreed.

"Maybe they just lost track of time?" Renny suggested as he climbed up onto the flight deck.

"Teison doesn't *lose track of time,*" Sasha insisted. "You get the port heat exchanger problem resolved?"

"It was just a stuck flow control valve," the engineer replied. "Easier than I thought. Shouldn't give us any more trouble."

"That's what you said about the inertial dampeners in the galley," Robert commented, a smirk on his face.

"Yeah," Sasha agreed. "I put a lot of work into that lasagna, only to have it tossed across the room during a routine braking maneuver."

"I'm still finding bits of it in the ventilation filters," Renny admitted.

"*New contact,*" Kasma reported over comm-sets.

"Please tell me it's the Falcon," Robert begged. "I've had enough excitement for one day."

"*It's the Falcon,*" Kasma assured him.

"*Striker One, Falcon,*" Lieutenant Teison called over comms.

"Falcon, Striker One," Robert replied. "You guys ready for a nap, Jasser?"

"*I wish,*" the lieutenant said. "*We've got a problem.*"

"I don't like problems," Robert said.

"*Sorry, but all four gunships disappeared about thirty minutes ago,*" the lieutenant began. "*We fell back a few light minutes to find their departure light and got a course heading and speed, and some more bad news.*"

"You suck at storytelling, Jasser," Robert commented.

"*Twenty octos quick-launched from the dreadnought and went with them. They're headed back on a reciprocal heading.*"

"So, they're heading for either Rogen or Orswella," Robert surmised.

"How the hell did they slip out without you noticing right away?" Sasha asked.

"*They must have been tracking us for some time,*" Lieutenant Teison replied. "*Probably since we made ourselves detectable on purpose.*"

"Whose bright idea was that?" Robert wondered.

"*Captain Scott's,*" the lieutenant replied.

"I should have known," Robert groaned. "How long since you broke contact from the dreadnought?"

"*If they were tracking us tracking them, then we missed our last track in their eyes.*"

"Okay, get back on schedule, and don't miss another track jump. I want you to look like they either missed your last contact, or you had a problem. We'll update command and then look for the gunships and octos."

"*Got it.*"

"And whatever you do, don't lose that dreadnought," Robert insisted. "This could be a diversion to help them lose their tail."

"*We won't lose them,*" the lieutenant assured him. "*Falcon, out.*"

"*I'm receiving the Falcon's tracking data now,*" Kasma reported.

"Copy it to a comm-drone, along with a situation update, and send it to command," Robert instructed. "We're going on the hunt."

* * *

Jessica entered Sanctuary's security

headquarters, pausing a moment after closing the door to look around.

"Lieutenant Commander Nash," the officer at the counter greeted. "Are you going to be civil, or shall I put the tactical response team on alert?"

Jessica smiled. "I promise to behave," she told him, crossing her heart.

"I'll give them a heads up, just in case," the officer stated.

"I was hoping to speak with Commander Manderon."

"About?" the officer wondered, still suspicious.

"About why the hell..." Jessica paused and took a deep breath, starting over. "Our ship was fired upon by *your* defense grid while it was *well* outside your defense perimeter." Again, she took a breath, realizing she needed to take it down another notch. "I was hoping to learn *why* this happened so we can *avoid* such an occurrence in the future."

"I'll see if the commander is available," the officer promised.

"Thank you," Jessica replied. She watched as the officer walked across to the back of the room and entered the commander's office. A moment later, he came back out and signaled to Jessica.

Jessica went around the end of the counter and across the room, passing the officer and entering the commander's office.

"Lieutenant Commander Nash," Commander Manderon greeted, rising from her chair behind her desk. "I understand your ship was fired upon?"

"Yes, while well outside your defense perimeter," Jessica replied, shaking the commander's hand. "I was hoping to learn why so we can avoid wasting your missiles in the future."

Commander Manderon laughed. "As confident as always, I'll give you that." The commander took her seat again. "We have recently upgraded our defense systems," she explained as she called up a report on her desktop view screen. "If *this* is your ship, then it violated our secondary defense perimeter."

"I thought you only had the one defense perimeter," Jessica said, "and that *is* our ship."

"We have two defense perimeters," the commander said. "One for standard vessels approaching this station and another for *warships* approaching this station."

"Is this something new?"

"The decision was made months ago but only put into effect last week."

"Why weren't we notified?" Jessica wondered.

"We are not in the habit of advertising our defense tactics to armed vessels," the commander explained, leaning back in her chair. "Had you approached in the approved manner, in an *authorized* vessel equipped with a properly issued transponder, there would not have been a problem."

"So, it's *our* fault?"

"Precisely."

"And if a ship just happens to wander by, with no ill intent, you just shoot it down without warning?"

"An *armed* vessel, yes," the commander replied adamantly. "We learned long ago that it was the only way to ensure our survival."

"With no concern for the people you are shooting at."

"We only fire without warning at warships violating our secondary perimeter. Such vessels usually have the ability to defend themselves."

"And if they don't?"

"Then, they may want to be more careful about which systems they enter," the commander insisted. "Sanctuary's location, as well as our aggressive defense posture, are well known throughout the sector, as well as neighboring sectors."

"What if an unarmed ship enters your secondary perimeter?" Jessica wondered. "Do you shoot them down, as well?"

"Unarmed ships are given a warning and an opportunity to change course," the commander explained. "If they fail to comply, then, yes, they will be destroyed, as well."

"And I assume that *all* ships entering your *primary* defense perimeter without a proper transponder are still dealt with in the same aggressive fashion."

"Indeed."

Jessica leaned back in her chair, as well, sighing. "How do you guys stay in business if you shoot down potential customers?"

"To *stay in business*, one must first continue to *exist*," the commander replied.

"Okay, so, what do we have to do in order to bring the Aurora into your system?" Jessica wondered. "Get one of those transponders for it?"

"Warships are not allowed in the Sanctuary system," the commander insisted.

"But we're the good guys," Jessica said, half joking.

"Very few people believe they are the *bad guys*," the commander countered.

"Good point." Jessica sighed. "So, how far out do we have to stay in order to avoid being fired upon by you?"

"Four light years," the commander told her. "However, if you intend on remaining within six light years of this station for any length of time, I would strongly suggest that you let us know, to avoid any... *misunderstandings.*"

"I'll pass that on to my captain," Jessica replied.

The commander tapped her interface a few times, then handed Jessica a small data chip.

"What's this?" Jessica wondered, taking the chip from her.

"A bill for the missiles your ship destroyed. The cost exceeds the limits of your house account and, therefore, must be paid in full immediately."

"Nice," Jessica replied, rising to depart.

Commander Manderon stood again. "Thank you for not using my staff for hand-to-hand combat practice this time, Lieutenant Commander."

"Right."

* * *

Nathan stood at the observation window, staring at his sleeping sister on the other side.

"Sorry to keep you waiting, Captain," Doctor Chen apologized as she entered the observation room. "I was reviewing Miri's latest scans."

"I thought she was awake," Nathan said.

"She was, but we chose to sedate her until you got here."

"I don't understand."

"She was in a state of panic, which is not uncommon after suffering such a sudden and severe trauma. She didn't recognize where she was or who the people were around her. I imagine the entire *room* looked unfamiliar, compared to what she would have expected on Earth."

"I should have been here," Nathan said.

"We still would have sedated her. The only

difference is that we've kept her sedated a bit longer, that's all."

"Does this mean she's going to recover?"

"Well, the fact that she actually woke is *huge*. I mean, it's practically a *miracle*, at least by our medical standards. Doctor Symyri doesn't seem to be as impressed by it, though, but then again, the medical care here is *far* more advanced than ours."

"Is she going to be okay?" Nathan asked again, rephrasing the question.

"It's too early to tell. Physiologically, her body is recovering, as is her brain, which suffered plenty of trauma on its own. What we don't know is how much that trauma has affected her *mind*."

"Her *mind*?"

"Doctor Symyri likes to use that term to refer to memory, personality, emotional patterns—the essence of the person. Sort of what we tend to call a person's *soul*. He prefers the term *mind*, since it doesn't carry any spiritual undertones and, therefore, does not risk offense."

"When will we know?" Nathan asked.

"Well, waking her will help us assess her condition, but again, we wanted to wait until *you* were here; someone she recognizes and trusts."

"What about her kids?" Nathan wondered. "Do they know she's woken up?"

"We haven't informed anyone but you, as of yet," Doctor Chen replied. "She's going to have questions: what happened, the status of her father, her kids, her sisters..."

"So, I get to tell her," Nathan said, sighing.

"Unfortunately, yes." Doctor Chen observed him for a moment. "You can take all the time you need,

Captain. Her being in a sedated state is not harming her progress in any way."

"*Time*, as usual, is the one thing I don't have."

"I trust everything is okay on the Aurora?"

"Yes," Nathan replied. "Actually, she's only a few light years away, at the moment."

"You brought the *Aurora here*?"

"She was the fastest way to *get* here," Nathan said. Noticing the confused look on her face, he added, "She's got a five-hundred-light-year jump range now."

"My God, that's incredible!"

"That's Abby," he stated, looking back at his sister. "So, when do you plan to wake her?"

"She's only being kept sedated by the use of a toeren drip," Doctor Chen explained. "The moment we cut it off, she'll wake again, so as soon as you're ready."

Nathan took a deep breath, letting it out slowly. "I don't think I'll ever be *ready*," he admitted, "but I guess I should get it over with before something else comes up."

"That bad?"

"It's been a rough couple of days."

"Maybe you'd like to rest up a bit, first?" she asked, noticing the bags under his eyes.

"I can't take the chance," Nathan insisted. "Her children need to see her, and more importantly, she needs to see them."

"I couldn't agree more," Doctor Chen replied. "Shall we, then?"

"Lead the way," he told her.

* * *

Cameron came out of the captain's ready room

onto the bridge, pausing at the comm-station. "Anything new?"

"Message from Lieutenant Commander Nash," Naralena replied. "They arrived safely. She spoke with the head of security on Sanctuary. Apparently, they shoot first and ask questions later with any ships that violate their primary perimeter without a transponder and any *warship* that comes within four light years."

"How friendly of them."

"Oh, and they're billing us for the wasted missiles."

"Only the ones that detonated, I assume," Cameron said.

Naralena smiled. "The lieutenant commander did not specify."

"Of course not." Cameron moved forward to the tactical station. "Lieutenant Kitweil."

"Threat board is clear, Captain," the lieutenant reported. "A small cargo ship did jump in about half a light year to starboard a few minutes ago, but they jumped away seconds later. Probably just a quick transition point on their way into Sanctuary."

"Any ID on it?"

"Nothing *we've* ever seen before, that's for sure," the lieutenant replied.

"I imagine that's not too surprising, considering we've never been in this part of the galaxy."

"Kind of exciting, when you think of it," the young lieutenant said. "I mean, I signed up expecting to patrol the Sol sector. Now, I find myself about fifteen hundred light years away from there." He shook his head in disbelief. "I'm going to have some amazing stories to tell my kids someday."

"Indeed, you will, Lieutenant," Cameron agreed.

"How far out do you think they go?" the lieutenant wondered.

"They?"

"Other human civilizations."

"Well, the average speed of most ships back then was five to ten times the speed of light, so, technically, they could be as far out as nine thousand light years."

"Incredible," he exclaimed. "You think we'll ever make contact with them all again? I mean, most of them probably don't even know the Earth recovered and that we're back out in space again."

"I think that, someday, someone will attempt to make contact with all the lost colonies of Earth. It only makes sense to do so."

"It just seems so impossible," the lieutenant said. "I mean, *nine thousand light years.*"

"The oceans that separated the continents of Earth once seemed just as vast until technology closed the gap," Cameron told him. "In the same way, the jump drive will close the interstellar gaps, as well. Someday, we'll be able to jump across the galaxy as easily as we now jump across a light year."

"You really think so?"

"I know so, Lieutenant," Cameron assured him, patting him on the back.

"My father felt the same way," Abby said, overhearing the conversation from the auxiliary station. "That very thought is what drove him."

"Contact," Ensign Ingram reported from the sensor station. "Comm-drone."

"It's from Rogen Command," Naralena reported.

"This can't be good news," Cameron said.

"Relay from the Falcon via Striker One and Rogen Command. Four Dusahn gunships and twenty octos broke off from the dreadnought at its last layover point. They departed on a reciprocal course. Captain Nash ordered the Falcon to continue trailing the dreadnought in case they, too, reverse their course. Striker One is now searching for the gunships and octos. Striker Two has been dispatched to assist in the search, and Rogen Command has sent Konay squadron *and* the Nighthawks to back up the Falcon and serve as a fast-attack force."

"I assume they've alerted the Orswellan system."

"The same message was sent to them, as well," Naralena assured her.

"Very well," Cameron replied. "Forward the message to Lieutenant Commander Nash."

"Yes, sir."

Cameron turned and headed forward. "Ensign Taub, plot jumps to both Rogen and Orswella, just in case."

* * *

Nathan sat beside Miri, her hand in his, studying her face. She looked so serene, completely different than the last time he had seen her: bruised, swollen, and suffering.

"She doesn't look like she was ever injured," he said in a near whisper.

"She can't hear you," Doctor Chen told him. "Besides being a paralytic, toeren blocks all sensory input."

"How long will it take for her to wake, once you discontinue the medication?" Nathan asked.

"Less than a minute," Doctor Chen explained. "For her, it will be as if she has awakened from a good night's sleep. She will be fully coherent almost immediately, assuming she has not suffered any permanent brain damage."

"How will I know?"

"It will take considerable testing to be certain, but I suspect you'll be able to tell right away if she's still all there."

"What do I do if she isn't?" Nathan wondered.

"How about we tackle that question if and when it comes up," Doctor Chen suggested. "Are you ready?"

"Yes."

"I'll discontinue the drip and then step back into the observation room so as not to confuse her further. If anything goes wrong, I am seconds away."

"Understood," Nathan replied, putting both his hands on his sister's face.

Doctor Chen pressed some buttons on the control console over Miri's bed and then exited the room.

Nathan watched his sister's face. After half a minute, Miri's eyes fluttered a bit and then slowly began to open. Her expression was peaceful, at first, then fear and confusion began to take hold again.

"It's alright, Miri," Nathan told her, squeezing her hand. "It's me, Nathan. I'm right here."

Miri's eyes darted about, taking in the unfamiliar room and all the strange equipment around her; her face full of abject terror until she saw her baby brother. "Nathan?"

Nathan smiled. "It's me, sis."

Miri's fear began to subside, but she still appeared confused. "Where am I?"

"It's a long story, but you're safe."

"Where are my..."

"They're fine," Nathan assured her. "They're close by, in fact."

Her fear finally subsided. "What happened to me?"

"There was a bomb," Nathan began, his voice breaking. He froze, unsure of what to say next.

"Dad?"

Nathan closed his eyes, trying to hold back his tears. He had blocked the death of his father and all of his sisters from his mind for two months now, not allowing himself to cry, but now...

"Oh, God," Miri said, tears forming. Then, the memory hit her: her entire family standing on the stage behind their father. "Oh, God," she repeated, the tears now flowing more freely. "All of them?"

Nathan leaned forward, sobbing as he put his arms around the only family he had left.

* * *

"I have spoken to several people," Commander Andreola told General Telles. "They are certain the Dusahn regularly dress some of their people in Orswellan clothing in order to observe our people covertly."

"Are they *absolutely* certain of this?" the general asked.

"Several persons have stated that they have seen the same individual in both Dusahn uniform and then in Orswellan clothing, on two different days."

"Perhaps they were simply off duty," General Telles suggested.

"The Dusahn are never *off duty*," Commander Andreola insisted. "The only time they were out of uniform was when they were bathing or spying on my people."

"That does not bode well," the general decided. "If they were already conducting covert monitoring operations, then at least some of their people would have the experience required to operate as covert agents after the Dusahn were defeated. They may have even had *plans* to do so."

"Just like they rigged our ships to turn against

our own world, should we abandon them," the commander surmised.

"Precisely. With a little training and a bit of equipment, a few men can do considerable damage, especially to such a centralized society."

"General," a voice called from the doorway.

"Yes, Sergeant," the general replied.

Sergeant Spira entered the room, handing a data pad to the general.

General Telles read the message on the data pad, a concerned look coming over his face.

"What is it?" Commander Andreola wondered, noticing the uncharacteristic change in the general's expression.

"It seems that four gunships and twenty octo-fighters have separated from the dreadnought and could be headed here."

"*Could* be?"

"While their departure course was in the opposite direction of their parent vessel, the ships have yet to be found. Until they are, their true destination cannot be known."

"You believe they are coming here?" Commander Andreola surmised.

"I have insufficient information upon which to base an opinion," General Telles replied. "However, I *do* believe we should assume that they are, indeed, on their way to Orswella and take appropriate precautions." The general turned to Sergeant Spira. "Has the Glendanon been notified?"

"The message was relayed through the Glendanon, sir. The Gunyoki have been alerted, as well."

"Very well," the general replied. "Alert me immediately of anything further."

"Yes, sir."

"What do we do?" Commander Andreola asked.

"Your people once fought a war with a neighboring world, did they not?"

"Yes, but..."

"Did your people build any shelters, in case of attack?"

"Yes, but they were decommissioned after the war ended. The Dusahn turned them into detention and interrogation facilities for dissidents."

"Are there still dissidents in captivity?" the general wondered.

"The last of them were executed more than a decade ago," the commander assured him.

"Then, the facilities are no longer in use."

"I assume so," the commander replied.

"Then, perhaps they could be used as shelters once again," the general suggested. "Can you show them to me?"

"Of course," the commander replied.

* * *

Nathan walked down the corridor of their suite on Sanctuary. The hour was late, and all but a few had retired for the evening. He removed his jacket, laying it over the back of one of the dining room chairs to his left as he headed through the entryway into the main living area.

"*Out here,*" Jessica called from the balcony.

Nathan walked across the living room out onto the balcony where Jessica, Marcus, and Lieutenant Rezhik were sitting around a table, enjoying the view. "The simulation really is breathtaking, isn't it," Nathan commented as he joined them.

"You can even smell the ocean," Jessica said.

"How are the kids doing?" Marcus asked.

"Neli's going to have a hard time getting them to

sleep, that's for certain," Nathan commented, taking a seat next to Jessica.

"It's been a long time since they've looked happy," Marcus said.

"They would've curled up next to their mother in her bed, had I let them," Nathan replied. "I expect you guys are going to be spending a lot of time at Symyri's medical center."

"Not like we weren't already," Marcus chuckled. "They've been visiting their mother twice a day since we got here."

"Captain, I believe Mister Taggart has made a local contact that could be of interest," Lieutenant Rezhik reported.

"Oh, really?"

"Kind of a strange, little guy who goes by the name of Gunwant Vout," Marcus explained. "He works for some big company called SilTek as a technology scout."

"A technology scout?" Jessica asked.

"He trolls the markets, looking for technologies that his company can make a profit from. I met him in the tech markets. I've had lunch with him a few times."

"What's this guy like?" Nathan wondered.

"Like I said, he's a strange, little guy. He acts like he's a nobody, but I get the feeling he's better connected than he lets on. After our first meeting, he checked us out and had us pretty much pegged. I tried to convince him otherwise, but I doubt he bought it."

"Did you check him out?" Jessica asked the lieutenant.

"I did," Lieutenant Rezhik replied. "As thoroughly as possible, which is not much, I'm afraid. As Mister

Taggart suspects, he has considerable influence on this station. Most likely due to the fact that he represents SilTek."

"SilTek?" Nathan said. "That sounds familiar."

"Apparently they are one of the largest companies in the entire quadrant," the lieutenant explained.

"They make the AIs that the Sugali fighters use," Marcus added. "That seems to be their thing—AIs, robotics, automation."

"They also make defense systems," Lieutenant Rezhik pointed out. "They have recently upgraded the detection and defense capabilities of this station, which, as best I can tell, is the reason they have so much influence here."

"Interesting food, too," Marcus said.

"Do they make weapons?" Jessica wondered.

"Only defensive ones," Lieutenant Rezhik insisted. "Mister Vout claims that SilTek refuses to make offensive weapons for reasons of self-preservation."

"Best way to defeat an enemy is to take out their weapons supplier," Jessica said.

"And you think they have something that can help us?" Nathan wondered.

"From what Gunwy has told me, their automated fabrication systems make ours look like a joke," Marcus said. "They crank shit out ten times faster than we can."

"Sounds like a good ally," Nathan decided.

"I got the impression that SilTek is not interested in becoming anyone's ally," Lieutenant Rezhik stated.

"Maybe they just need a little convincing," Nathan replied. He looked over at Marcus. "You think you can arrange a meeting for me?"

"As long as you're buyin', I'm pretty sure Gunwy

will hear you out," Marcus replied. "That guy loves to eat."

"Set it up, then," Nathan instructed.

"For tonight?"

"Better make it for lunch tomorrow," Nathan decided. "I'm way overdue for some *real* sleep."

"There are extra rooms available here," Lieutenant Rezhik suggested. "They are quite comfortable."

"I'd love to take advantage of them," Nathan assured the lieutenant, "but we need to get back to the Aurora."

Marcus looked confused. "There's no way you'll make it back in time for lunch tomorrow if you go all the way back to the Aurora."

"The Aurora's only four light years away," Jessica explained.

"I was not aware that the Aurora's jump drive was operational again," Lieutenant Rezhik stated, "but are you not putting the Rogen system at risk by bringing her all the way out here?"

"Oh, it's working again," Jessica said with a smile.

"*And* she's got a five-hundred-light-year jump range," Nathan added, also smiling.

"Impressive," the lieutenant congratulated.

"*Impressive?*" Marcus exclaimed. "That's downright *amazing!* Jesus, Cap'n, you know what we could've done with a range like that on the *Seiiki?*"

"The thought *had* crossed my mind," Nathan admitted, rising from his seat. "Set up the meeting, Marcus."

"You got it, Cap'n," Marcus replied.

"If you'll excuse me, gentlemen, my rack is calling my name," Nathan stated, heading for the exit with Jessica rising to follow.

Marcus sighed as he watched them depart. "Five hundred fucking light years. Can you imagine that?"

Lieutenant Rezhik cast a puzzled look at Marcus. "Yes, I can."

* * *

"Jump complete," Pip announced from the copilot's seat of Striker Two.

"*Starting scans,*" Jela reported over comm-sets from the sensor station.

"This is the last scan point before we reach the Rogen system," Pip said. "If we don't find anything here..."

"Then, that means they're headed for the Orswellan system," Gil said, finishing his copilot's thought.

* * *

"Welcome back, Captain," Cameron greeted as Nathan and Jessica stepped out of their shuttle. "How is Miri?"

"She is awake," Nathan replied.

"Then, she is going to be okay?"

"It's too soon to be sure, but it looks pretty good."

"How are the kids?"

"Happier than hell to hear their mother's voice again," Nathan said. "Any word from the Strikers?"

"Nothing yet," Cameron replied, falling in beside them as they headed across the hangar deck toward the forward hatch. "Did you find out why they attacked us?"

"Seems they've upgraded their defense systems," Jessica explained. "Their new perimeter is four light years. Oh, and they don't like warships anywhere near them."

"Good to know," Cameron replied. "Shall I set course back to Rogen?"

"Not yet," Nathan replied. "It seems Marcus has made contact with a potential ally. The same people who upgraded Sanctuary's defense systems. I've asked him to arrange a meeting for noon tomorrow."

"Don't you think we should head back?" Cameron asked, "All things considered."

"We're still within single jump range of both systems," Nathan reminded her.

"Yes, which means we can easily jump back for the meeting."

"If we jump back to Orswella now, and the attack occurs in the Rogen system, we won't have enough energy to jump from Orswella to Rogen to help them, at least not for a few hours," Nathan explained. "The same is true if we jump to Rogen, and they attack Orswella."

"We don't know that they *will* attack *either one*," Cameron pointed out. "Besides, the Weatherly and the Gunyoki can handle four gunships and twenty octos."

"Probably, but better not to take the risk," Nathan insisted as he stepped through the hatch into the central corridor.

"If they *are* going to attack, it should happen in a few hours," Cameron said.

"Let's hope not," Nathan replied. "I really need some sleep."

CHAPTER THREE

"How's it lookin', Leta?" Talisha inquired as she finished entering the next jump in their search grid.

"*I am not detecting any contacts.*"

"Kishor?" Talisha called over comms.

Twenty seconds later, her wingman replied. "*Nothing.*"

"On to the next grid," Talisha told him.

"*It would be more effective if there was more distance between us and Razor Four,*" Leta suggested.

"We have to fly the grid pattern we were assigned," Talisha replied.

"*Razor Four copies.*"

Talisha activated her jump drive, jumping her Sugali fighter ahead two light minutes.

"*Beginning new scan,*" Leta reported.

"We're practically there," Talisha said in frustration, checking her tactical display to ensure that Razor Four had also jumped.

"*Orswella is still ninety-two light years away. Based on the known jump range of both the Dusahn gunships and octo-fighters, they still have nine point two jumps remaining to complete their journey, assuming Orswella is their destination.*"

"So, ten minutes, then," Talisha said. "Like I said..."

"*I have detected several ships,*" Leta interrupted. "*Bearing one four seven by zero three five up relative, range of one point two seven light minutes. Profile indicates four Dusahn gunships and twenty octo-fighters, on course for Orswella.*"

"Razor Four, Razor Three," Talisha called over comms. "I've got them at one four seven, zero three five up, one point two seven light minutes, on course for Orswella. I'm staying on them and sending you their track data. You jump to Striker One's location and relay word, then rendezvous with me at grid... Four Seven Bravo."

"*Contacts are jumping,*" Leta added.

"Damn it," she cursed. "I hate comms lag. Remind me to get us some jump comm-drones when we get back."

Finally, her wingman confirmed her message. "*Razor Four copies your contact. Have received track data. Will jump to Striker One for relay, then rendezvous with you at Four Seven Bravo. Don't lose them, Tali.*"

"Oh, I don't plan to," she said to herself as she pressed her jump button.

"*Contact!*" Striker One's sensor officer reported over comm-sets.

"Tell me it's the Dusahn," Robert begged.

"*Negative,*" Kasma replied. "*Nighthawk.*"

"*Striker One, Razor Four. We found them at Four Five Alpha!*" Ensign Tellor reported over comms. "*They're headed for Orswella! Talisha is maintaining contact. She instructed me to relay the contact to you and then meet her back at grid Four Seven Bravo!*"

"I'm getting his tracking data," Robert's copilot announced.

Robert studied the tactical display as the icon appeared along with course and speed data. "Christ, they're less than ninety light years from Orswella." Robert tapped his comm-set. "Razor Four, Striker One. We're out of jump comm-drones. You warn the Nighthawks, and I'll relay to Striker Two."

"*What about Razor Three?*" Ensign Tellor asked. "*I was supposed to rendezvous with her.*"

"We'll meet her at Four Seven Bravo *after* we tell Striker Two, so they can send a comm-drone to Rogen Command. Tell the Nighthawks to go to Five Zero Charlie and wait for orders. If they don't receive instructions by..." Robert glanced at the clock, "... by zero five one four, they are to jump to Orswella to defend."

"*Understood,*" Ensign Tellor replied.

"*Razor Four has jumped away,*" Kasma reported.

"Orswella is only going to get a one or two-minute warning," Sasha advised.

"Can't be helped," Robert replied as he changed course. He quickly selected a new jump distance and pressed his jump button.

"Jump complete," Sasha reported.

"Give me a heading for grid Five Zero Charlie," Robert ordered.

"*Striker Two, dead ahead, three hundred kilometers and closing,*" his sensor officer added.

"Heading on your display," Sasha assured him.

"Two, One," Robert called over comms as he turned toward the rendezvous point. "Razor Three has located the gunships and octos. They're headed for Orswella. We're transmitting the track data to you now. I'm out of jump comm-drones. Please tell me you have some."

"*One,*" Gil replied.

"Notify Rogen Command, then go to rally point Five Zero Charlie and meet up with the Nighthawks. If no further by zero five one four, all forces at rally point jump to Orswella to defend."

"*Got it,*" Gil replied. "*Where are you going?*"

"I'm going to hook up with Razor Three at grid Four

Seven Bravo. We've got better sensors than she does, and we can follow the Dusahn more accurately."

"*See you at Five Zero Charlie*," Gil replied.

"See you there," Robert told him, pressing his jump button.

———————————

Commander Isaro began his watch at Rogen Defense Command in the usual manner: a report from the outgoing officer of the watch, a review of the communications log sheet, and a strong cup of bolka tea.

"Officer of the Watch!" the communications officer called. "Flash traffic from Striker Two!"

"Message reads?"

"They have located the Dusahn assault force. They are headed for Orswella and were eighty-two light years out at the time of the message."

The commander glanced up at the clock. "That was two minutes ago," he said to himself. "Alert the Aurora via jump comm-drone," the commander ordered. "Also, alert General Telles on Orswella," he added as he picked up a comm-handset and pressed a direct-channel select button. "Gunyoki Command, Officer of the Watch, Rogen Defense Command. Set alert status two."

"*Alert status two, aye*," the officer at Gunyoki command replied.

"Oversight officers, recommend all missiles at alert status two," the commander continued. "Confirm."

"Neramese confirms missile alert status two."

"Rakuen confirms missile alert status two."

"MDO," the commander barked. "Set missiles to alert status two."

"All missiles to alert status two," the missile defense officer acknowledged.

"Jump comm-drones have been dispatched to the Aurora and to Orswella," the communications officer reported.

"Very well," the commander replied, picking up his mug of tea and taking a sip.

"Alert two is a bit aggressive, don't you think?" the Rakuen oversight officer asked, half under his breath.

"It took them nearly an hour and a half to locate that assault force," Commander Isaro replied. "What if that dreadnought launched *forty* octos, and the Falcon only spotted *twenty* of them departing?"

"Good point."

———————

"You got 'em, Tee?" Ensign Tellor asked.

"*Razors One and Two; bearing two nine four; three point five degrees down relative; range of ten thousand five hundred and eight kilometers and closing,*" Razor Four's AI reported.

"Put us on a heading for the next group," the ensign ordered as he pressed his transmit button. "Razor One, Razor Four!"

"*Go for One,*" Commander Prechitt replied over comms.

"Positive contact, sir!" Ensign Tellor reported. "On course for Orswella! Grid Four Five Alpha! All Razors are to rally at grid Five Zero Charlie! If no further by zero five one four, all units are to jump to Orswella to defend!"

"*Understood,*" the commander replied. "*Where are you headed next, Ensign?*"

"Teri?" the ensign asked his AI.

"*Razors Seven and Eight,*" his AI replied, "*at grid Six One Delta.*"

"Grid Six One Delta, sir," the ensign told the commander. "Razors Seven and Eight."

"*Five and Six are on my way to the rally point,*" the commander replied. "*I'll notify them to save you time.*"

"Sounds like a plan, sir," the ensign replied as he moved his thumb to the jump button. "See you there!"

"*CO, Comms,*" Sergeant Spira called over the general's comm-set.

"Go ahead, Sergeant."

"*Flash traffic from Rogen Command. The missing Dusahn assault force has been located. They are on their way here. ETA: seven minutes. Rogen Command has sent word to the Aurora, but she is currently near the Sanctuary system.*"

"Understood," the general replied.

"What is it?" Commander Andreola asked, unable to read the general's expression.

"Four Dusahn gunships and twenty octo-fighters will be attacking this world in less than seven minutes."

Commander Andreola's eyes widened. "You must activate the alert system."

"Will your people even know what to do?"

"The elder portion will remember," Commander Andreola insisted. "The rest will turn on their view screens to see what's going on the moment they hear the warning sirens. We can *tell* them where to go."

"*You* will tell them where to go," General Telles insisted.

"Me?"

"You are one of them," the general explained. "It will be better coming from one of their own."

"What do I say?" the commander wondered.

"I will tell you what to say," the general assured him as he headed for the makeshift command center down the corridor. "We must move quickly."

"*Digger One, Command,*" Sergeant Czarny called over comms.

"Go for Digger One," Lieutenant Erskin replied from Digger One's copilot's seat.

"*Pick up One Red Alpha at LZ Echo One Four, and Two Blue Bravo at LZ Echo Two Five. Relocate both to shelter Alpha, and report on final to destination.*"

"Roger that," the lieutenant replied. "En route to Echo One Four."

"*Oh, and don't be surprised if air-raid sirens go off in the next thirty seconds. We've got bandits six minutes out, so be ready for incoming.*"

"Digger One copies," the lieutenant replied, exchanging glances with his pilot.

"Fletch, Mac?" Captain Hosick called over his comm-set. "Bad guys in six. Be ready for a wild ride."

"*Maigo One, Command,*" Sergeant Spira called over comms.

"Command, go for Maigo One," Tham replied while adjusting himself in the pilot's seat of his Gunyoki fighter as it orbited high above Orswella.

"*Bandits inbound,*" the sergeant reported. "*Four Dusahn gunships and twenty octos. ETA five-plus.*"

"Understood," Tham replied.

"That's *twenty-four* ships," his systems officer exclaimed from behind. "The octos, alone, will be a handful."

Ryk Brown

"Maigo Leader to all Gunyoki," Tham called over comms. "Four gunships and twenty octos are five minutes out, and we're all that stands between them and Orswella. The gunships will go straight for surface-bombardment runs, and the octos will fly cover. They'll be using hit-and-jump tactics, so if you have a shot, don't hesitate. One through Twelve will attack the gunships. Thirteen through Twenty-four will attack the octos."

"*What about backup?*" one of the other pilots wondered. "*Surely, they don't expect us to hold off that many ships...*"

"I'm sure backup will arrive shortly," Tham assured his squadron, "but the first few minutes will be up to us. Everybody takes the gunships first, then we split forces."

"*This ought to be fun,*" another pilot commented.

"What about the Aurora?" Gento asked from the backseat.

"She's in the Sanctuary system," Tham replied. "I'm sure she'll get here as quickly as possible."

———

"*I have a new contact,*" Leta reported.

"A straggler?" Talisha wondered, quickly counting the icons on her sensor display.

"*Negative. It is a Cobra gunship. Twenty kilometers to starboard, paralleling our course.*"

"*Razor Three, Striker One,*" Robert called over Talisha's helmet comms.

Talisha breathed a sigh of relief. "Go for Razor Three."

"*I've got everyone rallying at Five Zero Charlie. I'll move them all to Five One Alpha and ambush the targets when they arrive. You jump in behind them and attack from the rear,*" Robert instructed.

74

"Understood," Talisha replied.

———————

Air-raid sirens, that many people didn't even know existed, began to wail in the lavender sunset.

Like most Orswellans who were born after the Dusahn had invaded their world, Marli Ayers went straight for her view screen in the living room where, to her surprise, she was met with her father's face.

"Attention, people of Orswella. I am Commander Stethan Andreola of the Orswellan Guard. There is a small, Dusahn attack force headed our way. All who are able should head to the nearest public shelter. Those who cannot, should shelter in place. I urge you to hurry, as the attack will come in minutes. We will thwart this punitive action by the Dusahn, but there may be more damage incurred. Again, if you can get to a shelter, do so with great haste. If unable, shelter in place. Help one another, and we will get through this, together."

As she headed for the door, Marli decided to have her last name changed to Andreola.

* * *

Cameron came out of the ready room as she periodically did during the night shift. "Do you ever sleep?" she asked Naralena, surprised to still see her on duty.

"Ensign Orin wasn't feeling well," Naralena replied. "And I could ask the same about you."

"I've never been much of a sleeper," Cameron admitted. "Five, maybe six hours at the most."

"I used to be the same way. After returning to Volon, I swear, I was sleeping ten hours a day for months."

"Sounds blissful," Cameron admitted. "I've always been jealous of those who could sleep that long. I seem to function best when I'm slightly sleep deprived."

"Contact," Ensign Ingram reported from the Aurora's sensor station. "Comm-drone."

"Incoming message," Naralena added. "Flash traffic from Rogen Command. They have located the Dusahn assault force. They are headed for Orswella."

"ETA?"

"Based on the time stamp, two to three minutes, maximum."

"General quarters," Cameron instructed.

"General quarters, aye," Naralena acknowledged.

"Ensign Taub," Cameron continued as the accent lighting on the Aurora's bridge changed from blue to red, "plot a single jump to Orswella, five hundred thousand kilometers out. Helm, turn to as soon as you have a heading."

"Plotting a single jump to Orswella, five-hundred-thousand-kilometer entry point," the navigator replied.

"Turning toward Orswella and accelerating," the helmsman reported.

"General quarters, general quarters," Naralena announced over the ship-wide loudspeakers and intercom panels. "All hands to action stations."

* * *

"Jump complete," Sasha reported from Striker One's copilot seat. "We are now at grid point Five Zero Alpha."

"Let me know when everyone has arrived, Kas," Robert instructed over his comm-set.

"*Two is already in position on the far side of the grid,*" Kasma replied.

"Turn to one zero five, down eleven," Sasha instructed.

"Coming left to one zero five, down eleven," Robert replied. "Two, One, you got the back door, Gil?"

"*One, Two, we'll fry their asses,*" Captain Roselle replied over comms.

"*Razors One, Seven, Nine, and Ten have jumped into position,*" Kas reported. "*Three, Four, and Six are on the opposite side.*"

"And the trap is set," Robert stated as he finished his turn. "Be ready, people."

"*Multiple contacts!*" Jela reported over comm-sets. "*Gunships and octos; four and twenty! Transferring target data to you!*"

"They're dead ahead, three hundred and seventeen thousand clicks," Gil's copilot reported. "Attack jump is ready."

"Not yet," Gil insisted. "Bobby attacks first; gets their eyes forward. Just a few more seconds."

"*Dusahn forces have arrived,*" Commander Prechitt's AI reported.

The commander glanced at his tactical display as he adjusted his jump range.

"*Striker One is attacking,*" Max added.

"Here we go," he said over comms. "Alpha Razors, attacking."

Commander Prechitt pressed his jump button, instantly transitioning his ship a few hundred thousand kilometers, coming out less than a kilometer from the left-most octo-fighter in the formation. On either side of him, jump flashes appeared, indicating that the other three ships in his formation had joined the attack.

He pressed his firing trigger, holding it down, sending repetitive bolts of plasma energy streaking out from both sides of his Nighthawk's double nose. A split second later, his wingman joined in, sending his own stream of destructive plasma energy into the same octo the commander was targeting. The octo's shields flashed repeatedly as it tried to protect the target, but within seconds, it failed, allowing the plasma energy to reach the octo's hull.

The first octo exploded, followed by the second octo directly behind it, which had been targeted by Razors Nine and Ten.

"*I got one!*" Lieutenant Cristos exclaimed.

"*Whattaya mean, you got one?*" Ensign Siena argued.

Only five seconds after the attack had begun, those who were being attacked retaliated. The red-orange weapons fire, barreling toward the group of Dusahn ships from every direction, was met with an overwhelming amount of red energy weapons fire, lashing out at their attackers.

Commander Prechitt's shields lit up, flashing repeatedly and rocking his fighter as the incoming fire found his ship.

"*Forward shields down to sixty percent and falling quickly,*" Max warned.

"Damn!" Gil cursed as his plasma torpedoes tore through the first Dusahn fighter. "Those octos are willing to die to protect those gunships!"

"We got another!" his copilot exclaimed as an additional octo-fighter exploded in front of them.

Their own shields suddenly lit up as the enemy returned fire.

"Damn!" Gil cursed, his Cobra gunship shaking violently from the incoming weapons fire.

"*I got one!*" Cayle yelled with excitement from the port gunner's turret.

"Jesus!" Pip exclaimed. "Forward shields are already down twenty percent."

"*I'm counting thirty-seven different streams of incoming fire!*" Jela reported from Striker Two's sensor station.

"Christ!" Gil exclaimed. "There are nine of us attacking! How many damned guns do those bastards have?"

"Shields are down to fifty percent!" Pip warned. "We gotta jump, Gil!"

"Damn right, we do," Gil agreed, pitching up to jump clear.

"Holy crap!" Talisha exclaimed as the enemy ships retaliated.

"*What a shitshow!*" her wingman added.

Talisha's shields lit up as red, orange, and green bolts of energy flew in all directions, her Nighthawk rocking with the impacts.

"*Look at all the lights!*" Ensign Patyk said from Razor Six. "*It looks like Christmas!*"

"*Shields are down to thirty-seven percent and falling,*" Leta warned.

The octo Talisha had been attacking suddenly broke in half, with the back section exploding a second later.

"YES!" she exclaimed. "I got one!"

"*I got one, too!*" her wingman exclaimed as an explosion to Talisha's right lit up her cockpit.

"*Shields are down to twenty percent and falling,*" Leta warned. "*Recommend immediate escape jump.*"

"I'm outta here!" Talisha announced, pressing her jump button.

———————

"Ignore the octos and target the gunships!" Robert instructed as he jumped back into the fray.

Striker One dove between two Dusahn octo-fighters, taking a beating on both sides as they passed. As soon as they cleared the fighters, the gunships on the other side opened up on them, pounding their forward shields with bright orange pulses from their plasma cannon turrets.

Robert and Sasha held on tightly as their ship rocked, and their cockpit flashed bright orange with each impact against their shields.

"Shields down to thirty percent!" Sasha warned.

"*Gunships are turning!*" Kasma reported over comm-sets. "*They're splitting up!*"

"They're going to jump," Robert realized. A moment later, all four gunships disappeared behind bright, blue-white flashes of light. "Range!" Robert barked.

"*Best guess: two light years!*" his sensor officer replied.

"*Octos are jumping!*" one of the Nighthawk pilots reported.

Robert peered out the side window as octo-fighters also began disappearing behind flashes of blue-white light. "Striker One to all units!" he called over comms as he changed his jump range to two light years. "Targets are jumping," he added as icons began disappearing from his tactical display. "I'm going after gunship one. Gil, go after two. Nighthawks, chase the rest."

"*What about the octos?*" Talisha asked.

"To hell with the octos," Robert replied. "The octos can't attack Orswella! The gunships can!" he explained as he pressed his jump button.

"Shit!" Gil cursed as the gunship slipped from his sites. "I almost had him!"

"Turn to two seven five, up eight," his copilot instructed.

"Give me a range, Jela," Gil instructed as he rolled his gunship into a tight turn to port.

"*One point eight!*" his sensor officer replied.

"You sure?"

"*No.*"

"At least you're honest," Gil commented as he rolled out of his turn and pitched up a few degrees. "Eyes open, everyone," he added, pressing his jump button.

"Deshi, you and I are going after Gunship Three," Commander Prechitt ordered over comms.

"*Target course is one eight seven, twenty up relative,*" Max reported.

"*I'm with you, Commander,*" his wingman replied.

"Cristos, Siena, go after Gunship Four," the commander ordered as he rolled into his turn and began pitching up.

"*Gotcha, Chief,*" the pilot of Razor Nine replied.

"*Estimated jump range of target is two point five light years,*" Max added.

"Two point five," the commander confirmed, more out of habit than necessity. "You with me?"

"*I'm with you, boss,*" Deshi promised.

"*What about us?*" Talisha asked.

"You three go after the octos," the commander instructed.

"*Got it.*"

"Guns free, Max," the commander ordered as

he reached for his jump button. "You see him, you shoot him."

"*Guns free, confirmed,*" Max replied.

* * *

The lights in Nathan's quarters switched on as the intercom next to his bed beeped three times in rapid succession. At the same time, the trim lighting turned red, and the general quarters klaxon sounded in the corridor.

Nathan's eyes snapped open, still dreary and bloodshot. He sat up on the edge of his bed and tapped the intercom before speaking. "Report?" he inquired as he pulled on his boots.

"*Nighthawks found the gunships and octos,*" Cameron replied. "*They're five minutes away from Orswella. Ship is preparing for the jump, now.*"

"On my way," Nathan replied, grabbing his comm-set from the bedside table.

* * *

"*Got 'em!*" Kasma announced. "*Two one zero, ten down, eight hundred thousand clicks!*"

Robert immediately turned his gunship to its new heading while adjusting his jump range.

"*They jumped!*" his sensor officer added.

"How far?" Robert demanded.

"*Best guess...one point five light years.*"

Robert readjusted his jump range as he rolled out of his turn.

"That light is two point six seconds old," his copilot warned.

"I know," Robert replied as he pressed his jump button.

"Jump complete," Sasha announced.

"*Scanning,*" Kasma reported over comm-sets.

"Old light, same course and speed, he baby-jumped! Maybe thirty light minutes!"

"He's trying to shake us," Robert decided, dialing up a thirty-light-minute jump and pressing the jump button. "Scan again!"

"He's turning," Kasma announced, *"and accelerating!"*

"I need a course," Robert reminded him.

"He's still turning..."

"Which way?"

"To starboard! He's pitching up, as well!"

"Crap! He's jamming!" Kasma reported. *"New course! Three two five, eighteen up! Fuck! I lost him!"*

"Did he jump?" Robert asked.

"He must have!"

"How far?"

"I don't know!" Kasma replied. *"He was masking his jump!"*

"Damn it!" Robert cursed as he dialed up another jump.

"What are you doing?" Sasha asked.

"Best guess," Robert replied as he made another turn.

"But you're turning off the target's course."

"His last turn was away from Orswella," Robert said. "No way he's aborting. He's just trying to fool us into looking in the wrong direction."

"You have no way of knowing where he is now."

"If I try, I may fail," Robert replied. "If I don't try, I'll definitely fail." He pressed the button, jumping his gunship ahead one light year. "Start scanning, Kas. All directions, all ranges."

"Scanning," Kasma replied.

Robert could tell by his sensor officer's tone that it was a useless endeavor.

"What now?" Sasha asked.

"We scan for one minute, and then we jump to Orswella," Robert replied with a sigh. "What else *can* we do?"

A brilliant, blue-white flash of light appeared less than one hundred kilometers above Orswella, revealing a single Dusahn gunship. Within a few seconds of its arrival, the ship rolled over, bringing its guns toward the planet, and opened fire on the surface below. Bright orange bolts of plasma leapt from the gunship's barrels, streaking toward the undefended Orswellans below.

Another flash of blue-white light revealed a second gunship, followed by eight more, smaller, flashes announcing their escort fighters. The second gunship also rolled over and opened fire on the planet below as the octo-fighters spread out to better defend the gunships against any attackers.

The warning sirens on Orswella had been sounding for three minutes when the first strike came. Orange bolts of energy slammed into buildings and plowed through rooftops, the pressure waves blowing them apart from the inside out.

People in the streets screamed and scattered in all directions, panic overwhelming the city in the blink of an eye. One, two, three, four impacts at a time, followed by a few seconds of nothing but screams and the sounds of crumbling structures, and air-raid sirens. Then, the process repeated. One, two, three, four shots blowing apart everything they rained down upon. More screams, more panic, more smoke, more fire...then, the process repeated again.

Thirty seconds after the bombardment began, the

rain of fire doubled in its intensity and frequency. There was nowhere to run, nowhere to hide. For the people who had not yet reached the shelters, all they could do was pray they would be spared.

———————

"Jump complete," Pip reported from Striker Two's copilot seat.

"*Multiple bandits!*" Jela reported over comm-sets. "*Two gunships and eight octos!*"

"Where they at, Jela?" Gil inquired.

"*I'll give you three guesses,*" his sensor officer replied.

Gil glanced at his tactical display, then immediately turned toward Orswella and touched his jump button again, instantly transitioning from their arrival point, a few million kilometers from Orswella, to low orbit twenty kilometers behind the attackers. "I've got 'em...dead ahead, twenty clicks," Gil reported as he dialed up a nineteen-kilometer jump.

"*Gunyoki are maneuvering to attack,*" Jela warned. "*From the target's starboard side, forty-five degrees high.*"

"Let me know when the Gunyoki jump in," Gil instructed. "That way, their guns will be on the Gunyoki instead of us."

"*New contacts,*" his sensor officer reported.

"Two more gunships," Pip added, examining the tactical display. "Four octos, ten clicks behind us."

"*New contacts are opening fire on the planet,*" Jela reported. "*Gunyoki are jumping.*"

"Here we go," Gil said, pressing the jump button.

———————

Two Dusahn gunships and eight octo-fighters appeared directly in front of Tham's eyes as his

Gunyoki fighter came out of its attack jump. He immediately pressed the firing trigger on his flight control stick, sending red-orange pulses of plasma energy from the main guns, on the front of his port and starboard engines, toward the nearest gunship. "I'm on the lead gunship!" he announced as he continued to fire. "Gento, target anyone who turns to attack us!"

"No shit," Gento replied, locking their gun turrets on the two octos already turning toward them.

"*I'm on the second gunship!*" Kio reported over comms as he began his attack.

"Joay! Kio! On me!" Tham called over comms as he continued his attack on the lead gunship. "Kaori! Udo! On Ki! Everyone else on the octos!"

"New contacts!" Gento warned. "Gunships, octos, and Striker Two!"

"Striker Two! Maigo Leader! Target the gunships! We'll deal with the octos!"

"Striker Two is jumping!" Gento reported. "They're on their asses!"

"*Striker Two is on the gunships!*" Gil reported over comms.

"New plan!" Tham announced. "All Gunyoki find an octo and dance!"

* * *

Nathan left his quarters and entered the corridor just as Josh, Loki, and Kaylah jogged past him on their way to the bridge. Alarms still sounded, and the red warning lights pulsed all along the corridor as Nathan fell in behind his staff, following them to the bridge.

Nathan passed through the entrance airlock and onto the bridge.

"Captain on the bridge!" the guard at the door announced as his captain passed.

"Report," Nathan beckoned as he moved toward the command chair at the center of the bridge.

"I've ordered a course change toward Orswella," Cameron replied as she rose from the command chair and stepped aside. "According to the last message, we should have two minutes before the Dusahn reach Orswella. Waiting for the ship to reach general quarters before jumping."

"Ship is on course for Orswella," Josh reported as he replaced the C-shift helmsman and took his seat.

"Jump is plotted and ready," Loki confirmed, also taking his seat.

"All weapons are charged and ready," Jessica added, stepping up to the tactical console after having just entered the bridge.

"All compartments report general quarters," Naralena reported from the comm-station.

The general quarters alarm ceased, and the red warning lights at the bridge entrance stopped flashing.

"Shields up," Nathan ordered as he stood in front of the Aurora's command chair.

"Raising all shields," Jessica acknowledged.

"Mister Sheehan," Nathan called as he took his seat, "jump us to Orswella."

"Aye, sir," Loki replied. "Jumping in three......two......one......"

* * *

"Holy crap!" Sasha exclaimed as Striker One came out of their jump. Before them was the planet Orswella. In orbit above it, a battle had already begun. Twenty-four Gunyoki and one Cobra gunship were attacking Dusahn octos and gunships.

"*About time you got here, Bobby,*" Gil called over comms. "*Half the Gunyoki are veering for the group ten clicks back, to your port. Put the hurt on those goddamned gunships, and see if you can get them to stop pummeling the surface!*"

"We're on it," Robert replied. "Kas, is everyone here?"

"*I count four gunships and twelve octos,*" the sensor officer replied.

"What about the Nighthawks?" Robert wondered.

"*Not on my scope.*"

"Keep an eye out for them," Robert instructed as he turned toward the two gunships to port and pressed his jump button.

A split second later, two Dusahn gunships and four octo-fighters filled his front windows. Robert pressed the firing button on his flight control stick, sending four plasma torpedoes racing toward the lead gunship, lighting up its port shields. He held the trigger down, sending wave after wave of torpedoes, but the gunship's shields held. "Damn, they've got good shields," he complained, firing incessantly.

"*Octos have a bead on us!*" Kasma reported.

Striker One's shields lit up as incoming fire from the Dusahn octos slammed into them, the ship shaking violently with each impact.

"Shields are down to eighty percent," Sasha warned. "We can't take more than a few seconds of this!"

"*Contacts!*" Kasma called over comm-sets. "*Nighthawks!*"

———

Commander Prechitt turned his Nighthawk fighter toward the octos attacking Striker One the moment he came out of his jump.

"Four Dusahn octos are attacking Striker One," Max reported. *"Striker One is maintaining their attack, but their shields will give out before their target's shields fail."*

Commander Prechitt glanced at his tactical display as more Nighthawks came out of their jumps around him. "Razors!" he called over comms. "Attack the four octos attacking Striker One!" he ordered as he dialed up a micro-jump and pressed his jump button. Suddenly, the battle was less than a kilometer away from him, dead ahead. He angled his fighter slightly left, putting his targeting sites on the nearest octo. "Max, weapons free on all octos. Only shoot at what you can hit."

"I always do," Max replied, locking the Nighthawk's turrets on the two nearest octo-fighters.

Commander Prechitt opened fire, sending bolts of energy streaking toward the nearest octo. The enemy fighter's shields flashed as the bolts of energy slammed into them. The octo immediately turned away from his pursuit of Striker One, coming around quickly toward the commander. Just as he came around, the enemy fighter disappeared in a blue-white flash.

Four more blue-white flashes followed as the rest of the octos, and then the gunship, jumped away.

"Targets have jumped," Max reported.

"No kidding," the commander replied.

"Targets have reappeared," Max reported.

"Shit!" Gil cursed over comms. *"Get these assholes off of me!"*

"Razor Three is on it," Talisha announced.

"Razor Four is with you," Ensign Tellor added.

"Striker One has jumped forward to support Striker Two and the other Nighthawks," Max reported.

"Desh, let's join them," the commander instructed his wingman.

"*I'm with you, boss.*"

"*I'm hit!*" Joay yelled over comms. "*I'm coming ap...*"

"*Fuck!*" Natsu exclaimed. "*Maigo Five is gone! These bastards are all over...*"

"Jump!" Tham ordered.

"Six is gone!" Gento reported from Maigo One's back seat.

"All Maigos, Leader!" Tham barked. "Hit-and-run tactics! Five-second engagements! Don't let them gang up..."

Tham's ship suddenly rocked violently as multiple weapon blasts impacted his aft shields.

"Four octos on our six!" Gento warned. "We gotta..."

The Gunyoki fighter rocked again. Tham felt an incredible heat on his backside. Alarms began sounding all over his console, and his cockpit filled with smoke to the point that he could no longer see. Another explosion rocked his ship. Tham's helmet visor dropped down automatically, and the smoke filling the cockpit suddenly vanished. "Gento!" he yelled but got no response.

"*Tham!*" Krish, Tham's wingman, called over comms. "*Pitch down and jump into the atmosphere!*"

"I can't raise Gento!" Tham replied, feeling for the jump distance dial on his flight control stick, spinning it down to its minimum setting of one half kilometer, then rolling it back up, counting each click.

"*The back half of your cockpit is gone!*" Krish told

him. *"Gento's gotta be dead! Get down low and bail out!"*

"I can't see shit!" Tham replied while counting clicks.

"Two more octos are moving to your six! Jump now!"

Tham pressed the jump button, hoping he had dialed correctly and wouldn't jump right into the surface. There was a deafening thud and a sudden rush of air as he was thrown forward against his shoulder restraints. He could now see the surface rushing up toward him, much closer than he had hoped. Without hesitation, he reached down between his legs and grabbed the ejection handle, pulling up sharply.

An explosion went off all around him as his canopy blew away from his ship. Tham felt himself blown back against his seat by the rush of air. Then, a second later, another explosion underneath him went off, and he was rocketed from his doomed fighter.

"Targets have jumped!" Kasma reported over comm-sets.

"What the hell?" Robert exclaimed as the ship rocked violently.

"Two gunships just jumped in behind us!" Kasma reported as the ship continued to rock.

"Aft shields are down to twenty percent!" Sasha warned.

"One of the gunships is targeting Striker Two, and one of them is targeting us!" Kasma added.

"Aft shields are going down!" Renny warned.

"Octo escorts have jumped, as well!"

Robert adjusted the ship's pitch, bringing their

nose over to face behind them, opening fire on the attacking gunship.

"Aft shields are barely holding on at five percent!" Renny announced. *"One more hit, and they would've been history!"*

Robert glanced out the forward window as his fourth round of plasma torpedoes slammed into the closest gunship.

"The second gunship is maneuvering," Kasma reported. *"He's translating upward."*

Robert looked out the window again as the second enemy gunship, attacking Gil's gunship, rose up behind Striker Two and then disappeared in a blue-white flash.

"Contact!" Kasma warned. *"Directly behind us!"*

The ship lurched violently as something slammed into them from behind. Alarms began sounding, and warning indicators lit up all over the console as systems began failing throughout the ship.

"Aft shields are gone!" Renny reported.

"It's the second gunship!" Kasma added. *"They jumped just past us."*

Robert yanked his flight control stick back, attempting to pitch up ninety degrees in order to have a good shield facing each attacker, but his attitude thrusters were not responding as well as expected. "I've got a problem, here."

"Bobby!" Gil called over comms. *"Translate down and jump!"*

"Attitude thrusters are failing!" Robert replied. "She's sluggish as hell."

The ship rocked again as more energy bolts slammed into their unshielded stern.

"Port engine offline!" his engineer warned.

Again, the ship rocked; this time, so violently that Robert thought his restraints might fail.

"*Starboard engine has taken a direct hit.*"

Robert attempted to translate downward, but again, his thrusters were sluggish, at best.

"We gotta jump!" Sasha insisted.

"How long until we have a clear jump line?" Robert demanded, continuing to attempt to force his battered ship to translate downward.

The ship rocked again as more weapons fire slammed into the stern.

"*Hull breach!*" Renny reported. "*Starboard side! Just aft of the heat exchangers!*"

"*Twenty seconds to a clear jump line!*" Kasma answered.

"Shit!" Robert cursed as more weapons fire rocked his doomed gunship. He dialed up a two-light-hour jump. "Call the jump!" he ordered.

"Ten seconds!"

The ship rocked again, even more violently than before. A split second later, something deep inside the stern of his ship let go, exploding with incredible force.

"*We just lost half our backside!*" Renny reported.

"We're ending over!" Sasha warned.

Robert had no choice. One more shot, and they would be doomed. He pressed the jump button.

"Jump complete," Loki reported as the Aurora came out of its long jump from Sanctuary to Orswella.

"Planet is under attack," Kaylah reported. "Four gunships and ten octos."

"I thought we had two minutes?" Nathan said.

"I've got debris from three Gunyoki," Kaylah continued, "and from a Cobra gunship."

"Which one?" Jessica asked.

"Jump us to the engagement," Nathan instructed. "Tactical, gunships first, octos second. Comms, as soon as we come out of the jump, order all of our forces out of the battle zone. I don't want to take out any friendlies."

"Jumping to the battle zone," Loki reported.

"Torpedo firing control to the helm," Nathan ordered. "Make short work of those gunships, Josh."

"You got it," Josh replied.

"It's Striker One," Kaylah reported. "Half their stern section is gone...they jumped. Oh, my God!"

"Jump complete," Loki reported as the Aurora came out of its short jump to an orbit over Orswella, just above that of the enemy gunships.

"They must have collided with one of the gunships when they jumped!" Kaylah reported.

Josh swung the Aurora's nose onto the gunship closest to the wreckage of Striker One and opened fire, blowing it apart with a single round of four plasma torpedoes.

"Striker One is going down!" Kaylah reported.

"Can their hull take the reentry?" Nathan asked.

"Targeting all octos," Jessica reported. "Firing!"

Josh turned the Aurora slightly to port and angled it down a bit, bringing the ship's torpedo cannons onto the second gunship, pressing his firing button the moment the targeting reticle on the main view screen turned green. A split second later, the first round of four torpedoes slammed into the gunship's shields, overloading them, and causing them to fail. The second round tore into the enemy ship's hull, splitting it wide open, after which, secondary explosions broke it apart.

Nathan pressed the comm-controls on his

command chair arm, calling up a ship-to-ship channel. "Striker One, Aurora Actual!" Nathan called over comms. "Do you have any attitude control?"

"*Not much,*" Robert replied. "*Renny's working on it, but I'm afraid a controlled crash is the best we can hope for.*"

Josh fired again, destroying the third gunship with three rounds of plasma torpedoes.

"Fourth gunship has jumped," Kaylah reported.

"Pussy!" Josh exclaimed.

"Octos are jumping, as well."

"Show me Striker One's trajectory," Nathan ordered.

"One moment," Kaylah replied.

A moment later, an image came onto the screen, and a dotted line, showing Striker One's projected flight path all the way down to the surface, revealed Nathan's worst fear to be true. "Your present trajectory puts your impact on the far side of the city, about two kilometers short of the water," Nathan told him. "Is there any way you can do a burn of some sort? Thrusters? Vent a compartment? Anything?"

"*Negative,*" Robert replied, sounding somewhat fatalistic. "*Renny can't get any more power to the thrusters, and they're currently barely strong enough to keep our nose pointed in the direction of our flight, and that's going to get a lot more difficult once we hit the atmosphere.*"

"Can we nudge him?" Jessica wondered. "Or detonate something nearby?"

"Either one will probably make matters worse," Nathan told her.

"We have to do *something*," Jessica insisted.

"Scoop him up," Cameron suggested.

"What?" Nathan wondered.

"They fit on our flight deck," she explained. "Just scoop them up." She looked to Josh who had already turned around, surprised at her suggestion.

"That's why you put him at the helm, isn't it?" Cameron insisted. "For something like this?" She looked to Josh, again. "You can do it, can't you?"

"Damned right, he can," Jessica insisted.

"Of course," Josh replied. "No pressure," he muttered as he turned back around.

"Robert," Nathan called over comms. "Get everyone secured. We're coming to get you."

"*You're what?*" Robert asked, confused.

"We're going to scoop you up with the port forward flight deck."

"*Are you insane?*"

"You got a better idea?" Jessica asked over comms.

"*This was your idea, wasn't it?*" Robert accused Jessica.

"Actually, it was Captain Taylor's idea," Nathan corrected. "I know it sounds crazy, but I believe Josh can do it."

"*Captain, you can't risk the Aurora just to save us,*" Robert argued.

"Shut the hell up, Bobert!" Jessica scolded. "We're coming to get you, whether you like it or not!"

"Uh, it would help if they could stop wobbling," Josh suggested.

———————

"Did he say what I think he said?" Sasha asked.

Robert looked at his copilot. "He did."

"Is this going to work?"

"Beats the hell out of me," Robert admitted. "Renny, I'm going to need as much power to the thrusters as possible, to get us out of this spin, so they can scoop us up."

"*Come again?*" his engineer asked.

"The Aurora is going to try to scoop us up into their port forward flight bay."

"*Uh...*"

"It's either that, or we crash into the surface and take out a few blocks of the city."

"*I'll do what I can,*" Renny replied.

"Everyone else, start buttoning up the ship," Robert instructed. "It probably won't be a soft landing, and we're already a mess. Use emergency sealant on all hatches. Seal us in tight, just in case."

"How are they going to get to us once we're down?" Sasha wondered.

"I'm sure they'll figure out something," Robert replied.

"Don't those bays have emergency doors?"

"Yeah, but they don't come down that fast," Robert explained. "If we crack open, we'll depressurize in seconds."

"So, this plan pretty much sucks, then," Sasha concluded.

"Yup, pretty much," Robert agreed.

Vladimir entered the rescue trunk as teams suited up in preparation for the recovery of Striker One. "Chief, I've got men disconnecting the motors on the emergency outer doors."

"Uh, we're going to need that bay pressurized before we crack her open," the chief of the rescue team said.

"Those doors are too damned slow," Vladimir insisted. "With the motors disconnected, we can jack up the gravity levels across the threshold right after

Striker One crosses the line. The door should come down in seconds."

"And if it breaks?" the chief asked. "That thing's gotta weigh a ton."

"Four point two tons, to be exact," Vladimir replied. "I will dial the gravity back down just before impact. That should help. I've also got the pump safeties removed, so we can pressurize the bay in less than a minute."

"If it's alright with you, I'm going to take a few tanks of blow seal in with us."

"It will work," Vladimir insisted.

Commander Prechitt glanced at the port side of his canopy as another Nighthawk jumped in next to him.

"*What's going on?*" Talisha asked over comms.

"The Aurora took out three of the gunships and eight of the octos. The others jumped out," the commander explained. "The rest of us are flying cover, in case they come back, while the Aurora rescues Striker One."

"*Rescues?*" Talisha wondered.

"They're shot to shit and going down pretty much dead stick."

"*How are they going to rescue them?*"

"They're going to scoop them up in one of their flight bays."

"*You're kidding...*" Talisha replied in shock.

"Nope."

After a pause, she asked, "*Are things always this crazy with you guys?*"

"More often than not, yes," the commander replied.

"*Where do I sign up?*" Talisha joked.

"Unless Striker One can alter its attitude to parallel its flight path, you will have to approach from below the vessel in order to successfully capture it within the port forward flight bay," the voice of the Aurora's AI explained.

"I expect I'm gonna need your help on this, Aurora," Josh admitted.

"I believe this maneuver is well within your demonstrated piloting abilities, Mister Hayes. However, I stand ready to assist."

"I didn't say I *couldn't* do it," Josh replied, "but thanks."

"If we have to come up from below, our stern is going to dip into the atmosphere and create considerable drag," Kaylah warned.

"Can we come in from above?" Jessica wondered.

"Better to come in from underneath," Nathan insisted. "Her back end is a mess. If something goes wrong, and some of that mess catches the hull, it'll tear us open. Or, it could catch on the door frame, and they'd be stuck half in and half out. Better to enter the bay nose first."

"We're a fifteen-hundred-meter ship," Loki reminded them. "It's going to take a lot of thrust to keep our tail from dragging in the atmosphere and causing us to miss."

"If I may make a suggestion?" the Aurora asked.

"Please," Nathan replied.

"Allow me to handle the aft thrusters to compensate for tail drag in the atmosphere. That will allow Mister Hayes to concentrate on capturing the damaged vessel within the port forward flight bay."

"Josh?" Nathan asked.

"Sounds good to me," Josh replied, happy for the help.

"Very well, Aurora. Compensation for atmospheric drag is your responsibility."

"*Understood,*" the Aurora replied. "*I would also suggest that you channel additional power to all aft shields to prevent overheating of the outer hull, which could interfere with proper thruster operations.*"

"Jess?" Nathan called.

"I'm all over it," Jessica replied.

"If we're going to do this, it needs to be soon," Kaylah warned. "They're going to hit atmospheric interface in five minutes. Two minutes after that, they'll start burning up."

"Mister Hayes," Nathan said.

Josh took a deep breath. "Here goes nothing," he said as he pitched the ship up and began translating toward the planet.

"Striker One, Aurora Actual," Nathan called over comms. "You need to stop that rotation, Robert."

"*Got it,*" Robert replied. "*Give me a minute.*"

"Time is of the essence," Nathan warned. "In just over six minutes, you're going to start heating up."

"*You think I don't know that?*" Robert replied.

"I'm just saying..."

———

Robert struggled with his flight control stick, trying to get his battered ship's attitude thrusters to work well enough to stop their spin.

"You're over thrusting," Sasha said again.

"These damned things aren't working right," Robert replied. "Sometimes they respond, sometimes they don't. I can't find an input level that yields a consistent result."

"Try minimum inputs only," Sasha suggested.

100

"Thrust and wait. If that doesn't work, try it again, but don't give it *more* thrust."

Robert tried again, applying the tiniest bit of lateral thrust. As expected, nothing happened. He repeated the process, giving just the minimum control input. Two times, three times, four. On the fifth attempt, the thrusters fired for a brief moment. "Okay. That worked." He began twisting the input level wheel around the base of the flight control stick. "I'm going to lock it down and then back it off just a touch, to keep me from giving too much control input."

"Good thinking," Sasha agreed.

Robert finished twisting the wheel to its fully locked position and then backed it off a quarter rotation. After taking a deep breath, he was ready to try again. One input, two, three... "I've got thrust." He continued to apply control inputs but couldn't get any reliable response. "It seems random. Renny, why the hell isn't every control input getting to the thrusters?"

"*It's either a faulty control input processor or a short in the signal line,*" the engineer replied. "*I'm trying to boost the signal strength between the processor and the thrusters to compensate.*"

"What if we reprogrammed the processor to send only specific commands for thrust—both thrust time and level—regardless of the strength of the control input?" Sasha suggested.

"*That will only help if the problem is between the flight control stick and the processor,*" Renny said. "*I don't see how that could be.*"

"Do it anyway," Robert ordered, "and program it to only send a single thrust command through, regardless of the number of inputs from my stick."

"If I do that, you'll only be able to thrust once along each axis."

"Put a reset timer on it," Sasha suggested. "Maybe ten seconds?"

"Make it five," Robert decided. "I may need to apply a second thrust along the same axis more quickly."

"I can do the reprogramming," Kasma offered.

"Renny?" Robert asked.

"Great. That way I can work on the signal strength to the thrusters, themselves," the engineer replied.

"We need this done yesterday, guys," Robert reminded them. "We've got about four minutes."

———

The Aurora descended into an extremely low orbit over Orswella, sliding into position two kilometers beneath the still-spinning Striker One as it began to pitch upward.

Striker One stood in a vertical orientation relative to the planet below, both its nose and what was left of its stern were oscillating in opposite directions, parallel to the gunship's longitudinal axis.

———

"Striker One is still oscillating," Kaylah reported.

"How badly?" Nathan asked.

"It's spinning around its central axis, nose, and stern," Kaylah explained.

"Drawing circles," Cameron commented. "An expression from flight school."

"I remember that," Nathan said. "It was caused by an underpowered thruster that was reporting normal thrust."

"If you didn't catch the condition early on, it could become impossible to correct," Cameron finished for him.

"But Robert has tens of thousands of hours behind the stick," Nathan insisted. "There's no way he wouldn't notice a thruster problem."

"Considering the amount of damage to the stern of his ship, I'm surprised he even *has* thrusters," Cameron said.

"His CG is off," Josh said, looking at the image of the oscillating gunship sliding into view from overhead as their nose finished pitching upward.

"We're picking up tail drag," Loki warned.

"*I am compensating now,*" the voice of the Aurora's AI commented.

"It's going to be nearly impossible to maintain speed due to the drag, using only translation thrusters," Loki warned.

"*I have routed additional power to the acceleration chambers on all dorsal translation thrusters, proportionally, according to the amount of drag being induced by each portion of the ship,*" Aurora assured them.

"Well, alright, then," Josh said.

"The diameter of the stern oscillation is greater than the height of the port forward flight deck threshold," Kaylah warned.

"I can get 'em," Josh insisted.

Nathan didn't look as convinced. "How?"

"Uh..."

"*It is possible,*" the Aurora said, "*by entering the same type of spin pattern as the target, but at larger oscillation diameters, which must be reduced gradually during approach, so the pattern is identical at the time the target crosses the recovery threshold.*"

"Yeah, that's what I was gonna say," Josh insisted.

"Josh, you'd have to induce a dangerous spin," Nathan said, "one that is considered *so dangerous,*" most ships have automated systems to *prevent* that from happening."

"Including this one," Loki added.

"*The anti-oscillation features can be overridden,*" Aurora stated.

"You won't be oscillating around *our* longitudinal axis, Josh," Nathan reminded. "It will be around an imaginary axis drawn along the port forward flight deck's threshold. That means you'll have to adjust which thrusters you're using to control the ship, based on the current attitude of the ship at each second. *No one* can do that."

"*She* can," Josh insisted, pointing at the helm console. "I can fly the ship, and the Aurora can do the calculations and make the adjustments on the fly."

"Aurora, is this even feasible?" Nathan asked.

"*It is possible,*" the Aurora replied, "*but it is also quite risky. If my calculations are the slightest bit off...*"

"You're a computer," Jessica said. "How could your calculations be off?"

"*The Aurora is a complex vessel with hundreds of thousands of systems, all of which have minute variations in performance. This ship's thrusters, for example, have a point-zero-two-seven variation in thrust at any given moment. The same is true of all ships, but with time, such variations can be predicted and compensated for. I have yet to accumulate the experience necessary with this vessel in order to accurately make such predictions and compensations.*"

"We can do it," Josh, again, insisted.

Nathan pressed the button on the arm of his command chair, linking his comm-set to the ship-to-ship communications system. "Striker One, Aurora

Actual. Any chance you can reduce your rotation a bit more?"

"*Uh...I'm afraid not,*" Robert replied. "*We lost most of our propellant in the collision. We've already used up what we had left. We're pretty much dead stick right now.*"

"Yeah, that's what I figured," Nathan replied. "Listen, we've got an idea. It's not great, but it's all we've got at this point, and I don't have to remind you that the planet isn't about to move out of your way."

"*So, what's the plan?*"

"As you've probably already figured out, the diameter of your oscillations is wider than the flight deck threshold."

"*Everything is failing around here, so, no, I didn't know,*" Robert replied over comms, "*but I'm not surprised.*"

"We're going to try to match your oscillations in order to get you past the threshold."

After a pause, Robert replied, "*You're right; it's not a great idea.*"

"Well, our AI seems to think it can be done, so we've got that going for us."

"Gee, thanks," Josh said.

"Assuming it works, it's likely to be a rough landing," Nathan continued.

"*And if it doesn't?*" Robert wondered.

"Well, you won't have to worry about burning up in the atmosphere," Nathan replied.

"*What's the risk to the Aurora?*"

"I know the risks, Captain," Nathan replied. "No offense, but I wouldn't be suggesting this if I thought it might bring *us* down, as well. Whatever happens, we'll survive."

"*I don't suppose I've got time to think about it?*"

"Take all the time you want," Nathan replied. "What's your answer?"

Another pause. "*Well, I've trusted you this far. Let's get this done, Captain.*"

"Buckle up and button up, Robert. We're coming to get you."

———

Robert glanced over at his copilot.

"This is a terrible idea," Sasha commented.

"Got a better one?" Robert tapped his comm-set. "Listen up, people. The Aurora's going to try to scoop us up, so we need to button this ship up tight, and get everyone strapped in, pronto. Renny, apply emergency sealant around the airlock hatch. In our current spin, we could end up torquing that thing out of joint, which means we could lose all pressure before rescue crews can get to us. Close and lock everything. Stow everything, then strap your asses in."

"This ought to be fun," Sasha commented.

———

"*Calculations are complete, and I have implemented two compensation algorithms,*" the Aurora's AI voice reported. "*I can maintain the appropriate rate of oscillations while Mister Hayes conducts the capture maneuver.*"

"The ship is lined up, so to speak," Josh reported.

Nathan stared at the main view screen, watching Striker One oscillating just beyond the Aurora's nose to her port side.

"We are picking up a lot of heat on our stern," Loki warned.

Nathan pressed a button on his comm-panel. "You ready down there, Commander?"

"*We are ready*," Vladimir replied.

"How about you, Josh?" Nathan asked.

"I got this," Josh replied, exchanging a glance with Loki that belied his boast.

Josh eased his control stick forward slightly and then released it, applying just a touch of forward thrust. A moment later, the crippled, oscillating gunship began to drift toward them at a greater rate.

"*Initiating oscillation maneuver*," the Aurora's AI reported.

"Whoa," Josh said. "This is weird."

"Something wrong?" Nathan asked, becoming concerned.

"No, it's just weird," Josh replied. "The ship is doing things that I'm not telling it to do."

Nathan watched as the stars on the view screen began to move. "Try concentrating on the target and not the surroundings."

"Trust me, I am," Josh insisted, thrusting forward again.

"Closure rate is three meters per second," Loki reported.

"*Ten seconds to oscillation match*," the Aurora reported.

Nathan continued to watch as the constellations on the view screen slid out of view to the right, only to reemerge on the left. "Thank God the planet is under us and not in front of us," he mumbled.

"Hell, I'm not even *looking* at the view screen at this point," Josh replied, his eyes locked on the glass, heads-up display before him.

"Closure rate: four meters per second," Loki reported.

"How long until we get too deep into the atmosphere?" Nathan asked.

"In three minutes and forty-eight seconds, the atmospheric drag on our stern will exceed my ability to compensate, and we will most likely collide with the target."

"You have three minutes, Josh," Nathan warned. "Then, we abort by translating away from Striker One and jumping clear, understood?"

"I got it, I got it," Josh insisted, his concentration on the task at hand.

"I've got an abort timer running, Captain," Loki assured him.

Josh cast him a quick look of disapproval.

"Just in case," Loki assured his friend.

"Oh, my God," Robert muttered, staring out the forward window. Outside, the Aurora seemed to be coming right at them. It rotated around his view; one moment there, the next moment gone. Over the course of half a minute, the cycling slowed as the massive vessel matched his ship's oscillations.

"How the hell are they doing this?" Sasha exclaimed, also looking out the window. "Even *with* an AI helping, I couldn't do this."

"Neither could I," Robert admitted.

"Jesus, he's almost got it," Sasha declared as the bow of the Aurora was about to pass their own nose.

"Five-meters-per-second closure," Loki warned. "You need to start slowing down, Josh."

Josh stared at his heads-up display, mesmerized by the dance of the angles representing the Aurora and the battered gunship they were attempting to save. "Not yet," he insisted. "We're not matched yet, Aurora."

"I am attempting to avoid overcompensation in an

effort to ensure proper alignment at the last moment, when we will have no time to correct for drift."

"So, you're playing it safe, too," Josh replied as he made a final adjustment to their approach.

"*Of course.*"

"Bow threshold in ten seconds," Loki warned. "The distance between us and them will begin to decrease once we cross."

"No kidding," Josh replied.

"Three......two......one......"

Nathan watched the main view screen as the wounded gunship slipped past the port side of the Aurora's bow. Although the variation was small, the oscillations of both ships were still not quite synchronized.

"Switching to flight deck camera," Loki announced.

A rectangle appeared in the middle of the main view screen, filling most of it with the view from the back of the port forward flight bay, looking forward through its open end.

"Where are they?" Jessica wondered.

"They're still to port of the approach path," Loki explained.

"Translating to port," Josh reported as he adjusted his flight control stick.

On the main view screen, a small, light gray object moved into the camera view from the left side, slightly oscillating.

"Oscillations have increased," Kaylah warned.

"You need to slow down," Loki urged.

"Aurora?" Josh queried.

"*Compensating,*" the Aurora replied.

────────────

Sasha stared out the window in terror while the Aurora's hull moved frighteningly close to them as they passed, then away, then back again. "Jesus, that's close."

"Braking," Josh announced as he activated the Aurora's forward braking thrusters.

"Five-meters-per-second closure, four meters range to port, one meter off the approach line," Loki reported.

"I'm working on it," Josh replied.

"We need to move a meter to starboard," Loki urged.

"We need to match their oscillations," Jessica insisted nervously from the tactical station.

Cameron put her hand on Jessica's shoulder. "They've got this."

"Four meters per second; still need to move a meter to starboard," Loki reported.

"I know, I know," Josh replied.

"Drifting slightly low," Loki warned.

"Aurora?" Josh called.

"*Preparing for final compensation,*" she replied.

"Come on," Nathan mumbled to himself.

"This is insane," Talisha exclaimed as she watched the gunship sliding closely along the Aurora's port side. "Who the hell is piloting the Aurora?"

"*Josh Hayes,*" Commander Prechitt replied, "*with the help of the AI you gave us.*"

"They incorporated her into the Aurora?" she asked, shocked. "I thought you were just going to evaluate her code?"

"*I guess you could call it a field evaluation.*"

"Amazing," Talisha added. "I need to meet that guy."

"*Please, don't feed his ego,*" Commander Prechitt begged. "*It's big enough already.*"

———

"Three meters per second," Loki reported, "half a meter right of line, on elevation." Everyone on the bridge, with the exception of Josh and Loki, stood stock-still with their eyes fixed on the image of the battered gunship as it grew larger in the opening of the port forward flight bay, its nose still drawing small circles as it approached.

"Two meters per second, you're in the lane, drifting slightly starboard again," Loki reported. "Ten seconds to threshold."

Nathan tapped the comm-panel on the arm of his command chair, tying in the ship-wide channel as well as ship-to-ship. "All hands, brace for impact. Port forward flight deck, prepare for recovery."

"Five seconds, one point five," Loki reported. "Three......two......one......threshold."

His job now over, Josh took his hands off the flight controls and looked up at the main view screen as everyone on the bridge held their breath.

———

The Cobra gunship crossed the threshold of the Aurora's port forward flight bay, passing through the opening nose first, still wobbling.

Striker One's nose swung upward slightly as it continued to oscillate, crashing into a catwalk and ripping it from its mounts. The force of the impact drove the nose downward, disrupting its pattern of oscillations and sending it toward the deck and slightly inboard.

———

Vladimir stared out the window of the port forward control booth as the gunship plowed through the catwalk toward the deck. "NOW!" he yelled as the stern of the gunship passed the threshold. "GRAVITY AT FIFTY! DROP THE DOORS AND REPRESS!"

———

The emergency doors came down quickly, sliding down and outboard along their sloped tracks, drawn downward by the sudden activation of the flight deck's artificial gravity.

Striker One slammed into the deck and slid twenty meters at an angle across the bay, impacting the inboard bulkhead and bending the impacted area inward.

———

Robert's head slammed into the now-bent-in port window frame, cutting his forehead wide open. His vision went black as the sounds of bending and grinding metal filled his ears.

———

The emergency doors slammed closed, and air began to rush into the bay as the gunship bounced off the inboard bulkhead.

———

After bouncing off the damaged wall, Striker One continued sliding aft as it spun slowly on its belly across the deck, finally ramming its port side into the aft bulkhead of the flight bay.

———

"Move to airlock seven!" the rescue chief yelled to his rescue teams; the doors to their current airlock now bent inward from the collision and, therefore, were inoperable.

———

Robert groaned, his head ringing with pain. Sparks burst from the switch panel above his head, and he choked on the rancid smoke of burning circuits. "Sasha!" he cried out, unable to see his copilot through the smoke. "Renny! Kas! Someone! Sound off..." He coughed, and then everything went black again.

As the bay was still pressurizing, rescue crews wearing safety gear and breathing masks burst through the airlock door in the aft bulkhead of the flight bay, outboard of the wreckage of Striker One. The first ones in were the fire-suppression crews, dragging big, floppy fire-retardant tubes to be positioned strategically about the smoking vessel.

Hot on their heels, confident that their predecessors would be successful at containing any fires, were the rescue techs. Part medic and part extrication specialists, the four men had already reviewed the rescue procedures for the Cobra gunship and formulated a plan. Although badly crumpled, the bow of the ship, specifically the area over the copilot's seat, was still intact. The rescue team went straight for the copilot's side, climbing up onto the bow of the still-smoking vessel, quickly working their way up the hull to the copilot's window. Once there, they used power tools to unbolt the emergency access collar around the copilot's window, removing the entire window panel in less than a minute.

Once removed, smoke began to pour out of the open window, signaling to the rescue workers that there was a fire inside the gunship's cabin.

"*Interior fire!*" the chief yelled from behind his breathing mask. "*Let's move!*"

"Commander Kamenetskiy reports that Striker One is on the deck, and the bay is secured and pressurized," Naralena reported.

"Nice work, Josh," Nathan congratulated. "Now, get us some altitude, and quickly," he added.

"Aye, sir," Josh replied, getting to work. "Aurora, return all flight controls to normal, please."

"*All flight controls to normal operating parameters,*" the Aurora confirmed.

"Rescue chief reports both external and internal fires," Naralena added. "Rescue techs are entering Striker One now."

Nathan said nothing.

"I need to go down there," Jessica insisted.

"We're still at general quarters," Nathan replied calmly, a look of sympathy on his face.

"I can handle tactical, sir," Cameron suggested.

"You belong on the flight deck," Nathan insisted, looking toward the exit.

"Aye, sir," Cameron replied, exchanging a sympathetic glance with Jessica as she headed for the exit.

"Comms, call another tactical officer to the bridge, please."

"Aye, sir," Naralena replied.

"As soon as you are relieved," Nathan told Jessica.

"Thank you," she said, nodding her appreciation.

"Positive climb rate, sir," Loki reported.

"Very well," Nathan replied. "Get us back up into standard orbit."

"Standard orbit, aye," Loki confirmed.

––––––––––

Fire-suppression foam poured from the tubes onto the damaged stern of Striker One as the first rescue technician dropped through the open copilot's window.

The rescue tech dropped down inside, straddling the motionless body of Striker One's copilot. He reached for the man's Khannatid artery with one hand, while his other hand went to his chest to feel for respirations. "Copilot's alive but has asymmetrical chest expansion!" he reported. He quickly disconnected the copilot's restraint harness from the seat by pulling the emergency release rings from the back. As he did so, two straps with rescue clips on the ends came down through the open window. The rescue tech clipped them onto the rings at the top of the unconscious copilot's harness and then hollered, "Pull him out!"

The tech guided the copilot's unconscious body as the men outside pulled him through the window. As soon as the copilot's feet were through the window, the rescue tech turned around and checked Robert's motionless body in the same way. "Pilot's alive!" he called out. "Head lac! Possible arm! Possible lower leg! Good pulse, good respirations! Can you pop the window on the port side?"

"*Negative!*" the chief replied over comm-sets. "*Too much damage. Harness him up, and we'll pull him out through the copilot's window.*"

"Someone needs to splint his arm and leg, first!" the rescue tech warned.

"*Check the others!*" the chief insisted. "*We'll get the pilot out.*"

"On my way," the rescue tech confirmed, climbing back over the center console away from Robert and then dropping down the access ladder as the second rescue tech dropped in through the open copilot's window.

———

Vladimir rushed into the flight bay, stopping short once inside, aghast at the amount of damage to the once-proud Cobra gunship. "*Gospadee!*" He moved

115

quickly around the ship, being careful not to impede the fire and rescue crews attempting to secure the wreckage and ensure everyone's safety. "Don't forget to check the plasma torpedo generators!" he yelled as he made his way around the bow to the rescue chief. "Are they alive?" he asked the chief as two men carefully handed Sasha's unconscious body down to two medical techs.

"Pilot and copilot are alive but badly injured," the chief replied. "One of my men is working on getting the pilot out, the other is checking the crew deeper inside the ship, but it's still full of smoke."

"I'll see if I can get the purge system activated from the external maintenance panel on the starboard side," Vladimir offered.

"My guys are on it, sir," the chief insisted, putting his hand on Vlad's chest to stop him. "Let 'em do their jobs."

"Of course, of course," Vladimir agreed, frustrated that he could only watch.

"Hey! Hey! You with me, Sergeant?" the rescue tech yelled as he patted Kasma's face.

The sensor officer opened his eyes for a moment and then closed them again. The rescue tech felt his pulse, as well as his chest. "Sensors! Alive, weak pulse, shallow respirations," he reported as he patted the man down. "No outward signs of trauma. Probable smoke inhalation," he added as he pulled a pocket rescue breather out of his bag, placed it over Kasma's head, and then activated it. The bag inflated, filling full of oxygen in seconds. "Moving to ops!"

"Flight crew is alive," Cameron reported over comm-sets. *"So are the sensor officer and engineer."*

"What about the gunners?" Nathan asked.

"They're trying to get to them, now," Cameron replied. *"They have to cut in through the top of the port gun tunnel to reach them. The midship hatch is bent and won't open. If Vlad hadn't gotten the door down so quickly, they would have suffocated in seconds."*

"Keep me updated," Nathan told her.

"You got it."

"Message from the Gunyoki," Naralena reported. "They managed to chase down and destroy the last gunship, but the octos got away. They're asking for orders."

"Tell them to take up position in high orbit for now," Nathan replied. "I don't want to take anyone onboard to replenish until I'm certain everything is under control down there."

"Aye, sir."

"And patch me through to Telles."

"One moment."

Nathan sighed as he continued to stand in front of his command chair, directly behind the helm's center console.

"General Telles is on the line, Captain," Naralena reported.

"Telles, Actual," Nathan called. "How are you holding up?"

"There are no casualties among my men," the general replied. *"However, we do not have a tally of civilian losses, as of yet."*

"How bad was it?"

"Not as bad as we feared. Your losses?"

"We lost a few," Nathan admitted. "Not sure how many yet, but at least three that I know of."

"*Understood.*"

"Let us know if you need anything," Nathan added.

"*You will be remaining in orbit?*" the general wondered.

"Until the Glendanon arrives, yes."

"*Very well. Telles out.*"

"*Captain, XO,*" Cameron called over comm-sets. "*All six members of Striker One's crew are alive. Four are out, and the gunners are being extricated, now.*"

Nathan breathed a sigh of relief, as did everyone else on the bridge. "That's good to hear, Cam. Let me know as soon as that deck is secured. We have a lot of thirsty Gunyoki to recover."

"*Understood.*"

Nathan reached out and patted both Josh and Loki on their shoulders. "Nice work, guys."

"Thank you, sir," Loki replied.

"Don't forget to thank Aurora," Josh joked.

CHAPTER FOUR

Captain Gullen stepped onto the Glendanon's bridge, his morning cup of jola in his hand. It had been an uneventful thirty-seven-hour trip from Rakuen, and Edom was looking forward to his new assignment.

"Good morning, Captain," his helmsman greeted.

"Good morning," Captain Gullen replied. "How are things?"

"We are about to make the final jump to Orswella," the helmsman reported. "I was just about to contact you, to clarify how close in you wanted our arrival point to be."

Captain Gullen glanced at the flight display on the helm, doing the math in his head. "Let's try eight hundred thousand kilometers. We can do a long decel burn to drop into a tighter orbit after we arrive."

"Yes, sir," the helmsman replied. "I'll have the jump ready in a moment."

Captain Gullen stepped up to the operations station, pressing the intercom button. "Justan, you ready down there?"

"All four boxcars are loaded and ready for departure," his XO replied. *"Second, third, and fourth loads are lined up on deck, and fuelers are prepared for a quick turnaround."*

"Excellent. I'm sure the Ghatazhak will appreciate the rapid service."

"Jump is ready, Captain," the helmsman announced.

"We're about to jump, Justan. You're clear to launch, once we do so."

"Understood."

"Boxcars have their own jump drives, *and* they can get there more quickly," the helmsman commented. "Why didn't they just shuttle the supplies to Orswella while we were en route?"

"Because we have guns, and the boxcars do not," the captain explained, "and we have no idea how many Dusahn fighters could still be lurking in the area."

"Of course," the helmsman replied, embarrassed. "I didn't mean to question your judgment, Captain."

"It's quite alright, Mister Kondu," the captain assured his young helmsman. "This is your first interstellar jump ship assignment, isn't it?"

"Yes, sir, it is."

"Then, you should ask questions," the captain insisted. "It is how you learn."

"Yes, sir."

"Execute the jump to Orswella when ready, Mister Kondu," the captain instructed.

* * *

"Captain on the bridge," the guard at the entrance to the Aurora's bridge announced as Nathan passed.

"The Glendanon jumped in a few minutes ago," Cameron reported as she rose from the command chair. "They launched boxcars immediately upon arrival."

"I have Captain Gullen on comms," Naralena reported.

"Captain Gullen," Nathan called, after tapping his comm-set to tie it into the ship-to-ship channel. "Welcome to Orswella."

"*Thank you, Captain,*" the captain of the Glendanon replied.

"As soon as your decks are clear, I'm sure the

Gunyoki would like a place to park and stretch their legs from time to time," Nathan told him.

"It will take us a few hours to offload all that the Ghatazhak have requested, but after that, our decks will be theirs."

"Konay Squadron should arrive by then," Nathan continued, "as well as the four Orochi I have assigned to your command, for the time being."

"That is good news."

"Now, if you'll excuse me, Captain, I must return to Sanctuary."

"Yes, I was pleased to hear about the improvement in your sister's condition. Safe journey, Captain. We'll take it from here."

"Call if you need us, Captain. We're only a jump away." Nathan tapped his comm-set, smiling.

"You enjoyed that last line, didn't you?" Cameron commented.

"It's a pretty heady feeling, knowing you can jump a few hundred light years in the blink of an eye," Nathan admitted. "Mister Sheehan, a jump to Rogen if you will."

"Aye, sir," Loki replied.

"Shouldn't we retaliate against the Dusahn, first?" Jessica wondered.

"Attacking that dreadnought would be pushing our luck," Nathan insisted, "even with the Nighthawks."

"What about Takara?" Jessica suggested. "Plenty of soft targets, there."

"Takara would require a recharge layover," Cameron pointed out. "Plus, it would put us twice as far from Sanctuary as we are now."

"And we have an appointment there in four hours," Nathan added.

"The Dusahn have called your bluff," Jessica

reminded him. "If we don't respond, we'll just be inviting more attacks."

"Why does everyone always assume I'm bluffing?" Nathan wondered.

"Well…" Jessica said.

"We *will* retaliate," he promised, "just not right now."

"On course and speed for the Rogen system," Josh reported from the helm.

"Jump is plotted and ready," Loki added.

"Take us home, Mister Sheehan," Nathan ordered.

* * *

"Welcome back," one of her research assistants greeted as Abby entered her lab.

"Thank you, Aneko," Abby replied.

"Is it true?"

"Is what true?" Abby wondered.

"Did the Aurora really destroy four Dusahn battleships?" Aneko asked.

"Yes, she did," Abby confirmed.

"What was it like?"

"Terrifying, to be honest."

"I can't even imagine."

"Neither can I," Abby replied, "and I've been through worse. Where are we?" she added, intending to change the subject.

"We have several emitters mounted on test mounts inside safe tanks. They are fully connected and powered," Aneko told her. "We have running several tests, at various power levels and time durations, in order to build a baseline for the purposes of computer modeling."

"Excellent," Abby said. "Let's get started, then."

* * *

Marcus led Nathan and Jessica into the lobby of the Tekan restaurant on Sanctuary.

"No one would know this is a dining establishment," Jessica commented as they looked around the foyer. "No sign on the door. No maître d'. Not even a waiting area."

A man in monochromatic attire appeared from the interior doorway. "Mister Taggart," the man greeted. "I see you took my advice about Coroway's?"

"Yeah, pretty spiffy, don't you think?" Marcus replied, tugging on his new clothes with pride.

"Indeed. Is this your complete party? Just the three?"

"Just us," Marcus replied.

"Mister Vout is waiting," the man said. "If you will all follow me."

The man returned to the door, which slid open automatically, and led them inside. On the other side was a long corridor lined with evenly spaced doors on either side.

After passing several of them, the man stopped, turned, and opened the door to his left, gesturing for them to enter. "Mister Vout awaits."

Marcus was the first to enter, leading the others inside. "Gunwy," he called.

Gunwy stood, eager to meet his new guests. "Welcome," he greeted. "Welcome to you all."

"Captain, this is Gunwant Vout," Marcus introduced. "Gunwy, this is Lieutenant Commander Jessica Nash, and this is Captain Nathan Scott of the Aurora."

"A pleasure to meet you, Mister Vout," Nathan stated, extending his hand.

"I am most honored to meet you," Gunwy insisted, "both of you." Gunwy gestured to the collection of multi-colored pillows scattered around a low table in the middle of the room. "Please, make yourselves comfortable. I took the liberty of ordering for us," he added as he sat. "I hope you do not mind."

"I'm afraid I didn't bring an appetite, myself," Nathan admitted.

"Me either," Jessica added.

"I'll eat theirs," Marcus stated.

"I ordered a shared sampler plate of Tekan delicacies," Gunwy explained. "On my world, it is customary for first meetings between two potential business partners. Consumption is not required, nor is it an offense if you choose not to."

"Then, this is a business meeting," Nathan surmised.

"I assumed this to be the case," Gunwy replied, looking concerned. "Was I mistaken?"

"Not necessarily," Nathan replied. "While your company may have some products that we *might* be interested in purchasing or some manufacturing that we *might* be interested in contracting you to perform, we are primarily looking for allies."

"Against the Dusahn," Gunwy surmised.

"Yes, but not only the Dusahn."

"You have more than one enemy?"

"There are many enemies," Nathan explained. "Many of whom have yet to be discovered."

"Then, you are a crusader."

Nathan took a breath, letting it out in a long sigh. "Not by choice, I assure you. The problem is that the jump drive, like most great inventions, is a double-edged sword. It has the capacity to connect all the civilizations of humanity and improve the lives of everyone. Unfortunately, it has the ability to enslave us, as well. The Dusahn are just the first example."

"Such is the nature of humanity," Gunwy insisted. "To fight it is, well, somewhat idealistic, I'm afraid."

"Just because it is the nature of humanity does not mean we have to accept it," Nathan countered.

"Humans, like water, tend to follow the path of least resistance. Submission is far easier than resistance."

"True, but there are still good people who *will* resist injustice. I am surrounded by them."

"Then, you are a fortunate man," Gunwy congratulated. "But I'm afraid SilTek does not *ally* itself with anyone, the very least of whom are revolutionaries."

"I prefer to think of us as freedom fighters," Nathan corrected.

"Regardless, my people are only concerned with profit and opportunity."

"Both of which will be lost if evil is allowed to spread unchecked," Nathan argued.

"Possibly," Gunwy agreed, "but to ally with one side over the other creates enemies where none existed. In addition, it closes off potential opportunity with the other side."

"No offense, but your thinking is too *regional*. You must think on a much larger scale."

"There are limits to the range within which we can operate," Gunwy insisted. "The more that limit is exceeded, the lower the profit."

"Technologies change," Nathan argued. "You should know that better than anyone."

"True, but such changes generally take considerable time."

"What if I were to tell you that my ship can jump five hundred light years in a *single jump*?"

"No offense, Captain, but I would find that difficult

to believe. The power requirements for a ship your size to jump such a distance would be enormous."

"It's not about the power, Mister Vout, it's about the emitters."

"If what you are saying is true, then you must have some very good scientists," Gunwy admitted.

"We have the original *inventor* of the jump drive," Nathan told him.

"Interesting." Gunwy leaned back against his pillows for a moment. "As I said, SilTek is not interested in alliances, even with parties able to jump five hundred light years at a time. Profits and opportunity, those are our only interests."

Nathan thought for a moment. "What if I told you that we also possess the entire history of the Earth, from *before* the great plague, including all of its technology, much of which has yet to be reinvented anywhere in the galaxy. Is that enough opportunity for you?"

Gunwy studied Nathan for a moment. "I would require evidence of this."

"Not a chance," Nathan insisted, standing firm.

"You can't expect me to buy something without seeing what it is, first," Gunwy said.

"I'm not selling anything," Nathan replied. "I'm just asking to meet with your leaders."

"You want to *meet* with the leader of SilTek." Gunwy examined Nathan and Jessica further, failing to decipher their expressions. "No non-Tekan has ever met with the leader of SilTek," Gunwy insisted. "She would never agree to such a meeting."

"If SilTek is truly interested in opportunity and profit, she will make an exception."

"Captain…"

"All I ask is that you forward my request to your superiors," Nathan told him.

"I cannot *recommend* she meet with you, you understand," Gunwy explained. "I can only relay my impressions and the content of our conversation, that is all."

"That is all I ask," Nathan assured him. "Now, if you'll excuse me, I have other appointments on this station."

"You do not wish to sample Tekan delicacies, Captain?"

"I hope to do so *on* SilTek," Nathan countered as he and Jessica rose. "Thank you for your time, Mister Vout. I look forward to your leader's response." Nathan looked at Marcus.

"Oh, I gotta go, too?" Marcus got his answer from Nathan's expression and also stood.

"One more thing, Captain, if I may?" He waited for Nathan to face him before continuing. "Do you really believe you can defeat the Dusahn?"

Mister Vout's words were as much a challenge as they were a question.

Nathan stared at him with a confident expression, one that offered only the slightest hint of a smile. "I am certain of it," he replied before departing.

* * *

Deliza Ta'Akar entered hangar four of Ranni's research and development facility on Rakuen. "Sorry for the delay, everyone," she announced as she approached the group of technicians gathered around a Gunyoki fighter. "As you can see, this team is being retasked," she continued, picking up one of the Nighthawk grav-lift emitters sitting on a rolling cart. "Our new job is to figure out how to make these..." she explained, holding up an anti-

127

grav emitter, "…work in that," she ended, pointing to the Gunyoki fighter.

"Why?" one of the technicians asked.

"The original Gunyoki fighters were able to operate in both the atmosphere *and* in space. The current versions, although far more formidable, cannot."

"The Gunyoki *can* operate from the surface if they have to," another technician said.

"Not without using the majority of their tanked propellant. The Gunyoki are heavy and have no aerodynamic properties. The only way to make them capable of operating from the surface, *without* pre and post-atmospheric operation refueling, is to retrofit them with anti-grav systems."

"The Gunyoki's fight control systems are not designed to use anti-grav. It will require a complete retooling of their flight control systems."

"That's why you're all here," Deliza explained. "If all we had to do was slap some anti-grav emitters on them, I wouldn't need all of you eggheads. Now, shall we get started?"

* * *

"A pleasure to finally meet you," Commander Manderon greeted, shaking Nathan's hand. "Please, make yourselves comfortable."

"Thank you," Nathan replied as he and Jessica took their seats.

"I assume you have questions about your bill?"

Nathan laughed. "About the bill, no. My question is about why you think you have the right to fire on a ship that is well outside your system."

"We have the right to defend ourselves," the commander stated firmly.

"And we have the right to freely navigate

interstellar space without fear of attack," Nathan countered, "as should all vessels."

"Your ship was on a direct course for this station," Commander Manderon insisted.

"Had we hostile intent, we would have jumped *into* your system and attacked you directly, and believe me, had we done so, you would not be sitting here making such ludicrous assertions."

"Is that a threat, Captain?" the commander wondered.

"I don't make threats, Commander," Nathan replied. "I am simply pointing out the flaws in your tactical decisions, as well as your mistaken understanding of interstellar transit rights."

"I see," the commander stated nonplussed. "However, I believe it is *your* understanding that is mistaken. You see, the advent of the jump drive creates a completely different tactical picture, one in which we have very little time to respond to threats."

"While this may be true, you are overlooking the political aspects of your tactical situation," Nathan told her.

"Politics are not my concern," the commander insisted. "My responsibility is the defense of this station and the protection of its residents."

"Which is precisely why you should not be firing missiles, indiscriminately, at any ship that approaches your system, yet is still well outside any universally accepted boundaries."

"Sanctuary station is not bound by what you refer to as 'universally accepted boundaries'."

"Well, if you expect to continue interacting *and profiting* from the rest of the interstellar community, you might want to start."

"And if *you* wish to continue conducting business

on this station, *you* will be required to abide by our policies."

"Now it is you who is making threats," Nathan replied calmly. "Commander, the day will come when you will fire upon someone who does not care about your rules, nor about your right to exist. They will rightfully interpret this act as one of aggression and will level your station without batting an eye. Those are the kinds of people who are out there. Those are the kinds of people *we* fight, day in and day out. So, you might want to be a bit more careful about whom you launch unwarranted attacks against."

"I shall share your concerns with my superiors," Commander Manderon replied. "However, I doubt they will carry much weight. In the meantime, I should inform you that they have refused your request. You may continue to approach this station in an authorized vessel, equipped with a recognized transponder, but no armed vessel will be allowed to approach this station...period. Is that understood, Captain?"

"It is."

"Now, about your bill."

"We will honor your boundaries," Nathan told her, "despite the fact that you've changed them without reasonable notification. However, we will not pay for the missiles you wasted in your unwarranted attack."

"Captain..."

"Consider the event to be a test of your defense systems," Jessica suggested. "After all, a system is only good if it is regularly tested."

"Need I remind you that you still have people on this station," Commander Manderon said, "one of whom is in no condition to be moved."

Nathan's eyes narrowed, his demeanor changing.

He rose slowly from his seat, Jessica following his lead, and cast an ice-cold, deadly stare at the still-seated commander. "You should choose your next words *very carefully*. If you take any action against my family or my people, or make any further threats to do so, veiled or otherwise, you will see just how insufficient your defense system truly is. Do *you* understand?"

"Captain..." the commander began to backpedal.

"Do you understand?" the captain repeated more firmly than before. "Yes or no?"

The commander studied him for a moment, also glancing over at Jessica, whose gaze was just as menacing as her captain's. "Yes," she finally responded. "I understand."

"Good day, Commander," Nathan said, turning to exit.

Jessica just smiled and winked, before following her captain out of the office.

Nathan and Jessica walked across the open room, past the reception counter, and out into the corridor.

"That went well," Jessica commented as they strode down the hall.

"I've had better negotiations," Nathan admitted. "I just couldn't handle that woman's sanctimonious attitude."

"She's just a functionary, charged with protecting this station," Jessica pointed out.

"You think I went too far, then."

"I'm not saying she didn't deserve it," Jessica replied. "Hell, I probably would have kicked her ass, again."

"Again?" Nathan asked, staring at her as they walked.

"Long story," Jessica replied. "This may complicate

things for the Ghatazhak, though. She *did* authorize them to carry weapons."

"Only *their* weapons, and while wearing *their* uniforms," Nathan reminded her.

"Yeah, like that's ever going to happen."

"You know what I think?" Nathan asked. "I think Commander Manderon has more authority to make decisions about the security of this station than she lets on."

"Seriously?"

"She's just using it as an excuse to deflect resentment for her decisions to a bunch of nameless, faceless *superiors*."

"I hadn't thought of that," Jessica admitted.

Nathan glanced at her as they walked, surprised. "Think about it. If you were responsible for the safety and defense of this station, wouldn't *you* demand full authority?"

"Probably," Jessica agreed.

"I think we may have worn out our welcome on Sanctuary," Nathan decided.

"What about Miri?"

"We may have to make other arrangements. It's not safe to keep her here if these people are going to keep changing the rules on us, and there's no way we're paying for the missiles *they* launched at *us*; not unless we're allowed to recover and keep them."

"What do you want me to tell Rezhik?" Jessica wondered.

"Just bring him up to speed," Nathan instructed. "I'm sure he'll figure out how to deal with it."

* * *

Deliza entered the lab, surprised to find most of the lights off and no one around. "Hello?"

A familiar, blond-haired woman peeked out from

behind a desktop view screen. "Over here," Abby called.

"Where is everyone?" Deliza asked, walking across the lab to her.

"At dinner, I imagine."

"You don't eat dinner?"

Abby held up half a sandwich.

"Dinner is not just about eating, you know," Deliza stated as she came to stand next to Abby, looking at her view screen. "It's also about giving your brain a chance to rest."

"I can't stop now. I still haven't figured out how to make these things create the same interaction with energy shields as they do on the Nighthawks."

"Are you using the same power source?"

"Of course."

"Same level?"

"Everything is exactly the same as it is on the Nighthawks," Abby insisted.

Deliza studied the view screen more closely. "Not *everything.*"

"What are you talking about?"

"The Nighthawks have two noses, a little less than two meters apart, with an emitter in each nose. Leta told us they have to be spaced apart for balance purposes. Yours aren't even a meter apart."

"Jump missiles are only one point two four meters wide," Abby explained. "I was using them as if they were mounted within the nose cone's hull."

"Maybe that has something to do with it?"

"I suppose it's possible," Abby admitted, making the necessary adjustments in the computer model. "But they would still have to be mounted within the structure of the weapon."

"You're just trying to find out how they work at

this point, right?" Deliza said. "Figure out *how* they work, first, and then figure out how to *make* them work, later."

"Makes sense, I suppose," Abby admitted.

"It's sort of our motto when it comes to reverse engineering things."

"Huh," Abby said as she ran another simulation. "Look at that."

"Look at what?"

"There, in the area of field overlap between the two emitters. The wave patterns are distorted, but in a patterned way."

"The pattern looks almost like a harmonic resonance of some sort."

"Why didn't it do the same thing when they were closer together?" Abby wondered. "There was a lot more area of overlap."

"Maybe *that's* why?" Deliza suggested. "Maybe it takes a certain *amount* of overlap in order to generate those wave patterns."

"If it's just a wave pattern that's disrupting their shields and allowing the Nighthawks to pass through them, then it shouldn't be that difficult to recreate," Abby insisted, preparing another simulation.

"Got any more sandwiches?" Deliza asked, pulling up a chair.

* * *

"I can't believe you told that guy about the Data Ark," Jessica said. "I thought the only people given access to that information were allies."

"Which is precisely why I mentioned it," Nathan replied as he prepared their shuttle for departure.

"But he said SilTek doesn't make alliances, only business arrangements."

"Alliances *are* business arrangements," Nathan

told her. "Sanctuary, Alliance Shuttle, ready for departure from bay one five four," Nathan announced over comms.

"How so?" Jessica wondered.

"Alliances can generate profit for either party," Nathan explained. "Besides, profit is not the only reward from a business arrangement. Sometimes, it is for the increased *potential* for profit."

"*Alliance Shuttle, Sanctuary Control...*"

"This is it," Nathan said.

"What if they don't let us leave?" Jessica wondered. "Are we going to blast our way out?"

"*...Cleared for auto-departure from bay one five four. Expect clearance for departure jump at two point five million kilometers departure range.*"

"Sorry, no firefight today," Nathan said. "Sanctuary, Alliance Shuttle, auto-departing bay one five four," Nathan replied as he activated their shuttle's auto-flight system. "Expecting departure jump clearance at two point five million kilometers departure range."

"I guess your threat rattled her after all," Jessica decided.

"It was meant to," Nathan replied as their shuttle lifted off the deck and headed toward the exit.

* * *

"Captain on the bridge," the guard announced as Nathan and Jessica passed.

"Welcome back," Cameron greeted. "I take it your meetings went well?"

"One, maybe; the other, not so much," Nathan admitted.

"What happened?"

"Our captain used some rather firm language with

Sanctuary's chief of security," Jessica said. "Oh, and he refused to pay for the missiles they fired at us."

"Well, at least your meeting with the SilTek representative bore results," Cameron said. "We received a message from Mister Vout as you were landing. Ariana Batista, the CEO of SilTek, has invited you to visit their world and meet with her, at your earliest convenience. They even included their location, approach instructions, and recognition codes. I guess you impressed them."

"It wasn't me who impressed them," Nathan replied. "Naralena, send a response to Mister Vout. Thank him and inform him that we will arrive within the week."

"Aye, sir."

Nathan took a deep breath, allowing himself to relax mentally for the first time in hours. "Very well. We've got a gaggle of engineers waiting to install our second long-range jump drive, and they can't get much done while we're constantly jumping around, so let's get this ship back to Rakuen, shall we?"

"Yes, sir," Cameron replied. "Where will you be?"

"Sleeping," Nathan replied. "I hope."

CHAPTER FIVE

"How did you sleep?" Cameron asked as she met up with Nathan in the corridor outside the Aurora's command briefing room.

"Like a log," Nathan replied. "It was wonderful."

"Well, you *were* running on fumes."

"Yeah, I hope Commander Manderon realized that."

"Don't worry, I'm sure you weren't too harsh on her," Cameron defended as they entered the briefing room.

"Captain on deck!" the guard announced.

"As you were," Nathan insisted as he and Cameron headed for their seats. "I hope everyone finally got a good night's sleep," he said, taking his seat. "Let's start with you, Lieutenant Commander. What's the position of the dreadnought?"

"It is still in transit, about a day away from Takara," Lieutenant Commander Shinoda reported. "The octos that survived the Orswella attack rejoined the dreadnought just before their last jump, about two hours ago. If the dreadnought holds course and layover cycles, they should be back in the Takar system by this time tomorrow."

"And the Orochi?" Nathan wondered.

"What Orochi?" Jessica asked, confused.

"They will be in position in six hours," Cameron reported.

"What Orochi?" Jessica repeated. "In position where?"

"Outside the Takar system," Nathan told her. "They did call my bluff, after all," he added with a wry smile.

"Nice," Jessica nodded. "What are their targets?"

"Gunships, frigates, and about a dozen surface targets such as troop stations, communications infrastructure, propellant production facilities..." Lieutenant Commander Shinoda listed. "Just enough to anger them a bit."

"They deserve a lot worse," Jessica said.

"Perhaps, but at this point, it's better to maintain the status quo than to escalate it," Nathan told her.

"Should we proceed with the strike?" the lieutenant commander asked.

"Affirmative," Nathan replied. "Just make sure they know it's a hit-and-run operation."

"It's Orochis One through Four, led by Commander Kainan, so there shouldn't be any problems," Cameron assured him.

"Good," Nathan replied. "Where are we with the jump-missile defenses for the Rogen system?"

"Current inventory, as of this morning, is two hundred and twenty jump missiles, spread evenly amongst Rakuen, Neramese, and the Orochi, with the exception of One through Four, of course, which are carrying extra missiles for the attack on Takara," Cameron reported. "The sixth missile plant on Rakuen should be coming online in a few days, with the one on Neramese becoming operational shortly after. With the rate of production, and the additional plants that will be coming online over the next few weeks, we should reach full stock in approximately six weeks."

"Including us?" Jessica asked.

"Yes, including us," Cameron assured her.

"Which is precisely why we *don't* want things to escalate for a while," Nathan pointed out.

"I'm betting the Dusahn know this," Jessica said. "Or, at least, they'll figure it out quickly enough."

"I'm betting *they* could use some time to build up *their* forces, as well," Nathan countered. "Losing four battleships *and* their main shipyard has *got* to hurt."

"They'll be trying to figure out how we managed to get inside their shields, as well," Cameron added.

"Until they do, they're likely to avoid putting any of their best ships in harm's way," Nathan surmised. "Not until they're, once again, certain of their superiority."

"Typical bullies," Jessica commented, "only picking fights with those they know they can beat."

"Doctor Sorenson," Nathan called, "any progress on how the Sugali anti-grav systems are able to penetrate the Dusahn shields?"

"Actually, thanks to Deliza, I may have an answer," Abby replied. "At the distance the emitters are placed on the Nighthawks, a unique wave pattern forms where the anti-grav fields overlap. The waves only form at idle settings. Our working theory is that this wave form disrupts the Dusahn's energy shields, by somehow spreading the wave pattern through the immediate area of the enemy's shields."

"Why does it only work at slow speeds?" Nathan wondered.

"I suspect it has something to do with the rate at which the wave pattern spreads through their shields."

"That won't work for the jump missiles," Cameron observed. "The speed at which they leave the launch rails is already too fast. We'd have to be traveling in the opposite direction just to get them down to the correct speed."

"And due to their jump range limitations, we'd

have to be so close that we'd have only seconds to launch before detection," Nathan added. "Is there any way to make it work at higher speeds?"

"I've only just begun my experiments and have yet to discern all the variables involved, so I can't really speculate."

"Well, the sooner the better," Nathan suggested.

"Of course," Abby replied, nodding.

"Commander," Nathan said, looking to Vladimir, "you're up."

"The damage sustained over the last few battles is minimal," Vladimir reported. "Therefore, I have tasked all available personnel on the installation of the second long-range jump drive."

"How long until it's completed?" Nathan asked.

"As long as we don't run into any problems or get delayed by jumping around, about two weeks. Once complete, we will deal with the current battle damage."

"Until we have enough range to jump anywhere within our current operational area, engage the enemy, and jump back, we cannot take down the Dusahn," Nathan said. "So, you get the same instructions as Doctor Sorenson...the sooner the better."

"Two weeks," Vladimir repeated firmly.

Nathan turned to Deliza next. "Any progress on fitting the Gunyoki with anti-grav lift capabilities?"

"It should work just fine," Deliza replied. "We have some flight control system integration issues to deal with, but we'll figure it out. I expect to have a prototype ready by the end of the week."

"Excellent," Nathan replied. "Hopefully, we'll be back by then."

"About that," Cameron said. "Have you considered the risks? I mean, it *could* be a trap, after all."

"I'm so proud," Jessica joked.

"Seriously, as far-fetched as that might seem, it fits. What better way to lure us into a trap than to dangle some *super-tech* in front of us?"

"How would they know we were going to Sanctuary?" Nathan asked. "And if they *did* know, why not just ambush us there?"

"What if they already *control* SilTek?" Cameron suggested. "You could be flying into a Dusahn-controlled system."

"Lieutenant Rezhik already did some digging back on Sanctuary," Jessica assured her. "Everything indicates that SilTek is exactly what their representative says it is: the biggest tech company in the quadrant. There is no indication that the Dusahn are even *aware* of its *existence*."

"Regardless of the risk," Nathan said, "which I believe to be quite low, the potential for a new ally is worth it."

"Even when their representative swears they don't believe in alliances?" Cameron challenged.

"Even if all we get out of this are faster, more efficient manufacturing technologies, it will be worth it," Nathan replied.

"I still think you should take a squad of Ghatazhak with you," Cameron insisted.

"Everything indicates SilTek is a peaceful, corporate-owned world," Jessica told her. "I don't think we'll have any trouble."

"Well, if you do, we're going to be three max-range jumps away from you, so you're going to be on your own for at least twelve hours, assuming you can even get a call for help out to us."

"We'll leave a comm-drone somewhere in the SilTek system before we land," Nathan promised. "That way, we can call for help if needed."

"And if they find it?" Cameron wondered.

Nathan sighed, thinking for a moment. "It'll take us two days to get there. Figure at least two or three days there, then another two days back. If everything is on the up and up, then they shouldn't mind if we keep in touch with you. So, if you don't hear from us in a week, you'll know we're in trouble."

* * *

Nathan left his ready room and stepped onto the bridge, about to head out.

"New message from General Telles," Naralena reported as he passed.

Nathan paused, turning to face her. "Good news, I hope."

"What's up?" Cameron wondered, walking over to him.

Nathan quickly scanned the data pad Naralena had handed him. "The general is requesting personal weapons to arm the Corinari and create an interim police force, until a sufficient number of Orswellans can be trained to take over."

"Trouble on Orswella?"

"He's concerned that Dusahn operatives may be mixed in among the population and could conduct strikes against critical infrastructure, or worse."

"Or worse?"

"Orswella has several antimatter power plants," Nathan explained. "Any one of them, if sabotaged, could take out a large portion of the city, if not all of it."

"We don't *have* a stash of personal weapons,"

Cameron said. "At least not in the numbers he's talking about."

Nathan sighed. "I suppose we could fabricate them, but that would take some time."

"It would be a start."

"Naralena, send a message to Marcus on Sanctuary. Tell him we need guns...lots of them."

"Yes, sir."

"Marcus?" Cameron wondered.

"There are a lot of black-market weapons dealers on Sanctuary," Nathan explained. "Hopefully, one of them can handle a large order, quickly."

"Are you sure that's wise?"

"Nope. Got any better ideas?"

"At the moment, no," Cameron admitted.

"Then, Marcus is it," Nathan replied.

* * *

Nathan and Jessica stepped through the hatch into the Aurora's main hangar bay, each of them carrying a small duffel bag. To the starboard side, the Nighthawks were preparing for departure.

"Commander," Nathan called out as they drew near. "I'll catch up to you," he told Jessica. "Leaving already?" he asked the commander.

"Nothing personal, Captain," Commander Prechitt joked. "I promised Commander Verbeek I'd get his pilots back to him in a few days."

"Well, now that the Dusahn are back on their side of the playground, I suppose we can do without you, for now. Hopefully, Doctor Sorenson will figure out how to make our jump missiles penetrate their shields."

"That would certainly make things easier," the commander agreed.

"Tell Commander Verbeek and the rest of our

143

pilots that we look forward to their return," Nathan told him.

"I'll be sure to do so," the commander replied.

"I'd like to thank you, as well, Miss Sane," Nathan told Talisha. "None of this is your fight."

"I respectfully disagree, Captain," Talisha replied. "Stopping the Dusahn is *everyone's* fight. If not now, then eventually."

"If only *everyone* saw it that way," Nathan replied.

"Are *you* going somewhere, Captain?" Commander Prechitt wondered, noticing the duffel bag in his hand.

"Another diplomatic mission," Nathan replied. "To SilTek, this time."

"*SilTek?*" Talisha said.

"Yes, you've been there?"

"Oh, no," Talisha assured him. "You have to be fairly well connected to get permission to visit SilTek. But I *have* heard a lot about it."

"Oh, really? What can you tell me?"

"Only that it's supposed to be a very beautiful, and a very *advanced*, world."

"You know people who have been there?" Nathan asked.

"Oh, no, I don't generally run in such circles," Talisha assured him. "It's more like second, or even third, hand knowledge. I don't suppose you need a fighter escort," she added with a wink.

"Probably not the best way to make a good first impression, I'm afraid."

"Of course," she replied. "I had to try."

"What about your other three ships?" Nathan asked the commander. "The ones that were damaged?"

"One of them has been repaired enough to make

the trip home," the commander explained. "The other two are hitching a ride on the Weatherly."

"Ah, of course," Nathan replied.

"You know, I still cannot fathom a jump range of five hundred light years," the commander said, shaking his head.

"Twice that, once we get the second jump drive installed," Nathan boasted.

"It will open up a whole new era," the commander insisted.

"I'm just hoping it doesn't open up a whole new set of problems, as well," Nathan said, picking up his duffel. "Safe journeys."

"To you, as well, Captain," Talisha replied.

* * *

Lieutenant Rezhik entered the main living area of their suite on Sanctuary. "Mister Taggart, may I speak with you?" he asked Marcus as he headed out onto the patio.

"I was just getting comfortable," Marcus grumbled, rising from his recliner to following the lieutenant into the simulated outdoor space. "What's so important you took me from the game?"

"What game?" the lieutenant wondered.

"Ori-ball."

"I've never heard of it," the lieutenant admitted.

"A bunch of guys in padded tights flying around a sealed room on some kind of flying plank, trying to kill each other while also trying to whack a hovering ball into holes at each end."

Lieutenant Rezhik looked confused. "Do the players *actually* die?"

"No, but they do get busted up quite a bit."

"Unusual game."

"It's new. As far as I can tell, it only exists here, on Sanctuary."

"I have received a message from the Aurora. General Telles is in need of weapons to arm the Corinari, in order to form an interim police force to help protect Orswella."

"Protect them from what?"

"He suspects the presence of Dusahn operatives."

"How many guns does he need?"

"An exact number was not given, but considering their purpose, I would guess a few thousand, at least."

"Handguns and rifles, I suppose."

"Correct," the lieutenant confirmed. "Stun weapons would be of use, as well."

"Tall order," Marcus said, rubbing his chin. "Most of the gun dealers on Sanctuary deal in smaller numbers or specialty weapons. The only dealers who can move that kind of order are down in the Jungle."

"The *Jungle*?"

"The lower levels, beneath the environmental systems and the heat and humidity exchangers. They call it the Jungle because it is hot and humid down there. Stinks like a swamp, as well. Probably the most dangerous area on the station."

"You have been there?"

Marcus laughed. "Oh, yeah."

"If it is that dangerous, perhaps one of my men should accompany you?"

"Not if you want me to find a seller," Marcus argued. "They'll make your guys in a heartbeat. Better I go alone."

"Are you certain?"

"Yeah, you just have to know how to talk to these

people. The moment they sense weakness, they'll pounce."

"Yet another reason to call it the Jungle."

"You got it," Marcus replied. "How soon does the general need these guns?"

"As soon as possible," the lieutenant replied. "I'm afraid your ori-ball game will have to wait."

"That's okay," Marcus snickered. "It'll give me an excuse to miss out on whatever green crap Neli's making and get some *real* food down in the Jungle."

* * *

It had taken fewer than two days for the common markets to reopen after the Dusahn's failed retaliatory attack against Orswella. Even with the additional destruction the bombardment had brought, they were determined to take advantage of their newfound freedom.

The common markets were once the pride of Orswellan culture. Farmers, ranchers, and makers of any basic products that people used day in and day out were sold there. In the early days of the settlement, the markets had been the sole source of such products, and the original settlers had taken great pride in their wares. Over time, as with all the colonies of Earth, industrialization took over, and the common markets faded into near obscurity, their only patrons being the traditionalists, who were few in number.

The arrival of the Dusahn had given the common markets a resurgence. Their conquerors had usurped most of what Orswellan industry produced for their own uses. Rationing of basic needs had given the common markets a new customer base. The Dusahn had wisely chosen to ignore the markets, since their

147

existence served to ease the suffering of the people and helped to keep them in line.

Although the Dusahn were now gone, many feared an even greater shortage of food and water. Thousands swarmed the rows of traders, buying as much as they could for fear the credits they held would lose value, now that the government that backed them was gone.

On this day, there was a palpable feeling of hope among the patrons. Despite all they had endured over the last few days, and despite the sudden shortages of even the most basic needs, the market's ability to save them was inspiring. Shoppers carried all they could manage, with plans to return for more once they could get home and unload their goods.

The market was comprised of four intersecting streets, all of which met at a park in the middle. On some days, live musicians would perform in the center square. Today was no exception, and one of Orswella's most prominent musical groups had an audience of hundreds, captivated by their lilting melodies.

The unexpected number of patrons, as well as the popularity of the performers, forced the Ghatazhak to maintain a presence, as well. The sudden removal of a controlling power historically opened the door for criminals and opportunists alike. Until a police force could be mustered, the Ghatazhak were the only law enforcement available. Unfortunately, the crowd numbered in the thousands, and the Ghatazhak's total numbers were just over one hundred, the majority of whom were guarding Orswella's most critical infrastructures. Thus, the common markets had a minimal squad of Ghatazhak to handle security.

To make matters worse, their rules of engagement were even more limited than usual.

When a man wandering through the market appeared to have little interest in the vendors and their wares, no one noticed. When that same man wandered behind the open-air stage, where the majority of the crowd was gathered, no one noticed. No one was aware of the threat until it presented itself; when the man walked out onto the stage, grabbed the microphone from one of the vocalists and proclaimed, *"There are more ways to punish the disloyal than from the sky!"* The man pulled a remote out of his pocket, pressed a button, and the entire market, along with every person, disappeared in a brilliant, white explosion.

* * *

The Jungle was aptly named. Not only was it hot and humid, but there was a palpable 'predator and prey' environment down in the bowels of Sanctuary station. To anyone foolish enough to wander into the Jungle unaware, it seemed like a wonderland of sin and debauchery. While the upper levels were cleaner, more evenly lit, and far more regulated, the Jungle was the exact opposite. Although many areas were colorfully illuminated, shadows everywhere hid its ramshackle reality. The air was thick with numerous odors, some of them foul, and others meant to mask the unpleasant aromas. A low-hanging smoke wafted about, weaving in and out of makeshift booths and storefronts, generated by countless sources, the majority of which were illegal on most worlds...but not on Sanctuary and, especially, not in the Jungle.

It was said that those who entered the Jungle, left there forever changed. It was a place that hosted all the things humanity needed, but to which no one wanted to admit their dependence. Marcus had entered the Jungle for the first time at an early age; although, at the time, it had not been relegated to just the lower decks. In his heyday, most of Sanctuary was 'the Jungle', but of varying degrees. Even then, the lower levels had been the most dangerous and the most mesmerizing. His first visit had changed him, as well, introducing him to all the evils and ills of humanity; all of them assembled in a one-stop shopping environment. Most people could go a lifetime and never be exposed to a fraction of what the lower levels of Sanctuary had to offer. Just a few hours in the Jungle could expose one to a wide range of sins, even a few that most had never heard of. On his first visit, Marcus had remained for an entire week.

But that had been more than a century ago... or was it two? So much of his past had long been forgotten. Decades of faster-than-light travel while in suspended animation had that effect. Details were lost, time scales were altered...relativity was a bitch. At times, Marcus had cursed his early career choice. A long hauler didn't get to have relationships. Even the crews he worked with were mostly strangers, the majority of them signing on and then jumping ship once they reached their destination. Few were able to stick with the job, and those who did usually had their reasons.

For Marcus, it had been to escape the mistakes of his youth. He had fallen in with the wrong crowd at an early age and had done things he was not proud of. He had believed in the goals of the Golaran rebels, but in the end, they had been just another band of terrorists using false narratives of injustice, inequality, and oppression to recruit the young, the naive, and the idealistic dreamers, promising utopias that could never be delivered. Marcus had bought it hook, line, and sinker, and it had gotten him killed more than once...just not dead.

Few could safely walk the shadowy maze that was the Jungle. One needed to have *the look* that told the many predators hiding in those shadows that they were not an easy target and should be avoided. Marcus had that look about him most of the time, even when he was happy, but especially when he was drunk. Therefore, he stopped by one of the many saloons near the entrance to the Jungle, in order to chemically enhance his menacing expression.

Marcus rather enjoyed the frightened expressions he elicited from first-time visitors crossing his path. Even a few of the regulars shot him a double-take, unsure if he was one of them and, therefore, should not be considered prey. This game was yet another reason this part of Sanctuary had such a moniker.

Like every person who entered the Jungle—vendors and patrons alike—Marcus was followed by not only station security cameras, but by the eyes of watchers, hired by the various capis who ruled the lower levels. He noticed his watcher within minutes of leaving the saloon. They were generally skinny, unhealthy-looking, young men and women, most of whom had somehow found themselves indebted to a capi. What made them so easy to spot was the mere fact that had they themselves been patrons, they would have had someone watching *them*; more likely they would already be in the sights of one of the Jungle's many predators—worse yet, already a victim.

Marcus's watcher was average at best; a teenager who was jittery and always looking about, as if

151

she expected some creature to jump out at her at any moment—which wasn't far from the truth. On more than one occasion, the girl had let herself be distracted, forcing Marcus to wait for her to catch up. If he approached a Jungle rep for a major dealer without a watcher, he likely wouldn't get the time of day from them. Worse yet, he might get the business end of a pug.

Any arms dealers who could move large orders were often difficult to spot. Their booths looked like any other—laden with all sorts of weapons. From popguns, which were more noise than sting, to boomers that could bring down a building with a single shot. Of course, all of them had been properly and permanently disabled by station personnel upon arrival. Since the Jaton incident, all weapons were also fitted with a transponder, which immediately alerted station security if that device left its designated display or storage area.

The trick to spotting the real muscle was the *location* of their booths. All were directly in front of, or steps away from, a legit, unrelated business like a dunga shop, barrot lounge, or brothel. This allowed private conversations involving large-scale customers to be conducted within the confines of these businesses, away from the prying eyes and ears of station security, as well as the competition.

Although it had been a long time since Marcus had trolled the Jungle on a regular basis, he had been there a few times since his most recent arrival on Sanctuary. He had told Neli it was for business purposes; that he needed to scout the wares for the Alliance, just in case some unusual weapon, not available on the upper levels, was to be found. Mostly, that had been true. Despite his new, almost-legal life, and the comforts that it brought him at times, he still longed for the adventure and adrenaline rush that a visit to the Jungle provided.

Marcus had chosen to make his first pitch to a dealer who was only displaying the basics, and not the military-grade stuff. Such vendors were usually eager to service large orders because one deal could sustain them for months. Theirs was a hard lot, as their customers were usually looking for a single weapon, and an inexpensive one at that. Unfortunately, for that very reason, most of them did not have the connections necessary to move a few thousand weapons, although several of them tried to convince him otherwise. Luckily, Marcus could smell the bullshit before it even left their mouths.

Eventually, his wanderings landed him at a booth displaying the weaponry he sought, as well as several pieces that, while more appropriate for heavy assault, might also be of use. He asked the scruffy-looking man behind the displays the usual questions, testing his knowledge and salesmanship, both of which were sorely lacking. In fact, the man seemed downright uninterested in selling anything to Marcus, at all.

"You know, seein' as how no one's even givin' your shit a second look, you might want to seem a bit more interested in those who do," Marcus finally told the man.

"Piss off, old man."

"Nice sales tactic," Marcus replied, undaunted.

"How about fuck off?" the younger man suggested. "That work better for you?"

Marcus laughed. "Good thing there's a big-ass table between us."

The younger man stared at Marcus for a moment

and then looked over at one of the men standing to the left side of the booth. "Tell you what, pops, you leave now, and I'll let you live. Hell, I might even let you keep all your big, fat, fucking fingers."

"And here I was gonna buy a few thousand of these," Marcus replied, picking up one of the display weapons. His eyes followed the man moving around the left side of the table while still staring at the scruffy smartass smiling at him from behind it.

"I believe you were asked politely to leave," the second man growled as he approached Marcus from the left.

"Yeah, he asked me to leave," Marcus conceded, "but there weren't nothin' polite about it." Marcus turned to stare the second man in the eyes. "In fact, it was downright rude, if you ask me."

"No one was asking you," the second man argued, staring right back. "We were *telling* you...to leave... now. Is *that* clear enough for you?"

Marcus stared at the second man, their gazes still locked. "I ain't goin' nowhere," Marcus stated confidently. "The only person here that's goin' anywhere is you, and that's two fucking steps back while your legs still work. Is *that* clear enough for *you*?"

The second man stared at Marcus for a moment, then smiled and glanced back at the scruffy guy behind the table. "I like this old fart. He's got guts."

"Or he's stupid," his cohort stated, signaling the watcher who was standing behind Marcus, across the corridor.

The skinny, young woman hurried over, moving around Marcus and the second man as they continued to stare at each other. She went up to the scruffy man behind the table and whispered something to him, causing him to pick up his comm-unit from the table behind him and place a call.

"*Yeah?*" the man on the comm-unit asked.

"It's Bose. We've got a live one out here."

"*How live?*"

"Live enough."

After a moment, the man on the comm-unit replied, "*Send him back.*"

The scruffy man ended the call, setting the comm-unit back on the table behind him. "I guess you get to keep your fingers, pops."

The second man, standing nose to nose with Marcus, smiled and stepped aside.

"Lucky me," Marcus said, moving past the man and heading for the seedy-looking business behind, and to the left of, the booth.

"Good luck, old man," the scruffy-looking man said as he passed. "You're gonna need it."

* * *

General Telles sat in his office in Orswella's capitol building, studying the footage of the attack in the common markets only hours ago.

"I have a preliminary report on casualties," Commander Kellen announced as he entered the room.

"How many?"

"Five thousand three hundred dead; three thousand eight hundred wounded. The numbers are approximate and are expected to grow."

"Have we confirmed the identity of the bomber?" the general asked.

"He does not exist in the Orswellan population registry," the commander replied. "We can only assume he was Dusahn at this point, based on his final words."

"And the bomb?"

"The blast signature suggests multiple devices, all detonated simultaneously. Blast residue in various places shows traces of kentite."

"Which is used in Dusahn warheads," the general surmised. "There was no way for them to know that the reopening of the markets would draw such a crowd. We didn't even know about the musicians until an hour before they opened."

"Which suggests the bombs were placed by more than one person, and that there is a supply of them on hand."

"An ample supply," General Telles added. "Otherwise, they wouldn't waste them on crowds of people; they'd use them against infrastructure."

"Unless they're stupid," Commander Kellen joked.

"We must assume they are following a plan, of sorts. If it's not designated targets, then there's a list of suggested target types."

"They may even have explosive devices pre-planted. We should fully scan all critical infrastructure targets, as well as places where large numbers of people regularly gather."

"Let's start with the power plants, water treatment facilities, and communications," General Telles instructed. "After that, we go to the hospitals. I fear we will need them."

* * *

Marcus stepped through the door and was immediately surprised. Instead of the usual dingy, poorly lit, foul-smelling shop selling all manner of vices, he found an elegant, well-adorned, clean lobby that looked more like a hotel than a seedy front for an enterprise of questionable legality.

"How can I help you, sir?" the well-dressed, young man at the reception desk asked politely.

Marcus squinted a moment, his mouth twisting unnaturally as he tried to make sense of things. "Uh, I'm not sure I'm in the right place," he admitted, cautiously approaching the counter. "I was looking to buy...uh..." Marcus lowered his voice to a near whisper before continuing, "...*guns...lots of them*?"

The young man smiled, holding back his laughter. "You don't have to whisper, sir. There is nothing illegal about selling guns on Sanctuary."

"I feel underdressed," Marcus admitted.

"Not at all, sir. Name?"

"Uh...Taggart. Marcus Taggart."

"If you'll make yourself comfortable, Mister Taggart, Mister Ruef will be with you shortly. Feel free to help yourself to something at the courtesy bar."

"Over there?"

"Yes, sir."

"Right." Marcus straightened his jacket and walked over to the waiting area, pausing to pick up a pastry at the courtesy bar on his way. Moments after wolfing down the treat in a single bite, a well-dressed, young man with perfect hair appeared from a hidden door.

"Mister Taggart?"

Marcus stood, again straightening his jacket. "That's me."

"If you'll come this way, sir."

Marcus headed over to the previously hidden doorway, following the man into the corridor. "Where are we going?"

"All volume purchases are handled by the head

157

of our organization," the man explained as he led Marcus down the hallway and around the corner.

Once around the corner, the man stepped aside, taking position alongside a door, which he opened. "If you will please wait in here, Mister Koren will be with you shortly."

Marcus stepped cautiously through the doorway, into another well-appointed room. There was a round table surrounded by six chairs, and a sim-window covering an entire wall. Marcus walked around the table, pausing to pick up the remote for the sim-window, flipping through several simulation views before finally settling on a downtown skyline of some unknown city. He continued wandering around the room, checking two other doors and finding them locked. Finally, he returned to the table and took a seat.

Marcus felt tired, more tired than usual, and he wondered if the few drinks he had consumed, prior to beginning his exploration of the Jungle, had been a mistake. It had been weeks since he had anything stronger than a glass of ale with lunch, and he was not as young as he had once been. Then again, he had been a hard drinker most of his life and doubted that a few watered-down cocktails would do him in. It had been a long couple of days with Miri awakening, Nathan's visit, and their meeting with Gunwy. Add to that his usual lack of quality sleep, and it was no surprise that he was so tired.

I'm gettin' old.

A door opened, and two men, both of whom, though well dressed, would have looked more comfortable in the same type of attire as Marcus. Immediately, he pegged them as muscle, which was expected. Despite the respectable trappings of this particular business, gun runners were gun runners. They generally operated out of places like Sanctuary because they obtained their inventory using less-than-legal methods. While the sale of weapons might not be illegal on Sanctuary, volume sales were subject to much greater scrutiny; hence, the Jungle.

The two men stepped to either side of the door, and a middle-aged man, also wearing a business suit, although one with a bit more flair, entered the room.

"Mister Taggart," the man greeted, "I trust you weren't waiting long."

"Not really," Marcus replied, trying to seem indifferent to their attempts to appear as a legitimate business. Marcus knew damned well they were just gangsters in business suits, and the scar on the side of the man's face confirmed it. He'd seen it all before, just not with the fancy offices.

"I am Dinesh Koren," the man said, offering his hand, "the leader of this...organization."

"Marcus Taggart," Marcus replied, rising to shake the man's hand. "Nice place you got, here. Not sure why you need it."

"Just because we deal in the shadows does not mean we must live in them," Mister Koren replied, moving to his seat at the head of the table.

"Then, you *live* here," Marcus surmised.

"It's an expression, Mister Taggart. I'm told you wish to purchase a large number of weapons."

"Straight to the point," Marcus replied. "Finally."

"What type of weapons?" Mister Koren asked, ignoring Marcus's comment.

"Sidearms, rifles, maybe some stunners. Nothing too heavy."

"You looking to start a revolution somewhere?"

"I don't see how that's any of your business," Marcus replied, looking indignant.

Mister Koren placed his elbows on the table, his fingers spread wide and touching those on the opposite hand, tapping his index fingers together as he eyed Marcus with mild disapproval. "It *is* my business," he corrected. "This is *all* my business," he continued, spreading his arms wide as he leaned back in his chair, "and since you're asking me to sell you enough firepower to threaten *my* organization, *why* you need the weapons is *my* business, as well."

"How about *humanitarian reasons*," Marcus suggested. "Does that work for you?"

"If you expect me to sell a few thousand guns to you, you'll have to be more forthcoming, I'm afraid."

"Maybe I should take my business elsewhere," Marcus decided, rising to depart.

"With whom?" Mister Koren wondered. "Bezel, Owyang, the Zant brothers?" Mister Koren smiled. "One call, and they'd rather slice you open than take your money."

Marcus shook his head as he stood. "Put an ape in a suit, and he's still an ape."

"I suggest you sit back down, Mister Taggart."

"Or what?" Marcus asked, glaring at him.

"Or the other two apes in suits will *make* you sit."

Marcus turned to glare at his muscle, as well. "You think just because I'm older than the two of you fucks combined, that I'm an easy mark?"

"Do you feel tired, Mister Taggart?" Mister Koren asked.

Marcus turned to look at Mister Koren, who was still seated. "What?"

"You should," he continued. "You see, that pastry you inhaled was laced with verazentalin. It's made from a flower that grows only on Para-Allen Four. They use it as a sleep aid, but in larger doses, it's quite effective at taking the *fight* out of our guests. In fact, you might want to sit back down, before you *fall* down."

Marcus felt dizzy. "Classy," he said, plopping back down into his chair, feeling as if his legs were about to give out. "You don't know who the fuck you're dealing with."

Mister Koren rose, confidently walking over to Marcus. "Perhaps," he said as he leaned down, coming nose to nose with him, "but I promise you; we will find out."

* * *

To be a Ghatazhak meant many things. Above all, it meant having complete control over one's body and mind. To Torren Rezhik, nothing exemplified this concept more than how a Ghatazhak slept: perfectly flat on one's back, hands at their sides.

When a Ghatazhak slept, he did so lightly. There was a balance point when sleeping. Too lightly, and the full benefit of slumber was unrealized. Too deeply, and one might not respond swiftly enough to a sudden threat. Such mental discipline while sleeping took considerable practice, but once the balance was achieved, a Ghatazhak could sleep anywhere, in any position, and still be able to switch from slumber to combat in the blink of an eye. In the field, this gave a Ghatazhak considerable peace of mind.

Many Ghatazhak achieved this balance in a variety of sleeping positions, even Lieutenant Rezhik. However, he preferred the supine position whenever possible, despite the fact that his fellow Ghatazhak often teased him for what they called *sleeping at attention.*

Ryk Brown

When the knock came at his door, the lieutenant's eyes popped open. In one smooth motion, he was upright, on his feet and headed for the door, reaching it before the second knock.

Neli was startled by the quickness at which the lieutenant had responded. "Oh, good, you're not asleep yet."

"What can I do for you, Miss Ravel?"

"I'm worried about Marcus," she replied. "It's not like him to be out this late without calling."

"Have you tried contacting him, yourself?" the lieutenant queried.

"About a hundred times," she insisted. "I think his comm-unit is turned off."

The lieutenant stepped back, returning to his nightstand to retrieve his own comm-unit.

"Why would he do that?" she asked, following him inside.

"I can think of several reasons," the lieutenant assured her, hoping to calm her nerves. The truth was that none of the reasons that came to mind were very good. After a moment of working with his own comm-unit, he announced, "His comm-unit is not turned off, it is disabled."

"What?" Neli was nearly beside herself with concern. "How can you tell?"

"The tracking chip in the Sanctuary-issued comm-unit continues to work even when the device is powered down. In order to disable the chip, you must remove it, which is *not* something that is done *accidentally*."

"Why would he *do* that?" Neli wondered.

"He would not," the lieutenant replied as he picked up his data pad.

"You think something is wrong?" Neli asked.

162

"It is possible," the lieutenant admitted.

"I knew it was a bad idea for him to go to the Jungle," Neli said. "Why did you let him go by himself?"

"His reasons for wanting to go alone were sound," the lieutenant explained, "and no one is more qualified to *read* that particular situation than Marcus."

"What are you doing?" she asked, noticing how intently the lieutenant was studying his data pad.

"All Ghatazhak wear a ring."

"Yeah, I noticed, but what does..."

"It contains a small transponder, which emits a signal that can only be detected by our tactical awareness systems."

"I don't understand," Neli said, frustrated. "What does that have to..."

"I gave Marcus one of our rings before he departed. This data pad is tied into my tactical helmet," the lieutenant explained, pointing to his helmet hanging on the wall. "He is still in the Jungle."

"Then, he's alive?" Neli asked, hope slipping into her voice.

"I cannot determine his condition. However, he has not moved in more than an hour, which is not a good sign."

"You don't know Marcus," Neli said, struggling to hold onto the hope that he was alright. "That man can sit in one place and watch the world go by for hours on end, as long as he doesn't need to use the toilet."

"Then, there is hope," the lieutenant said as he picked up his comm-set and placed it on his head. "Attention all Ghatazhak. Condition Three. Rally in the main living area in two minutes."

"What are we going to do?" Neli asked with pleading eyes.

"We're going to find him," the lieutenant replied confidently.

* * *

Blood and sweat were making Marcus's eyes sting whenever he opened them. His wrists were sore from the restraints holding his hands behind his back, unable to defend himself. He had lost count of the number of blows they had inflicted upon him and the number of times they had made precise incisions in locations designed to elicit maximum pain but minimal bleeding.

"It is only a matter of time before you break and tell us everything we want to know," Mister Koren said from his comfortable vantage point a few meters away.

Marcus forced his left eye open, followed by his right, suffering through the stinging. "You know... nobody beats...information...out of people...... anymore," he said, barely able to get the words out through the pain. "They use...drugs......or tech...... I guess...you're just...too stupid...to know that."

"Let's just say I prefer the *old-school* methodologies," Mister Koren replied. "You see, there's a *psychological* aspect to physical torture. It creates *fear*, both in the one being tortured, as well as his cohorts. It is always there, silently gnawing at their consciousness, affecting their decision-making processes."

Marcus laughed. "The joke's...on you...asshole...... I ain't...that deep."

"I beg to differ."

"Besides..." Marcus continued, "I already...told you..."

"...That you work for the Karuzari Alliance, and that you need weapons for the people of *Orswella*, wherever the hell *that* is, so they can police themselves after your people so *heroically* liberated them from Dusahn subjugation. Sorry, Mister Taggart, but I'm still not convinced."

"That's your...fucking problem."

"Again, I beg to differ," Mister Koren replied, signaling one of his men to continue the torture.

Marcus screamed as another electrical shock coursed through his body. His fingers outstretched, his toes curled, his neck tensed...every muscle in his body cried out in protest. It was only for a few seconds, but each shock seemed to last an eternity. The only thing getting him through the pain was knowing they had no intention of killing him, not if there was any chance of making a profit from him. "God damn you!" he cursed once the electricity was shut off again.

"You have spirit, old man," Mister Koren congratulated. "Most men would not have lasted as long."

"I already told you......I work...for the...Karuzari... Alliance!"

Mister Koren rose from his seat, strolling casually toward Marcus as he spoke. "We have run your DNA through our database, Mister Taggart, or Wallace, Hayes, Tedan, or one of the many names you have used throughout your remarkably long life. You know, you may have done business with my great-grandfather. He sold arms to the Crispin Rebellion, of which you were one of its more ruthless members. In fact, there may still be a reward for your head on that world."

"You should…give them…a call," Marcus replied, trying to sound indifferent.

"Oh, I have, I assure you," Mister Koren replied. "Fortunately, the hour is late in their capital, so we have time to explore the possibilities."

"Possibilities?" Marcus wondered, spitting blood from his mouth as he spoke.

"Yes, you see, it has been some time since my men have had the chance to torture someone. So, they've had ample opportunity to discuss various strategies of physical abuse and its effectiveness in the retrieval of information."

Marcus smiled, spitting more blood. "Lucky me."

"Continue," Mister Koren said, turning to return to his chair.

Marcus forced his eyes open wide, first studying the man to his right, then to his left.

"What are you looking at, old man?" the man to Marcus's left asked.

"Just gettin'…a good look," Marcus replied, "so I know…who to kill…later."

CHAPTER SIX

Buildings, a dozen stories tall, lined the streets of Orswella's business district, each of them interconnected by a myriad of overhead breezeways at various levels. Traffic ebbed and flowed around them, pulsing through the intersections in disorderly fashion as Orswellans went about their routines. Despite the previous day's terrorist bombing of the common markets, the business leaders and industrialists were determined to restore their newly liberated world to its former glory. The Dusahn were gone. All that remained were their covert operatives bent on punishing the rightful occupants of the planet. But their numbers could not be many, and the Orswellans were determined to outlast them, no matter the cost.

Corporal Venezia and Specialist Brummett walked along the main street of the business district. As always, their heads were on a pivot, and their vision was split between their tactical displays and the view beyond.

"I couldn't do it," Specialist Brummett said.

"Couldn't do what?"

"Work in the same place every day. Do the same *thing* every day."

"Isn't that what we do now?" the corporal wondered.

"You know what I mean."

"It doesn't seem so bad to me," Corporal Venezia said.

"Now I *know* you're lying."

"That obvious, huh?"

"How do they do it?"

"Just different kinds of people," the corporal replied. "My father was like that. He was an accountant his entire life."

"What does he do now?"

"I have no idea," the corporal admitted. "I haven't spoken with anyone in my family in years. As far as I know, my father could be doing the Dusahn's books right now."

The tram, connecting the western residential areas to the business district, pulled up to a stop at the elevated platform. The doors opened, and more than a hundred people disembarked from every car.

Orswellans in business attire flooded onto the platform, spilling down the stairs that led to the street below. Among them were eight men in dissimilar dress, their only similarity being the matching satchels they carried.

"That's funny," Specialist Brummett said.

"I wasn't kidding," the corporal insisted. "He could be..."

"No, I just picked up a weapons signature, but it disappeared a moment later."

Corporal Venezia tapped the side of his helmet, activating his comms. "Faulds, Prisk, you guys picking up any weapons signatures?"

"*Negative,*" Specialist Faulds replied.

"*You got something, Vinnie?*" Sergeant Morano asked, picking up the comms traffic.

"Brumms did, but only for a moment."

"*Direction?*" the sergeant asked.

"Tram platform south of us," Specialist Brummett replied.

Sergeant Morano checked the tactical display on his helmet visor as he stood in the central square, visually scanning the passersby. "That would be the one at Parker and Alla," he decided. "Faulds, you and Prisk head toward the platform. Take Wellesly to Alla. Once you round the corner, you should have a clear sweep."

"*You got it, Sarge,*" Specialist Faulds replied.

"Vinnie, you guys backtrack. See if you can pick up the signature again," the sergeant added.

"*Two Blue Alpha One and Two are backtracking south on Parker,*" the corporal confirmed.

"Don't forget to call out your locations," the sergeant reminded them. "Until we figure out what it is about the Orswellans's communications gear that's fucking with our tactical sensors, we need to call out everything."

"*Brummsy just farted,*" Corporal Venezia announced, smiling. "*Did you want me to report that, as well?*"

"Funny."

A man in a dark business suit, carrying a satchel over his shoulder, exited the stairwell on the sixth floor, pausing to orient himself, and then strode across the hallway into the nearest office.

"Good afternoon, sir," the young lady behind the reception desk greeted. "Do you have an appointment?"

"I'm afraid not," the man stated as he walked around the desk.

"What are you..." The young lady never got to finish her sentence; the attacker grabbed her head, snapping her neck with a quick, expert twist.

He dropped her onto her desk, quickly heading

into the corridor behind her. As he passed the side offices, a few people poked their heads out, curious about the thump they had heard.

He continued down the corridor, paying no mind to the onlookers as he opened the door to the office at the end, stepping inside and closing it behind him.

"I beg your pardon," the woman behind the desk objected as the unknown intruder locked the door. "You can't just come barging in here like this," she continued as she stood.

The man turned around, his right hand flicking something toward her. A small, disc-shaped object zipped across the room, six tiny emitters popping out as it spun. The emitters charged the instant they deployed, creating a blue halo around the disc as it sailed across the office, separating the woman's head from her body before deactivating and bouncing off the window behind her.

The man stepped behind the desk, pushing the headless corpse aside, and kicked the disembodied head to the corner of the room.

Placing his satchel on the desk behind him, he opened it and pulled out two identical devices, which he stuck to the wall on either side of the window overlooking the street below.

After activating the devices, the man reached into his satchel and pulled out two more objects: a window cutter and a folded-up laser rifle.

———

A red triangle appeared on Corporal Venezia's tactical visor, accompanied by descriptive symbology indicating the type of threat the icon represented, along with its position and elevation. "Hot target," the corporal announced. "Are you seeing this, Sergeant?"

"I am," Sergeant Morano replied over comms. *"Looks like the target's in a building at two four five Parker, six floors up. Weapons data indicates precision laser. Probably a sniper rifle."*

"If he just charged up, then he's about to..." Another triangle appeared. "Second hot target," he announced, quickening his pace. "Opposite side of the street, same altitude."

Two more triangles appeared on his tactical visor. At the same time, the high-pitched *zing* of laser fire could be heard as tiny bolts of bright red laser energy began dropping people in the streets below.

"Active shooters!" the corporal reported, bringing his weapon up to his shoulder and breaking into a combat jog.

In the streets, people scrambled, screaming in terror. Tiny, red bolts of laser fire slammed into one victim after another, boring holes through their heads, shoulders, chests, and abdomens. Some were killed immediately; others fell to the ground, crying out in agony. Those who bravely tried to help the injured were rewarded with their own injuries, becoming easy targets for the snipers above.

People began running into buildings, seeking shelter through any open door, but the laser fire followed them, burning through windows in order to find their targets on the other side, driving the people deeper inside.

"How many?" Telles barked as he entered the makeshift command center in the Orswellan capitol building.

"Four active shooters," Sergeant Spira replied. "Two on either side of Parker and two more on Alla.

Ryk Brown

Sergeant Morano suspects the shooters came from the tram platform at Parker and Alla. Blue Alpha is responding. Gold Alpha and Charlie are en route. Alpha is three out, Charlie is five."

"Shut down the trams," General Telles ordered. "I don't want any more shooters joining the party."

"You want EMS to stage?"

"Not yet," the general instructed. "Put them on alert but tell them to wait for orders before they roll. There could be additional shooters waiting to ambush them as they approach."

"We've already got dozens of casualties," Sergeant Spira said.

"Have both Diggers pick up squads from quiet areas and bring them in. Put them on the rooftops. Get all the civilians inside and then lock down the buildings."

"If we get a shooter moving around in a locked-down building, it's going to be a bloodbath."

"If they get out, it would be the same result, just over a wider area," the general pointed out.

"*Digger Two, evac One Blue Charlie from LZ One Eight Two, to rooftop of one four five Parker,*" Sergeant Spira instructed over comms.

"Digger Two, copy evac squad from LZ One Eight Two to rooftop of one four five Parker," Captain Orrock responded as he started his turn.

"*Digger Two, destination is hot, four shooters. Suggest approach from southeast.*"

"Digger Two will approach rooftop from southeast," the pilot acknowledged. "Got the jump plugged in, Hume?"

"Punch it."

Captain Orrock rolled out of his turn, lining up

his flight path indicator with the jump path line. Once the jump line turned green, the pilot pressed his jump button. A split second later, the cityscape below changed, and an entirely new set of streets, parks, and buildings were now beneath him.

"LZ One Eight Two, dead ahead, two clicks," the copilot reported.

"One Blue Charlie, Digger Two, dropping in for pickup," the pilot announced over comms.

"Digger Two, One Blue Charlie, ready."

_____

Corporal Venezia and Specialist Brummett opened fire on both sniper positions as they ran down the center of the street, moving from one abandoned vehicle to the next, using them briefly for cover as they advanced.

"We can't get a clean shot from here!" Corporal Venezia reported as he peppered the sniper's position on the right side of the street. "The building's structure is blocking our angle of fire!"

Red-orange blasts of plasma energy slammed into the car's rooftop and hood, forcing the corporal to duck for cover. "Where the fuck did that come from?" he yelled as a fifth red triangle appeared on his tactical visor.

"Two Blue Alpha One and Two are pinned down twenty meters north of targets one and two!" Specialist Brummett reported over comms as laser fire rained down upon their position. "We have a fifth shooter! Repeat! We have a fifth shooter, a heavy!"

"That's no sniper rifle!" Corporal Venezia yelled, rolling away from the vehicle being torn apart by the incoming plasma weapons fire.

"He's on the rooftop to your left!" Sergeant Morano warned.

"No shit!" the corporal retorted as he fell against the car, behind which Specialist Brummett was taking cover.

"*He can use the elevated breezeways to move to any rooftop,*" the sergeant continued.

Another round of plasma bolts slammed into the car they were hiding behind, this time from the opposite direction.

"He doesn't have to!"

"*I'm picking up a sixth shooter!*" Specialist Faulds reported over comms.

"Two Blue Alpha One and Two are falling back to Alla!" Corporal Venezia announced, tapping Brummett on the shoulder. "I'll cover you!" he added as he rose up and opened fire, alternating his bursts between the buildings to the right and left.

Specialist Brummett took off, running between vehicles back in the direction they had come, passing two of them before turning around and opening fire himself. "Go!"

Corporal Venezia ceased fire, turning and running in a crouch between the vehicles, passing Brummett by one vehicle before turning and opening fire again. "Go!"

"*Faulds! Prisk!*" Sergeant Morano called over comms. "*Can you get an angle on the rooftop shooters?*"

"*Negative,*" Specialist Faulds replied. "*Same problem. The rooftop shooters will cut us down before we get anywhere near.*"

"They're trying to keep us *out* of the buildings," Corporal Venezia announced as he and Specialist Brummett finally reached safe cover.

"Two Gold Alpha is one block out, taking fire from

two new shooters, rooftops, just east of the original targets."

Captain Orrock exchanged worried glances with his copilot as his Digger touched down at LZ One Eight Two.

"*You hearing this, Busby?*" Corporal Wimpfen asked over comms as he and the other three members of One Blue Charlie squad ran up Digger Two's aft cargo ramp.

"Yup," Captain Orrock replied as he advanced his lift throttles, his Digger ascending once again.

"*Whattaya say we do something about it?*"

"What have you got in mind, Corporal?"

"*Think you can fly this thing backwards?*"

Captain Orrock looked over at his copilot again, smiling. "No problem," he replied, yawing his ship around one hundred and eighty degrees as they climbed out.

———

"They've got us blocked on three sides," Commander Kellen declared, pointing to the large tactical display on the wall of the makeshift command center. "Four rooftop shooters, four snipers, and all those breezeways... If they're smart, they can keep us at bay for as long as they want."

"What about the river on the west side?" the general wondered.

"There's no egress point nearby," the commander replied.

General Telles studied the display. "Why *this* location, and why at *this* particular time?"

"It's one of the busiest parts of the city, and at this time of day, everyone is out getting lunch. Lots of targets in the streets. Lots of panic."

The general pointed at the panel of view screens

displaying the various security cameras located all over the Orswellan business district. "This event is less than five minutes old, and the streets are practically empty already. This isn't a sniper assault." General Telles turned toward Sergeant Spira at the communications desk. "Contact the managers of every building in that area, and tell them to be ready to evacuate on our call."

"Yes, sir," the sergeant acknowledged.

"If we don't take out those snipers, first, they'll cut people down as they come out," Commander Kellen warned.

A blue-white flash appeared just south of the center of the business district, revealing a Contra ship, flying backwards, its cargo ramp coming down. Two Ghatazhak soldiers walked carefully out onto the ramp; the mag-locks on their boots holding them firmly against the wind. Once to the corners, they braced themselves and raised their weapons.

The snipers on the rooftops below immediately spotted the threat and turned to open fire, but it was too late.

Corporal Wimpfen and Specialist Samudio fired two shots each, dropping all four targets before any of them could defend themselves.

"Rooftop shooters are eliminated," the corporal announced over comms, smiling.

"*Badass, Corporal,*" Captain Orrock congratulated from the cockpit. "*Badass.*"

"*Two Gold Alpha, take the shooters in the windows,*" Sergeant Morano's voice called over their helmet comms as Corporal Venezia and Specialist Brummett continued to take fire. "*Two Blue Alpha, advance and enter buildings when able. Two Blue Alpha One and Two take the north building; Three and Four, south."*

Corporal Venezia peered around the corner of the building as four Orswellans, trapped behind an abandoned vehicle, prepared to make a break for it. "STAY DOWN!" he yelled, gesturing at them with his left hand. Four laser blasts struck the corner of the building, showering him with chunks of concrete and forcing him to duck back. "I've got four civilians trapped in the street," he called over comms. "Polke! I need cover fire now!"

"Twenty seconds!" Corporal Polke replied.

"STAY DOWN!" Corporal Venezia repeated, drawing more fire to himself.

"Two Gold Alpha, in position," Corporal Polke reported as his squad reached their positions and opened up on the snipers in both buildings.

The areas around the windows, from which the snipers were firing, flashed as the incoming fire from the Ghatazhak impacted the buildings.

"They're shielded!" Corporal Polke yelled. "Switch to full power!"

Bolts of plasma energy streaked from the other end of the street up to the snipers above. Corporal Venezia immediately stepped out from behind the corner of the building and ran toward the four trapped Orswellans. Laser fire, from the left and above, slammed into the ground around him as he zigzagged his way down the street, returning fire as he went.

Specialist Brummett also stepped out but, instead, darted across to the opposite corner as he too fired, hoping to draw the attack of at least one of the snipers away from his cohort.

Corporal Venezia dove behind the vehicle shielding the four terrified Orswellans. "How are you all doing?" he asked as he scrambled over to them. "I'm Corporal Venezia, and I'm going to get you all to safety," he explained, laser fire continuing to pummel their position.

All four of them stared at the corporal as if he was crazy.

"They'll kill us before we get halfway," the elder of the two men insisted.

"We'll be fine," the corporal replied, smiling. "Trust me."

The two women seemed to believe him, even if the men did not.

"Listen carefully," he instructed as weapons fire peppered the roof of the vehicles around them. "I'm going to use my personal shield to protect us all, and we're all going to walk quickly, but *orderly*, back to that corner, over there. All four of you will need to huddle together as we move, and I mean *close*. Like one big group hug, got it?" Three of them nodded, but one man was cowering down, flinching from the incoming fire. "Hey!" the corporal barked, tapping the guy on the head. "Are you listening?"

"Group hug!" the man repeated. "I got it!"

"You sure?" the corporal asked. "I'm going to be walking backward. If you go too fast, I won't be able to protect you, and you'll get cut down by those assholes. If you aren't close enough together, they'll cut you down from the sides. One big group hug!"

"You gotta move, Vinnie!" Specialist Brummett hollered as he continued firing toward the snipers.

"Sooner or later, one of those bolts is gonna find its way through your cover!"

"We're moving!" Corporal Venezia assured his partner. "You guys ready?" he asked the group, using the controller on his forearm to set his personal shield to its maximum spread. "On three... One...... two......THREE!"

Corporal Venezia stood up, activating his personal shield as he rose, bringing his weapon up to fire on both sniper positions, one after the other. "GROUP HUG!" he barked over his shoulder as laser bolts bounced off his personal shield, causing it to flash brilliantly with each impact. "LET'S GO, LET'S GO, LET'S GO!"

All four of the trapped Orswellans rose, coming together clumsily. Immediately, one man let himself get too far from the others and was grazed in the arm by a laser bolt. He screamed out in pain, falling to his knees as the group began to move. One of the women grabbed him while, as a group, they baby-stepped away from their cover and toward the distant corner. She pulled the stricken man back to his feet, with the other man grabbing hold of him, as well, as the group continued to move.

Corporal Venezia stepped backward carefully, constantly checking on the group's progress behind him as he fired away at the sniper positions. "THAT'S IT!" he barked. "YOU'RE DOING IT! STAY TOGETHER!" He glanced at his visor display, noting that his personal shield strength was already down to fifty percent. The maximum coverage and constant barrage of laser fire was quickly taking its toll. "LET'S PICK UP THE PACE, PEOPLE!" the corporal barked.

"How's your shield strength, Vinnie?" Specialist Brummett asked as he, too, poured weapons fire into the two sniper positions, causing their shields to flash.

"Not good!"

The injured man lost step with the group, again exposing himself to the snipers. Two shots struck him, one in the shoulder, the other in the chest, dropping him.

"STAY TOGETHER!" Corporal Venezia ordered them, but his warnings fell on deaf ears.

One of the men tried to grab his fallen friend, taking a laser bolt to his left forearm, causing him to fall backwards, tripping up the entire group.

"Son of a bitch!" Corporal Venezia cursed, stopping and crouching to protect the entire group as best he could.

"VINNIE!" Brummett yelled, seeing the pileup.

"I'm down to thirty percent!" Corporal Venezia yelled.

"You gotta bail on them!"

Corporal Venezia glanced over his shoulder as a laser blast ricocheted off his armored, left combat boot. He could feel the heat penetrating his armor. Now, both snipers were focused on him and him alone. If they got *his* shield down, they would *all* die.

With no one shooting at him now, Specialist Brummett activated his own personal shield and ran out to assist his fellow Ghatazhak. He cared little about the Orswellans and even less about the fallen one. His concern was with the life of his comrade.

Brummett crouched down next to Venezia to protect both him and the three remaining Orswellans. "Let's get this done!"

"MOVE PEOPLE, MOVE!" the corporal barked as laser fire rained down upon them, lighting up both personal shields. "Twenty percent!"

Two streams of red-orange plasma joined in the assault on the sniper positions, but from the opposite end of the street. The effect was a slight reduction in the amount of laser fire they were taking, but not by much.

Suddenly, a third Ghatazhak appeared, taking position on Corporal Venezia's right side, opposite Specialist Brummett. "Thought you two could use a little help!" Sergeant Morano exclaimed.

"What took you so fucking long?" Corporal Venezia joked as they continued backward, protecting the three remaining Orswellans.

"How low are you?"

"Ten percent!" the corporal replied.

"Step behind me and shut your shield off!" the sergeant ordered. "Brumms, hold one!" he added.

Both men held their position for a few seconds, moving closer together as the corporal stepped back, joining in the group hug to guide them.

"Move!" Sergeant Morano ordered.

"Everyone together!" Corporal Venezia repeated to the group.

Sergeant Morano and Specialist Brummett continued their backward retreat toward the corner while Corporal Venezia, his armored back protecting the group, wrapped his arms around them, guiding them smoothly around the corner to safety.

"General!" Sergeant Spira yelled. "Six of eight building managers in the engagement area report that all their exits are locked, and they can't get them opened!"

"They're going to blow the buildings," Commander Kellen realized.

General Telles was one step ahead of him. "Have the Diggers put anyone on the rooftops yet?"

"Negative, sir," the sergeant replied. "Digger Two is about to."

"Abort," the general instructed.

"Digger Two, Digger Two," the sergeant called over comms, "Abort! Abort! No one goes on the rooftops! Repeat! No one goes on the rooftops!"

"Digger Two, aborting insertion," Captain Orrock acknowledged.

"Digger One, you copy the abort?"

"Roger that," Captain Hosick replied. *"We just jumped in, holding at fifty meters, just west of the engagement area."*

"Both Diggers are to blast the sniper positions," General Telles ordered. "Maximum force. Blow holes in those buildings."

"Diggers One and Two, Control," Sergeant Spira called over comms. "Fire mission..."

"...Hit both sniper positions! Maximum force! Blow holes in the buildings if you have to! Just eliminate the targets!"

"Go!" Sergeant Morano instructed the three Orswellans. "Down the street and around the corner! Get as far away from here as you can!"

"Busby, I'll take the east target," Captain Hosick said over comms.

"I'll take the west target," Captain Orrock agreed.

"All Ghatazhak! Clear the area!" Sergeant Spira instructed. *"Double-time it!"*

"Let's move!" Sergeant Morano yelled. Heading off in the same direction he had just sent the rescued Orswellans.

"You believe the snipers have the detonators?" Commander Kellen asked the general.

"I honestly do not know," General Telles admitted. "If they do and we take them by surprise, we may have a chance to get those people out."

"If not?" the commander wondered.

General Telles looked at the commander. "Then, we're going to have to step up our game."

———

Captain Orrock guided his Digger up and over the rooftop, coming to a hover in a position allowing just enough room for the turret under their nose to get a clean line of sight on the sniper position across the street and a few floors down. "Let 'em have it," he instructed his copilot.

Lieutenant Westwood selected the sniper position, easily locking his weapon onto the energy field created by the sniper's portable shields. "Target locked, max power...firing."

Captain Orrock leaned forward just enough to see the sniper's window become engulfed by a rapid barrage of plasma fire. The side of the building around the sniper's window exploded, sending chunks of concrete flying outward as it fell to the empty streets below.

At the same time, Digger One, hovering over the building that Digger Two was targeting, also opened fire on the sniper's position in the building below Digger Two.

After ten seconds of constant fire, Captain Orrock gave the order. "Cease fire."

The barrage stopped. When the smoke cleared a few seconds later, a massive hole, large enough to include parts of the floor above and below it, appeared where the window had once been. *Control,*

Ryk Brown

Digger One," Captain Hosick called over comms. "*Target eliminated.*"

An explosion sounded to Captain Orrock's left, causing him to turn his head. "Uh-oh..."

"Control, Digger Two," Captain Orrock added. "Target eliminated."

One after another, all eight buildings on Parker street— four on each side—exploded from within, collapsing to the ground in terrifying clouds of dust, debris, and fire that rose so quickly, it nearly engulfed the Diggers as they jumped away to safety.

Corporal Venezia and his men found themselves thrown forward by the shock wave, tossed against the building in front of them. Had it not been for their body armor and the assistive bodysuits, all three of them would have been killed.

The corporal shook off the blast, rising to his knees and looking about. "You okay, Sarge?"

"My ears are ringing," the sergeant replied, struggling to his feet, "but other than that..."

"Brummsy?"

"Nothing a nanite booster won't cure," the specialist replied, rolling over onto his back.

"...Fuck," the sergeant cursed.

Corporal Venezia looked in the same direction as the sergeant, his expression crestfallen as he spotted the source of his dismay. Smashed against the wall a few meters ahead of them were the three Orswellans they had just rescued; their bodies torn apart by the shock wave and splattered on the wall. Had it not been for the remnants of their clothing, he would not have recognized them. After sighing, he

184

declared, "We really need to find these fuckers and kill them all."

"Agreed," Sergeant Morano responded.

———————

General Telles stared at the images of destruction being displayed by the few surviving security cameras in the area.

"What do we do now?" Sergeant Spira wondered, looking over at the general.

"We lock this fucking city down," General Telles replied. "Everyone still alive goes home and stays there. Only vetted EMS, fire, and hospital staff will be allowed on the streets, but only with Ghatazhak escorts."

"Martial law?" the commander asked.

"*Ghatazhak* martial law," the general replied. "I will not give those bastards another target."

* * *

Nathan entered instructions into their shuttle's auto-flight system, preparing for their final jump into the SilTek system.

"We about ready?" Jessica asked as she stepped over the center console and wiggled her way into the copilot's seat.

"I've got the final jump loaded, and we've just about finished decelerating to our initial approach speed," Nathan replied as he activated the new auto-flight instructions.

"How far out is the arrival point?"

"I have no idea."

Jessica looked surprised. "They gave you coordinates, didn't they?"

"Yes, but we have no data on their system," Nathan explained. "Assuming their system and world are both analogous to Sol and Earth, and the

185

position of the jump point in relation to that of their star, we should be jumping in close to their orbit."

"That's reassuring," Jessica quipped.

"If they use the same approach system as most of the industrialized systems seeing regular jump traffic, then they are probably bringing us into a low-traffic zone reserved for first-time visitors. I'm *hoping* they've assigned us a private arrival point, one they haven't given to any other ship."

"You're *hoping*?"

"Jumping into a system is dangerous, no matter how you look at it," he told her. "Especially one you know nothing about. Hell, jumping period is dangerous. Luckily, even *interplanetary* space is so vast that the odds of jumping in dangerously close to the position of another ship are astronomical."

"Yet, on the second jump ever in the history of the jump drive, you managed to do so," Jessica reminded him.

"My claim to fame," Nathan joked. "Don't worry, I'm sure they wait a reasonable amount of time before assigning the same arrival location to another vessel."

"I *wasn't* worried until you started talking about it," Jessica pointed out.

"We're at approach speed," Nathan reported. "Punch the code they gave us into the transponder."

"You got it," Jessica replied, entering the proper code.

"Shall we?" Nathan asked, looking over at her.

"Let's do it."

Nathan turned back to his flight controls and activated the jump sequencer. "Jumping in three...... two......one......"

The cockpit windows turned opaque for a second

and then cleared, revealing the stars once again. Nathan studied his navigational display for a moment and then announced, "We're here. It looks like we're about five hundred thousand kilometers beyond the orbit of SilTek," he added as the sensor display began populating. "Damn, there's a *lot* of traffic in this system."

"Newly arrived shuttle squawking code One Four Seven, Two Five Zero, Zero Eight Four Five, SilTek Approach Control. Identify yourself."

"SilTek Approach Control, Karuzari Alliance Shuttle, Captain Nathan Scott. I believe we are expected?"

"Karuzari Alliance Shuttle, SilTek Approach Control, affirmative," the controller confirmed. *"Your comms designator for the duration of your stay will be Kilo Alpha Two Six. Please state identities of all occupants."*

"Kilo Alpha Two Six, two souls, Captain Nathan Scott and Lieutenant Commander Jessica Nash," Nathan replied.

"Understood. Is your vessel armed or carrying any weapons, Captain?"

"Our vessel is unarmed, but we do have a weapons locker containing four sidearms."

"Kilo Alpha Two Six, please secure your sidearms and prepare for landing. Do you have remote auto-flight capabilities and textual data communications?"

"Kilo Alpha Two Six, affirmative to both."

"Excellent," the controller replied. *"Transmitting authorization codes and control frequencies now. Please configure your auto-flight system for full, remote-automated landing and stand by for activation."*

Ryk Brown

"Uh, I'd prefer to keep override control local, if you don't mind," Nathan replied.

"Sorry, Captain, but SilTek is a high-traffic corridor, and your vessel is not equipped with anti-grav lift systems. Should a problem with auto-flight occur, we will release control to you."

"Understood," Nathan replied, setting up his auto-flight to accept the codes and frequencies now displayed on his textual communications display.

"You sure that's a good idea?" Jessica asked.

"I'm not crazy about it, no," Nathan admitted. "If Josh were here, he'd be livid, but it's understandable, given the amount of traffic here."

"Kilo Alpha Two Six, SilTek Approach Control. Remote auto-flight control confirmed. We now have control of your flight systems. You will be landing in iso-bay one two five, at the Bayside Spaceport. ETA: twenty-seven minutes. Enjoy the ride and welcome to SilTek."

"Thank you," Nathan replied. He leaned back, looking at Jessica. "You heard the lady...enjoy the ride."

* * *

The entire team stood watching the holo-display in the living room as Master Sergeant Farrish flipped through the station's security monitoring archives. "He comes out of the bar here," the master sergeant explained, calling up the video of Marcus exiting the bar near the entrance to the Jungle. "He immediately picks up a tail," he added, calling up another camera view showing a skinny, poorly dressed young woman.

"Well, I doubt she took him down," Corporal Vasya commented.

"Don't let her looks deceive you," the master

188

sergeant warned. "She's had some training, at least at shadowing a mark, anyway."

"She's a watcher," Neli told them. "How did you get access to all this?"

"I established a fake account with command-level access. Took all of two minutes," the master sergeant replied.

"What's a watcher?" Lieutenant Rezhik asked.

"The capis track the movements of everyone who comes into the Jungle. They have an army of them."

"You've been to the Jungle?"

"No, but I've been to places *like* it on other worlds," Neli replied. "They don't have access to the camera feeds, so they use watchers."

"Then Marcus knows of them, as well," Rezhik surmised.

"I'm certain of it," Neli insisted.

"I'm pretty sure he was aware of her," Master Sergeant Farrish told the lieutenant. "She got distracted a few times, and Marcus had to make an effort *not* to lose her."

"I guess she isn't *that* skilled, then," Neli commented.

"I guess his level of impairment due to his visit to the drinking establishment was minimal," the lieutenant surmised.

"It takes a *lot* to impair Marcus," Neli assured him. "Trust me. I've seen him drink twice his volume and still be kicking."

"Anyway, he wanders around the market for a while and finally ends up here." The master sergeant called up a map of the Jungle with a flashing red dot indicating Marcus's position at the time. "After a few minutes, he moves to a business front, just behind the vendor booth and slightly to the left. At that point, his signal strength drops by seventy percent. He moves around a bit, changing his position by about ten or twenty meters, finally stopping at the back side of the section, where he has been for the last eighty-seven minutes."

"Any idea what level he is on?" Sergeant Viano wondered.

"His signal strength is too low to get vertical movement readings," the master sergeant replied. "They must be using some sort of sensor jamming system."

"But you're still getting his signal, right?" Neli wondered, concerned.

"It was probably designed specifically for Sanctuary's security sensors, not our transponders. The drop in signal strength is not uncommon, depending on where you're located on the station. However, since there was no movement pattern suggesting the use of stairs, my guess is he's still on the main level. At most, one level up. Unfortunately, there's no way to know for sure."

"Based on movement, *could* he be on a different level?" the lieutenant inquired.

"It *is* possible," the master sergeant admitted.

"Do we have any data on that section?" Sergeant Viano asked.

"Only that it is leased by the Rayzion Corporation," the master sergeant replied. "We also have the basic floor plan for every level, but no indication of who the occupants are. They could have just the main level or all four levels in that section."

"Rayzion is probably a separate organization that just subleases space to others," Neli suggested. "That's how they do it on other worlds. It masks the identity of the people leasing the business space."

"There are several businesses on the main level, all of similar ill repute, so they could be part of the same organization," Specialist Brill suggested.

"Or not," Specialist Deeks added.

"We need more intel before going in," Lieutenant Rezhik decided. "We can only send in a few of us without leaving Miri and her children insufficiently protected."

"You think this is a diversion op?" Sergeant Viano wondered.

"It *is* a possibility," the lieutenant admitted.

"What's the plan, LT?" Master Sergeant Farrish inquired.

Lieutenant Rezhik took a breath, letting it out in a long sigh as he studied the images on the holo-display. "She is our target," he decided, pointing at the image of the skinny, young woman who had been tailing Marcus. "Vasya will make contact with her, with Brill as backup."

"Why me?" Corporal Vasya wondered.

"Because you haven't cut your hair since we arrived; therefore, you look less like a Ghatazhak than any of us."

"I'm trying something new," the corporal mused.

"You also have the additional advantage of being a pretty boy, which may appeal to her feminine side."

"Hey, it's a gift," Vasya bragged.

"What if she likes girls?" Specialist Brill wondered.

Lieutenant Rezhik looked at Brill, then at Vasya. "Still good," he added with a slight grin.

* * *

Nathan and Jessica gazed out the forward cockpit windows as their shuttle flew over the city on a gradual descent into the Bayside Spaceport complex.

"This world is incredible," Jessica exclaimed.

"Everything looks great from the air," Nathan commented, "but I have to admit, it does look better than most I've seen."

"I keep forgetting about your life as Connor," Jessica admitted. "You've probably visited a *lot* of different worlds."

"Not as many as you might think," Nathan admitted. "Thirty or forty of them, I'd guess. Most of the time, it was the same ten or fifteen worlds, though. Still, I have to admit, this tops all of them." Nathan scanned further ahead, noting a large complex. "That must be the spaceport. It's bigger than I expected."

"If they felt they needed to tell us *which* spaceport we were going to, then they must have more than one," Jessica surmised.

"Like I said, a *lot* of traffic."

They continued to peer out the windows as they descended into their final approach to the Bayside Spaceport. Nathan glanced at his flight displays at regular intervals, ensuring that the remote auto-flight system was performing properly.

Once they passed over the outer fence, their shuttle dropped down to thirty meters above the surface and turned toward one of the many wheel-and-spoke style terminals that made up the spaceport.

"Aren't we kind of high?" Jessica wondered.

"I don't think they like our lift thrusters," Nathan replied. "Probably burns their pretty, green grass. They'll likely drop us in directly over our landing spot, to minimize thruster damage to the rest of the tarmac."

"Do our thrusters actually do that much damage?" Jessica asked, finding it difficult to believe.

"No," Nathan replied, "they're probably just

playing it safe. Same reason they're putting us in an isolation bay."

As expected, their shuttle steered to a position directly above a small landing pad, after which they descended to it, touching down gently.

Nathan immediately began the engine shutdown process.

"Kilo Alpha Two Six, Bayside Ops."

"Go for Kilo Alpha Two Six," Nathan replied.

"You may disembark when ready. Upon exit of your ship, proceed to decon-lock for decontamination."

"Understood," Nathan replied. He looked over at Jessica. "You ready to get naked?"

"What are you proposing?" she teased back.

* * *

Corporal Vasya and Specialist Brill had entered the Jungle separately, each of them through a different hatch, dressed in common civilian attire, purchased on Sanctuary, and wearing hats. A little slouching and avoiding direct eye contact with others had been enough to avert undue attention from most. However, as expected, each of them had picked up a watcher of their own.

Specialist Brill's had been a good one, sticking with him through every twist and turn, yet always at a distance, making him difficult to notice. Corporal Vasya's watcher, on the other hand, seemed to have very little experience. It had taken the corporal all of ten minutes to lose the kid, circling back and coming in behind him, and watching the poor sap wander deeper into the Jungle in search of his lost mark.

After losing his watcher, Corporal Vasya took a seat at an open-air café of sorts. There, he could watch passersby in an inconspicuous fashion. With several other patrons on the dining patio, none of the Jungle's upper echelon would be able to tell that the corporal had no watcher tracking him.

"How you doing, Mori?" the corporal asked over his hidden comm-set, keeping his voice low to avoid being overheard.

"*Nothing yet,*" the specialist reported. "*I'm surprised this place is so busy this late.*"

"I don't think this hellhole gives a crap about night and day," the corporal said.

"*Yeah, a lot of interesting characters in this place.*"

"Did you see the guy with that huge mane of hair?"

"*The one in the exoskeleton? How could I miss him?*"

"The guy looked like a pella-cat."

"*I heard someone talking about him,*" Specialist Brill replied. "*They called him a 'Noji'. They live on a world with really low gravity.*"

"That explains the exoskeleton, but what about all that facial hair?"

"*I don't know. Maybe it's fashionable there.*"

"I don't know how much more of this freak show I can take," the corporal admitted.

"*Hey, I think I may have something,*" Brill reported. "*Skinny, little, dirty blond. I can't tell if she's tailing anyone just yet.*"

"Should I head toward you?" the corporal asked.

"*Not yet,*" the specialist replied. "*I'm not even sure it's her, and I'm not very far from your location, anyway.*"

"Move to a better angle."

"*Already doing so,*" Brill replied.

Corporal Vasya waited patiently, continuing to watch the collection of criminals and social outcasts who populated the Jungle.

"It's her," Specialist Brill reported.

"What's the plan?" Vasya asked.

"Head for the service corridor between sections forty-seven and forty-eight. I have an idea."

"I'm on my way," Corporal Vasya replied, rising from his seat and heading out.

———

Specialist Brill followed the young woman for a minute, in order to clearly determine her mark. Once satisfied, he moved past her, eventually coming to stand next to the man she was tracking. "I'll make this brief," he explained to the man without looking at him. "I'll give you one hundred station credits if you take a stroll down that service corridor behind you and then go through the maintenance hatch on the right."

"Why the fuck would I be dumb enough to do that?" the guy grumbled, continuing to examine the weapon he had been looking at.

"Because you'll get paid, *and* you'll lose your watcher."

"There's much better ass available in nearly every one of the brothels around here, and for about half the price."

"I'm not looking to fuck her," Brill assured him. "I just want to ask her a few questions. Do you want to make some easy credits, or not?"

The man finally looked up at Brill. "Two hundred... up front. And if this is a trap, I'll kill you and whoever you're working with."

"In position," Corporal Vasya reported over Specialist Brill's hidden earpiece.

"Fair enough," Brill replied, placing two chips, worth one hundred credits each, on the table in front of the man.

The man picked up the chips, discretely placing them in his pocket. "You station security?"

"A very loose affiliation," Brill replied, "and if *you* cross *us*, we'll kill *you*."

The man flashed a toothless grin. "Fair enough," he replied, turning and heading for the service corridor behind him.

Brill picked up a weapon on the display table, looking it over, pretending to be interested; at the same time, keeping an eye on the girl as she followed her mark down the service corridor. "She's on her way to you, now," he told Vasya over comms. "I've got her six."

Brill followed the girl from a safe distance, keeping visual contact on her, but staying far enough behind so she wouldn't notice him. As soon as she disappeared through the hatch to the right, he quickened his pace.

"Hi, there," Corporal Vasya greeted, stepping out from behind a vertical support beam. "Looking for someone?"

The skinny, young woman stopped dead in her tracks. "Uh, I thought I saw a friend of mine come in here..."

The girl's mark stepped out, as well, grinning. The girl immediately turned to run but was blocked by Specialist Brill, who had just stepped through the hatch behind her.

"Fuck," she cursed, pulling a knife from under her loose-fitting coat.

"That would be a mistake," Corporal Vasya assured the girl.

"Oh, this is getting good," her mark stated, moving over to the side to watch.

"Let me go, or I'll cut you both."

"Cut away," Corporal Vasya said, walking toward her confidently with his arms wide.

The girl lunged at him, knife first. In a flash, Corporal Vasya blocked the knife to one side, plucked it from her hand, spun her around, and trapped her with one arm around her neck, her knife held at her throat.

"I don't like being threatened," Corporal Vasya warned her. "Apologize, and I will not kill you."

"Fuck you!" she cursed, trying to get free.

The corporal tightened his grip further, forcing her to stop. "Apologize."

She struggled a bit longer but started to get weak from lack of oxygen. "Alright," she finally squeaked, "I'm sorry."

Corporal Vasya released her, letting her step back. "You have two options," he told her. "Answer my questions, or I turn you over to this guy to do with you what he wants." Vasya looked at the man she had been following. "And if you ask me, he looks pretty shady."

"You, sir, are an excellent judge of character," the man declared, his eyes traveling up and down the skinny, young girl's body.

* * *

Nathan stepped out of the decontamination chamber, stark naked, still wet from the cleansing spray at the end of the cycle. The next compartment was shared by four decon chambers, another of which opened, revealing Jessica, also naked and dripping wet.

"Quit gawking and hand me a towel," Jessica told him.

Nathan picked up a wash cloth from the bench and tossed it over to her.

"Funny," she replied, throwing it back at him.

Nathan picked up two towels, handing her one. "That was the strangest decon procedure I've ever been through," he commented as he toweled off.

"I'm pretty sure we were scanned in there, as well."

"*Please don your robes and proceed to the next compartment,*" a voice prompted.

Nathan handed a robe to Jessica. "After you," he said, putting on his own robe.

Jessica slipped into her robe and stepped up to the door, which opened automatically. On the other side was a large chamber, surrounded by windows. There was a table and several chairs in the corner, in front of a kitchenette, a few overstuffed sitting chairs, and what appeared to be fold-out beds along one wall.

"I have a feeling this is going to take longer than we thought," Nathan stated as he followed her into the room.

* * *

"What's your name?" Corporal Vasya asked the skinny, young lady they had cornered.

She studied each of them, still unsure of what to do.

"Surely, it can't hurt to tell me your *name*?" the corporal insisted.

"Sila," she answered reluctantly. "My name is Sila."

"Nice to meet you, Sila. I'm Kit, that's Mori, and I don't actually know this guy," Corporal Vasya admitted, pointing over his shoulder to her mark.

"People call me Fang."

Kit turned slowly, looking at Fang. "Seriously?"

"You got a problem with that?" the man asked.

"No problem at all, *Fang*," Kit replied, turning back to Sila. "Earlier tonight, you were following an old guy. Heavyset, angry-looking, with black hair, scruffy beard, wearing brown pants and a black jacket..."

"Yeah, I remember him," Sila replied.

"He went into a business in section two-thirty-five," Vasya told her, "and he hasn't come out."

"How do you know he hasn't?" she wondered.

"Don't worry yourself about that; just tell me about that business."

"It's not a business," she told him. "It's offices."

"Offices for whom?"

"I don't know."

"You were watching someone for them, weren't you?"

"I don't work for the vendors," she explained. "I work for Mama Lewicki."

"Who?" Kit asked.

"The Lewicki family runs the Jungle," Fang chimed in. "Mama Lewicki is the matriarch of the family. She is one mean, old witch."

"Good to know," Kit said, turning back to Sila. "You spoke to the guy running the vendor booth in front of that office."

"I just gave him a watch report, that's all," she assured him. "That's my job."

"All the capis pay a percentage of their profits to Mama Lewicki," Fang explained. "Watchers are one of the services she provides in exchange for her cut. What section did you say this office was in?"

"Two-thirty-five," Kit replied.

"A scruffy-looking guy with a bad attitude?"

"Our friend?"

"No, the guy working the booth," Fang explained.

"Yeah, I believe so," Mori said. "Skinny, too."

"That's Dinesh Koren's operation," Fang realized. "The guy's a real asshole. What was your friend looking to buy?"

"A few thousand guns," Kit replied.

"Well, Koren's about the only guy in the Jungle who can handle that kind of volume, but if he doesn't already know you, he's more likely to kill you than sell you something."

"Honestly, I don't know anything about Koren or your friend," Sila insisted, suddenly becoming nervous. "All I know is that I followed the old guy around and then reported on where he had been when the vendor asked."

"Did you see our friend go into Koren's offices?" Kit asked.

"I saw him go inside an office in section two-thirty-five, but I don't know *whose* office it was. I don't even know who this *Koren* guy *is*. I'm just a watcher, I swear."

"Koren has the entire first level of that section," Fang told them.

"Does he have any of the upper levels?" Kit asked.

"I don't know," Fang replied. "A friend of mine used to work for him a few years back. He told me about the lavish offices they had in there. I don't remember him ever talking about a second level, but that don't mean there ain't one."

Kit studied Sila. "This guy is more help than you."

"I told you, I'm just a watcher."

"She's lyin' to you, you know," Fang told him.

"I am not!"

"I've seen her coming and going from Koren's place," Fang added.

"That's not true!" Sila insisted.

"My ass."

"You lying fuck!" Sila yelled, lunging at Fang.

Kit grabbed her by the throat, pushing her back against the bulkhead, sliding her up a few centimeters until her feet were no longer touching the deck. Sila grabbed at his hand, trying to break free as she struggled to breathe.

"I see no reason for Fang to lie about your association with Koren," Kit explained calmly, maintaining his stranglehold on the girl. "However, I can see plenty of reasons for *you* to be lying."

"She's probably fucking one of his goons," Fang told him. "Most of the female watchers hook up with capi muscle to keep regulars from hitting on them all the time. Some of them even get pimped out by them."

"I can't breathe," Sila squeaked.

Kit turned back to look at Sila as she gasped for air. "You will tell me everything I need to know," he said, his tone taking on great menace, "or I will kill you *right* here, *right* now. The choice is yours."

CHAPTER SEVEN

The exit door to their room in the decon facility slid open, and a woman in medical attire entered, carrying two sealed pouches. "Welcome," she greeted in a pleasant, yet obviously artificial, voice.

Nathan examined her a little more closely, immediately realizing she was not human. "Thank you," he replied, intrigued by the humanoid robot.

"I am your quarantine assistant," the woman stated. "You may call me Orana."

"You're not real, are you," Jessica stated rather bluntly.

Nathan shot Jessica a disapproving glance.

"What?" Jessica defended. "She isn't."

"You are correct, Lieutenant Commander," Orana confirmed. "I am a medical service android, series one four seven. I am assigned to provide for you both, to make your time in quarantine more comfortable. These are for you to wear. They have been sized according to your physical scans, so they should fit appropriately."

"How long are we going to be in here?" Nathan asked as he took the pouch handed to him.

"A minimum of twenty-four hours," Orana replied.

"Why?" Jessica asked, opening her pouch.

"Your scans revealed several organisms within your bodies that are new to us. Our pathologists require time to determine the threat level to the general population, if any."

"We were both given medical exams prior to departing our ship," Nathan assured her. "We were both clean."

"It is merely a precaution," Orana insisted, "for both the people of SilTek and yourselves."

"For *ourselves*?" Nathan wondered.

"There are organisms on *our* world that could be dangerous to you and the lieutenant commander."

"We're willing to take that chance," Nathan assured her.

"We are not," Orana replied in a matter-of-fact tone. "Sustenance and water are available in the kitchen area," Orana continued, walking around the room, pointing out the amenities. "Lavatory facilities are in there. Should you require privacy, use the lavatory or simply touch the windows to obscure them, and touch them again to clear. Lighting controls are near the exit. If you require rest, the beds deploy with a touch," she added, touching one of the beds, causing it to fold down from the wall. "If you require any assistance, there are call buttons located all about the compartment." Orana walked back to the exit and turned to face them, striking a preprogrammed pose. "Will there be anything else?"

"No, thank you," Nathan replied.

"Welcome to SilTek," Orana stated before exiting.

"Two days in a shuttle, and now a day in here," Jessica grumbled, opening her pouch. "Great, pajamas," she added as she examined the bright red attire. "Why red?"

"Probably to identify that we are in quarantine," Nathan suggested as he pulled on his baggy, red pants. "Not exactly a tailored fit," he joked as he donned the pullover top. "Comfortable enough, I suppose."

"Do you think they'll let us keep them?" Jessica joked as she unabashedly dropped her robe and donned her red pajamas.

Nathan peered out the windows. There were similar quarantine rooms on either side and across the corridor, each of them with multiple occupants. "I guess we're not the only ones in quarantine," he said, pointing at the other rooms. "I wonder where they're all from and why they're here."

* * *

"The place is owned by a capi named Dinesh Koren," Corporal Vasya informed Lieutenant Rezhik. "He's the only high-volume guns dealer on Sanctuary, but apparently, he doesn't like to do business with strangers."

"Since we're continuing to receive a signal, Marcus is still alive," the lieutenant said.

"How do you know that?" Neli inquired.

"Our transponder rings are powered by our bodies," Lieutenant Rezhik explained. "If Marcus were dead, his signal would be lost. They are probably interrogating him. Did you learn his location within the complex?" he asked the corporal.

"He's probably being held in a room on the second level," the corporal explained. "A room they call 'the box'. If we're going to rescue him, we need to move quickly. According to our sources, once this Koren fellow has gotten all the information he needs, he'll most likely kill Marcus."

"Any idea as to number and armaments?" the lieutenant asked.

"We know he's got at least a dozen goons working for him as muscle, but there's no way to know how many will be in the facility at any given time," Corporal Vasya explained. "As to armaments, Fang told us they probably have what he called 'popguns'. Some kind of projectile weapons. If someone is hit in the wrong spot, they can be deadly."

"Maybe we should notify security," Neli suggested. "After all, Marcus wasn't doing anything wrong."

"Armed criminals are holding him hostage for merely making an inquiry," Lieutenant Rezhik stated. "On a station that is supposed to be weapons-free and safe. His best chance of survival is with us."

"But they're armed," Neli reminded him.

"As are we," the lieutenant replied, moving over to the closet. He reached up onto the shelf and pulled down a large, locked case. After placing it on the table, he opened it and began handing out sidearms to his men.

"Where did you get those?" Neli asked.

"We brought them with us," the lieutenant explained. "They were in Miri's stasis chamber."

"Won't security detect them?"

"These use extremely high-pressure air to launch select projectiles," the lieutenant explained. "Since they do not use any energy, they are undetectable by station weapons sensors, and they have the additional advantage of being quiet, in comparison with energy weapons or other projectile weapons. They are *precise* and can be *quite* deadly."

"Then, this is a kill mission?" Corporal Vasya asked.

"If necessary, yes," the lieutenant replied.

"It'll piss off security if they catch wind of it."

"I don't much care," the lieutenant stated bluntly. "Neli, get the kids ready to move."

"Why?"

"This could be a diversion to pull the five of us away from you and the kids. We will escort you to the medical facility where Team Two can guard everyone. Farrish, you will take command of Team Two while Team One and I rescue Mister Taggart."

"You got enough of those for all of us?" Master Sergeant Farrish asked.

* * *

"This is one well stocked fridge," Jessica exclaimed. "You hungry?" she asked, pulling snacks out of the mini-fridge.

"Not really," Nathan replied as he opened the door to the lavatory and peeked inside. "Nice head."

"Leave it to a guy to check the toilet, first," Jessica joked as she placed a selection of food on the table. "They've got all kinds of fruit here, some of which I've never seen before."

"Leave it to you to check out the fridge, first," Nathan retorted.

"*Hello, Captain Scott,*" a female voice greeted.

Nathan turned toward the voice and spotted a woman in what appeared to be a Tekan business suit, standing on the other side of the window next to the exit.

"*I am Caitrin Bindi, special assistant to Ariana Batista. On behalf of the leadership of my world, I would like to welcome you both.*"

"Thank you," Nathan replied, walking toward her. "Are we going to meet with Missus Batista?"

"*Missus Batista is a busy woman; however, I am certain she will make an effort to speak with you in person. In the meantime, might I inquire as to the nature of your visit?*"

"No offense, Miss Bindi, but I would prefer to discuss such things with Missus Batista."

"*I understand,*" Miss Bindi replied. "*However, the nature of your discussion dictates the type of advisors Missus Batista will need to have on hand. It would be more efficient if she had some idea of your intent prior to meeting.*"

"Very well," Nathan agreed. "I lead an alliance of three worlds attempting to defend against a conquering force and liberate about a dozen worlds they have illegally occupied. I was hoping to add SilTek to that alliance."

"Then, you believe this invading force is a threat to SilTek, as well?"

"The Dusahn Empire is a threat to everyone," Nathan insisted. "They are ruthless and well armed, and they destroy those who reject their rule."

"We are aware of the Dusahn Empire," Miss Bindi assured him. *"I assume Mister Vout warned you that SilTek does not take sides in the disputes between others."*

"He did," Nathan admitted. "I am hoping that your leader will make an exception in our case."

"That is doubtful, I'm afraid."

"Then, perhaps we can come to a business arrangement?" Nathan suggested. "We have many technologies that would be of advantage to your company."

"I shall convey this information to Missus Batista," Miss Bindi promised, turning to depart.

"One more thing," Nathan called.

"Yes?"

"Orana," he began, "is she self-aware?"

"If you are asking if she is sentient, then the answer is no. She is aware of her own existence, just as all androids are. She knows what she is and what her purpose is. Her programming, although quite complex, is designed to perform the tasks required for her position; nothing more, nothing less."

"Then why make her so human, yet obviously *not* human?" Jessica asked.

"Androids, tasked to interact with humans, are

207

humanoid in design to put those with whom they interact at ease," Miss Bindi explained. *"However, they are given obvious marker-traits to remind us that they are not human. We find this helps our people avoid developing emotional attachments to the android workforce. We believe that simulations and automation should help people, not fool them."*

"I see," Nathan replied. "What happens after we are released from quarantine?"

"I have arranged transportation and comfortable accommodations for the duration of your stay on SilTek. Now, if you'll excuse me, I must return to my duties."

"Of course," Nathan replied.

Jessica watched as Miss Bindi departed, then turned to Nathan. "You think this place has room service?"

* * *

Once again, each Ghatazhak entered the Jungle separately and from different hatches. Dressed differently, their only common trait was their steely, confident look. Luckily, there were many people in the Jungle, both men and women, who had similar looks. Most had killed or witnessed killings and other acts of violence.

Lieutenant Rezhik was the last to enter the seedy marketplace. Within the first minute, a watcher had begun to track his movements. He would be easy to follow.

The lieutenant moved deliberately down the main aisle of the Jungle, not bothering to stop and observe the myriad of weapons being offered. He had no interest in their wares. His role required a direct approach, and he was comfortable with that.

"Any eyes on me?" Corporal Vasya asked over his hidden comm-set.

Specialist Brill glanced around, surveying everyone within one hundred degrees on either side. No one appeared to be paying any undue attention to the corporal ahead of him. "Just your watcher, about ten meters behind you," he reported.

"Going in."

Specialist Brill continued his lazy pace, watching Vasya out of the corner of his eye as the corporal ducked into the service corridor behind the section containing Dinesh Koren's offices. As expected, his watcher followed him. "Watcher is coming your way," he reported, picking up his pace and heading toward the same corridor. A quick glance over his shoulder confirmed that his own watcher was quickening his pace, as well.

The lanky, redheaded, young man peeked around the corner, unsure about entering the shadowy service corridor. For a moment, he wondered if his mark had actually entered it. What possible reason could he have to go in there?

A sound further down the corridor caught his attention, and his heart sank. He had no choice but to follow his mark, his employment depended on it. It would be a mistake.

By his second step, he felt a sharp pain in his neck. Before he could turn around, everything went black.

"He looks comfy," Specialist Brill commented as he entered the service corridor and found Vasya's mark, curled up in the corner, sound asleep.

"Poor kid must be overworked," Vasya replied with

Ryk Brown

a smile, moving back into the shadows to prepare for the arrival of Brill's mark.

Specialist Brill moved to the opposite corner, leaning nonchalantly against the bulkhead.

A moment later, his mark entered the service corridor, stopping short when he spotted one of his fellow watchers, curled up, asleep on the deck.

"Looking for me?" Specialist Brill asked.

His watcher turned to his left, realizing he was had as he too felt a sharp pain in his neck.

Vasya caught the second watcher as he collapsed and dragged him over to the first watcher. "These guys were too easy," he declared as he laid him, cuddled up, next to the first watcher.

"I wonder what they'll think when they find them," Specialist Brill wondered, stepping over them to follow Vasya down the service corridor.

"Probably that they make a cute couple," Vasya joked as he headed down the corridor.

———

Sergeant Viano hovered over the display of weapons at the booth in front of Dinesh Koren's offices. From his position, he could monitor three men, of the five in the area, who could be guards. Specialist Deeks, currently talking up a salesman at the booth two doors down, had a clear line of sight on the other two.

"*One and Two are in position,*" Corporal Vasya reported over comms.

The sergeant glanced to his left, spotting Lieutenant Rezhik as he approached the man standing at the door to Koren's offices. "Five is at the door," he said under his breath.

———

"Where do you think you're going?" the man

guarding the office door challenged, putting his hand out to block Lieutenant Rezhik's advance.

"I need to speak with Mister Koren," the lieutenant told the man.

"No one enters unless they're invited."

"It would be in your employer's best interest to speak with me... *now*."

"Oh, really," the man said, chuckling. "And who the fuck are you?"

"I am Lieutenant Torren Rezhik of the Ghatazhak," the lieutenant stated, staring confidently at the man, "and I am here to discuss the release of my comrade, Marcus Taggart."

———

"*Five is inside,*" Sergeant Viano reported over comms.

"You about done, there, Brilly?" Corporal Vasya questioned as he checked up and down the service corridor to ensure that no one had spotted them.

"Pretty stupid of them not to have any security cameras back here," Specialist Brill commented as he worked on the keypad on the back door to the offices. The door suddenly clicked and swung inward a few centimeters. "Got it."

"One and Two are entering," Vasya announced over comms as he drew his weapon.

"*Don't forget to use tranq rounds first,*" Sergeant Viano reminded them.

"Tranq rounds are for pussies," Vasya joked as he set his weapon to fire tranquilizer rounds instead of kill shots.

"*Which is precisely what these guys are,*" Sergeant Viano commented.

"It's like going to a party with no wine or women,"

Vasya complained as he stepped through the doorway, his sidearm held at the ready.

The very moment the door closed behind him, Lieutenant Rezhik launched into action, planting his boot into the back of his escort's right knee. The man howled in pain as the joint dislocated, and he fell to the floor, pulling his weapon as he fell. The lieutenant moved swiftly, kicking the weapon out of the man's hand as he pulled out his own, firing a tranq-round into the man's chest, then turning to plant another in the shoulder of the receptionist. Within seconds, both of them were unconscious. "Lobby secured," he reported over comms. "Moving inward."

"*One and Two are in the back corridor, sweeping the first level,*" Corporal Vasya reported.

Lieutenant Rezhik moved over to the inner door, turning the latch and slowly pushing it open. Two shots rang out, one of them ricocheting off the inside of the door, the other passing through the opening, just above the lieutenant's head, and slamming into the acoustical paneling on the front wall. "Five has contact," he called over comms. "One shooter." There was a subdued pop from the corridor on the other side of the door, followed by a thump.

"*Five, One, shooter down, your corridor is clear,*" Corporal Vasya reported. "*Sweeping right.*"

"Five is entering the corridor, sweeping left," the lieutenant reported as he opened the door and entered the corridor

---

Sergeant Viano spotted two men who suddenly turned and ran toward the office door. "Two going in," he reported under his breath.

"I've got them," Specialist Deeks reported. The sergeant glanced to his left, spotting the specialist as he walked around the back side of the booth, pulled his sidearm, and fired twice, his weapon barely audible in the noisy marketplace. The men fell through the open front door, both of them struck by Specialist Deeks's tranq-rounds.

The scruffy salesman, at the booth Sergeant Viano was standing in front of, noticed the men falling through the front office door and grabbed his weapon.

"Bad idea," the sergeant warned.

The scruffy man turned to look at the sergeant, his eyes widening when he saw the discrete sidearm pointed at him.

The sergeant pulled the trigger, firing a tranq-round into the scruffy man's chest, knocking him backward into his chair, where the man passed out and appeared to be sleeping. "Night night," the sergeant said as he hid his weapon and headed toward the office door.

———

Marcus's head hung down, his face dripping with blood. A man grabbed his hair, pulling his head back sharply so the other man could strike him, yet again.

"Who the fuck is Lieutenant Rezhik?" Mister Koren demanded. "And who the fuck are the Ghatazhak?"

Marcus laughed and was rewarded with another blow, sending another one of his teeth flying.

The door burst open, and a man ran in, panicked. "I've lost contact with Jigger and Dal!"

"What?" Mister Koren exclaimed.

"And someone has breached the back entrance!"

"Tell Basqer and Yont to cover the front," Mister Koren ordered.

"Basqer! Tolman!" the man called.

"Who the fuck are the Ghatazhak?" Mister Koren repeated, stepping up and raising Marcus's head by his hair.

Marcus looked him straight in the eyes. "You should've done business with me, asshole," he laughed.

This time, it was Mister Koren who struck Marcus, and with all his might, knocking him and the chair to which he was bound to the floor.

"They're not answering!" Tolman reported.

"Bon, go with Tolman and see what's going on," Mister Koren ordered.

Tolman turned to exit but stopped when something struck him in the chest. He turned around to face his boss, his eyes crossing as he dropped to the floor.

The other two men drew their weapons as Lieutenant Rezhik burst into the room. The first man fired at the intruder but was not quick enough. The lieutenant dodged to the right, the man's rounds passing by his left ear.

Corporal Vasya appeared in the doorway, firing two shots, dropping both of the armed men in the room.

Dinesh Koren went for his own weapon but stopped when he realized that both of the intruders had him in their sights. After a moment, he slid his partially-drawn weapon back in its holster, and moved his arms slowly down to his sides. "Gentlemen."

Corporal Vasya immediately went over to Marcus as Specialist Brill moved into the doorway behind him, his weapon now trained on Dinesh Koren, as well.

"Hey, old man," Corporal Vasya said as he cut

away the plastic restraints that held Marcus to the fallen chair. "You making friends, again?"

"Shut up and give me a hand," Marcus grumbled as Vasya cut him free.

Vasya took Marcus's hand and helped him to his feet. "You look like shit," he said, seeing the beating Marcus had taken. "You want a load of nanites?"

"Nanites are for Ghatazhak weenies," Marcus grumbled, wiping the blood from his mouth. He turned his head to glare at Mister Koren and then moved toward him, one unsteady step at a time.

"I believe we can do business," Mister Koren announced.

"Oh, yeah?" Marcus replied as he approached. "There's just one thing." Marcus rammed his knee into Koren's groin, causing the man to double over. Marcus raised his right hand, thumping Koren on the head and knocking him to the floor.

"Marcus," Lieutenant Rezhik began, "what are you doing?"

Marcus dropped down to one knee, grabbing Dinesh Koren's hair and raising his head with his left hand as he raised his right. "Negotiating," he replied as he began striking Koren in the face, again and again. After a dozen blows, he paused, looking at Mister Koren's bloody face, deciding whether or not the beating the capi had received was equal to the one he had been given. Finally, he released him, leaving him on the floor, bleeding. "Now we can do business," Marcus said, struggling back to his feet.

"Clean him up and get him out of here," Lieutenant Rezhik instructed.

"Come on, tough guy," Corporal Vasya said, putting Marcus's arm up over his shoulder to support him. "Let's get you home. Neli's worried about you."

"She fucking should be," Marcus sputtered.

Lieutenant Rezhik waited for Vasya and Brill to remove Marcus from the room and then moved over next to Mister Koren, who was lying on the floor, his face bloodied, barely conscious. He squatted down by the man, checking his face. "Looks like you'll live. Your nose is probably broken, but I'm certain a man of your means can afford to have it fixed."

"You think this is over?" Mister Koren gasped, nearly choking on his own blood.

"That is up to you, Mister Koren," the lieutenant calmly explained. "No one has died here, today. None of your men and none of mine. My advice to you is to consider this a misunderstanding and supply us with the weapons we require...*at a fair price*. Any other course of action could have dire consequences." The lieutenant studied the man for a moment and then added, "Are we clear?"

Dinesh Koren glared back at the lieutenant. Never had he seen such a confident look in a man's eyes, and he regularly associated with some of the deadliest men in the entire quadrant.

"Are...we...clear?" the lieutenant asked again.

"Yeah......we're clear," Mister Koren finally confirmed.

"We'll be in touch," the lieutenant said as he rose and headed out the door.

* * *

Nathan tapped the window, causing its obscuring field to disappear, making the window clear again. He looked up and down the corridor outside their quarantine suite. All the lighting was dimmed, and every occupied suite had their windows obscured.

"The hardest part of away missions is having to adapt to completely different time cycles and day lengths," Nathan said as he tapped the window a second time, causing it to become obscured once again.

"Just go to sleep," Jessica complained from her bed.

"I can't," Nathan replied.

"You were flying for two full days, with only catnaps. You *must* be tired."

"I am, I just can't sleep," Nathan replied. "Don't you ever get to a point where you're so exhausted that your mind won't shut down?"

"Never. I can sleep anywhere, anytime."

"Then, why aren't you asleep now?" Nathan wondered.

"Because you won't shut up."

"I thought you said you could sleep anywhere, anytime?" Nathan challenged.

"Don't make me knock you out," Jessica warned.

"Don't make me knock you out...*sir*," he retorted. Nathan looked around the room again. "Isn't there a view screen around here, or something? I need something to watch to help me fall asleep."

"Just lie down and close your eyes."

Nathan tapped the intercom button on the wall.

"*How may I help you?*" Orana asked over the intercom.

"Hi, Nathan Scott here. Sorry to bother you, but I was wondering if there is any kind of visual entertainment device in here. I'm having a little trouble falling asleep. Some kind of view screen that shows news, or vid-plays, or something?"

"*I can provide medication to help you relax,*" Orana suggested. "*It is commonly used to help visitors synchronize their circadian rhythms to SilTek's time cycles. However, it does come with some side effects.*"

"Like what?"

"You will be impossible to awaken for the first few hours, and you will be somewhat groggy for the first full day after use."

"I think I'll pass," Nathan replied.

"As you wish, Captain. As to your inquiry, we do not have view screens, as you call them. Entertainment on SilTek is provided using virtual reality immersion systems. The equipment is located in the nightstand by your bed. Simply place it on your head and select the desired program. It is quite intuitive. You can even share your selected program with friends. All they have to do is select you as the source, and they will be sharing the same experience with you."

"Maybe I'll give it a try," Nathan replied. "Thank you."

"You are most welcome," Orana assured him. *"Please feel free to contact me if you need anything further."*

Nathan walked back to his bed and sat down, opening the drawer. Inside, he found a wire-thin headset with two pinpoint electrodes on each side and a small control box on top. Next to it was a small, handheld remote. He picked up the headset, examining it for a moment. "Is this the headset she was talking about?"

Jessica rolled her head toward him. "Yup."

"She said it's some kind of virtual reality entertainment system," he said, placing it on his head. "We can both share the same program. You want to try it with me?"

"It's probably best if one of us stays in the real world," Jessica pointed out. "This *is* an unknown world to us, after all."

"Good point," Nathan admitted, picking up the

remote. He pressed the power button, and within seconds, his view of their quarantine room became obscured by a gray, semi-opaque field blocking the center of his visual field, but leaving his peripheral vision unaffected. "Okay, this is different," he said. "The instructions are in English," he added, "or something close to it." He scrolled through a menu, first selecting settings. "You can choose your immersion level," he announced, taking note that the current setting was at fifty percent. "I'll start with seventy-five percent," he decided aloud. He made the selection, and the obscuration of his visual field became fully opaque, expanding to cover all but the very fringes of his periphery. He then selected a demo program. A loading indicator appeared, and a second later, he found himself standing in a colorful, lush garden. "Whoa," he exclaimed. "Not bad." He looked around, turning his head left and right, and then up and down. "Say something," he asked Jessica.

"Why?"

"I want to make sure I can hear you over the audio."

Jessica pretended to snore.

"Funny."

"How real is it?" she asked, humoring him.

"It's pretty good," Nathan admitted. "You can tell it's not real. There's an orientation icon in the upper, left corner of your visual field, something in the upper right that looks like a program name, and two time references. One of them is obviously the program's run time and remaining time, and I think the other is the current local time." He moved his head back and forth again. "It tracks pretty well." He held up the remote in front of his face, and the system opened up a hole in his visual field so he could see his hand with the remote in it. "That's handy," he said, pressing the zoom button. "When you zoom in on things, it becomes a little more obvious that it's a simulation."

"*Sorry to interrupt, Captain,*" Orana said.

"Wow, it's like you're standing next to me," Nathan replied.

"What?" Jessica asked.

"Not you, Orana."

"What?"

"She's talking to me through this VR thing," Nathan explained. "Yes, Orana?"

"*If I might make a suggestion?*"

"Please."

"*It is customary for one to lay supine, either on a bed or in a recliner, while using the virtual reality immersion system, especially if one is new to the experience. It helps to avoid loss of balance due to disassociation issues between the virtual and the real worlds.*"

"How do I move around the demo program?" he wondered.

"*The system will sense you are in the proper position and intercept your motion impulses. You will think you are moving your arms and legs, but in reality, you will not be.*"

"Interesting," Nathan replied. "Then, how do I use the remote?"

"*Think or say the word 'remote', and the impulses to move your hand holding the remote will no longer be intercepted, allowing you to move the remote in front of your face again. Once you replace your hand to your side, the impulses to that hand will once again be intercepted. If you wish to leave the immersion,*" *simply use the remote or say, 'Exit immersion,' and all will return to normal."*

"Thank you, Orana."

"You are most welcome, Captain. Enjoy your program."

"Can I sleep now?" Jessica wondered.

"Just stay awake for a few more minutes while I try this thing out a bit more," Nathan pleaded.

"Five minutes, but no more," Jessica replied, rising from her bed. "I'm going to the head."

Nathan lay down on his bed, his hands at his sides. "This is pretty sweet," he said to himself as he began walking around the virtual garden. He could smell the flowers around him. He could feel the warm, afternoon breeze on his face. He could even feel the unevenness of the dirt path under his feet as he walked. As long as one could ignore the telltale signs that it *was* a simulation, one could easily become lost in this world.

Luckily, the markers were everywhere, and it wasn't just the data indicators in the upper corners of his field of vision. Everything was extremely clean. The plants were trimmed and balanced. The edges of the dirt pathways were smooth, blending perfectly into the ground cover along them. The rhythm of the breeze was consistent and predictable. In short, everything was *too* perfect. In the real world, *nothing* was perfect.

"Remote," Nathan said, raising his right hand. Just as Orana had said, his hand appeared in front of him, holding the remote. He pressed the command button.

"State command," a voice prompted.

"Increase immersion level to one hundred percent," he instructed.

"*Immersion level to one hundred percent,*" the voice confirmed.

Nathan placed his hand back at his side, and his field of vision increased, filling in his periphery, as well. At the same time, the data displays in the upper corners disappeared. Yet the overall perfection, which made it seem real, yet unreal, was still there.

His finger still on the remote's command button, Nathan pressed it again.

"*State command,*" the voice repeated.

"Can you add people?" Nathan asked.

"*Specify type and number.*"

"I don't know, maybe ten, scattered throughout the garden. Like it was a public garden, or something."

"*Specify type.*"

"Typical citizens of SilTek," Nathan instructed. "Men, women, and children."

"*Adjusting program,*" the voice confirmed.

Nathan continued walking, spotting a man and a woman to his right. He took a side path in order to intercept them, nodding as he passed. "Good afternoon."

"*Good afternoon,*" the man replied.

"*Lovely garden, isn't it?*" the woman added.

"Indeed," Nathan replied, continuing on.

"Who are you talking to?" Jessica asked.

"Some people in the garden program," Nathan explained.

"There are people in there?"

"Yeah, I had to ask for them, though."

"How real are they?"

"Pretty real, but again, you can tell they're *not* real," he told her. "You should try this."

"Maybe tomorrow," Jessica replied. "I'm going to sleep. You should turn that thing off."

"I suppose you're right," Nathan agreed. "Exit immersion," he said. The garden disappeared, and his view of the interior of their quarantine suite returned. Nathan pulled the wire-thin headset off, turning to look at Jessica who was lying back down on her bed. "That was pretty interesting."

"You can tell me all about it," Jessica said, "in the morning."

"Good night, Jess."

"Good night."

Nathan took a deep breath, letting it out slowly as he closed his eyes to attempt to sleep.

* * *

"Oh, my God!" Neli exclaimed as Specialist Brill and Corporal Vasya helped Marcus into Doctor Symyri's medical facility.

"It looks worse than it is," Marcus insisted as they helped him to the exam bed.

"It couldn't possibly be as bad as it looks," Neli insisted. "What the hell did you do, pick a fight with everyone in the Jungle?"

"It could have been worse," Marcus insisted.

"Not by much," Doctor Symyri declared as he studied his medical scanner after passing it over Marcus's body. "You have a flail segment, your right arm is fractured, your *skull* is fractured..."

"Someone actually managed to crack that hard head of yours?" Corporal Vasya joked.

"Took 'em more than an hour," Marcus bragged.

"Are you stupid, or something?" Neli scolded. "You could've been killed, you old fool!"

"I did what had to be done."

"You *had* to get your ass beat?" Neli questioned.

"If that's what it took to close the deal, then, yes," Marcus insisted.

Neli shook her head, looking to Lieutenant Rezhik. "You should have sent someone with him."

"He insisted on going alone," Lieutenant Rezhik replied.

"And you listened?"

"In retrospect, it may have been a mistake."

"It wasn't a mistake," Marcus insisted. "Neli, I knew I was gonna get my ass kicked when I entered the place. I *also* knew that the lieutenant would rescue me."

"Then why the hell did you do it?"

"Because it had to be done," Marcus insisted.

"You're not making any sense."

"You don't understand how the Jungle works," Marcus told her. "My beatdown, rescue, and then *his* beatdown, established our rep. Now, nobody will fuck with us."

"Getting your ass beat and killing a bunch of them establishes your *rep*?"

"For the record, we didn't *kill* anyone," the lieutenant corrected.

"I thought you said it was a 'kill mission'?" Neli said.

"*If necessary*," Lieutenant Rezhik said, "which it was *not*."

"I thought you said you beat someone down?" Neli asked Marcus.

Marcus grinned from ear to ear. "I did."

"He stopped short of killing their leader."

"You think *I* look bad," Marcus grinned, revealing his recently knocked out teeth.

"Then, I take it I can expect another patient?" Doctor Symyri asked as he pushed Marcus back on the bed.

"I doubt he can afford you," Lieutenant Rezhik stated, almost laughing.

CHAPTER EIGHT

After a good night's sleep, Jessica opened her eyes, pushed off her covers, and stretched. She turned to look at Nathan who was lying on his bed, hands at his sides, with the wire-thin virtual reality gear on his head. "Oh, my God, have you been wearing that thing all night?"

"Good morning to you, too," Nathan replied, unmoving. "And, no, I put it on about twenty minutes ago."

"I think you might be developing an addiction," Jessica said as she swung her feet off the bed and sat up.

"It's not realistic enough for that," Nathan insisted.

"Please tell me you're not watching porn."

Nathan reached up and removed the headgear, glaring at her. "Seriously?"

"Just checking."

"It's actually a very good tool to learn about this planet," Nathan informed her, putting the headgear back on. "I'm taking a historical tour right now, learning about how this world was settled, how it was almost wiped out, and how it eventually became a corporate-owned, and managed, society. It's actually quite fascinating. You should give it a try. You *are* an intelligence officer, after all."

"And intelligence officers know better than to get their information from propaganda vids," Jessica commented.

"You have to start somewhere."

"Can I pee first?" Jessica asked as she disappeared into the bathroom.

Nathan, ignoring her, was already back on his VR tour. "This particular program is clearly aimed at newcomers like us," he said, assuming she could hear him. "It's a pretty condensed version of SilTek's five-hundred-year history, and not anywhere near as immersive as the garden simulation I was in last night. It's more like watching a documentary."

"*You're such a history geek,*" Jessica mocked from the open bathroom.

"Yeah, I can't help myself," he admitted.

Jessica returned from the bathroom, headed over to the nightstand by her bed, and pulled out her own VR headgear and its remote. "So, how do I use this?"

"Just put it on your head and use the remote," Nathan explained as he picked up his own remote. "It's pretty intuitive."

Jessica placed the wire-thin device on her head, then picked up her remote and pressed the power button. Immediately, the center area of her field of vision became obscured by an opaque, gray cloud with a menu prompting her to select a language. After choosing English, she asked, "What program should I select?"

"Choose 'Join Session', and then select my name."

"Damn," she exclaimed as she followed his instructions. "It looks like everyone around us is using this thing. What happens if I choose the wrong one?"

"I don't know," Nathan admitted. "I'm guessing the system will ask the source user's permission before sharing their session with someone else."

Jessica selected Nathan from the list of active sessions.

"Yup, it's asking my permission for you to join."

A moment later, Jessica found herself standing in

the middle of a serene shopping area, surrounding a beautifully manicured park. The setting was full of shoppers. She looked up, taking in the brilliant topaz sky, and then looked to her left, spotting Nathan.

"Hi," Nathan greeted, waving at her.

"Wow, your avatar *really* looks like you," Jessica exclaimed.

"So does yours," Nathan replied.

"Except your hair is never that neat," she added. "How does it make such good avatars?"

"I'm guessing it uses the data from our medical scans to recreate our bodies."

"I'm not crazy about the outfit it selected for me," Jessica complained, noticing her avatar's clothing, "but other than that, it's pretty impressive," she said, looking around further. "How do you move around?"

"Just lie back on your bed, and place your hands at your sides, then just think about moving," Nathan instructed.

Jessica lay back on her bed, hands at her sides, and began walking around in the simulation. "This is weird."

"Yeah, it takes some getting used to," Nathan admitted.

"How does it work?"

"When you're supine, hands at your sides, the system takes over and intercepts your brain's impulses to move your body, sending them to the simulation instead."

"Then how do I get *out* of the simulation?" Jessica wondered.

"Just say, 'Exit immersion,'" Nathan explained. "You can also hold down any button on the remote and then raise your hand, holding the remote up to your face to see it, and press any button."

"Exit immersion," Jessica commanded. The immersion faded away, and Jessica pulled the headgear off.

"What are you doing?" Nathan wondered, pulling off his own headgear. "You barely started."

"I haven't even had breakfast," Jessica complained.

* * *

"I have no idea what that was, but it tasted pretty good," Nathan said, picking up his empty tray and placing it in the waste processor.

"I want to say *omelet* or *frittata*, but it wasn't really either," Jessica commented as she took her last bite. "Any idea what those little red things were? I could swear they tasted different every time I ate one."

The door opened, and Orana entered their quarantine suite carrying two bags. "Good morning," she greeted. "I trust you both slept well?"

"Yes, quite well," Nathan replied.

"What's in the bags?" Jessica wondered.

"The clothing you arrived in," Orana answered, handing one of the bags to Jessica. "They have been cleaned and sterilized, as have all of the belongings you brought with you for your stay on SilTek. I thought you might like to change before your departure."

"Then, we're cleared from quarantine?" Nathan asked.

"That is correct, Captain," Orana replied, handing the other bag to Nathan. "SilTek has sent a transport to take you to headquarters. It seems our leader wishes to welcome you, herself."

"When can we go?" Nathan wondered.

"As soon as you are ready," Orana explained. "The transport is already here."

"Then, we didn't bring any little germs with us?" Jessica quipped.

"Nothing out of the ordinary, no," Orana assured her. "You are both very healthy specimens; especially you, Captain Scott. You both would have been cleared much sooner, had it not been for the nanites in the lieutenant commander's system. Those required closer examination."

"They are nothing more than medical nanites," Nathan explained. "They cannot replicate, and once outside of the host, they instantly become inert."

"So we eventually determined," Orana replied. "I apologize for the delay. I hope you were not too inconvenienced."

"Not at all," Nathan replied. "I needed a good night's sleep. Being in quarantine gave me the perfect excuse."

"I am happy to hear that," Orana told him. "Once you are ready, I will escort you to your transport."

Ten minutes later, Nathan and Jessica followed Orana out onto the rooftop transportation platform where a large, black vehicle waited for them on the pad.

"Is that for us?" Nathan asked Orana.

"Yes," she confirmed. "It was an honor to serve you both," she added with a respectful nod.

Nathan moved toward the awaiting vehicle, and its doors opened. He paused a moment, then turned back to Orana. "Where's the pilot?"

"Transports on SilTek are automated," Orana explained. "It is perfectly safe, I assure you."

"Of course," Nathan replied, continuing toward the waiting vehicle.

"Good day to you both," Orana waved, before turning and heading back inside.

"Ladies first," Nathan said, gesturing for Jessica to enter the vehicle.

Jessica climbed inside and took a seat in the back. "Nice. Comfy, but not ostentatious."

Nathan climbed in next, and the doors automatically closed.

"*Welcome aboard,*" a voice announced. "*Our destination is SilTek headquarters in the Asburton district. Our flight time will be twenty-seven minutes and forty-two seconds. Please sit back and enjoy the flight.*"

The vehicle began to hum as it slowly lifted off the rooftop deck. Inching forward as it rose, the vehicle rotated ninety degrees to the right and then accelerated away from the arrival facility, climbing more rapidly.

Within seconds, their transport had reached its cruising altitude, only a hundred meters or so above the flowing terrain. Other transport vehicles cluttered the sky, traveling in different directions and altitudes. Large and small, in a variety of shapes, colors, and styles, multiple transports ascended and descended, entering and exiting the traffic patterns in an orderly fashion. There were dozens of them nearby and probably hundreds, if not thousands, more in the distance.

"There aren't any roads," Jessica observed, looking at the surface below.

"Probably would've been difficult," Nathan commented. "This place is all rolling hills, forests, and rivers."

"Still, how do they haul stuff around? Surely they must have service roads."

"They eliminated the need for surface roads a few hundred years ago," Nathan explained. *"Everything is flown.* This has allowed them to spread their population out over most of the planet. Most people live in small districts, where they can walk to most places. All of this reduces the overall impact on their environment."

"But they still have actual *cities*, right?"

"Like I said, they call them *districts*, not *cities*. Some are larger than others. For example, the Asburton district, where SilTek's headquarters is located, is one of the largest districts on the planet, large enough to require public transit systems."

"Why do they need public transit when they have flying cars?" Jessica wondered.

"The larger districts have more restrictions on aerial traffic. They only allow arrivals and departures to and from certain points within them. Kind of like airports. Some of the larger buildings also have transit platforms on their rooftops, much like the one atop the arrival facility we just left. They have massive underground garages."

Jessica cast a sidelong glance at Nathan. "How long did you spend in that VR thing?"

"It's a fascinating world," Nathan insisted. "Its political and economic systems are unlike anything we've ever come across."

Jessica rolled her eyes. "At least, I know you weren't trolling VR strip clubs."

* * *

"We are approaching SilTek headquarters," the transport's autopilot announced. *"Please prepare for landing."*

"Not as impressive as I'd expected," Nathan

231

commented as their transport descended toward the rooftop flight deck.

"What *were* you expecting," Jessica wondered, also gazing out the window at the complex below, "a crystal palace?"

"Throughout history, organizations holding considerable power over others have chosen to headquarter themselves in structures *reflecting* their level of influence, as a way of reminding those they control of that power," Nathan explained.

"Maybe they're not as big as Mister Vout wants us to believe?"

"Doubtful," Nathan disagreed. "If that were the case, why show us their modest administrative offices?"

"There's nothing *modest* about this world," Jessica insisted. "It may not be covered with skyscrapers and ornate palaces, but it *is* quite nice."

"From what we've seen so far," Nathan added as their transport gently touched down. Nathan's door opened, and he climbed out of the transport, offering Jessica his hand.

"What a gentleman," she teased, accepting his gesture.

"Welcome to SilTek headquarters," Miss Bindi greeted as she walked toward them. "I hope you enjoyed the ride over."

"Indeed, we did," Nathan replied. "You have an amazing world, Miss Bindi. Is your entire planet as clean and well landscaped?"

"Oh, no," Miss Bindi chuckled. "Only the populated areas, which covers roughly one third of our planet's landmass. The rest is agricultural land and wilderness, the latter of which we try to leave as undisturbed as possible."

"A difficult task for a growing society," Nathan commented.

"Our growth rate is strictly controlled," Miss Bindi stated as she led them toward the rooftop foyer. "We achieved a balance between population needs and planetary resources more than a hundred years ago."

"Yet, you seek to expand your area of sales," Nathan commented. "Does that not require increasing your population, as well?"

"We use automation to fill that void," Miss Bindi explained as they entered the foyer. "Our population has remained constant for the last one hundred and twenty-seven years."

"How do you *control* population growth?" Jessica wondered.

"Procreation is not a right on SilTek, it is a privilege," Miss Bindi responded as she led them across the foyer to the elevators. "Tekan males are born unable to impregnate a female. The sterilization is easily reversed but requires a procreation permit that is good for at most two children, one of each sex. After the children have been born, the sterilization is reinstated to avoid accidental impregnation."

"What if a couple wants a larger family?" Jessica asked.

"Permits for additional children are available, but on a very limited basis. The idea is to keep the population of our world well within our planet's natural carrying capacity."

"But accidents *must* happen from time to time," Nathan posited as they entered the elevator.

"Of course," Miss Bindi admitted as she activated the elevator. "That is why we keep the population well *below* SilTek's carrying capacity."

"Seems like a reasonable solution," Nathan admitted.

"You seem somewhat surprised," Miss Bindi realized.

"It's just that you're the first world we've come across that limits procreation. Most worlds are still struggling to *grow* their populations to full industrialization levels," Nathan told her.

"That's because they lack our level of automation," Miss Bindi replied. "That is one of the reasons we are trying to sell our automation to other worlds."

The elevator slowed to a stop and then began traveling sideways.

"This elevator moves *laterally*, as well as vertically?" Nathan wondered.

"Yes, however, we do not refer to them as *elevators*; we call them *cubes*. They allow us to spread our facilities out, rather than building vertically, while still being able to move about with ease."

"I would have thought you would use more telepresence than *actual* presence," Nathan commented.

"Telepresence has its place," Miss Bindi admitted. "However, we value the *actual* over the *virtual*, whenever possible. Transport cubes make that possible."

"So, you'd rather take the time to ride a cube across the campus, to have a brief conversation with someone, than just call them over a communications device?" Jessica wondered. "Seems kind of inefficient."

"We believe any efficiency that robs us of our humanity, and leads to the deterioration of our interpersonal relationships, actually makes us *less* efficient in the *long* run," Miss Bindi explained.

"*Speed* is not the end goal, rather *quality*. Quality of our products, our society, and our *lives*. *Those* are the core beliefs that *all* Tekans live by."

The cube doors opened, revealing a large lobby with several reception desks. "If you'll follow me," she prompted, leading them out of the cube.

Nathan surveyed the surroundings as they followed Miss Bindi across the lobby. Much like its exterior, the interior of SilTek's headquarters, although well appointed, was not unduly so. The decor was stylish, but not ostentatious like most seats of power. He was unsure what this difference meant, but it left him with a positive impression.

After crossing the lobby, Miss Bindi led them into a private meeting area with a large picture window at one end.

"Missus Batista will be with you shortly," Miss Bindi told them. "Meanwhile, can I get you anything? Something to eat or drink, perhaps?"

"I'm fine, thank you," Nathan replied.

"I'm still full of whatever it was we had for breakfast," Jessica admitted.

"As you wish. Please, make yourselves comfortable. I'm certain she will not be long."

Nathan strolled over to the picture window as Miss Bindi disappeared through a side door. "Nice gardens, at least."

"What do you mean?"

"I mean, they have a nice garden," Nathan said, gesturing toward the window.

"*At least?*"

"I'm just not sure what to make of all this," Nathan explained. "Their world seems ideal, at least from the air. They seem to be very efficient, with very little waste, and yet are also very cognizant of how the use of technology impacts their civilization."

"Seems like a good thing, if you ask me," Jessica declared as she made herself comfortable on one of the three couches in the room.

"It is," Nathan continued, "but it's also very uncharacteristic of humanity."

"I never pegged you for a pessimist," Jessica said.

"Humanity has been trying to create utopian societies since before recorded history, and it always ends in failure for pretty much the same reason."

"Which is?"

"Everyone has a different *idea* of utopia," Nathan explained. "The whole reason behind the initial push to colonize extrasolar worlds was to enable humans to create their own *perfect societies*, free from the restraints of the unified Earth government of the twenty-second century. The idea was that starting over was the only way to build a perfect society, because the trappings of the past always got in the way. But no one ever really succeeded because of the one common denominator: humans."

"An imperfect species cannot create a perfect society," Jessica stated. "I remember that from philosophy class."

"*You* studied *philosophy*?" Nathan asked, shocked.

"Not because I wanted to, I assure you."

"I wonder how much their automation had to do with all of this," Nathan wondered, gazing out the massive window.

"Quite a lot, actually," a female voice replied.

From the side door, a middle-aged woman, dressed in gray and white business attire, entered the room. She had shorter hair, cropped just above her shoulders, with only the slightest hint of gray, which she appeared to wear with pride. She was confident and graceful, and at first glance, reminded Nathan of his mother. "Captain Scott, Lieutenant Commander Nash, I am Ariana Batista, leader of SilTek. It is a pleasure to make your acquaintance."

"The pleasure is all mine," Nathan replied, shaking her hand politely. "Thank you for seeing us on such short notice."

"Normally, I do not do so," Ariana admitted. "As you might expect, I am a very busy woman. However, since I suspect you are equally as busy, I thought we might have a preliminary discussion to sort of *feel each other out*, so to speak. You see, I rarely meet with anyone without a team of advisors at my side. But unless I know for certain what you are proposing, I know not *which* advisors to have on hand."

"Understandable," Nathan replied, following her to the center of the room.

"They tell me *you* are the Aurora's chief of security and the protector of Captain Scott," Ariana said to Jessica as she shook her hand. "Are the stories I have been told true? Are you *really* a *badass*?"

"Yes, ma'am," Jessica replied with equal confidence.

Ariana nodded. "I *am* impressed, Lieutenant Commander." Ariana looked at Nathan. "The stories of *your* exploits are as equally impressive, Captain Scott. I must admit, however, I had not heard of you prior to receiving your request to meet. Needless to say, it made for some interesting reading. So," she continued, taking a seat on the couch across from Jessica, "what type of business arrangement do you seek?"

"I was hoping to convince your world to join our

alliance," Nathan admitted, taking a seat next to Jessica.

"I'm sure Mister Vout informed you that SilTek does not get involved in conflicts between other worlds. We consider neutrality an important element of our ongoing business success, especially now that the jump drive has reached our corner of the galaxy."

"He did, and I appreciate your decision, however shortsighted it may be," Nathan replied.

"You don't hold back, do you, Captain," Ariana observed, one eyebrow slightly raised.

"I'm afraid I can't afford that luxury."

"I suppose this is where you explain to me that the Dusahn are a threat to everyone, and that it is only a matter of time before they come knocking at our door, as well."

"I would not dream of insulting your intelligence," Nathan assured her. "I trust you have done your research on the Dusahn, as well."

"I have. As expected, they are frighteningly ruthless and have little regard for human life."

"They see humans as resources," Nathan explained, "to be exploited in order to achieve their own goals."

"And what are those goals?"

"One cannot be certain," Nathan admitted. "However, based on their history and their actions, I can only assume they seek to build an empire that cannot be defeated."

"So, you expect them to expand their sphere of control."

"I don't think they care about the number of worlds they control," Nathan clarified. "I believe they care more about the number of *industrialized*, *technologically advanced* worlds they control. This makes SilTek a prime target."

"Would you be surprised to learn that the Dusahn are not the only threat out there?" Ariana asked.

"Honestly, I would not."

"*Really?*" Ariana examined her guest for a moment. "I would have pegged you for an optimist, Captain Scott. After all, you are taking on an *empire* with only a single warship."

"I am a student of history," Nathan replied. "Humans are a ruthless species, capable of evil, as well as good. We are able to convince ourselves that one plus one equals four if we *need* it to be true. This is how we survive against all odds. The problem occurs when we become so convinced that our beliefs are justified, that we stop listening to, and respecting the opinions of, those who do not believe as we do. The Dusahn are such people. They are so convinced in their *right* to rule over all others that they see no action serving that goal as unjust. Sadly, they will not be the last, since history is replete with such men *and* women."

"Mostly men, I suspect," Ariana added with a smile.

Nathan also smiled. "Yes, mostly men."

"And what happens when the next would-be ruler rears his ugly head? The galaxy cannot always count on another Nathan Scott coming to its rescue."

"And it shouldn't have to," Nathan agreed. "History is also replete with attempts to form coalitions aimed at preventing the rise of such people, to protect the liberty of all its members. The trouble is that they, too, usually failed."

"Any idea as to *why* they failed?"

"I actually wrote a paper on that very subject in

college. My position was that they failed because they continually tried to impose their *collective* beliefs onto *all* member nations. Later, because of their might, they would impose those same beliefs on *nonmember* nations, as well."

"It doesn't seem like an unreasonable way to ensure order," Ariana said.

"When you negotiate a business deal with another company, do you tell them how to dress, or how to do their accounting, or whom they should associate with? No, because those issues are not germane to the deal."

"But common ideals lead to better relations between entities," Ariana insisted.

"Perhaps, but there are limits," Nathan argued, "and those limits are breached when such coalitions believe they have the *right* to tell others how to live and what to believe. Wars are generally fought over one of three things: political beliefs, religious beliefs, or resources. I believe that humanity, now that it has the jump drive, can finally overcome those three causes of conflict."

"I think you put more faith in the jump drive than it deserves, Captain," Ariana argued. "After all, as wonderful an invention as it is, it still has its own limitations. It is simply a faster method of transportation than linear FTL."

"What if I told you that its range is potentially unlimited?" Nathan replied. "And that it is still in its infancy?"

"I would ask for proof to back your claims."

"Not only have we developed a *stealth* version of the jump drive, but we have also managed to increase the Aurora's single-jump range to over *five hundred* light years, and within weeks, it will have a *two-jump* range of more than *one thousand* light years."

"I would wonder how you had managed that on your own," Ariana replied, failing to hide her curiosity.

"We have the inventor of the jump drive working *with* us."

"Doctor Sorenson is a member of your alliance?" Ariana was in shock.

"Abigail Sorenson is a personal friend. She and Deliza Ta'Akar are the leaders of our research and development division. In fact, we are currently developing a jump missile able to penetrate the Dusahn's shields; technology that recently helped us defeat *four* Dusahn battleships with barely a scratch on the Aurora."

Ariana studied Nathan for a moment before replying. "I would say...we need to schedule further discussions."

* * *

"What do you think?" Jessica queried as they rode the cube across the SilTek campus toward the product pavilions.

"She seems quite certain in her position and beliefs, and she doesn't seem easily swayed," Nathan replied.

"But the fact that she is willing to talk further is a good sign, right?"

"Well, I suppose it's better than being shown the door, but I wouldn't get your hopes up just yet."

"That was a good idea to drop Abby's name," Jessica complimented, "but why Deliza?"

"Because she probably doesn't know her, so she'll have her people do some research before we meet again," Nathan explained. "Then, she'll know that not only is Deliza a genius in her own right, but is also the leader of a successful, interstellar tech company, as well as the rightful heir to the throne of Takara. Once the Dusahn *are* defeated, Deliza Ta'Akar is going to be a woman Ariana Batista will want as a friend."

"Wouldn't it have been easier to just *tell* her that?"

"It will have more of an impact if she learns it on her own," Nathan explained. "That will give us an edge."

"I'm not following," Jessica admitted. "How exactly will that work in our favor?"

"My father once told me that people in positions of power usually believe they are smarter than everyone else. If she believes that we don't realize how valuable a business relationship with Deliza could be for her, she'll feel like she has the advantage going into negotiations."

"So, you're playing stupid," Jessica decided.

"Something like that," Nathan replied. "Trust me, it's better for her to *believe* she's smarter than us."

"Is she?"

"Probably," Nathan admitted.

The cube came to a stop, and the doors opened.

"Why are we here, again?" Jessica wondered as they started down the corridor toward the first of five product pavilions.

"This is supposed to be a series of showrooms of SilTek products," Nathan explained. "I'm pretty sure Ariana recommended we come here to impress us with their product lines before beginning negotiations."

"Like what? A bunch of android nurses?" Jessica's jaw dropped as they reached the end of the corridor and entered the first pavilion. "Oh...my...God."

Before them was a dome-shaped pavilion at least

twice the size of the Aurora's main hangar bay and nearly as tall. All around the perimeter were different types of automated equipment, all of them designed for military use. In the middle of the pavilion, on a massive, raised, rotating stage was an array of modules, all of which were designed to fit onto the same tracked mobility system. The modules were being rotated around, automatically being loaded and unloaded onto the mobile platform at the center of the stage. Nathan and Jessica both watched in fascination as the first module was lowered onto the tracked vehicle and, in seconds, was ready for action.

"Welcome to the military pavilion," a male voice greeted.

Nathan turned in the direction of the voice, finding a male android in a SilTek uniform smiling at him.

"My name is Bernard. You must be Captain Scott and Lieutenant Commander Nash. I was told to expect you. If you have any questions, I'd be happy to answer them."

"Hi, Bernard," Nathan replied. "What is this thing?" he asked, pointing toward the massive rotating display in the center of the pavilion.

"Impressive, isn't it," Bernard stated, almost bragging. "That's our modular mobile tactical system. It's capable of swapping out the service module in less than a minute. Missile launcher, ion cannon, plasma cannon, rail guns, rocket launchers, all manner of smart weapons and artillery, as well as anti-personnel modules, troop movers, sensor platforms...you name it, we have a module for it. The system allows for maximum flexibility to meet changing defense conditions, without the investment in dedicated mobility platforms. Imagine the flexibility..."

"How fast does the mobility platform travel?" Jessica wondered.

"Eighty kilometers per hour over smooth terrain, forty over rough terrain. Load the first few platforms with auto-graders and ground fusers, and you can create new roads at a rate of three kilometers per hour."

"So, the mobility platform isn't just for use by military modules, then," Nathan surmised.

"The mobility platforms come in many different sizes and configurations," Bernard explained, leading them toward another exhibit. "There are crawlers, wheeled platforms, hover platforms, just about every method of mobility you can imagine. And all of them come in a variety of sizes. Better yet, they are all manufactured using extremely precise, fully automated systems. This ensures that *every* unit operates *exactly* the same, meeting the *same* performance tolerances."

"What are those?" Jessica wondered, pointing to a few ungainly looking vehicles.

"Those are automated garbage collector-compactors."

"I'm confused," Nathan admitted. "SilTek doesn't have any roads. Don't all of these things need roads, or at least open terrain, in order to operate?"

"These products aren't designed for use *on* SilTek," Bernard explained. "They are for use on other worlds."

"What does SilTek use to collect garbage?" Jessica wondered.

"All garbage on SilTek is compacted at the source and then transported through an automated underground collection network to centralized facilities, where it is broken down into its base elements and then reintegrated into society."

"One hundred percent recycling," Jessica realized. "Nice."

"I can think of a few worlds who could use *that* technology," Nathan chuckled.

"I would love to know which worlds," Bernard said. "I could forward their names to our sales department."

"I was joking," Nathan told him. "Sort of..."

"This is all very impressive, but do you make any *offensive* weapons?" Jessica asked.

"SilTek does not create, or sell, offensive weapons," Bernard assured her. "We do not promote the use of military force in lieu of diplomacy."

"Some would say that military conflict is a *form* of diplomacy," Nathan countered.

"A *bad* form, yes."

"There are times when force is the only option," Jessica added.

"I would not know," Bernard replied. "The use of physical or military force is contrary to my programming."

"Good to know," Jessica said.

"What about automated manufacturing?" Nathan asked. "Do you have fabricators that can be fed designs and raw materials, which will then produce the parts needed to assemble into a larger product?"

"SilTek offers entire lines of automated fabrication and manufacturing, requiring no human participation, and can produce complex items with great precision and speed," Bernard bragged. "They are on display in pavilion three."

"Can you take us there?" Nathan asked.

"It would be my pleasure, Captain," Bernard replied enthusiastically. "If you'll please follow me."

"What kind of company doesn't make offensive weapons?" Jessica muttered to Nathan under her breath as they followed Bernard.

"I don't care," Nathan replied. "Especially if they can sell us a system that can make weapons *for* us faster than we can already make them. Can you imagine being able to manufacture shield-penetrating jump missiles in our cargo bay, automatically, twenty-four seven? What does it take the factories on Rogen now, about a week? What if they could do it in hours?"

"Now, who's getting their hopes up?" Jessica countered as they transitioned to the next pavilion.

This time, it was Nathan's jaw that dropped. "Holy shit."

"Welcome to the automated manufacturing pavilion, where we showcase the latest in high-speed, high-precision, high-tech fabrication and manufacturing systems," Bernard greeted as if introducing the next act in a variety show.

Nathan looked over to Jessica, grinning from ear to ear. "Vlad would shit his pants."

* * *

The black transport vehicle descended smoothly from its cruising altitude toward the rolling hills below.

"Do you see a hotel?" Jessica wondered, scanning the hillsides.

"Nothing but residences," Nathan replied. "Nice ones, but no hotels."

"Pilot, where are we going?" Jessica asked the automated transport.

"*SilTek maintains a number of luxury guest*

residences. You have been assigned to the one at two four seven five Bora Creek Way, in the district of Etimone. We will arrive in two minutes."

"Are all these homes guest residences?" Nathan wondered.

"No, there are only two guest residences in the Etimone district. The remainder of residences are occupied by citizens of SilTek."

As the transport closed on its destination, the view of the residences below improved, revealing all of their features and landscaping.

"Wow," Nathan exclaimed softly. "These places are amazing. Does everyone on SilTek live like this?"

"These are upper-level homes," the automated pilot replied. *"However, mid and lower-level homes have many of the same amenities shared among them."*

"It looks like every one of these has a pool, hot tub, and some sort of athletic court," Jessica realized.

"Please prepare for landing."

Nathan peered out the window as their transport continued its descent. "That one must be ours."

"It's *huge*," Jessica exclaimed.

"It is approximately four thousand square meters," the automated pilot reported.

The hum of the transport's gravity-lift systems increased as it slowed its rate of descent. Ten seconds later, the transport executed another perfect landing.

"Welcome to your residence," the pilot announced. *"Your bags have already been delivered. This transport will remain on the pad, available to you whenever you need it."*

The door on the transport opened, and Nathan climbed out, pausing to take in the landscape. The entire property was surrounded by an assortment

247

of trees, all of which were expertly chosen for their color, shape, and size, all complementing one another. There were flowering bushes along the perimeter, mixed in with ornate little planters full of flowers. Nathan slowly rotated around, noticing that he could not see a single neighboring residence. "This is unbelievable. It's even nicer than our family estate in Vancouver."

"I keep forgetting that you grew up with a silver spoon in your mouth," Jessica commented as she climbed out of the transport.

"It was stainless steel," Nathan corrected, heading toward the front door.

"Our house was more like a collection of add-ons, but it *was* walking distance from the beach," Jessica commented as they followed the winding path leading to the front door. "This place must require an army of landscapers."

As they approached the main entrance, the double doors swung open automatically. "*Welcome, Captain,*" a voice greeted as he entered.

Nathan looked around for the source of the voice but found no one. "Tell me you heard that," he said, looking at Jessica.

"Heard what?" she joked.

"*I am the residence's automated systems interface,*" the voice continued.

"Now, I *know* you heard *that*," Nathan insisted.

"Is that a male or a female?" Jessica wondered.

"*My voice has been designed as genderless,*" the voice explained. "*All residences on SilTek have an artificial intelligence as a systems interface. I control all automated service and maintenance systems throughout the residence and property. If you need anything, feel free to ask.*"

"What do we call you?" Nathan wondered.

"My default name is Ory. However, you can assign any name you wish."

"Ory is fine with me," Nathan said, looking to Jessica.

"Fine with me, too."

"This home has four bedrooms, each with its own bath, and a fully automated kitchen with a personal chef. If you wish to conduct business from home, there is a dedicated office space complete with virtual reality communications systems. For entertainment, there is a game room, an outdoor activities court, pool, and hot tub, as well as a system of trails that winds its way throughout the district."

"Which bedroom do you want?" Nathan asked Jessica.

"Doesn't matter to me," she replied.

"Captain Scott, you have been assigned to bedroom number four, which is the last door down the corridor to your right," Ory explained. *"Lieutenant Commander Nash has been assigned bedroom number three, directly adjacent. Your bags have already been delivered, and your closets have been stocked with appropriately sized clothing, with outfits for every conceivable activity while on SilTek."*

"Thank you, Ory," Nathan replied.

"You are quite welcome. If you require anything, again, please ask."

"Ory? Do you know when we are scheduled to meet with Missus Batista again?" Nathan wondered.

"Your next meeting with Ariana Batista is scheduled for tomorrow at fourteen hundred hours. Would you like me to give you a reminder tomorrow, prior to your appointment?"

"Thanks, that won't be necessary."

"*Holy crap!*" Jessica yelled from her bedroom.

Nathan ran into bedroom three and found Jessica rummaging through a large walk-in closet, stocked with women's clothing. "What's wrong?"

"Nothing!" she laughed.

"Why did you yell?"

"I haven't had a wardrobe like this since...well, *ever!*" she exclaimed as she stripped off her uniform. "Hell, I haven't owned a *dress* in *years!*" She pulled a sleek, black dress off the rack, pulling it on over her head and sliding it down over her body. "What do you think?" she asked, turning to face Nathan.

Nathan smiled. "Brings back memories."

* * *

By the time they had left the restaurant, the sun had set, and the sky had taken on an eerie pale blue from its primary moon, with tinges of red from its smaller, secondary one.

The center of their district was just as Ory had described it, with lots of shops and restaurants on the first floors, and service businesses and offices on the upper levels. It had taken them only fifteen minutes, at a medium-paced walk, to make the journey from the residence, and now, after tasting numerous Tekan delicacies, they were glad to have the chance to walk some of it off.

"That was some dinner," Nathan declared as he and Jessica walked along one of the many trails that wound through the woods separating the homes in their district.

"I think we pissed off the waiter with all of our questions."

"I still haven't figured out what that purple stuff was."

"I'm guessing it was some kind of fish," Jessica decided.

"Tasted more like a slug to me."

"Eaten many slugs, have you?"

"The wine was good."

"I can't believe we went through two bottles," Jessica giggled.

"Well, it's not like we're on call, or anything," Nathan replied. "You know, this is the first time I've been able to forget about everything and just enjoy myself."

"It's also our first *real* date, you know," Jessica pointed out.

"What? No..."

"Yeah..."

"But..."

"Doesn't count," Jessica insisted. "That was a one-night stand between strangers. I didn't even know your name."

"I suppose you're right."

"You ate a ton of that shellfish, you know."

"Hey, it was delicious."

"It's also supposed to *increase your libido.*"

"Where'd you hear that?" Nathan wondered.

"I heard the older couple behind us talking about it," Jessica explained. "Apparently, it led to their second child."

"The people here seem nice," Nathan commented, hoping to change the topic. "Very happy."

"Too happy," Jessica insisted.

"How can you be *too* happy?" Nathan wondered.

"I don't trust people who are too happy."

"You didn't answer the question."

"You can be *too* happy," Jessica insisted. "Things need to go wrong once in a while, or you don't appreciate when they go right. Even worse, if you're happy all the time, and something *does* go wrong, it can be devastating."

"You're not making sense."

"Yup. Too much happiness makes you *weak*."

"You're drunk."

"Doesn't mean I'm not right," Jessica insisted. "You, sir, are a perfect example."

"What are you talking about?"

"You were a spoiled, little, rich boy with no responsibilities in the world," she explained. "Getting all drunk because you didn't like how daddy treated you."

"Careful," Nathan warned.

"No, no, no," she defended, "it's a good thing. You see, bad shit happened, and you became tougher. Hell, you've done *incredible* things. *Unbelievable* things, none of which you would've accomplished if bad stuff hadn't happened to you. So, you see, too much happiness is bad for you."

"Who says I wasn't happy during all that?" Nathan asked.

"Well, you were always moping around feeling sorry for yourself, for one."

"Only in the beginning," Nathan defended.

"More like the entire time," Jessica insisted.

"It was a stressful period," Nathan argued, "and I wasn't trained for any of that."

"But you stepped up and got it done," Jessica pointed out, "and *that's* my point."

Nathan paused at the fork in the trails. "Which way was it?"

"Left."

"Are you sure?"

"Nope."

"Let's go right," Nathan decided, continuing on.

"You're the captain, Captain."

They walked silently for a moment, enjoying the glowing flora of SilTek.

"What about *this* time?" Nathan asked.

"*This* time?"

"You know, since you and Telles showed up and told me who I really was."

"This time, you're different," Jessica said. "You were still a bit whiny in the beginning, but once you were transferred into this body...well...you've changed."

"How?"

"You're more confident now," she admitted.

"Really?"

"Don't let it go to your head," Jessica warned. "You still have your self-absorbed moments. They're just few and far between."

"Good to know."

"You think faster now, as well," Jessica added. "You even *move* faster. I used to be able to kick your ass with one hand tied behind my back."

"And you need both hands now?" Nathan laughed.

"No, but at least I break a sweat now."

"Well, you *are* getting older," Nathan taunted.

"Technically, *you're* older than *I* am," Jessica defended.

"*Technically*, I'm not. *Chronologically*, I am."

"That's because you cheated," Jessica said.

"Hey, it was your idea." Nathan stopped at the next fork, a confused look on his face. "Didn't we pass this fork a few minutes ago?"

"Some leader you are," Jessica giggled, heading down the trail to the left. "I told you we should have gone left."

"Fine, we go left," Nathan agreed, following Jessica.

"Why did you do it?" Jessica asked.

"I honestly thought the trail to the right was the way home."

"I mean, why did you agree to lead us this time?" Jessica clarified as she led them down the trail. "You could have just headed further out, found an area where they hadn't yet heard of the jump drive, and made a fortune. That's what your crew wanted to do."

"That's what Neli wanted to do," Nathan replied. "Dalen didn't much care, and Marcus and Josh were just babysitting me, probably under *your* orders."

"Then, why didn't you?" she asked.

"Would you believe me if I said it felt like the right thing to do?"

"Partly," Jessica replied. "Hey, I think I see our place up ahead."

"Finally," Nathan sighed. "I was afraid I'd gotten us lost."

"Yup, this is it," she said, opening the gate into their yard. "Just in time, I was starting to get cold."

"In that skimpy, little dress, I'm not surprised."

"Hey, I look hot in this dress," Jessica insisted.

"Damned hot," Nathan replied with a grin.

Jessica glanced back over her shoulder as she opened the patio door, smiling at Nathan. "You haven't answered the question," she added as she entered the house. "Why *did* you decide to lead us this time?"

Nathan took a deep breath, letting it out with a long sigh as they headed down the corridor toward their bedrooms. "It *was* partly because I felt like it was the right thing to do," he insisted, "but it was also because I didn't feel *whole*. I felt like I'd been missing a part of my life, and I'd pretty much accepted that I was never going to get it back." They stopped at the end of the corridor, each of them leaning their backs against their respective doors. "It made me feel like I was just going through the motions of life. I couldn't tell if my goals were *mine*, or if they were what I was *told* were mine. Then, you came along, and you were so beautiful and so familiar, and you were *so* confident in *me*...more confident than *I* was in *myself*. It was a way to find out who I *really* was."

"How come you've never told me all this?" Jessica wondered.

"I guess because I felt guilty," Nathan admitted, looking down. "It was about me. I wasn't even going to stay around after I got my memories back."

"But you did," Jessica said, "and you know why?"

"Because you're hot?" Nathan said, flashing his usual, charming smile.

"Well, that, but mostly because you're Nathan Scott. *You're Na-Tan*. You're a *savior*. Not *the* savior, but a savior, nonetheless. It's what you do. You save those who need saving, and you're willing to sacrifice your *own* life to do so. In fact, you did."

"Not my best plan ever," Nathan joked.

"*That's* why the Ghatazhak follow you. That's why we *all* follow you."

"Is that why *you* follow me?" Nathan asked.

"That, and because I love you."

Nathan smiled, saying nothing.

"You're not going to say anything?" Jessica wondered.

"You already know how I feel about you."

Jessica smiled, moving closer to him. "You know,"

she said, reaching behind him to open his door, "it seems a shame to mess up two beds."

"Yeah, I'd hate to make the robot-maid do extra work," Nathan agreed.

CHAPTER NINE

Nathan's eyes opened slowly. The bedroom was bathed in the soft, amber light of SilTek's dawn. He felt rested and relaxed, more so than he could ever remember.

Nathan turned his head slightly, taking in the smell of Jessica's hair. She felt so soft, so warm, cuddled up next to him, their naked bodies sharing one another's warmth. He couldn't help but smile. In that brief moment, there was no Alliance, no rebellion, no war.

But there was a sound...like a door closing.

Jessica's eyes popped open, her head rising slightly.

"You heard that?" Nathan whispered.

"I'm a light sleeper," she whispered back, still listening. "Someone's here," she stated, immediately climbing out of bed.

"It's probably just the android maid, or something."

Jessica ignored him, donning her robe as she headed for the door.

"Jess," Nathan called, also rising from the bed.

The door suddenly flew open. Jessica stepped to the left, out of instinct, as two armed officers stormed into the room.

"SILTEK SECURITY! DO NOT MOVE!"

Nathan reached for his robe as the officer on the left opened fire. A bolt of pale blue light struck Nathan's left arm, causing it to go completely numb and fall limp at his side. The sudden sensation took him by surprise, throwing off his balance and causing him to tumble to the bedroom floor.

Meanwhile, Jessica sprang into action, dropping

down to her side and sweeping her leg under the other officer, tripping him up. As he fell, she snatched his weapon from his hand and fired at the other guard as she rolled away, paralyzing him and dropping him to the floor, as well.

Nathan scrambled to the other side of the room, grabbing the dressing stool with his still-functioning right hand and holding it in front of him like a shield as another pair of guards followed the first two into the room, opening fire, as well.

Jessica continued to fire, dropping the second pair of guards in seconds. She then dropped down, with one knee on the neck of the still-conscious guard, whom she had tripped up. "Check the corridor!" she ordered Nathan.

Nathan scrambled to his feet, his left arm still numb and dangling at his side. Still naked, he charged into the corridor and crossed into the opposite bedroom, which had windows facing the transit pad in front of the residence.

"There're two security vehicles on the pad!" Nathan yelled as he headed back into his bedroom.

"What are your orders?" Jessica yelled at the trapped officer, her knee threatening to choke him out.

"I...can't...breathe," the officer struggled to reply.

"Our vehicle is gone," Nathan added as he reentered the bedroom.

"You might want to put something on," Jessica commented as she turned the power setting on her captured handgun to its maximum setting. "I wonder what a max-power hit feels like," she threatened, placing the muzzle against the officer's forehead, at the same time easing the pressure on his throat.

"We were ordered to apprehend you both and

deliver you to flight ops," the officer admitted, his eyes focused on the muzzle on his forehead.

"Why?" Jessica demanded.

"I don't know, I swear," the officer assured her. "All I know is that all hell is breaking loose!"

Jessica dialed the weapon back down, then stood up and shot the officer, rendering him unconscious. She turned and shot the remaining still-conscious officer and then turned to look at Nathan. "What the hell is wrong with your arm?"

"That one caught me with a shot. It's numb as hell."

"We have to get out of here," she said, grabbing her evening dress.

"You're going to wear that?" Nathan wondered as he struggled to pull on his pants.

"I don't think our uniforms are going to be very covert," she replied.

"Maybe, but an *evening* dress?"

"Maybe you're right," she admitted, tossing the dress aside and heading for her bedroom.

"Why the hell are they trying to arrest us?" Nathan yelled to her as he pulled on his shirt. "What did he mean by 'all hell is breaking loose'?"

"*I don't know,*" Jessica yelled back from the other room, "*but I'm not about to wait around to find out.*"

"Maybe you shouldn't have attacked them," Nathan remarked as he pulled on his shoes.

"*I prefer to shoot first and ask questions later,*" Jessica replied. "How's the arm?" she asked as she returned to the room, wearing pants and a comfortable shirt.

"Still numb, but I can move it a little," Nathan replied, standing up. "Nice outfit."

Jessica ignored him as she squatted down and

began searching one of the unconscious officers. She pulled a comm-unit from the officer's ear and a card from his shirt pocket.

"What's that?" Nathan wondered.

"I'm guessing it's some kind of security card," Jessica said, slipping it into her pocket and continuing to search the man. "Hopefully, it will come in handy."

"I'm assuming you have some kind of plan?"

"Get someplace secure and lie low until we figure out what's going on and what our options are," Jessica explained. Satisfied there was nothing else of value on the one man, she moved to the next officer.

"Maybe we should just call Ariana Batista's office and ask *her* what's going on," Nathan suggested.

A low wail sounded in the distance, climbing in volume and pitch within seconds.

"What the hell is that?" Nathan wondered.

"All hell breaking loose," Jessica responded, rising to her feet. "Let's move."

"It's locked," Nathan said with surprise as he tried to open the front door.

"Well, unlock it."

"I can't," he insisted, struggling with the lock.

"Ory," Jessica called out, "unlock the front door."

"*I apologize for the inconvenience, Lieutenant Commander,*" Ory replied, "*but the building has been secured according to SilTek security protocol one four seven dash two five, subsection five B.*"

"What the hell is security protocol one four seven dash two five, subsection five B?"

"*SilTek security protocol one four seven dash two five, subsection five B requires all building control systems to secure their building to prevent persons*" *who present a severe threat to the public's welfare from escaping."*

"Are you saying that *we* are a threat?" Nathan asked.

"I am not programmed to make such determinations," Ory explained. *"The security protocol requires that I restrict ingress and egress to only those possessing SilTek Security access credentials."*

"Ta-da!" Jessica declared, pulling out the security card she had taken from the unconscious officer.

"It can't be that easy," Nathan insisted.

Jessica stuck the card into the slot below the door handle, and the door unlocked. "Never underestimate humanity's potential for poor planning," she stated as she headed out the door, her stunner at the ready.

Nathan followed Jessica down the path leading from the front door to the transit pad, coming to a stop at the nearest of two black security vehicles. Now that they were outside, the distant alert sirens seemed louder and numerous, coming from all directions. "Those sound like air-raid sirens," Nathan commented.

Jessica stuck the security card into the slot along the vehicle's doorjamb, causing the doors to unlock. "These people know nothing about multi-layered security," she announced as she climbed into the pilot's seat.

"Maybe they don't have the *need*," Nathan suggested. He glanced through the side windows of the security vehicle, noticing two energy rifles attached to a rack between the seats.

Another sound caught Nathan's attention, also in the distance: more sirens, but different. He looked skyward, spotting two sets of flashing blue and red lights descending toward them at a rapid rate. "Move over," Nathan insisted.

"Why?"

"I'm the pilot, you're the shooter," he said, pointing at the incoming security vehicles.

Jessica leaned forward, looking skyward through the front window. "Oh, shit," she said, climbing over the center console into the front passenger seat.

Nathan hurried into the pilot's seat, scanning the console while Jessica moved over. "How the hell do you start this thing?"

Jessica jammed the security card into the slot at the upper center of the dashboard, and the console lit up. "*State destination,*" the vehicle's auto-flight system requested.

"Manual control!" Nathan ordered, closing his door.

"*Flight controls set to manual operation,*" the system confirmed.

"Uh...lift...attitude...horizontal speed..."

"Do you know how to fly this thing?" Jessica wondered.

"I think so," Nathan replied, grabbing the controls.

Jessica looked skyward again. "They're nearly on top of us!"

"Here goes nothing," Nathan announced, grabbing the throttle and twisting the lift collar all the way around the throttle handle.

The vehicle leapt skyward, pushing both of them down in their seats. It shot straight upward, climbing at a frighteningly rapid rate, nearly colliding with the two incoming security vehicles, both of which had to swerve to avoid colliding with the climbing vehicle.

"Whoa! Too much!" Nathan exclaimed, twisting the lift throttle back a bit to slow their rate of climb.

The ship reacted more quickly than expected, lifting them both up out of their seats, causing them to hit their heads on the ceiling. "Maybe we should buckle up?" Nathan suggested, putting on his restraints.

"Good idea," Jessica agreed, reaching for her own restraints.

"*This is SilTek Security,*" a voice called over comms. "*You are ordered to land your vehicle and surrender, or we will be forced to disable.*"

"Forced to disable?" Jessica said. "What the fuck does that mean?"

"Where's the auto-flight," Nathan wondered, searching nervously.

"*Receiving request for remote operations,*" the auto-flight system announced. "*Switching to...*"

"No!" Nathan yelled in frustration, finally finding the auto-flight control display and punching at the buttons.

"Look out!" Jessica exclaimed as she smashed the auto-flight control display with the butt of her sidearm.

"Are you insane?" Nathan yelled. "How the hell am I..."

"*Auto-flight system malfunction,*" the auto-flight system reported. "*Flight controls set to manual.*"

"Get us out of here!" Jessica exclaimed, looking behind them, and down, at the security vehicle circling back around toward them.

Nathan jammed the throttle forward, causing their vehicle to accelerate suddenly, this time throwing them against their seat backs.

"Jesus! Take it easy, slick!" Jessica yelled, grabbing hold of whatever she could to steady herself.

"This thing is *really* sensitive!" Nathan exclaimed defensively.

"Then, maybe you shouldn't jam the controls to the max!"

Nathan eased back on the throttle, moving the flight control stick in his left hand from side to side, up and down, and twisting it left and right, trying to get the feel of the vehicle's flight characteristics.

"They're both on our tail," Jessica advised.

"Hold on," Nathan warned, putting their vehicle into a forty-five-degree dive and easing back on the throttle enough to keep their airspeed from dramatically increasing.

Jessica turned back around to peer out the front window, her eyes widening at the sight of the hills rushing up toward them. "What are you doing?"

"Just seeing what she can do," Nathan replied, struggling to remain calm. He continued his dive, pointing their vehicle toward a hill with a valley on either side.

"What are you doing?"

"How many times are you going to ask me that?" Nathan wondered as he pushed his throttle forward and twisted his lift throttle a bit more, pulling back on his attitude control. "Hang on."

Jessica braced herself as their vehicle barely cleared the top of the hill; the tips of the trees brushing the underside of their hull. "Was that *really* necessary?"

"Yes...and no," Nathan replied as he rolled the ship into a tight turn toward the canyon on their left. "I just needed to know how well this thing would pull out of a dive before I started snaking the deck."

"I don't think I want to know what *snaking the deck* means," Jessica said as she took one of the energy rifles out of the rack between them.

"What are *you* doing?" Nathan asked as he pulled

out of the turn, taking the vehicle even lower into the canyon.

"I'm the shooter, remember?"

"I don't think shooting down a few of their security vehicles is going to win us any points with Missus Batista," Nathan said.

"I stopped caring about what that bitch thought the moment she sent armed goons to arrest us."

"I'm sure she has her reasons."

Jessica tossed a disapproving glance his way. "I'm going to pretend you didn't say that," she commented as she reached up and pressed the overhead hatch control.

The hatch slid open, sending a gush of forced air into their vehicle. Jessica stood up, turning around to face aft as her head popped up through the hatch. The slipstream pushed her against the back edge of the opening, forcing her to brace herself with her left hand as she pulled the rifle up through the hatch. After wrapping the weapon's shoulder strap over her body, she spread her feet and braced herself, raising her rifle to take aim at the nearest of the two security vehicles pursuing them from above and behind as Nathan jinked their vehicle back and forth. She pressed the charge button on the weapon and toggled the safety. A moment later, a green light appeared on the top of the weapon. "Hold it steady for a moment!" she yelled down to Nathan.

"I still don't think this is a good idea!" Nathan told her.

"You can *snake the deck* all you want!" she argued. "They're just going to follow us from a safe distance until we run out of options or reinforcements arrive!"

Nathan's eyes suddenly widened. Ahead of them, massive bolts of red-orange plasma began raining down from above, slamming into the planet ahead of them, causing massive explosions with each impact.

Jessica pulled the trigger, sending a green ball of energy at the nearest pursuer, slamming into its underside.

"Jess!" Nathan yelled.

The nearest pursuing ship rolled right, smoke pouring from its underside.

"Got one!" she declared triumphantly.

"JESS!"

A bolt of red-orange plasma struck the other vehicle, blowing it apart. Jessica felt Nathan grab her, pulling her down into the vehicle and knocking the rifle from her hands. "What the fuck!" she exclaimed as she fell into her seat.

Nathan rolled their vehicle into a sharp right turn, diving their ship into a valley covered with homes. "LOOK!" he yelled.

Jessica recovered, straightening out in her seat and looked forward. "Holy shit!"

"This world is under attack!" Nathan exclaimed.

"By who?"

There was a thud as something struck the back of their vehicle, causing their back end to drop violently. Warning alarms and red lights began appearing all over the console.

"Uh-oh," Nathan said as he struggled with the controls.

"What the hell was that?" Jessica wondered.

"I don't know. Maybe debris from the second vehicle," Nathan replied. "Whatever it was, it damaged our aft port side grav-lift emitter. I don't think I can keep us in the air."

"Then, put us down!" Jessica insisted. "There's no one chasing us now, anyway!"

"Believe me, I'm trying!" Nathan replied, twisting the lift throttle to full power. "I'm not getting any response on the lift throttle!"

"Nathan!" Jessica yelled, pointing to the trees ahead of them.

"Brace yourself!" he warned just before they plowed into the tops of the trees. The ship bounced and then flipped over, tumbling downward. Branches cracked as their ship slammed into them, breaking from the impact. Nathan felt himself being thrown to one side, then forward, slamming his head into the corner of the forward windshield frame. Finally, the ship hit the ground, and he blacked out.

Nathan woke to the sound of distant sirens and explosions. He immediately turned to find Jessica, who was lying against her door, not moving. "Jess!" he yelled. "Jess!"

"Nice landing, flyboy," she groaned.

"Are you hurt?"

"We just crashed into a forest," she replied angrily. "Of course, I'm hurt."

"How bad?"

"I'll survive," she insisted, moving toward the open overhead hatch. "What about you? Can you move?"

"Yeah, I'm okay."

"You've got a cut on your head," she pointed out.

"Bumps and bruises," Nathan insisted. "I'm good."

"Let's get out of here," Jessica said. "Some of those sirens could still be for us."

"Right behind you."

Jessica pulled herself up through the hatch,

pushing a fallen branch out of the way and surveying the area.

Nathan was next, climbing up through the hatch and sliding down the side of the vehicle onto the ground. "Now what?"

"We need to put some distance between us and this crash site," Jessica told him. "If they're still coming after us, this is where they'll start looking."

"I think they have more important things to worry about right now," Nathan insisted. "I think we should find a way to get off this world. We need a ship, *preferably* one with a jump drive."

"We could try to get back to the Bayside Spaceport to our own ship, but we'd probably have to shoot our way in *and* out."

"Yeah, probably not the best idea," Nathan agreed.

"We'll use the trails. If they have satellite or drone surveillance, it will give us at least intermittent cover," Jessica advised as she headed off. "Hopefully, with all that's happening, they'll be busy looking elsewhere."

"Where are we going?" Nathan asked, following her through the broken branches.

"We need a place to hold up until we can figure out what the hell is going on and who is attacking SilTek."

"And *why* they wanted to *arrest* us," Nathan added.

* * *

Nathan followed Jessica down the trails between homes, staying in the shadows as much as possible. "Why are we heading *away* from the spaceport?"

"Because the spaceport is exactly where they would *expect* us to go," Jessica replied.

"For good reason," Nathan insisted. "We *need* to

get *off* this world, and pronto. It *is* under attack, after all."

"And this attack is why we're still free. The moment it ends, they'll devote all available resources to finding us."

"We don't even know *why* they're looking for us."

Jessica stopped dead in her tracks. "Someone's coming," she whispered, moving around behind some bushes.

Nathan followed her, hiding behind the same bush. A moment later, a young man came running down the path, darting into one of the gates just after passing their hiding place.

Jessica jumped out, heading for the same gate.

"Wait..." Nathan called out in a whisper. Jessica disappeared through the gate a moment later, leaving Nathan no choice but to follow. He glanced upward, checking for security vehicles and search drones, and then darted down the path and through the gate after her.

Once inside the gate, he spotted Jessica on the other side of the yard, crouched down behind a bush, a few meters from the back door of the house where the young man she had been following was punching in an access code to enter.

The back-door control panel beeped, and the door opened for the young man. Jessica leapt into action, charging out from behind the bush and rushing up behind the unsuspecting young man.

The young man spun around, his eyes wide, as Jessica grabbed him by the collar, pushed the muzzle of her sidearm against his face, and shoved him inside.

Nathan again searched the skies, checking for surveillance, and then dashed across the open yard, up the steps onto the back patio, and through the open door.

"Who are you?" the young man demanded as Jessica pushed him up against the kitchen wall. "Are you Section Twelve?"

"Shut up," Jessica insisted. "Close the door," she called back over her shoulder to Nathan.

"What are we doing?" Nathan asked.

"As automated as this world is, every home is probably locked," she explained, "and if we tried to break into one, we'd just be telling them where we're hiding."

"What the hell is going on here?" the young man asked again, looking bewildered.

"I thought I told you to shut up," Jessica said, flashing him a menacing look.

"You're not Section Twelve, are you," the young man realized.

"What is Section Twelve?" Nathan wondered.

The young man looked confused. "You're not Tekan."

"What gave it away," Jessica sneered.

"Tekans don't run from bobo..." His eyes widened. "Are you *Subvert*?"

Jessica looked at Nathan, confused.

"Don't look at me. I'm still wondering what Section Twelve is."

"If you don't know what *Section Twelve* is, and you don't know what *Subvert* is, then you're *definitely* not Tekan," the young man deduced.

"What's your name?" Nathan asked.

The young man looked at Jessica, then back to Nathan. "Dylan. My name's Dylan."

"What is Section Twelve?" Jessica asked.

"Uh... They're probably who's after you."

"Look, Dylan," Nathan began, "we don't know *who* is after us, or even *why*. So, any information you could give us would be helpful."

"Well, first, you should turn off those zappers," he suggested. "They can track them, you know."

Nathan looked at Jessica. "Shouldn't *you* have thought of that?" he scolded as he powered down his sidearm.

Jessica shrugged, powering down her weapon.

"If you've got tainers, you should power those down, as well," Dylan added.

"What are *tainers*?" Nathan wondered.

"VR sets?"

"We don't have any," Jessica told him.

"Then, you're *definitely* not Tekan," Dylan chuckled.

"*What* is Section Twelve?" Nathan asked again.

"*Secret* security," Dylan replied. "They're not subject to corporate bylaws. You do *not* want to be on their scope, *trust me*. Is *that* who is hunting you?"

"Like I said, we have no idea *who* is hunting us," Nathan reminded him.

"Where did you get those zappers?" Dylan asked, pointing to the sidearm tucked in Nathan's belt. "They're standard security issue."

"Uniformed security officers burst into our guest house this morning," Nathan told him.

"How the hell did you get away?" Dylan wondered, looking confused.

"It wasn't difficult," Jessica bragged.

"*It wasn't difficult?*" Dylan repeated. "Are you *kidding* me?"

Jessica shrugged.

"Who *are* you people?"

"*Who* is attacking your world?" Nathan asked.

"They didn't say," Dylan replied. "The warning sirens went off, and my comm-unit instructed me to take shelter."

"Then, why didn't you?" Nathan wondered.

"This *is* my shelter," Dylan explained. "Or, at least, it's *downstairs*."

"Your home has an *attack shelter*?" Jessica asked in disbelief.

"Every home has one," Dylan explained, surprised that she didn't know. "Every home, every building... they're everywhere. We're taught to head to the nearest shelter when the alert is sounded. I was already on my way home, so I just kept going."

"Isn't that risky?" Nathan wondered.

"Less risky than my mom finding out I was at Lan's house," Dylan replied. "Besides, they always attack the spaceports and defense systems first, so I figured I had time."

"Who's Lan?" Nathan wondered.

"My friend," Dylan explained. "My mom doesn't like him much, and, well, I'm sort of grounded."

"How often does your world get attacked?" Jessica asked, curious.

"A few times a year," Dylan replied.

"By whom?" Nathan asked.

"Usually the Benicasi, but sometimes the Yachi or the Ristani. Last year, we even got attacked by the *Sinato*." Dylan studied the two of them. "Which one are you?"

"I haven't heard of *any* of them," Nathan insisted.

"Neither had we, until the jump drive was invented," Dylan explained. "Now, every world with a few jump-equipped warships wants to try and steal our tech."

"Why doesn't SilTek stop them?" Nathan asked.

"They do," Dylan replied. "At least, they have so far, but many of us believe that it's only a matter of time until someone comes along who can defeat our defenses. Many Tekans believe our government should go on the offensive. You know, *show* them we can *strike back*."

"That strategy doesn't always work as well as you might think," Nathan warned.

"It's better than hiding in our shelters and hoping for the best," Dylan insisted.

"Then, *you're* one of the many who believe SilTek should go on the offensive," Jessica surmised.

Dylan held up both hands. "I didn't say that."

"Relax," Jessica told him. "We're not *Section Twelve*."

"We're visitors to your world," Nathan explained. "We were invited by Ariana Batista. We're supposed to be negotiating a...*business arrangement*."

"It must not have gone well," Dylan said.

"I guess not," Nathan admitted.

"Why are you here?" Dylan wondered. "Why *my* house?"

"We needed someplace to hide while we figure out how to get off your world," Nathan told him.

"We spotted you on the trail and figured it was an easy way in," Jessica added.

"You can't *hide* from SilTek," Dylan said. "They know where *everyone* is, at *all* times."

"How?" Nathan wondered.

"There are no cameras inside the homes," Jessica pointed out. "Only in public places."

"True, but the house AIs know who is on their property and will report that knowledge if lawfully queried by security."

"Then, your AI knows we're here?" Nathan surmised.

"Yes."

"Then, I guess we'd better keep moving," Jessica decided.

Nathan sighed. "Sorry if we scared you, Dylan."

Dylan watched as Nathan and Jessica turned to depart.

"I can shut down our AI's comm-link to the main hub and make it look like an equipment failure," Dylan offered. "That should at least buy you some time, if it hasn't already been queried, of course."

"How can you tell?" Jessica wondered.

"It's all in the logs," Dylan bragged, "*if* you know how to *read* them."

"Your AIs have *logs*?" Nathan asked, surprised.

"All AIs have logs," Dylan replied as if it were common knowledge. "They're written to local data banks that cannot be altered by the AIs, themselves. It's a legal requirement. It's how we monitor our AIs, to make sure they're performing as designed." He gestured toward the corridor. "I can show you."

Nathan looked to Jessica.

"If you're hoping for a better idea, you're looking at the wrong person," Jessica told him.

"Looks like we're in your hands, Dylan," Nathan told the young man. "I have to warn you, though, the stakes are far higher than you could possibly imagine."

Dylan swallowed hard. "You could've kept that part to yourself, you know."

Nathan gestured for Dylan to lead the way, falling in behind him as he headed down the corridor.

"The AI is downstairs," Dylan explained, opening

the door to the stairwell. He led them down the stairs and into another corridor.

"What's in there?" Nathan asked, pointing at another door as they passed.

"The garage," Dylan replied. "The AI is down the hall, just inside the entrance to the shelter."

Nathan and Jessica followed Dylan down the corridor, pausing at the entrance to the shelter as Dylan entered the access code.

"It's in here," Dylan announced as he entered the shelter and opened another door just inside.

"Stay out here, just in case," Nathan ordered Jessica. He stepped into the shelter and looked inside the door Dylan had opened. On the other side was a closet full of electronic equipment. Dylan flipped up a small view screen revealing an input station. The screen lit up, and data began scrolling quickly across it.

"There," Dylan said, pointing to an entry on the screen. "This is where I unlocked the back door and the three of us entered. Here, it shows my identity, but it shows you and your friend as unidentified persons."

"What's that last line?" Nathan asked.

"That's where I logged on to view the logs," Dylan explained. "There are no entries showing any queries by security, so they don't yet know you're here," he added as he began typing furiously.

"What are you doing?" Nathan asked.

"I'm setting it up to send error codes if queried," Dylan explained.

"It's *that* easy?" Nathan asked, unsure if he believed the young man.

"It is if you know what you're doing," Dylan replied, obviously bragging.

"And *you* know what you're doing," Nathan said, still a bit skeptical.

"Everyone has a skill," Dylan replied. "Hacking AIs is mine." He stopped typing for a moment, glancing at Nathan and smiling. "On a world run by AIs, the ability to *hack* them is *very* valuable."

"Probably very *illegal*, as well," Nathan commented.

"There's that, yeah," Dylan conceded, returning to his typing. After a few moments, he stopped. "That should do it," he announced, turning back to Nathan again. "But that's only going to buy you ten or fifteen minutes."

"Why?"

"Because once the attack is over, they'll be able to conduct a full search," Dylan explained. "Any AI that doesn't answer a lawful query will go to the top of the search list."

"How long do these attacks usually last?" Nathan wondered.

"Never more than half an hour," he replied, "at least, not in *my* lifetime."

"It's already been twenty minutes," Nathan pointed out.

"Hence, the ten or fifteen minutes I quoted."

"I don't suppose you could hack the AI that runs the Bayside Spaceport, could you?" Jessica asked from the shelter hatchway.

"I'm good, but I'm not *that* good," Dylan admitted. "Is that where your ship is?"

"Yup," Jessica replied.

"Does it have to be *your* ship?" Dylan wondered.

"Preferably," Nathan said. "However, at this point, I'd be happy with any ship with a jump drive."

"*That*, I might be able to help you with," Dylan said, grinning.

* * *

The door to the garage opened, and the lights came on. "Old, FTL, light-cargo haulers converted into jump ships," Dylan explained as he led them inside. "Since they're so old, they need a *lot* of ongoing maintenance, so, rather than tie up space at the spaceports, they keep them in maintenance yards located all over the planet. There's one about one hundred kilometers from here. They usually have two or three of them there."

"How do you know all of this?" Jessica wondered.

"The mother of a friend of mine works there as an environmental systems specialist."

"If we only have ten or fifteen minutes, then we don't have enough time to get there before they figure out where we were and where we're headed," Nathan pointed out.

"Oh, we'll get there in time, *barely*," Dylan bragged.

"Uh, the transports we've seen don't go that fast," Nathan argued.

"This is not your ordinary ride," Dylan boasted as he placed his hands on the vehicle's cover. He yanked the cover off, revealing a cherry red, shiny, sporty-looking transport, unlike anything they had seen on SilTek.

"Whoa," Jessica exclaimed.

"Is this *yours*?" Nathan wondered, equally impressed.

"I wish," Dylan replied as he tossed the cover aside. "It used to be my grandfather's, but my pop inherited it when he died. He only takes it out once a month."

"Where are *your* parents?" Jessica wondered.

"Probably sheltering at work, like good little Tekans."

"And your father doesn't mind if you borrow his... whatever you call this?" Nathan asked.

"It's a DX-Four, Corbin Speedster, circa thirty-four twenty-five...limited edition, only twenty of them still in existence," Dylan bragged, "and no—no way in hell he'd let me borrow it. That's why you're going to *steal* it."

Jessica laughed. "I'd rather steal another security cruiser. It would be far less conspicuous than this hot rod."

"You *stole* a security cruiser?" Dylan laughed. "You two are *insane*! No wonder they're looking for you!"

"That was *after* they tried to arrest us for no reason," Nathan defended.

"This is *wild*!"

"How fast can this thing go?" Nathan wondered, circling around to the pilot's side.

"At least six hundred kilometers per hour at full throttle, but that kind of speed *will* attract attention. So, if you're going to take it, you need to do it now, while they're still busy with the attack."

"Let's do it," Nathan decided, opening the door with a grin on his face.

"Just one condition," Dylan said. "I'm driving."

Nathan looked at the kid. "How old are you?"

"Seventeen...in two months."

"You ever flown supersonic?" Nathan asked.

"No."

"How about superluminal?"

"Uh, definitely no."

"Well, I have, so *I'm* the one doing the flying."

"But..."

"That's non-negotiable," Nathan said, cutting him off.

Dylan thought for a moment. "I get to come along, though, right?"

Nathan studied Dylan for a moment and then looked over at Jessica.

"Bad idea, Nathan."

"Your name's Nathan?"

"We might need him, Jess," Nathan said.

"You'll definitely need me," Dylan insisted. "Who's going to help you hack into the ship's AI to take control?"

"You looking to become a criminal?" Jessica asked Dylan.

"Technically, I already am," Dylan replied. "I just haven't been caught yet."

"Well, the day is still young," Nathan said, climbing into the pilot's seat. He looked over the interior of the vehicle and its console, both of which were just as impressive as the vehicle's exterior. "Well, are you guys coming, or what?"

Jessica stepped up to the front, right door and opened it.

"Uh, I have to sit in front," Dylan told her.

"I don't think so," Jessica sneered.

"I can't hack the AI and start it from the back."

"Get in the back, Lieutenant Commander," Nathan instructed.

Jessica rolled her eyes, stepping aside to let Dylan sit in front.

"You outrank her?" Dylan asked, taking his seat.

"Yeah, I have to keep reminding her of that," Nathan commented.

"I heard that," Jessica snapped as she took her seat in the back.

Dylan leaned over and began punching commands into the dashboard keyboard. After a few moments, the rest of the dashboard lit up, and the overhead doors began to part.

"Are all residential garages underground?" Nathan wondered.

"Where else would they be," Dylan responded.

"I guess we didn't have to steal that cop car, after all," Jessica stated from the back seat.

"You *can* fly SilTek transport vehicles, right?" Dylan checked.

"I can fly pretty much anything," Nathan replied. "Buckle up," he warned, "this might be more than you're used to."

"Uh, if everyone is supposed to be in their shelters, aren't we going to be the only civilians flying around?" Jessica wondered.

"There are always people flying around during an attack," Dylan replied. "Like I said, they happen often enough that people don't really take them seriously, anymore."

"They don't take buildings blowing up seriously?" Jessica wondered as the speedster started to rise.

Dylan turned around to look at her. "You saw buildings blowing up?"

"Uh, yeah."

"That means the defense grid is down," he uttered, a look of horror on his face.

"I take it that's never happened before," Jessica surmised.

"I changed my mind," Dylan insisted. "I want to stay here."

"Too late," Nathan replied as the speedster cleared ground level. He twisted the lift throttle and pushed the vertical speed throttle all the way to the stops, causing the shiny, red speedster to leap into the air and accelerate forward at a frightening rate.

"OH, MY GOD!" Dylan exclaimed as he was pushed back into his seat.

"These things need inertial dampeners, if they're able to accelerate this fast," Nathan chuckled. He glanced over at Dylan's face as he backed off on the lift throttles, settling the speedster into the valley ahead.

Dylan's eyes were as big as plates, and his mouth was hanging open in abject fear. "What the hell are you doing? Climb!"

"If we stay under the ridgelines, we can evade their sensors," Nathan explained.

"But flying this low is *illegal*," Dylan insisted, "not to mention *dangerous!*"

"So is stealing a security cruiser," Jessica laughed.

"Uh-oh," Nathan said as the valley came to a dead end. "Hold onto your breakfast!" Nathan pulled back on the attitude control stick as he twisted the lift throttle, increasing the grav-lift to help gain altitude more quickly.

"That's not the way you're supposed to do it!" Dylan warned. "You climb with the grav-lift, not pitch and power!"

"It climbs faster if you use both," Nathan explained calmly. "Relax, kid, I've got this."

"Oh, my God," Dylan exclaimed again as they popped up over the ridgeline. He glanced to his right and spotted the rain of red-orange plasma bolts tearing apart the downtown district. "Oh, my God," he repeated as the speedster dropped back down the other side of the ridge and settled into the next valley. "It's true, they took it down. Subvert was right."

"Who the fuck is Subvert?" Jessica wondered.

"Does this thing have any kind of terrain mapping?" Nathan wondered. "Something that would show me a low-level route to that maintenance yard?"

"It's not designed to *do* that," Dylan replied, his voice stressed. "Minimum flight altitude is one thousand meters, not treetop level!"

"Surely, it at least *displays* terrain altitudes and curvatures," Nathan insisted. "What happens if your grav-lift fails and you can't reach minimum altitude?"

"Then, you fucking land!" Dylan insisted. "At least that's what *sane* people do!"

"Seriously?" Jessica said. "High-tech SilTek and no terrain maps?"

"Well, yeah, you can call up terrain maps," Dylan admitted, "but at this speed..."

"Then, call them up and find a route that will get us to the maintenance field without having to climb up over the ridgelines!" Jessica insisted.

"I don't know," Dylan replied, looking like he was going to throw up.

"Hey, you wanted to sit in the big-boy seat," Jessica chided.

Dylan leaned over again and began entering commands into the console keyboard. "Okay, I think this might be what you're looking for," he said, the ship jinking back and forth as Nathan weaved his way through the canyon. "I might be able to force the AI to plot a route at low altitude, if I override the legal flight restrictions, but I can't promise it will work."

"I'm only asking you to try," Nathan told him.

"Uh...this canyon's going to run out in two kilometers, as soon as you round the next turn," Dylan warned.

"See, *now* you're helping," Nathan congratulated. "Just tell me where to go after we pop up over the next ridgeline, preferably something that will get us all the way there at low level."

"I'm working on it," Dylan promised, "but it would help if you held it more steady!"

"Don't blame me, blame the canyon!" Nathan defended as he rounded the next turn. "Oh, shit!" he exclaimed, again pulling his nose up and adding grav-lift power.

Something smacked the underside of their speedster, making a terrible sound.

Dylan looked over at Nathan. "What was that?"

"Which canyon," Nathan barked, "left or right?"

Dylan looked back at the display. "Uh...left!"

"Are you sure?"

"Yes...NO, right!"

"What?"

"Go to the right!"

Nathan eased their nose back down and to the right, backing off on both power and lift as he guided the speedster down into the canyon. Once they dropped below the ridge, he backed off on the grav-lift and pushed the throttles back to full power, leveling off again.

"I've got it!" Dylan exclaimed as a jagged magenta line appeared on the wide map view. "Well, almost."

"What do you mean, *almost*?" Nathan wondered as he guided the speedster through the next canyon.

"The maintenance field is on a plateau; no hills for at least ten kilometers in all directions."

"It will have to do," Nathan decided.

"Nice work, kid," Jessica congratulated.

Dylan leaned back against his seat, trying not to

be terrified by the speed at which the outside world was streaking past them. "You fly this way often?"

"I'm not gonna lie, it's been a while," Nathan admitted.

"Sorry I asked."

* * *

The shiny, red speedster popped up from the last canyon, staying less than one hundred meters above the open plains to the south of the city.

"Everyone working at the maintenance field will be down in the shelter until the all clear is given," Dylan explained as they sped along, "but the moment we descend into the facility, their AI will sense us and notify security."

"How long after that until they arrive?" Jessica asked.

"I'm guessing a few minutes, at the most," Dylan replied, "assuming they haven't already detected us and have cruisers on the way."

"Even if the attack is still in progress?"

Dylan turned around, noticing that the red-orange rain was still falling on the city behind them. "It's never lasted this long before."

"Any chance all those people you mentioned joined forces against SilTek?" Nathan wondered.

"The Benicasi and the Yachi, *maybe*, but the Ristani *hate* the Benicasi *and* the Yachi, and the Sinato hate *everyone*. Even if the Benicasi and the Yachi *did* join forces, they still shouldn't be able to bring down our defense grid. They only have a handful of warships between them." Dylan watched the approaching maintenance field, becoming concerned. "Uh, you might want to start slowing down. Corbins are not known for their high rate of deceleration."

"Good to know," Nathan replied, easing back on the main throttle. "I *really* like this vehicle," he added. "Any chance you can give us the design specs?"

"What the hell are you going to do with it?" Jessica wondered.

"I don't know," Nathan replied, grinning, "fit it with a jump drive and use it as my personal jump speedster."

"Oh, that would be *sweet!*" Dylan exclaimed.

"Here we go," Nathan warned as he eased the vertical thrust throttle back and slid the speedster over the fence line.

"That one looks good," Dylan said, pointing to the second ship in the line.

"Are you *kidding?*" Jessica exclaimed. "*None* of them look *good.*"

"Okay, *not as bad?*" Dylan offered.

"If these ships are here for maintenance, how do we know they'll even fly?" Nathan asked as he maneuvered the speedster and began descending in front of the second cargo ship.

"This is a light maintenance facility," Dylan explained. "They don't do jump drive or main drive work here. Only internal systems like sensors, navigation, environmental, that kind of stuff."

"Oh, is *that* all?" Jessica said.

"Well, at least they'll fly *and* jump," Dylan defended. "Isn't that enough?"

"I'd like to be able to *breathe*, as well," Jessica replied as the speedster set down.

"If environment is down, you can always put on pressure suits," Dylan suggested as he opened his door and climbed out.

"Great, a two-day trip in pressure suits."

Nathan climbed out, pausing for a moment to look

at the old light-cargo vessel in front of him. "Pretty sure it's going to take more than a couple days to get home in that thing."

"If you want to get this thing started and off the ground before bobo gets here, we have to hurry," Dylan warned, heading straight for the cargo ship's boarding ramp.

"Why the hell are you helping us?" Jessica wondered as she followed Dylan up the ramp.

"Are you kidding?" Dylan replied. "This is better than *any* VR game! It's like Guns and Glory, and Night Runner, all rolled into one!" he exclaimed as he overrode the hatch lock, opened the boarding hatch, and headed inside.

Jessica glanced back at Nathan. "There's something not right about this kid."

"I kinda like him," Nathan said as he passed.

"You can't keep him," Jessica warned, following them inside.

"The cockpit is up two levels and all the way forward!" Dylan yelled from further down the corridor.

"Where are you going?" Nathan wondered.

"To the main power plant! It's the only place you can start up the ship's reactor!"

"How the hell does this kid know all of this?" Jessica wondered.

"I'm guessing he doesn't get out much," Nathan said as he started up the ladder.

Jessica followed Nathan up the ladder, climbing past the main level to the upper deck before stepping off.

Nathan headed forward, passing several compartments before reaching the ship's flight deck. Once inside, he found a standard cockpit, similar to that of the Seiiki, only much roomier. "This is *nice*," he commented as the consoles began to light up. "I guess he got the reactor up," he added as he headed for the pilot's seat. "That's encouraging."

"*That's* not," Jessica said, pointing out the port window.

In the distance, four black transports, with flashing red and blue lights, were quickly approaching.

"See if you can slow them down," Nathan ordered.

"With what? Stunners?" Jessica replied. "Damn, I wish we would've kept those rifles!"

"You'll find heavy blasters in the locker on the boarding deck," Dylan told her as he came scurrying out onto the flight deck.

Jessica reached out and put her hand on his chest, stopping him in his tracks. "How the hell do you know so much about this ship?" she asked in an accusatory tone.

"Are you *kidding*? It's a retro-fitted XK series, interstellar, light-cargo hauler; the exact same ship as in Night Runner! I know *everything* about it! It's like my all-time favorite VR game!"

"Go!" Nathan ordered her.

"I'm gone!" Jessica replied, heading out.

"You remind me a lot of a friend of mine back on my ship," Nathan told Dylan as the kid slid into the copilot's seat.

"You have a *ship*?" Dylan said. "How big is it?"

"A *lot* bigger than this bucket," Nathan replied. "Now, let's get this thing started."

"Got it," Dylan responded, pulling a small device from his pocket and attaching it to the console.

"That's the second time you've used that thing," Nathan realized. "What is it?"

"A digital code-pick," Dylan replied. "My mom is

Ryk Brown

always locking up my stuff to punish me. She thinks it works."

"Not anymore," Nathan told him.

"Yeah, I guess I'm kind of screwed, now."

"*Please state your authorization code,*" the ship's AI requested.

"Uh-oh," Dylan said.

"What, uh-oh?"

"My code-pick must've activated the ship's AI."

"We *need* the ship's AI, don't we?" Nathan wondered.

"Yeah, but I don't have the code yet. That's what this thing is for."

"You just informed the AI that we're trying to obtain an authorization code illegally," Nathan pointed out.

"The cockpit mic is *muted,*" Dylan assured him. "I'm all the way to level *twenty-eight* in Night Runner. You don't get that far being *stupid.*"

"*Please state authorization code,*" the AI repeated.

"What do we do?" Nathan wondered. "She's going to get suspicious if we don't respond."

"She'll get more than suspicious," Dylan warned. "She'll permanently lock us out if we don't give her the full code in under a minute."

"Great."

The first number appeared on Dylan's device, then the second, and then the third. "It's working."

"*Please state authorization code,*" the AI asked for the third time. "*Failure to provide proper code will result in security lockout in thirty seconds.*"

"Give her the code," Dylan instructed, pushing the un-mute button.

"Authorization code one...five...seven uh... two... seven...five...seven." When the AI did not respond,

288

Nathan pressed the mute button. "Are you sure that was the right number?"

"*Please state the final number,*" the AI instructed.

Nathan looked at Dylan, who shrugged.

"*Please state final number,*" the AI repeated.

Nathan released the mute button and blurted, "Nine?" He looked to Dylan, both of them holding their breath as they waited for a response.

"*Authorization code...accepted,*" the ship's AI replied. "*How may I be of assistance?*"

Nathan slumped back in his seat, breathing a sigh of relief.

"Rapid start for immediate liftoff and subsequent jump to orbit!" Dylan ordered.

"*Initiating quick start on all engines,*" the AI confirmed. "*Reactor currently at twenty percent and rising rapidly. Energy levels required for liftoff will be available in two minutes. Jump to orbit will be possible in four minutes.*"

Dylan pressed the mute button, looking at Nathan, dumbfounded. "How did you know the last number?"

"I didn't," Nathan admitted, shrugging his shoulders.

Dylan shook his head in disbelief.

"*Please state final destination,*" the AI added.

Nathan released the mute button. "The Rogen system."

"*The Rogen system does not exist in this ship's navigational charts. Please state a valid destination.*"

"How about *Sanctuary*?" Nathan suggested. "Can you get us there?"

"*Affirmative,*" the AI confirmed. "*Destination set as the Sanctuary system. Sixty-four jumps will be required. Transit time will be six days, fifteen hours, forty-seven minutes."*

"Not exactly a speedster," Nathan commented.

"How many jumps would it take *your* ship to get to Sanctuary?" Dylan wondered.

"The big one or the small one?"

"There's more than one *Sanctuary*?"

"Which *ship*," Nathan corrected.

"You have more than one?" Dylan asked in disbelief. "The big one, I guess."

"One jump," Nathan replied as he scanned the console, trying to familiarize himself with the displays.

Dylan's eyes widened. "Sanctuary is like three hundred and sixty light years away!"

"Okay, then, less than one jump," Nathan replied.

Dylan's jaw dropped open.

* * *

Jessica grabbed the handle of the weapons locker in the boarding compartment and jiggled it. "It's locked!" she yelled.

There was a *click* sound, and then Dylan's voice came over the intercom panel. *"Try it now."*

Jessica opened the locker, pulling out one of the six energy rifles, and then headed toward the exit.

"Two security cruisers are descending to port," Nathan warned over the intercom.

"I'm on it," she replied, heading down the ramp.

Once outside, Jessica moved quickly across the yard, forward of the ship, wanting to find a secure position to fire from, ensuring that it was far enough away from the ship they were about to steal to prevent it from being damaged by return fire.

Taking position behind a service vehicle, she raised her rifle and opened fire on the closest security cruiser as it descended to land to the port side of the ship. Both shots landed on the underside of the cruiser, blowing apart its underside light bar and damaging the front, right corner of its dorsal hull. The black cruiser dipped slightly, rotating around quickly. One more shot, which struck its back side as it spun around, was enough to cause it to climb again, albeit at an odd angle, moving outside the fence line before giving up and coming to a rough landing.

Meanwhile, the second cruiser passed overhead, swinging around to its right, and turning sideways. Its side door opened, and an officer inside stuck his weapon out and took aim.

Jessica ducked back behind the service vehicle as two blasts struck its back end, sending sparks and small pieces of metal flying. She ran around to the other side of the vehicle, quickly raising her own weapon and firing at the second cruiser, causing it to abort its own landing attempt and veer away from their ship.

Two blasts zinged past her, coming from her right, causing Jessica to duck back behind the front end of the vehicle. A quick peek around it was all she needed to spot the two men from the downed first cruiser, opening fire through the fence, which now had gaping holes.

The hum of the second cruiser's grav-lift systems, which had been moving away to her left, suddenly disappeared, telling Jessica that the cruiser had probably landed further away. Another peek around the front end of the vehicle, behind which she was taking cover, elicited another round of energy blasts from the two security officers who were now coming through the holes in the fence they had created moments ago.

Without looking, Jessica held her weapon out, aiming around the corner, and squeezed her trigger, sending a barrage of energy bolts toward the approaching officers, causing them both to scramble in opposite directions, looking for cover. A second later, both officers found cover and returned fire, determined to keep her pinned down, or better yet, to force her to retreat back toward the other officers.

It was a typical strategy, one that usually worked on the unsuspecting, which Jessica was not. She quickly ran to the back end of the vehicle, looking toward the cockpit windows of the ship they were stealing. She could see Nathan and Dylan, both with their heads down, as they prepared the ship for liftoff.

Something caught her eye on her left, causing her to duck back just as energy bolts struck her cover vehicle. The officers were closing their trap.

Jessica tried waving to Nathan but got no response. "Son of a bitch," she cursed to herself as she adjusted the setting on her energy rifle to its lowest setting, took aim, and fired two blasts at the upper edge of the cockpit windows.

* * *

"Jesus!" Nathan exclaimed, flinching from the two blasts ricocheting off the window in front of him. He looked outside and spotted Jessica waving frantically.

"Did she just shoot at *us*?" Dylan wondered in dismay.

"I think she's trying to get our attention," Nathan said.

"By *shooting* at us?"

Nathan glanced to the left, then to the right, realizing what she was trying to tell him. "She's going to get cut off," he said, climbing out of his seat. "Does this ship have comm-sets?"

"What's a comm-set?"

"Some kind of portable communications gear so we can talk to each other," Nathan explained.

"If you're in the ship, or outside within a few meters, the intercoms will pick you up," Dylan replied. "If you have to go further, there are portable comm-units in the weapons locker—top shelf."

"Great!" Nathan said as he headed for the exit. "Don't take off without us!"

"What?" Dylan glanced over his shoulder. "Where are you going?" He was too late. Nathan was already sliding down the ladder. Dylan glanced outside, spotting two more cruisers less than a kilometer out. "They invited friends!" he yelled.

———

Nathan slid down the access ladder, descending two entire decks in seconds. He ran forward, jumping through the hatch to the boarding compartment, and grabbed both a comm-unit and an energy rifle from the weapons locker on his way out.

He activated the comm-unit and shoved it in his pocket, bringing up his rifle and pressing the power button as he headed down the ramp. By the time he had traveled far enough down the ramp to get a clear line of fire, SilTek Security officers were already firing at him from both sides.

Nathan fired four shots to the left, two at each officer, causing them to duck down behind cover. A moment later, he fired four more shots to the right and then jumped down off the ramp to starboard, taking cover behind the cargo ship's forward starboard landing gear.

Red bolts of energy slammed into the landing strut dorsal hull and the ground around Nathan, forcing him to stay hidden. The screech of additional weapons fire was heard, but from forward, not from either side. *Jessica's providing cover fire.*

Nathan crouched and ran aft, firing to port as Jessica fired to starboard to cover him. He turned to his left, diving behind a service vehicle as the officers to port spotted him and opened fire again.

Nathan scrambled on his belly, moving under the back end of the vehicle and over to the next as incoming fire ricocheted off the previous vehicle. He quickly got to his knees and peered around the edge of the vehicle, spotting two officers exchanging fire with Jessica.

After ducking back, Nathan took a deep breath. *One shot, one kill,* he thought to himself. In one smooth motion, he raised his rifle to his shoulder, rose, and swung around to fire. One...two quick shots, and both officers were down.

Nathan's eyes widened in surprise. "Shit, it worked," he said to himself, turning back around and running for the next vehicle, aft of their ship, to get a better angle on the two officers to port.

Jessica watched the two men fall to Nathan's fire. "Nice."

"*GO!*" she heard Nathan holler from the other end of the ship.

Jessica didn't hesitate, running out from her cover, her energy rifle blazing as she headed to the right of the last two officers on the ground.

Two more black security cruisers, their light bars

flashing blue and red, flew over at ten meters above the fence. Jessica broke off her attack of the officers on the ground, firing two shots into the underside of each of the passing cruisers, before ducking behind a large storage bin. She quickly circled around the back side of the bin, stepped out, and fired two more shots, dropping the last two officers. "CLEAR!" she hollered, heading back to the ship.

Nathan swung his weapon skyward, firing a barrage of shots at the two black security cruisers passing over him as they peeled off in opposite directions. As he headed back forward, he grabbed the comm-unit out of his pocket and hollered into it. "Is this bucket ready to lift off yet?"

"*Thirty seconds!*" Dylan replied.

Nathan ran forward, reaching the boarding ramp at the same time as Jessica.

"Nice shootin', Tex," she joked.

"Let's get the hell outta Dodge, shall we?" Nathan replied, gesturing for her to lead the way up the ramp.

* * *

A warning tone sounded on the cargo ship's sensor display, catching Dylan's attention. "Oh, no, no, no..."

"What?" Nathan asked as he and Jessica stepped onto the flight deck.

"*There are four security interceptors headed toward us,*" the AI reported. "*They will reach effective intercept in fifty seconds.*"

"That is *not* good," Dylan warned. "That is *so* not good!"

"Let me guess," Nathan said, climbing into his seat. "Interceptors are *bad*?"

"*So* bad," Dylan droned.

"Then, let's get this thing off the ground."

"Those cruisers have a different idea," Jessica warned, pointing out the port window.

Nathan glanced outside, spotting one of the cruisers sliding into a hover over the port-forward engine nacelle, attempting to block their liftoff.

"There's one on my side, as well," Dylan reported. "What do we do?"

"Open a comm-channel," Nathan suggested.

"What?"

"I want to talk to them," Nathan explained.

"He wants to talk to them," Dylan mumbled to himself, patching the ship's communications system to SilTek's security channel. "Talk away."

"Security cruisers, move off, or we'll plow right through you," Nathan warned.

"*This is Sergeant Meden of SilTek Security. You are ordered to shut down your engines and surrender.*"

"These the lift throttles?" Nathan asked.

"Yes, but..."

Nathan grabbed all four lift throttles and advanced them slowly as he turned his head and watched the cruiser hovering over their port forward engine nacelle. The cruiser held its position, refusing to move off, as the clunky cargo ship began to rise.

"This one's holding position!" Dylan exclaimed excitedly.

"So's this guy," Nathan announced as the top of their port forward nacelle bumped into the underside of the cruiser. The black security vehicle tipped over, spun around, lost control, and fell toward the ground, crashing into the fence before bouncing off the surface once, then settling onto the ground, inverted.

Their starboard forward nacelle bumped into the underside of the cruiser to starboard, but its pilot was prepared, taking the hit like he was catching a pass.

The cargo ship suddenly dipped to starboard, its forward starboard landing gear striking the surface and bending backward with a terrible groan of flexing metal.

"This guy's playing rough!" Nathan realized, jamming his lift throttles all the way forward, then grabbing the throttle for their main drive and easing them forward, as well.

The cargo ship leapt upward, accelerating forward as it climbed. The other security cruiser bounced off the starboard forward nacelle, spinning around and nearly losing control as the cargo ship pushed up and forward through him.

"I warned you!" Nathan exclaimed as they continued to climb.

"Fifteen seconds to intercept," the AI warned.

"XK cargo vessel climbing out of Sina maintenance yard!" one of the interceptor pilots called over comms. *"Activate your auto-flight systems and set to remote operation immediately, or we will shoot you down."*

"They'll do it," Dylan warned.

"Is the jump drive ready?" Nathan asked.

"Yeah, but..."

Nathan pulled up on their nose. "AI, jump us to orbit...*immediately!*" Nathan ordered.

"Jumping to orbit in three..."

"See ya," Nathan said over comms.

"Two..."

"They'll just jump to orbit, as well," Dylan warned.

"One..."

"And we'll jump again," Nathan told him.

"*Jumping.*"

The windows suddenly went black, and stars appeared. Nathan tipped their nose back down, even with the horizon. That's when he saw them. "Oh, shit."

* * *

"What the hell are those?" Dylan asked, staring out the forward windows at several enormous, menacing, black and crimson warships bombarding his planet from orbit.

"*Those* are Dusahn warships," Jessica replied.

"This day just keeps getting better," Nathan grumbled as he started scanning the console. "Does this thing have a snap jump setting?"

"A what?" Dylan wondered.

"I'll take that as a no," Nathan replied. "AI, can we jump toward Sanctuary from here?"

"*Negative,*" the AI replied. "*There are two ships directly in our flight path.*"

"How long to get to a clear jump line?"

"*Five minutes, thirty-eight seconds.*"

The sensor display beeped a warning.

"We're being targeted," Dylan warned.

"We don't have five minutes and thirty-eight seconds," Nathan said.

"*If you wish to jump sooner, you must specify an alternate destination in a direction that has a clear departure jump line.*"

"Jesus!" Nathan cursed. "Who the hell designs a jump-nav system this way?"

"This isn't a combat ship," Dylan reminded him.

"No shit," Nathan replied. "Do we at least have shields?"

"Yeah, but..."

"But nothing, raise them!"

"Raising shields," Dylan replied, activating the ship's shields.

"Four more contacts," Dylan warned.

"Let me guess, the interceptors?" Jessica guessed.

The ship rocked violently as sparks flew from the overhead panel to Nathan's left.

"I thought you raised shields!" Nathan scolded, shielding himself from the shower.

"I did!" Dylan defended. "That's what I was trying to tell you! XK's shields are designed to protect against pebbles and debris, and maybe a few hits from the kind of weapons most pirates have..."

The ship rocked as the interceptors fired again.

"*Warning, starboard aft anti-grav lift emitters are damaged,*" the AI announced.

"We need a new destination to jump to," Jessica reminded them.

"I have no idea what's around!" Nathan admitted as their ship took yet another hit.

Four flashes of blue-white light lit up their cockpit, nearly blinding them, and four black and crimson fighters streaked overhead, firing away at the interceptors attacking them from behind.

"They're attacking the interceptors!" Dylan exclaimed. "Are they friends of yours?"

"Hardly," Nathan replied. "Those are Dusahn octos."

"As soon as they finish off those interceptors, they'll do the same to us," Jessica added.

"Tergeron!" Dylan exclaimed.

Nathan looked at him.

"I just remembered! It's to starboard, and it's a single jump away! We can jump there and slingshot around its fifth planet. It's a massive gas giant. I do it all the time in Night Runner! You can pick up a ton of speed and quadruple your jump range!"

"Why didn't you say something before?" Nathan yelled.

"I didn't think of it!" Dylan defended. "Give me a break! I'm not used to being shot at!"

"Level twenty-eight, huh?" Jessica taunted.

"Okay, *twenty-two*," Dylan admitted as he punched in the new destination.

The incoming weapons blasts stopped.

"Uh-oh," Jessica said, realizing what that meant.

"We need to jump, *now*!" Nathan urged.

"I'm working on it!" Dylan assured him.

"The octos are coming about!" Jessica warned, pointing at the sensor display.

"*New destination accepted,*" the AI announced. "*Adjusting course. Jumping in forty seconds.*"

"We don't *have* forty seconds!" Nathan exclaimed.

"This is a *cargo* ship!" Dylan yelled back. "It can't turn that fast!"

"All four octos are on our six!" Jessica warned.

The ship rocked again as the octo-fighters opened up. Sparks flew, and smoke spewed, from a console behind Dylan.

"We've got a fire back here!" Jessica exclaimed, grabbing the fire extinguisher by the hatchway.

"*Aft shields have failed,*" the AI reported.

Jessica pointed the bottle at the smoking panel, but nothing happened when she pulled the trigger. "What the fuck!"

The ship rocked again, after which all four octos streaked overhead, passing from aft to forward, and peeling off in pairs in opposite directions.

"*Shield generators are down,*" the AI added.

"Reactor containment at forty percent. Jump drive offline."

"Great!" Nathan exclaimed. "I'm taking evasive action!" He yanked his flight control stick hard left and adjusted his throttles. The ship groaned, trying to respond to the radical stick inputs.

"You can't fly it that way!" Dylan warned.

Another warning beeped from the sensor display.

"Oh, shit," Dylan gasped.

Nathan looked at the display. "Missiles?"

"Two of them," Dylan replied.

"I don't suppose this thing has escape pods," Nathan commented.

"Thirty seconds to impact," Dylan reported.

"AI? Any chance you could get the jump drive working in fifteen seconds?" Nathan wondered.

"Negative," the AI replied. *"This vessel is not equipped with automated maintenance and repair systems."*

"We're screwed, aren't we?" Dylan asked, knowing the answer.

"We're not dead until we're dead," Nathan insisted, yanking his control stick in the other direction. "Can we jettison anything?" he wondered. "Maybe reduce our overall mass?"

"We're not carrying anything to jettison," Dylan replied. He glanced down at the sensor display again. "Ten seconds."

"Jess!" Nathan called, reaching back for her.

Jessica stepped up, grabbing his hand as the missiles closed in on them.

The sensor display beeped another warning as a large blip appeared directly behind them.

"What the..." Nathan was cut off when a barrage of reddish-yellow weapons fire streaked over them, slamming into the incoming missiles, blowing it apart.

The explosion rocked the ship more violently than before, knocking Jessica to the deck, and nearly bouncing Nathan and Dylan out of their seats.

"What just happened?" Dylan wondered, his eyes wide.

The cockpit suddenly darkened as a massive ship flew over them, slowing as it passed less than a hundred meters above them.

"YES!" Jessica exclaimed as she climbed back to her feet.

"*Nathan, is that you?*" Cameron called over comms.

Nathan laughed out loud. "YES!" he replied earnestly. "What the hell are you doing here?"

"*No time!*" she replied. "*Starboard bay! Quickly!*"

"I'm on it!" Nathan replied, grabbing his flight controls again.

"Who the hell is that?" Dylan wondered.

"It's the Aurora!" Jessica exclaimed.

"Who?"

"It's our ship!" Nathan added.

"That's *your* ship?" Dylan said in disbelief as Nathan guided their busted-up vessel across the Aurora's underside, passing to starboard and climbing up her side. The Aurora's shields flashed brightly as a hail of red-orange energy weapons fire slammed into their forward shields, courtesy of the Dusahn warships directly ahead of them.

As their beleaguered cargo ship climbed above the Aurora's midsection, Nathan fired his thrusters to translate their vessel to port, sliding into line with the Aurora's starboard aft landing bay.

"*Captain!*" Cameron called. "*We have to turn ten degrees to starboard to get a clear jump line!*"

"Go for it," Nathan replied. "We're on final. You can jump in ten seconds."

"*Are you sure?*"

"No," Nathan replied, easing his throttles forward to accelerate and begin a ten-degree turn to starboard.

They all watched out the front windows as the Aurora began to slip to the right. Nathan struggled to keep up with the turn as their ship accelerated toward the landing bay entrance.

"We're not going to make it," Jessica warned.

Nathan did not reply; all his concentration was on forcing the battered cargo ship to keep up with the Aurora's turn. "Easy, Josh," he called over comms.

The Aurora kept slipping to the right, leaving them headed directly for the inboard edge of the landing bay's entrance.

Another alarm sounded.

"We just lost maneuvering," Dylan announced.

"Brace for impact!" Nathan warned, his eyes widening as the edge of the landing bay came hurtling toward them.

At the last second, the Aurora stopped drifting right, then shifted back, slightly left. The cargo ship's nose slipped inside the landing bay entrance, but their port lift nacelle was unable to clear and slammed into it.

The ship lurched violently, yawing left as it entered the landing bay. A brilliant, blue-white flash filled their cockpit momentarily, and the ship slammed down onto the Aurora's landing deck.

The cockpit was filled with the sound of metal grinding on metal, bulkheads twisting, and systems coming apart all over the doomed cargo ship. The sickening sounds continued for several seconds as the ship shook violently, sliding across the landing deck. Finally, they came to a stop. The grinding sound was gone, and all that was left was the hiss of leaking systems and a cacophony of warning alarms.

Dylan looked over at Nathan, his eyes pleading. "Can I go home now?"

CHAPTER TEN

Nathan climbed up through the emergency hatch, helped by two rescue technicians atop the wrecked Tekan cargo ship, which was lying on the Aurora's starboard aft flight deck. Once out, he climbed down the access ladder to the deck below.

"Welcome aboard, sir," the rescue chief greeted.

"Thank you, Chief," Nathan replied, looking aft at the closed emergency doors. "Are those doors going to hold?" he wondered. "We smacked the tracks pretty good on our way in."

"We had a hard time getting them closed, but they'll hold," the chief assured him.

Nathan turned to find Jessica and Dylan standing a few meters away. "You guys okay?" he asked, heading toward them.

"I'm good," Jessica replied.

"Me, too," Dylan said, looking at the wreckage, "I think."

"Any landing you can walk away from," Nathan said, patting Dylan on the shoulder as he passed.

"Bridge?" Jessica asked.

"Where else," Nathan replied.

"What do you want us to do with this heap?" the chief asked Nathan.

"Jettison her," Nathan replied.

"It might have some useful tech," Jessica reminded him.

"We can't afford to tie up a landing bay," Nathan explained. "We can come back for the wreckage later, if we're still alive," he added, turning to head for the exit.

"What about him?" Jessica asked, pointing back at Dylan.

"With us," Nathan replied, his stride unbroken.

Dylan looked confused. "Who, me?"

"Yeah, him?" Jessica agreed, equally confused.

"He's the only Tekan contact we have right now," Nathan replied as he walked.

"Come on, kid," Jessica instructed Dylan as she turned to follow Nathan.

"Where are we going?" Dylan asked, following Jessica and Nathan, while looking around the massive landing bay.

"To the bridge," Jessica responded.

"Sweet," Dylan said, jogging a few steps to catch up with them.

Nathan stepped through the midship hatch, into the rescue trunk connecting the starboard aft landing bay to the main hangar bay.

"Your comm-set, sir," Sergeant Dixon said, handing Nathan a comm-set as he passed.

"Thank you, Sergeant," Nathan replied, donning the comm-set.

"Lieutenant Commander," the sergeant said, handing Jessica one, as well.

"Thanks, Dix," Jessica replied.

Nathan tapped his comm-set as he stepped through the next hatch into the main hangar bay. "Cam, we're aboard."

"*Nice landing,*" Cameron congratulated sarcastically.

"You saw that?"

"*We all did. Not your best.*"

"What's our status?"

"*A few overloaded circuits, a bit of a drain on*

several shield sections, but nothing Vlad can't handle."

"What the hell are you even *doing* here?"

"*Our operatives on Takara picked up some unusual comms traffic about distant operations. Shinoda put two and two together, and figured out that the Dusahn were on their way to SilTek. We didn't know when they would arrive, so we just jumped immediately.*"

"How did you know it was us in that freighter?" Nathan wondered.

"*It was the only ship being targeted, so I figured it was a pretty good bet,*" Cameron replied.

"Remind me to give you a raise, later," Nathan joked. "We'll be there shortly," he added, tapping his comm-set again to end the call.

"Holy..." Dylan exclaimed in awe as he entered the main hangar bay. "How big *is* this ship?"

"About one and a half clicks long and half a click wide," Nathan replied.

"What's a *click*?"

"Kilometer," Jessica explained.

"And this ship can jump more than three hundred light years at a time?"

"Nearly twice that," Nathan replied as they walked around the end of a row of Reapers and headed forward.

"That's incredible!" Dylan exclaimed. "What are these?" he wondered, pointing at the ships to their right.

"Reapers," Jessica replied.

"Ominous name. Are they fighters?"

"Multi-role, combat utility craft," Nathan explained as they neared the forward hatch. "Our fighters are out on assignment."

"You're awfully curious," Jessica commented suspiciously.

"It's my first time on a spaceship," Dylan defended. "On *two* spaceships... Hell, in *space!* Can you blame me?"

* * *

"Captain on the bridge!" the guard at the entrance announced as Nathan entered.

"Welcome back," Cameron greeted, rising from the command chair.

After Jessica passed, the guard stepped in front of Dylan, giving him a death stare.

"Uh, Jess?" Dylan squeaked.

"He's with us," Jessica told the guard.

"Yeah, I'm with them," Dylan repeated.

"Just stand there, by the comm-station," Jessica instructed.

"Here?"

The guard pushed him over next to Naralena's console. "Here, and don't move. I'm watching you."

"You bet."

"I take it your negotiations did not go as expected," Cameron commented.

"We only met with the leader of SilTek briefly," Nathan replied. "We were supposed to meet again with her later today. Frankly, I don't know *why* they were trying to arrest us."

"Is it possible they think you led the Dusahn *to* them?" Cameron suggested.

"Anything is possible," Nathan replied, tapping his comm-set. "Vlad, how's my ship? Can she fight?"

"*Good to hear your voice, Nathan,*" Vladimir replied. "*Shield power is fully restored, and we're working on the minor damage now, but you've only got about five percent remaining in our jump banks,*" *and our recharge rate is going to be reduced if we're pumping energy into shields and weapons."*

"Run the ZPEDs at one hundred twenty percent if you have to."

"That is not advisable during combat," Vladimir warned.

"It can't be helped," Nathan insisted, ending the call. "How far from SilTek are we at the moment?"

"About five light years," Cameron replied. "Are you planning to *return* to SilTek?"

"How much range do we have left, Loki?" Nathan asked his navigator.

"Thirty-two point six five light years," Loki replied.

"So, we have enough to put up a good fight and still be able to escape if we have to," Nathan surmised.

"Barely," Josh commented.

"Nathan," Cameron cut in, "I'm not sure that's a good idea. Both the Rogen and Orswellan systems are vulnerable right now, and it's going to be hours before we can jump back if they need us. And now, the Dusahn have *four more ships* than we originally thought; *two* of which are *battleships.*"

"SilTek is *loaded* with technology that can be used *against* us, should that world fall to the Dusahn," Nathan explained.

"Maybe, but even if we manage to drive them off for now, they'll come back, and we don't know how many more ships they might have or where they are located. They could be a single jump away from Rogen *right now*, just *waiting* for us to jump away."

"In which case, the Rogen system is *already* doomed," Nathan pointed out.

"I don't think so," Jessica argued from her position at the tactical station. "We spent *days* interrogating the crew of Andreola's ship. Their account of how many ships had been built or upgraded with jump drives in the Orswellan shipyards *was* a bit varied, but it pretty much lined up with our accounting of Dusahn ships."

"Then, these four *additional* ships are *not* a surprise?" Nathan asked.

"Yes, but not by much," Jessica replied. "The point is, I *strongly* doubt there are more."

"Are you willing to bet an entire *world* on that?" Cameron challenged.

Nathan sighed. "I don't see that we have a choice. If the Dusahn take SilTek, there's a good possibility they'll become too powerful to defeat."

"Doesn't SilTek have defenses?" Cameron asked.

Nathan looked to Dylan.

Dylan looked at the guard. "Can I..."

The guard gestured for him to step forward.

"Uh, SilTek *has* defenses, but not against *battleships*."

"What do you know about battleships?" Jessica wondered.

"Well, *nothing* really," Dylan admitted, "but I *do* know that one has never *attacked* us, until now. Hell, no one in this *quadrant* even *has* a warship that big."

"But you said you get attacked frequently," Jessica pointed out.

"Yeah, by gunships and fighters," Dylan replied. "One time, there was this big-ass pirate ship, maybe half as big as yours, but their guns weren't worth a damn. Just how big *is* a battleship?"

"Pretty big," Nathan assured him.

"Bigger than *this* ship?"

"Three to four times bigger," Jessica added.

Dylan's eyes widened, taking a step toward Nathan. "You have to go back and stop them!" he urged. He caught himself and turned back toward the guard, looking guilty.

"It's okay," Jessica assured the guard.

"Captain," Dylan said, "you are the captain, right?"

"Yes."

"Then you *must* help us. Even *one* of those ships can wipe us out, and you said there are *four* of them?"

"Two battleships and two cruisers," Cameron replied. "Who is this kid?" she asked Nathan.

"This is Dylan," Nathan explained. "He helped us escape."

"I don't suppose cruisers are much smaller," Dylan surmised.

"Not by much," Jessica replied.

"Please," Dylan pleaded. "My *family* is there. Everyone I *know* is there."

"You're going to have to choose which world you're going to put at risk," Cameron told Nathan.

"We're going back to SilTek," Nathan insisted.

"Nathan..."

Nathan held up his hand, cutting Cameron off. "If the Dusahn attack the Rogen or Orswellan systems, we'll lose them, and millions will probably die, but if we lose *SilTek*, we'll lose the *war*, and billions, possibly *trillions,* will die on all the worlds they will eventually conquer. There is no choice here, Cam. We *must* defend SilTek."

Cameron sighed. "I agree."

"You do?" Nathan replied, surprised.

"I do. I don't *like* it, but I do."

"Our only chance here is to hit them hard and fast, and then jump away quickly," Nathan announced, taking his seat. "We have to try to draw them off and spread them out. If they stay together, they can defend one another. We'll concentrate our strikes against the outlier. That should force them to rotate their ships around to give them time to recharge their shields."

"Or we could use our jump missiles," Jessica suggested.

Nathan looked at her, surprised, then at Cameron. "We have jump missiles? I thought..."

"I commandeered forty of them before we left," Cameron explained. "I figured we might need them."

"You figured right," Nathan agreed, smiling.

"This would be a lot easier if the Sugali fighters were still on board," Jessica commented as she reviewed the Aurora's weapons status.

"You use Sugali fighters?" Dylan wondered. "They make those on SilTek, or at least they did. But surely those would be useless against a *battleship*?"

"There's something about their grav-lift emitters that allows them to pass right through the Dusahn's shields," Nathan explained. "We used ten of them to defeat *four* battleships a few days ago."

Dylan's mind was racing. "P-Seventy-Twos use the same emitters."

"What's a P-Seventy-Two?" Nathan wondered.

"It's a single-seat vehicle—a real hot rod. Its nickname is *Lightning*. Their owners *love* to race them. There's even an organized league for it. They use the same emitters as the Sugali fighters. A *lot* of small and midsize vehicles use those same emitters."

"Unless they can operate in space, I'm afraid they won't be much use to us," Nathan told him.

"What if they could?" Dylan asked. "What if they could even *jump*?"

Nathan looked at Dylan. *"Can they?"*

"Well, not the *stock* ones, no," Dylan explained, "but the ones Subvert has can."

"You mentioned that name when we first met you," Jessica realized, her eyebrows furrowing. "Who are they?"

Dylan looked uncertain. He glanced at the guard, who was also staring at him. "They're a group that opposes SilTek's refusal to make offensive weapons or create a military that can attack other worlds. They believe the existence of a strong offense *is* the best defense."

"They have P-Seventy-Twos that can operate in space?" Nathan asked directly.

"Yes. They have been converting P-Seventy-Twos into jump fighters that use swarm technology to attack enemy ships. They want to demonstrate that technology can be more lethal than large warships, when used correctly. They were going to use them to launch a retaliatory attack against the next world that attacked *us*, to show that there will be consequences for doing so."

"And your leaders *allow* this?" Cameron wondered.

"Oh, hell no," Dylan assured her. "Subvert is totally underground."

"Does SilTek even *know* about them?" Jessica asked.

"Oh, they know. They've been hunting them for years, but like I said, they're *underground*. I mean, *really* underground, like in caves and tunnels, and stuff."

"How do you know all this?" Jessica wondered, growing more suspicious of him with each passing moment.

"I uh......uh..."

"You're one of them, aren't you?" Jessica guessed.

"Not *officially*," he insisted, "but I have a *friend* who is a member. I've been helping him with their swarm AI code. That's what I was doing when the attack started."

"Let me get this straight," Nathan said, "Subvert has makeshift jump fighters that use the same grav-lift systems as the Sugali fighters?"

Dylan looked confused. "Isn't that what I just said?"

"Any chance you could contact them?" Nathan wondered.

"Shouldn't be too hard," Dylan insisted. "Hell, if I know Zeller, he's getting ready to launch right now."

"How many operational P-Seventy-Twos do they have?" Jessica asked.

"At least four, for sure," Dylan promised.

"If those ships can get inside their shields..." Cameron began.

"Then, we might have a chance," Nathan finished for her.

* * *

"Reapers are away," Naralena reported. "Flight reports aft starboard landing bay will be clear in five minutes."

"How are they managing that?" Dylan wondered.

"Turn off the artificial gravity and use a few thruster packs to float it out of the bay into space," Nathan explained.

"You're just going to leave it behind?" Dylan asked in disbelief. "Can't it be fixed?"

"No time," Nathan replied. "Besides, we can come back for it later, assuming we're still in one piece."

Dylan suddenly felt the need to shut up.

"Comms, patch me through to Reaper One," Nathan instructed.

"One moment."

"Did you get that message recorded?" Nathan asked Dylan.

"Yeah," Dylan replied. "She compressed it so the entire message can be sent as a single-burst transmission."

"Reaper One is on your comm-set," Naralena reported.

"Reaper One, Aurora Actual," Nathan called.

"*Aurora Actual, go for Reaper One,*" Lieutenant Commander Manes replied.

"Sit tight here," Nathan instructed. "If you don't hear from us within the hour, head for the Orswellan system and report to General Telles."

"*Aye, sir,*" the lieutenant commander replied.

"And don't assume that either the Orswellan or Rogen systems are safe," Nathan added. "For all we know, the Dusahn could have already attacked them."

After a moment of silence, the lieutenant commander asked, "*And if they have?*"

Nathan sighed. "Find a way to survive."

"*Are you sure you don't want us to come with you?*"

"No insult intended, Lieutenant Commander, but I don't think your Reapers would turn the tide on this one. Besides, if things go south, I suspect that the Ghatazhak could make use of your ships."

"*Understood,*" the lieutenant commander replied. "*Good hunting, sir.*"

Nathan tapped his comm-set, ending the call, and then turned around to query Jessica and Cameron at the tactical station. "Any ideas?"

"Start every pass with jump missiles, but

don't always strike from the same side," Cameron suggested.

"Isn't that counterproductive?" Nathan wondered. "Isn't the entire purpose of striking with jump missiles to weaken their shields?"

"Yes, but if we always lead with jump missiles and then attack the same side, they'll figure it out in a hurry and be ready for us. We need to vary our tactics. Single-point, multi-point, opposing sides, same sides...maybe even do something obvious to trick them into leaving one side uncovered."

"I don't think we have that kind of time," Nathan replied, "and unless we can get them to split up, which I highly doubt, they'll just rotate the weak to the inside, never allowing us more than a single shot at the same shield section."

"You're assuming their commanders are skilled tacticians," Jessica pointed out. "If they had to resort to automating as many systems as possible, that means they lack manpower. That *could* mean their commanders are inexperienced."

"Would *you* send an inexperienced captain to capture a world like SilTek?" Nathan asked. "And that same automation could also be *dictating* their tactics."

"We haven't seen any evidence of AI-driven tactics in the past," Jessica commented.

"It makes sense that they would use AI against AI," Cameron added.

"How many times have *you* beaten the ship's computer at chess?" Nathan challenged. "We have to assume they'll use good battle tactics. If they do *not,* then we'll jump on that opportunity."

"Flight reports the landing bay is clear," Naralena announced.

"First four jump missiles are on the cats and ready for launch," Jessica added. "Second four are on the deck and in line for launch."

"Very well," Nathan replied, taking his seat. "Mister Sheehan?"

"On course and speed for return jump to SilTek," Loki replied. "Insertion point will be five light minutes out."

Nathan looked over to Lieutenant Commander Yosef at the sensor station.

"It will only take me about twenty seconds to detect the enemy targets and calculate their course and speeds."

"Two minutes to reload the cats and launch the second wave," Cameron reported.

"Make our insertion point three minutes out," Nathan decided. "Put a three-minute jump delay on the first round, and one minute on the second, so they come in one minute apart."

"Three minutes means they'll detect us just as we're about to attack," Jessica warned.

"That's the idea," Nathan replied. "I'd like to start this battle by looking stupid."

"We most certainly will," Cameron grumbled under her breath.

"Jump plot updated," Loki reported. "Ready to jump."

"All decks show battle stations manned and ready," Naralena announced.

"Very well, let's go defend SilTek," Nathan said.

"Executing insertion jump in five seconds," Loki replied. "Three..."

Nathan glanced at the tactical displays on the lower corners of the main view screen...

"Two..."

His ship was armed to the teeth and ready for action...

"One..."

But their success lay in the hands of an unknown element...

"Jumping."

He only hoped that Subvert would answer their call.

"Jump complete," Loki reported as their jump flash faded, and the light inside the Aurora's bridge returned to normal.

"Scanning with passive sensors," Kaylah announced. "Don't want to make it *too* obvious."

"Launching first four jump missiles," Cameron announced. A few seconds later, she added, "Four jump missiles away."

Nathan observed the Aurora's bow at the bottom center of the view screen as two pairs of jump missiles streaked ahead on either side.

"Four contacts," Kaylah reported, "two battleships and two heavy cruisers. Ships are in high orbit over SilTek, line abreast, fifty-kilometer spacing, with the cruisers on the outside. They're bombarding the surface. Transferring target data to tactical."

"What are they targeting?" Nathan wondered.

"Nothing," Kaylah replied. "Firing patterns indicate they are attempting to cover the most surface possible."

"They're carpet-bombing?" Cameron asked.

"They're not trying to capture SilTek," Nathan realized. "They're trying to glass it."

"Why glass it?" Jessica wondered.

Nathan turned to look at Dylan. "Every building has a shelter, right?"

"Yes, but..."

"What about SilTek's manufacturing facilities?"

"They're all underground, as well," Dylan replied.

"They're trying to make the surface uninhabitable," Nathan realized. "Pound them into submission."

"They can glass the entire planet, and all of the manufacturing facilities will still be at their disposal," Cameron concluded.

"SilTek isn't just lying down and taking it," Kaylah reported. "They're fighting back."

"Second group of four jump missiles ready to launch," Cameron announced. "All eight still need targeting data."

"We're at a minute thirty," Jessica warned.

"They're launching their own jump missiles from the surface," Kaylah continued.

"Are they having any effect?" Nathan asked.

"Minimal," Kaylah replied. "All their power is going to their ventral shields."

"What side of them are we facing?"

"The starboard side, slightly below," Kaylah replied. "We're basically pointed at SilTek's southern pole."

"Helm," Nathan snapped, "pitch up twenty degrees and prepare to jump us to a position directly above the targets. Turn into them as soon as we come out of the jump."

"Pitching up," Josh replied.

"Hold the second wave of missiles," Nathan added. "First wave launches at plus three point five; target is the nearest cruiser."

"Plotting jump," Loki confirmed.

"Holding second wave," Cameron replied.

"The second wave will target the battleship nearest the targeted cruiser," Nathan added. "Dorsal side, just aft of midship, and get a third wave up and ready; same target as the second wave, ten seconds after."

"Understood," Cameron replied as she entered the targeting data.

"Pitch maneuver complete," Josh reported.

"Jump plotted," Loki added.

"Snap jump," Nathan instructed.

"Jumping," Loki replied as the wave of blue-white light swept over them. "Jump complete..."

"...Turning into the targets," Josh added.

"Launch second wave as soon as we come around," Nathan ordered.

"Dorsal shields on *all four* enemy ships are at twenty percent!" Kaylah exclaimed.

"Perfect," Nathan commented.

"Finishing our turn," Josh reported as he rolled the ship out of its turn.

"Launching second round of jump missiles," Cameron announced.

"Transferring track data to tactical," Kaylah reported.

"Four missiles away," Cameron announced. "Reloading all cats."

"I've got the track data," Jessica added. "Passing targeting data to second group of missiles."

"As soon as the third wave of missiles is away, I want to go *back* to our original insertion position and execute our attack jump from there, but twenty seconds *after* all three waves of jump missiles have struck," Nathan instructed his flight crew.

"Got it," Josh replied confidently.

"I thought you wanted to look stupid," Jessica taunted.

"They beat me to it," Nathan commented.

"We're at two point five minutes," Jessica warned.

"Launching third group," Cameron announced.

"I've already given them their targeting data," Jessica added.

"Four more missiles away," Cameron followed.

"Turning," Josh announced.

"Get us back to square one," Nathan urged.

"Jumping in five seconds," Loki replied. "Three......two......one..."

"Turn complete," Josh replied triumphantly.

"...Jumping."

"Turning back to original attack plot," Josh reported as the jump flash faded.

"Jump complete," Loki reported.

"Attack jump one...when ready," Nathan ordered.

"Attack jump one, in twenty seconds," Loki replied, checking his navigation display.

"First missile impacts in five seconds," Cameron warned.

Nathan fought to regulate his breathing, trying to control his body's release of adrenalin and remain calm.

"Missile impacts...now," Cameron reported.

"Jumping in five seconds," Loki announced.

"Three..."

"Let's hope this works," Cameron said.

"Two..."

Dylan clutched the side of the comm-station with all his might.

"One..."

"Here goes nothing," Nathan joked uneasily.

"Jumping."

The blue-white jump flash washed over the bridge momentarily, and the main view screen was filled with the planet SilTek and the four Dusahn warships bombarding it from orbit.

"First cruiser, all tubes, fire at will," Nathan instructed.

"Targeting cruiser," Jessica replied.

"Comms, start your transmission," Nathan ordered.

"Transmitting to Subvert on all known channels and frequencies," Naralena replied.

"Cruiser's midship and aft starboard shields are down to twenty percent," Kaylah reported.

"Jess," Nathan called.

"Got it!" Jessica assured him. "Firing all tubes."

"We're being targeted," Cameron warned as the bridge lit up with red-orange flashes, waves of plasma torpedoes racing from under the Aurora's nose toward the first cruiser.

Four flashes of blue-white light appeared on the main view screen, a kilometer above the battleship on the other side of the nearby cruiser.

"Second wave impact in five seconds," Cameron added.

"Multiple missile launches on the surface," Kaylah warned.

Nathan watched the screen as plasma torpedoes continued to traverse the distance to the first cruiser, lighting up their starboard shields with each impact.

"Battleship has activated point-defenses," Kaylah reported.

"Against us or them?" Nathan wondered.

"Both!"

"Nice," Nathan replied.

Two small explosions appeared above the battleship, followed two seconds later by two brilliant flashes as two of the four missiles struck the battleship's underpowered dorsal shields.

"Two got through!" Cameron exclaimed.

"Battleship's shields are down to ten percent!" Kaylah added.

Four more jump flashes appeared above the battleship.

"They're not engaging the third wave," Cameron realized.

"Their targeting sensors haven't had time to recover," Kaylah surmised.

Four more brilliant flashes appeared, lighting up what was left of the battleship's dorsal shields. Explosions appeared all over her topside as shield emitters overloaded and blew apart.

"Battleship One has lost all midship dorsal shields!" Kaylah announced.

"Hold fire," Nathan ordered. "Helm, pitch up ten and roll ninety to port. Jump us to the battleship, one click away, passing one click over."

"Pitching and rolling," Josh responded as he started the maneuver.

"Preparing micro-jump," Loki added.

"Jess, all guns to port, add in the broadsides, and fire as we pass," Nathan added. "You're only going to get about ten seconds; make them count."

"I plan to," Jessica assured him.

"The second battleship is launching short-range missiles at us," Cameron warned. "Impact in ten seconds."

"More surface launches," Kaylah announced. "They're jump missiles!"

"Loki?" Nathan called.

"Ready."

"Stand by to jump," Nathan ordered. He counted for a few seconds in his head and then gave the order. "Jump."

The blue-white flash washed over the bridge, and

the battleship appeared in their view screen on the left side, sliding aft.

"Targeting," Jessica announced.

"Missiles passed under us!" Cameron exclaimed.

"Battleship is rolling to port," Kaylah warned.

"Firing!" Jessica reported.

Nathan stared at the left side of the main view screen, watching the black and crimson battleship slowly roll over as they passed. Red-orange bolts of energy streaked from the Aurora's forward plasma turret, slamming into the hull of the massive warship.

"Incoming fire!" Cameron warned.

The Aurora began to shake violently, the left side of the view screen flashing as their shields protected them from the incoming fire.

"She's rolling too fast," Cameron reported. "We're losing the angle."

"SilTek jump missiles! Coming up the other side of the battleship!" Kaylah warned.

"Point-defenses!" Nathan barked.

"Already on it!" Jessica assured him.

"I count six missiles!" Kaylah added.

"I've lost the angle," Jessica warned. "Firing broadsides into their starboard shields!"

"Five still coming!" Kaylah warned.

"Two down!" Cameron announced. "Three! Four! Brace!"

"All hands, brace for impact!" Nathan ordered over the ship-wide intercom.

The last missile found the Aurora's port midship shields; the explosion lurched the ship sideways and nearly knocked Nathan from his command chair.

"Another eight right behind them!" Kaylah announced.

"Christ!" Nathan exclaimed. "Someone, tell them we're on their side!"

"Ten seconds to impact!" Kaylah reported.

"We're past the firing solution," Jessica added.

"Get us out of here, Loki," Nathan ordered.

"Activating escape jump," Loki announced as the blue-white flash filled the bridge again.

"Jump complete," Loki sighed.

"Naralena," Nathan called.

"Try to hail SilTek on our next pass and suggest they hold their fire when we're attacking?" she anticipated.

"That would be great," Nathan confirmed.

"Coming about," Josh reported.

"Straight attack on the second cruiser," Nathan instructed. "We jump in five seconds behind our missiles."

"Yes, sir," Loki replied.

"Four of them?" Cameron asked.

"Yes, but spread them out before they jump, and set them to jump in at five hundred meters."

"That won't give them enough room to make final course corrections," Cameron reminded him.

"It also won't give the Dusahn enough time to intercept them," Nathan replied. "I'd rather miss than have them blown away."

"Either way is ineffective," Jessica said, partly to herself.

"Finishing our turn," Josh reported from the helm.

"Let's pass under, this time," Nathan decided. "Bring us out of the jump one kilometer aft, one down, and one off the target's port side. Pitch, yaw, and roll so we come out of the jump with our nose on the target."

"They'll be smaller targets," Jessica warned.

"But they've got fewer guns pointing aft," Nathan added. "They'll also be expecting us to attack the same side as the missiles."

"On course for jump missile launch," Loki reported.

"Launch another round of four, Cam," Nathan instructed.

"Targeting data loaded," Cameron replied. "Launching four."

Four missiles streaked away on the main view screen.

"Missiles away."

"Adjusting course," Josh announced.

"Jump plotted and ready," Loki added.

"Missiles will jump in fifteen seconds," Cameron reported. "Executing final course adjustments for target intercept."

"Make sure you get that message to SilTek," Nathan urged.

"On course and speed for attack jump two," Josh announced. "Pitching up and to port," he added, twisting his control stick counterclockwise, pulling back slightly, and tipping it to the right a bit to add some roll.

"Five seconds," Cameron reported.

"All weapons are pre-aimed and ready," Jessica announced. "Broadsides are set for full-power triplets. We should have time for a single round at each target as we pass."

"Assuming we can linger that long," Cameron added.

"Ready to rip," Josh reported as he finished his yaw and pitch maneuver.

Four blue-white flashes appeared in the distance on the main view screen.

"Missiles have jumped," Cameron reported.

"Weapons hot, execute jump," Nathan ordered.

The blue-white flash washed over them, and again, the Aurora was back in orbit over SilTek, this time passing the second Dusahn cruiser slightly below and from its port to starboard.

"Firing all forward torpedoes," Jessica announced.

"Sending burst transmission," Naralena added.

"Cruiser Two has no port shields!" Kaylah reported.

"I have an idea," Josh said, nearly cutting her off. "I need a hot stick, though."

"SilTek Defense, this is the Aurora..." Naralena called over comms from the back of the bridge.

Nathan didn't hesitate. As crazy as his friend could be at times, he was a gifted pilot, and the AI assisting him only made him better. "Jess, make his stick hot."

"...Do not target us..."

"Your stick is hot, Josh," Jessica announced. "Don't miss."

"...We are trying to defend you..." Naralena continued.

"You just be ready on all your other guns," Josh replied as he pushed the main throttles forward.

Nathan's eyes widened as the cruiser on the main view screen grew closer, passing from right to left. The cruiser slid up the screen slightly, then back down as Josh pitched the Aurora up while they closed on the cruiser.

"...I repeat, do not target us..."

"Firing," Josh reported, pressing the firing button on his flight control stick. Four sets of triplets leapt from under their nose, slamming into the port ventral aspect of the cruiser's hull, ripping it open. Secondary explosions deep within its hull spread fore and aft, breaking it up further.

"More missiles from the surface!" Kaylah warned. "Twenty seconds to impact!"

"Firing point-defenses!" Jessica announced.

"I need full power to all forward and dorsal shields!" Josh demanded as he translated the ship upward, pitching back down as the ship rose.

"You got it," Cameron assured Josh.

The view screen flashed brightly as thousands of bits of debris from the doomed cruiser impacted the Aurora's dorsal shields.

"Are they hearing us?" Nathan barked.

"I'm transmitting on every known channel and frequency," Naralena assured him.

Undaunted, Josh held his course, plowing through the debris, rocking the entire ship in the process.

"I'm about to give you a clear shot," Josh announced.

"*This* was your great idea?" Cameron asked.

"I never said it was *great*," Josh defended.

"Target the second battleship with four jump missiles, set to jump as soon as they are away, and come out five hundred meters from target," Nathan ordered.

"I already am," Cameron assured him.

Suddenly, they were through the debris with a clear shot at the second battleship.

"Dial up a one-hundred-kilometer jump for me, Lok," Josh urged.

Loki glanced over his shoulder at Nathan.

"You heard the man," Nathan said.

"You got it," Loki replied.

"Missiles rea..." Cameron began to announce.

"Launch four!" Nathan ordered before the words left her mouth.

"Firing!" Cameron replied, pressing the launch button. "Four away!"

The view screen lit up as two jump missiles on each side of the Aurora's bow vanished behind blue-white flashes of light. A split second later, four flashes of light appeared ahead of them in the distance, followed immediately by four brilliant, yellow flashes as they impacted the second battleship's shields.

Josh pulled back slightly on his flight control stick, pitching the Aurora up to get a clear jump line. He pushed the throttles for the main engines all the way forward, then reversed them back to zero thrust, pushing his stick back forward hard, swinging their nose back down quickly.

"Missile launch!" Kaylah warned. "Eight jump missiles..."

"Josh..." Nathan started to say.

"Jump us!" Josh ordered Loki.

Loki pressed the jump button, sending the Aurora ahead, instantly transitioning to a point beyond the incoming missiles, the battleship that had fired them, and the other battleship they had already damaged on their first pass.

Josh held his stick back, waiting until the very last second to push it forward and apply counterthrust to stop their pitch-down maneuver. He glanced at the targeting reticle on the clear screen, on the front edge of his console, adjusting the ship's attitude until the piper in the center turned green. "Firing!" Josh announced, pressing his firing button again and holding it.

Three waves of four triplets streaked away from under the Aurora's nose, resulting in brilliant flashes of red as they struck the first battleship's shields.

"More missiles!" Kaylah warned. "From all three ships *and* the surface!"

"Escape jump!" Nathan ordered.

"Wait!" Josh exclaimed.

Loki ignored his helmsman, following his captain's orders, and executed the escape jump, getting the Aurora out of the path of countless jump missiles.

"Damn it!" Josh cursed. "I almost had that son of a bitch!"

"Couldn't risk it," Nathan told him, "but it was a great maneuver."

"If it makes you feel any better, you *did* drain their shields down to five percent," Kaylah consoled.

"Not really," Josh replied.

"Jump us to the rally point," Nathan instructed.

"Aye, sir," Loki replied.

"Load another four," Nathan instructed Cameron. "Same arrival range as before. Target the other cruiser."

"Turn complete," Josh announced.

"Targeting now," Cameron replied.

"You don't really expect them to be there, do you?" Jessica wondered.

"Not really," Nathan admitted as the jump flash washed over them. "But we have to try."

"We're at the rally point," Loki announced.

"Scanning," Kaylah added.

"We won't be able to keep this attack up for more than a few more passes," Cameron warned, "not unless we take out *one* of those battleships, and soon."

"How are our shields holding up?" Nathan wondered.

"After two passes, most of our shields are down to about sixty percent, on average," Cameron replied.

"They've dropped *that much*?" Nathan said in disbelief.

"Don't forget, we're still diverting a lot of power to recharging our jump energy banks, in case we need to jump back to an allied system sometime soon."

"What if we alternate power usage?" Nathan suggested. "We could channel everything to shields during our attack runs and then to the jump energy banks during transitions."

"The net result is pretty much the same," Cameron explained.

Nathan sighed. "Anything?" he asked Kaylah.

"No contacts within five hundred thousand kilometers," Kaylah replied.

"We're on course for the next attack run, Cap'n," Josh reported.

"Jump is ready," Loki added.

"Very well," Nathan replied. "Launch the next round of missiles," he instructed.

"Launching four," Cameron reported as she launched the next group of jump missiles. "Missiles away."

Nathan waited until the missiles jumped away and then gave the order. "Take us in again, Loki."

"Jumping."

Nathan's brow furrowed as the jump flash subsided. "Where's the cruiser?" he queried, seeing nothing but a black, starry field and a sliver of the planet's horizon along the bottom edge of their view screen.

"Cruiser is beneath us!" Kaylah warned. "Twenty kilometers! They're closing ranks!"

"What about our missiles?" Nathan wondered.

"Still running hot and true," Kaylah replied. "They missed, sir," she added, turning to look at the captain, "all four of them."

"Roll one-eighty," Nathan ordered.

"Flippin' over," Josh replied.

"What about our torpedoes?" Jessica questioned.

"No time," Nathan insisted. "Hit them with turrets and broadsides as we pass."

"They must have begun closing ranks the moment we jumped out," Jessica noted as she assigned the cruiser as a target for the Aurora's plasma cannon turrets.

"Damn it!" Nathan cursed, momentarily losing his composure.

"Even if we'd jumped them in at normal range, they still would have missed," Cameron assured him.

"More missiles from the surface," Kaylah added.

"Are we still hailing them?" Nathan asked Naralena.

"I have the message on a loop broadcast," she replied.

"Battleship Two is climbing," Kaylah announced. "Cruiser One is descending."

"They're trying to get more guns on us," Cameron surmised.

"We're being targeted by multiple guns," Jessica warned.

"Surface missiles are altering course!" Kaylah realized. "They're targeting the battleships!"

"Firing all weapons on the cruiser," Jessica reported.

"All three targets are firing," Kaylah warned.

The ship began to shake violently as multiple streams of energy weapons fire impacted their dorsal and port shields.

"Shield strength is falling," Jessica warned. "Firing broadsides."

"Four new contacts," Kaylah announced. "Unknown type. Based on size, I'd call them fighters."

A computer-generated profile appeared in a window on the main view screen.

"That's them!" Dylan exclaimed, pointing at the screen. "Those are P-Seventy-Two Lightnings!"

"See if you can raise them," Nathan instructed Naralena.

"Aye, sir."

"Cruiser's port shields are gone," Kaylah reported.

"Target their port side and hit them with..."

"Contacts are attacking the cruiser!" Kaylah interrupted. "They're in our firing line!"

"Belay last!" Nathan barked. "Hold fire!"

"Holding all fire," Jessica replied.

"One of the contacts has been destroyed," Kaylah reported.

"We can't just sit here and get pounded without shooting back," Jessica insisted.

"Target Battleship One and open fire," Nathan suggested.

"I'm losing the angle on Battleship One," Jessica warned.

"Comms, tell Subvert to disengage and jump to the rally point!" Nathan instructed.

"Another one is gone!" Kaylah reported. "Their shields *suck*!"

"Dorsal shields are down to thirty percent," Cameron warned. "Starboard average is at thirty-eight."

"Lightnings have jumped away," Kaylah reported with relief.

"Retarget that cruiser," Nathan began.

"Cruiser is rolling, bringing her good shields toward us," Kaylah added.

"We can dive under them," Josh suggested.

"Negative," Nathan replied with a sigh. "Jump us clear and then jump us to the rally point."

"Aye, sir," Loki replied as he pressed the jump button.

"The Lightnings were not headed for the rally point when they jumped," Kaylah told him as their jump flash washed over the bridge.

"Neither were we," Nathan replied.

"Jump complete," Loki reported.

"Turning toward the rally point," Josh added.

"Your friends aren't terribly bright," Jessica told Dylan.

"I never said *they* were my friends," Dylan defended, "and I'm pretty sure they were just trying to defend our world."

"By attacking a much stronger enemy with insufficient firepower?" Jessica retorted. "That's not brave, it's stupid."

"Easy, Jess," Nathan said, feeling sympathy for Dylan. "What I don't understand is why SilTek isn't making more headway defending themselves. Surely, they must have more than enough jump missiles. Launch enough of them, and you'll bring down their shields, even on the battleships."

"Turn complete," Josh reported.

"Jumping to the rally point," Loki added.

"We don't keep a large inventory of missiles," Dylan explained as the jump flash washed over the bridge. "No one with this kind of firepower has ever attacked us before."

"I'm afraid those days are over," Nathan replied, turning to Kaylah. "Anything?"

"Negative," Kaylah answered. "No contacts within five hundred thousand kilometers."

"Comms, drop a buoy with instructions for Subvert. Tell them to remain here until we return with instructions."

"Aye, sir," Naralena replied.

"We'll jump back and finish off the cruiser, then return to the rally point," Nathan added.

"Comm-buoy away," Naralena reported.

"Attack jump on the cruiser plotted and ready," Loki reported.

"Weapons ready," Jessica added.

"Let's make this quick," Nathan instructed. "Execute your jump."

"Jumping," Loki replied as the jump flash washed over the bridge.

"They've reversed their altitudes!" Kaylah reported urgently.

"Helm, pull up hard forty degrees," Nathan ordered. "All power to ventral shields."

"Pulling up hard," Josh acknowledged.

"Transferring all available power to ventral shields," Cameron confirmed.

The bridge lurched violently as a series of explosions rocked the ship.

"What the hell was that?" Nathan wondered.

"Missiles!" Kaylah replied. "I never even picked up their launch!"

"Up forty complete!" Josh reported.

"Jump us one click!" Nathan ordered.

"One-click jump, aye," Loki replied.

"Pitch back down, bring our tubes onto that cruiser, and fire at will," Nathan instructed as the jump flash washed over them.

"Pitching back down!" Josh acknowledged.

Bolts of red energy slammed into their shields, rocking the ship further.

"Aft ventral shields are down!" Cameron warned. "Midship ventrals are at ten percent!"

"Decks C and D, sections forty-seven and forty-eight report complete loss of power and life support," Naralena reported.

The ship lurched again as more plasma bolts struck the hull.

"Hull breach!" Naralena reported with alarm. "Aft ventral section!"

Another explosion shook the ship, knocking several people to the deck.

"Aft propellant tank just took a direct hit!" Cameron exclaimed, using the side of the tactical console to steady herself as she reached to pull Jessica back to her feet. "Heavy damage to engineering sections eighteen and twenty!"

"I'm getting thrust level warnings on the port outboard main drive," Loki warned.

"Get the shot, Josh!" Nathan urged.

"Five seconds!" Josh replied.

"How's our jump line?" Nathan asked.

"It's clear!" Loki replied.

"Missile launch!" Kaylah reported urgently. "Eight inbound from Battleship One! Ten seconds!"

The targeting piper on Josh's weapons screen turned green. "I've got a lock!" Josh declared. "Firing!"

Four sets of triplet plasma torpedoes leapt from the underside of the Aurora's nose, streaking across the ten kilometers separating the Aurora from the target. Two seconds later, they slammed into the cruiser's unprotected hull, blowing it open. Josh pressed the button again, holding it down and sending three more groups of triplets toward the doomed vessel.

"Escape jump!" Nathan barked. "NOW!"

"Jumping!" Loki replied as the blue-white jump flash washed over the bridge, yet again. "Jump complete."

"Fire in engineering section twenty!" Cameron reported.

"Evacuate and vent the entire section," Nathan ordered.

"We'll have to take the outboard port main drive offline," Cameron warned.

"That'll make our turns to port slow as hell," Josh complained.

"Damage Control, Captain," Nathan called over his comm-set. "How soon can you get fire teams to engineering twenty?"

"*Bulkheads one four seven and one five eight auto-sealed the moment the fire broke out,*" the chief explained. "*The only way to get a fire team in there is externally. Good news is, the Cheng automated everything down there, so no one is stationed in that section.*"

"Understood," Nathan replied. "Vent it," he instructed Cameron.

"Venting," Cameron replied.

"Helm, get us to the rally point," Nathan instructed.

"Turning to the rally point," Josh acknowledged.

"Cheng, Captain," Nathan called. "How long to restart port outboard main after the compartment is vented?"

"*I do not know,*" Vladimir admitted. "*When the port aft propellant tank blew, we lost all control and data links to that drive. I'm getting a repair team into pressure suits now. Once the fire is out, they can go in and reestablish the control links. Hopefully, that is all that is wrong.*"

"Get that engine up, Commander," Nathan ordered. "I don't like fighting with a limp."

"*Aye, sir!*"

"Jumping to rally point," Loki reported as the jump flash washed over the bridge.

"I think I can reroute power to the aft ventral shields," Cameron reported. "All but three of the emitters are still intact. It won't take more than one or two hits to knock it out again, but it's better than nothing."

"Do what you can," Nathan agreed.

"Two contacts!" Kaylah reported. "Lightnings!"

"Raise them," Nathan instructed Naralena.

"P-Seventy-Two Lightnings, this is the Aurora. How do you copy?" Naralena called over comms.

"*Aurora, this is Del Shelton of Subvert. How is it you know of us and our assets?*"

"Patch me in," Nathan ordered.

"You're connected," Naralena replied.

"Mister Shelton, this is Captain Nathan Scott of the Karuzari Alliance ship, Aurora. How we learned of your organization and its assets is a long story that I'd be happy to share with you later, assuming we all survive. For now, I need you to listen. Can you do that for me?"

After a moment, Del replied, "*Go ahead.*"

"The ships attacking you are the Dusahn. If they take your world, and its technology, we will be unable to stop them from growing and conquering the entire

338

galaxy. By ourselves, our chances of defeating those last two battleships are slim, at best. But with your help, I believe we have a chance to *save* your world."

"*We just lost two ships attacking a cruiser,*" Del replied. "*I don't see how we can be of help against two battleships.*"

"Your ships use the same type of gravity emitters as the Sugali fighters. When flown at extremely slow speeds, with their grav-lift systems at idle, they are able to pass *through* the Dusahn's shields. We've used them to get inside their shields and disable their shield emitters, allowing us to defeat *four* of their battleships."

"*And you believe our ships can also penetrate their shields,*" Del surmised.

"To be honest, we don't know for sure. In fact, you'd have to fly in backwards to make it work," Nathan told him.

"*Backwards?*"

After a moment of silence, Nathan continued. "I know it sounds crazy, but that's the reality of the situation."

Another moment of silence.

"*Captain Scott, I believe it only fair to tell you that SilTek Security has issued a level-one warrant for your arrest.*"

Jessica looked over at Dylan.

"Level one means 'dead or alive'," Dylan explained.

"*Our sources inside the government tell us that the Dusahn have promised to destroy our world unless we turn you over to them.*"

Nathan turned to Kaylah as he tapped his comm-set to mute it. "Keep a sharp eye out for contacts." He tapped his comm-set again and continued. "The Dusahn's jump range is very limited, so it had to have taken them weeks, if not months, to get here," he explained. "We only learned of your world about a week ago. So, the only way the Dusahn could know we were on your world would be if someone in *your* government *told* them."

"*Or someone in yours,*" Del replied.

"If you knew what my people have been through recently, you would not say that," Nathan assured him.

"*Fortunately for you, we of Subvert have little faith in our government, not since they began selling off our jump missile inventory, thus putting our own world at risk.*"

"Then, you'll help *us*, help *you*?" Nathan surmised.

"*I will, but I cannot speak for my cohort,*" Del replied.

"*I'm in,*" the other pilot replied.

"What is your name, sir?" Nathan asked.

"*Alair Hainen,*" the pilot replied. "*Why?*"

"I like to know the names of those who are willing to put their lives on the line for the sake of others."

"*Perhaps you can send us instructions on what we are to do,*" Del suggested. "*I am eager to get this over with so I can hear more about how you learned of us, and about your alliance.*"

"Thank you, Del," Nathan replied. "My helmsman has personally flown the Sugali fighters through the Dusahn shields. He will instruct you on the procedure," Nathan told him, snapping his fingers and pointing to Josh, signaling Naralena to patch Josh in.

"You're on, Josh," Naralena said.

Nathan walked over to Kaylah as Josh began explaining the procedure to the Subvert pilots. "How's it look?"

"They're still the only two contacts in the area," she replied. "But their shields are pitiful. There's no way they'll survive this."

"They have to use their swarm tech," Dylan said, having overheard them. "I'm sorry for eavesdropping, Captain, but... Well, they have to use the swarms."

"What exactly *are* the swarms?" Nathan asked.

"They're robots, kind of like spiders, with cutters and tiny plasma cannons. They're only about ten centimeters wide, but they're deadly as hell."

"They don't *sound* very deadly," Nathan disagreed.

"By themselves, no, but they use a *hive* AI. They work together to accomplish a goal. Once the Lightnings are inside the Dusahn's shields, they can release them. Then, they'll latch onto the enemy's hull, find their shield emitters, and bring them down."

"I doubt the Dusahn could even *target* anything that small," Cameron said, overhearing the conversation as she came up behind them. "*We* can't."

"If either one of those fighters comes anywhere near us, let me know," Nathan instructed Jessica.

"If they were going to use their swarms against you, they would've already done it," Dylan assured him.

"They're ready, Cap'n," Josh reported.

Nathan took a deep breath and sighed, tapping his comm-set to rejoin the conversation. "Gentlemen, my sensor officer informs me that your shields are inadequate against the Dusahn's weapons."

"*Yeah, we sort of figured that out, already,*" Del admitted.

"I believe your best chance of survival is to penetrate their shields, release your swarms with instructions to disable the target's shield emitters, and jump out as quickly as possible. If you remain within their weapons range for more than ten to fifteen seconds, well…"

"*Understood,*" Del replied. "*I'll want to hear about how you know about our swarm technology, as well, Captain.*"

"Deal," Nathan replied. "One Lightning per battleship. Go for their ventral side, just forward of their main propulsion heat exchangers. You'll have the fewest number of point-defenses on you, there."

"*Understood.*"

"We attack in two minutes," Nathan added. "Good luck."

"*To you, as well, Captain,*" Del replied.

"Helm, take us to a position directly above the targets, and set up for the attack jump," Nathan ordered.

"*Above?*"

"Yup."

"You got it," Josh replied.

"How are we doing on jump missiles?" Nathan asked Cameron.

"We've burned through half our load," Cameron replied.

Nathan sighed. "Then, we'll save them until the end," he decided. He looked over at Jessica as the Aurora jumped to its next turning point. "One shot, one kill."

"Damn right," she replied, smiling.

"Coming about to attack course," Josh reported.

"Attack jump in one minute," Loki announced.

"What's your plan B?" Cameron asked.

"I don't know…*ram them?*"

"Not funny," Cameron scolded.

Dylan looked concerned. "This will work, right?"

"You wrote the code, didn't you?" Nathan replied. "You tell me."

"I didn't *write* the code," Dylan insisted. "I just helped clean it up a bit."

"Why didn't you have the AI write the code?" Nathan wondered.

"AIs aren't allowed to sacrifice themselves," Dylan replied. "They're also not allowed to coordinate thought between AIs. That's one of their primary laws."

"And Subvert took it upon themselves to break it," Nathan surmised.

"They didn't have much of a choice," Dylan defended. "This attack confirms that."

"I suppose you're right," Nathan agreed.

"Coming up on attack jump," Loki reported.

Nathan returned to his command chair. "Let's do this," he confirmed as he took his seat.

"Jumping in three......two......one......jumping."

Nathan watched the main view screen as the blue-white flash washed over the bridge. In the blink of an eye, the view changed from the empty blackness of deep space to the image of SilTek filling the screen, with two small, long, black triangles making their way across it, a wave of impact explosions trailing behind them on the surface.

"Jump complete," Loki reported.

"Two battleships, dead ahead," Kaylah reported. "Twenty kilometers, passing from port to starboard."

"Any sign of our friends?" Nathan wondered.

"Negative," Kaylah replied.

"Maybe they're not as dumb as I thought," Jessica said half to herself.

"Wait, I have one of them. Just jumped in two

hundred meters from Battleship One. He's flying backwards and decelerating. He's..." Kaylah's tone changed. "He's gone. They shot him down."

"All turrets on Battleship One," Nathan instructed.

"What about Two?" Jessica asked.

"He jumped in too far out," Josh commented.

"We can't fire on him until the other P-Seventy-Two makes his attack run," Nathan explained.

"You have to arrive no more than fifty meters from their shield perimeter," Josh continued, "or you're still in their defense zone."

"You *told* them that, right?" Nathan asked.

"Of course, I told them," Josh defended. He looked at Loki. "I did, didn't I?"

"Yes, you did," Loki assured him. "I heard you."

"Battleship One is rolling to port," Jessica reported. "He's trying to protect his dorsal midship shields."

"Battleship Two is launching short-range missiles," Kaylah warned. "Eight inbound; fifteen seconds to impact."

"Engaging point-defenses," Jessica announced.

Nathan watched the main view screen as trails of point-defense cannon fire streaked toward the incoming missiles. "Helm, five degrees to port. Prepare to jump eight clicks."

"Five to port," Josh acknowledged, initiating the slight course change.

"Eight-click jump, ready," Loki added.

"Ten seconds to impact," Kaylah warned. "Battleship One is targeting us, as well."

"Where the hell is the other Lightning?" Cameron cursed as the first volley of energy weapons fire impacted the Aurora's shields, shaking them violently.

"He'll be here!" Dylan assured her, not sounding entirely convinced, himself.

"Five seconds to impact," Kaylah announced, her tone rising in urgency.

"Jump us," Nathan ordered.

"Jumping," Loki responded as the jump flash washed over the bridge.

"Ten degrees to starboard," Nathan ordered. "Helm has fire control. Target Battleship One and fire when ready."

"Helm trigger is hot," Jessica confirmed as Josh started his turn back to starboard.

"New contact!" Kaylah announced. "The other P-Seventy-Two just penetrated Battleship Two's starboard forward shields! He's flipping over and releasing something!"

"The swarm!" Dylan cried out as more incoming fire rocked the ship. "He's releasing his swarm!"

"We really need to think of a better name," Jessica grumbled. "Sounds like the title of a really bad creature vid."

"Firing!" Josh exclaimed as he sent the first wave of plasma torpedoes toward Battleship One.

"Target is reversing his roll," Kaylah warned.

"Oh, no, you don't," Josh muttered under his breath.

"Keep pounding him, Josh," Nathan urged.

"The other P-Seventy-Two is jump..." Kaylah stopped mid-sentence and sighed. "They took him out as he was jumping."

"Keep firing," Nathan ordered his helmsman. "What about the swarm?" he asked Kaylah.

"I saw them release, but I lost them in the background clutter off the surface of the battleship," Kaylah explained.

"Is there any change in their shields?" Nathan wondered as the ship rocked from more weapons fire.

"Negative," Kaylah replied.

"Forward shields are down to forty percent!" Cameron warned. "Average overall shield strength is down to fifty percent and falling."

"Battleship One is firing missiles!" Kaylah warned. "Seven seconds to impact!"

"Engaging with point-defenses!" Jessica reported.

"Hard to port and roll ninety!" Nathan ordered. "Escape jump as soon as your line is clear!"

"Hard rolling turn to port!" Josh acknowledged as he ceased fire and pushed his flight control stick hard to the left, pulling it back, as well, as he jammed the throttles forward.

"Three seconds!"

"She's turning slow!" Josh warned.

"Brace for impact!" Nathan announced.

Three explosions rocked the ship, nearly shaking Nathan out of his command chair.

"Clear line!" Loki announced as he pressed the jump button.

The jump flash washed over the Aurora's bridge, and the violent shaking stopped. For a moment, there was relative silence; with only the sounds of various alarms warning them of failing systems all over the ship.

Nathan took a breath and spoke. "Damage report."

"Port outboard engine is still offline," Cameron replied. "Forward shields are down to twenty percent, aft port ventral shields are still down. All other shields are at maximum of forty percent."

"What's our remaining jump range?"

"About fifty light years," Loki replied.

"Discontinue the recharge, and divert that power to shields," Nathan instructed.

"Then, we're going back in," Jessica surmised.

"I admit we have a chance at taking out Battleship One," Cameron said, "a few of their shield sections are already down, but Battleship Two is another story."

"We still have twenty jump missiles," Nathan reminded her.

"And they still have point-defenses," Cameron countered. "Even if *half* our jump missiles made it through their defenses, every single one would have to impact the same shield section to bring it down."

Nathan looked to Kaylah for confirmation.

"She's correct, sir," Kaylah told him. "The Dusahn's newer battleships have *very* good shields and *very* thick hulls."

Dylan stepped forward, forgetting about the Ghatazhak guard who was watching him. "You can't stop now," he insisted. "What about the swarm?"

"We don't even know if they made it to the hull," Cameron told him.

"You have to give them time," Dylan insisted. "This is their first use. They have no data on the enemy. It takes *time* for them to figure out *what* to do."

"How *much* time?" Nathan asked, turning to face Dylan.

"I don't know," Dylan admitted, looking at Nathan. "You *can't* let them conquer SilTek, you said so yourself."

"There is more at stake than just *your* world," Cameron told him, trying to appear sympathetic.

"Helm," Nathan began, still facing aft, "ninety to port, and jump five light minutes."

Josh paused a moment, exchanging a glance with Loki. "Ninety to port," he acknowledged as he initiated the turn.

"Five-light-minute jump," Loki added.

"Three-point, time-on-target attack," Nathan said to Cameron. "Four missiles per point. Two on each target. Set them to arrive one hundred meters outside their targets' shield perimeters. We jump in two seconds after impact, directly off Battleship One's starboard side, snap-launch four of them from five hundred meters, dive under, jump across to Battleship Two, and launch the last four from the same range." He looked at Kaylah again. "Will *that* be enough to bring down their shields?"

"It might," Kaylah replied.

"Assuming they don't miss," Cameron added.

"Turn complete," Josh reported.

"If they miss, we jump clear, put all power into recharging, and limp our way back home," Nathan promised.

"Jumping five light minutes," Loki announced.

"That's an awfully big risk," Cameron argued as the jump flash washed over the bridge.

"Jump complete," Loki reported.

"Bet big or go home," Nathan told her. "Helm, turn in toward the targets."

"Aye, sir," Josh acknowledged.

Cameron sighed. "Calculating a three-point, time-on-target attack," she reported as she began running the calculations.

"Then, you're not giving up?" Dylan asked.

"Not yet," Nathan replied, "but there's a very good chance that we'll have to, after this next attack pass."

"Loading targeting data and jump-delay timings

to first group," Cameron announced. "I've already sent the next two launch points to the helm."

"I've got them," Loki confirmed.

"First four missiles are ready to launch," Cameron reported.

"Start the attack clock and launch," Nathan instructed.

"Launching four," Cameron announced as she pressed the launch button. "Attack clock is running. Missiles away."

"Turning toward second launch point," Josh announced as he began a turn to starboard.

"Loading next group of missiles."

Jessica looked to Nathan, doubt in her eyes.

"Turn complete," Josh reported.

"Jumping to second launch point," Loki announced.

"This will work," Nathan assured her as the jump flash washed over the bridge.

"Jump complete."

"Turning back toward targets," Josh announced.

Jessica said nothing further, returning her attention to her tactical console, preparing for the final attack pass.

"On course for launch," Josh announced.

"Launching four," Cameron said, pressing the launch button. "Missiles away, loading next group of missiles."

"Turning to third launch point," Josh announced as the missiles sped away.

Nathan exchanged a glance with Dylan.

"The swarm will work," Dylan promised, seeing the doubt in Nathan's eyes. "I *know* it."

"Turn complete," Josh announced.

"Jumping to third launch point," Loki added.

"I hope you're right," Nathan said as the jump flash washed over them again. "I truly do."

"Jump complete."

"Turning toward targets," Josh announced.

Dylan leaned toward Naralena. "What's a *time-on-target* attack?"

"Missiles launched from different directions, arriving at the targets at the same time," Naralena explained.

"It makes it more difficult for the targets to defend against them," the Ghatazhak guard added, overhearing the conversation.

Dylan looked at the guard, surprised that the frightening-looking man had offered any information.

"On course and speed for final launch point," Josh reported.

"Move up the jump timing of the last group of missiles by ten seconds, and increase their arrival range to two clicks," Nathan instructed.

Cameron exchanged glances with Jessica. "Launching final group," Cameron reported as she pressed the launch button. "Missiles away. Jump time moved ahead by ten seconds, arrival point: two clicks."

"Turning toward attack jump point," Josh announced, initiating his turn.

"Loading next group of missiles," Cameron announced. "Set for snap jump."

"You're sacrificing four missiles as decoys," Jessica surmised.

"Turn complete," Josh reported.

"A deke before I take my shot," Nathan explained.

"Jumping," Loki announced.

"It used to work great when I was kid," Nathan added as the jump flash washed over them.

Jessica said nothing, only smiled.

"Jump complete," Loki announced.

"Turning to final attack jump course," Josh reported.

"Twenty seconds to attack jump," Loki added.

Dylan leaned toward Naralena again. "What's a deke?" he whispered.

Naralena shrugged her shoulders.

Dylan looked to the Ghatazhak guard.

"Third group is jumping now," Cameron announced.

"A deceptive move intended to cause one's opponent to execute a desired action, thus creating an opportunity to achieve an intended result."

"Right," Dylan replied, still confused.

"Jumping in five seconds," Loki announced. "Three......two......one......jumping."

Nathan took a deep breath, letting it out slowly as the jump flash washed over them.

"Jump complete," Loki announced as the first round of energy weapons slammed into their forward shields, shaking the bridge.

"No kidding," Josh grumbled, adjusting their course to bring the plasma torpedo tubes onto their target.

"Launch missiles," Nathan instructed calmly.

"Target lock!" Josh announced. "Firing on all tubes!"

"Launching missiles!" Cameron replied with equal demeanor.

"Firing all forward plasma turrets," Jessica added.

"Missiles away," Cameron reported.

The main view screen lit up as all four missiles jumped away after leaving the launch tubes. Red-orange bolts of plasma energy flew back and forth between the two ships as each tried to subdue the other. A split second after the jump missiles flashed away, they reappeared, right at the edge of Battleship One's shield perimeter, resulting in brilliant yellow-white explosions as they detonated, dumping all their energy into the enemy warship's shields.

"Reloading jump missiles," Cameron reported.

"Battleship One's shields are failing!" Kaylah exclaimed.

"Dive under the target," Nathan ordered. "Pitch up and hit them with all tubes as we pass under."

"Diving under!" Josh replied, pushing his flight control stick forward.

Nathan watched as the beleaguered Dusahn battleship slid up the main view screen; the exchange of energy weapons fire continuing. As the warship began to slide overhead, Josh pulled back on his flight control stick, pitching the ship back upwards, causing the image of the battleship to slide back down to center.

"I'm picking up fluctuations in Battleship Two's shields!" Kaylah reported.

"Which ones?" Nathan asked eagerly.

"*All* of them!" she replied. "There are detonations occurring all over their hull, right where their shield emitters are located!"

"It's the swarm!" Dylan exclaimed, his excitement getting the best of him, charging forward to the edge of the tactical console. "It's working!"

"Target lock reestablished!" Josh announced. "Firing!"

"Pound them, Josh!" Nathan urged.

Josh said nothing, his focus on his flight controls, keeping the Aurora's nose pointed at the battleship as they passed under it. Only once did he glance up at the main view screen, resulting in a satisfied grin at the sight of the underside of the mighty warship being torn open by his plasma torpedoes.

"Battleship One is breaking up!" Kaylah reported.

"Helm, pitch back down, tubes to bear on the second battleship," Nathan ordered urgently. "Jump us to five hundred meters off their starboard beam."

"Bringing tubes to bear on the second battleship!" Josh replied as he ceased firing and pushed the Aurora's nose back down toward her path of flight.

"Stand by to..."

The Aurora pitched downward sharply as something slammed into her topside. The main view screen flickered and then went black.

"What the hell happened?" Nathan demanded.

"We've collided with a large part of Battleship One!" Jessica replied.

"One is coming apart...*violently*!" Kaylah warned.

"Jump us forward!" Nathan ordered.

"We're losing power on all decks!" Cameron announced.

"We're losing all shields!" Jessica added.

"Multiple hull breaches on..."

"Jumping!" Loki replied as the jump flash washed over them.

"...decks B and C," Cameron finished.

"Jump complete!"

"Launch missiles!" Nathan ordered as the main view screen flickered and then came back to life, revealing the starboard side of the massive second battleship growing larger with each passing second.

"Both cats are down!" Cameron added. "Unable to launch!"

"Jump them in the tubes!" Nathan instructed.

"If they so much as brush the sides of the launch tubes on their way out..." Cameron warned.

"DO IT!" Nathan insisted.

"Jumping all four in the tubes!" Cameron replied as she pressed the snap jump button.

Four blue-white flashes of light appeared before them, immediately turning into yellow-white flashes as the missiles impacted the hull of the second battleship and detonated a split second after coming out of their jump. The battleship's midsection cracked open, prompting a series of secondary explosions deep within the doomed vessel.

"Missile launches on the surface!" Kaylah reported.

"We are too close to the target!" Cameron warned. "If one of those missiles misses..."

"Helm," Nathan barked, "pitch up to a clear jump line and get us the hell out of here!"

"I can't!" Josh replied, trying to get his flight controls to respond. "I've lost all maneuvering! All I've got are the mains!"

"Then, plow through them!" Nathan ordered.

"*Captain!*" Jessica exclaimed, "Our *shields* are *down!*"

"No choice," Nathan replied, pressing the ship-wide button on the comm-panel, on the right arm of his command chair.

"Surface missiles have jumped!" Kaylah reported.

"All hands! Brace for impact!" Nathan announced, clutching the armrests.

The main view screen flashed multiple times with blue-white light as a wave of surface-launched jump missiles slammed into the underside of the last Dusahn battleship, breaking it apart into multiple sections and sending debris, both large and small, in all directions.

The Aurora shook violently as it plowed through the debris field, unprotected. Equipment shorted out all over the bridge, and overhead ducting and conduits ripped from their mounts and came crashing down. Within seconds, the bridge was filled with acrid smoke, and the lights had gone out, leaving only the faint illumination of the emergency, battery-powered lighting. Then, as suddenly as it had started, it stopped.

Nathan found himself on the floor, a large section of the overhead air duct on top of him. Every inhalation made him choke. His eyes stung from the smoke, forcing him to keep them closed.

A whirring sound started, becoming louder in seconds, and the smoke quickly cleared. Someone lifted up the ducting from him and grabbed his left hand, pulling him from the floor.

Nathan opened his eyes, revealing Loki standing in front of him.

"Are you okay?" Loki asked.

"Yeah," Nathan replied. "I think so." He looked around briefly. "Where'd the smoke go?"

"Emergency ventilators," Loki reminded him. "Are you sure you're alright?"

"Yeah, I'm good," Nathan insisted. He looked to the helm where Josh was pushing fallen debris aside so he could return to his station. "Sound off!" he barked, his eyes still burning.

"XO!" Cameron barked from behind him.

"Helm!" Josh replied.

"Ops!" Loki followed.

Nathan looked toward Kaylah, expecting her to sound off. She was slumped forward, her body draped over her console. Nathan stepped over a fallen beam to reach her, pulling her back carefully. Her head was smashed, and her neck was broken.

"Nathan!" Cameron yelled, grave concern in her tone.

Then it dawned on him. *Jessica.*

Nathan turned aft, quickly climbing back over the fallen beam to make his way through. He stepped over the lifeless bodies of both the Ghatazhak guard and Dylan, finally coming up behind Cameron, who was crouched over Jessica's unmoving body.

Nathan stepped over to Jessica's opposite side, falling to his knees beside her. He stared at her for a moment, his mouth agape in disbelief. "Oh, my God, no," he whispered. "Jess."

Jessica's eyes opened, a blank stare in them. She coughed, blood sputtering up from her mouth, a gurgling wheeze coming from her with each labored breath. "Nathan?"

Nathan reached down for her, carefully lifting her upper torso, and cradling her head and shoulders in his arms as he shifted to a seated position on the deck next to her. "I'm here," he told her, his eyes welling up. "I'm here."

She coughed again, spraying blood everywhere, her eyes still a blank stare. She tried to laugh, but only gagged on her own blood. "I guess...you can... kill a Nash," she commented. She reached up with her bloody right hand, putting it to Nathan's cheek. "Don't ever give up, Nathan. Promise me..."

Nathan swallowed hard, fighting back his tears. "I promise," he whispered as she passed. He pulled her into his chest, sobbing. "What have I done?"

Cameron put her hand on his shoulder. "You did what you *had* to."

Nathan looked up at her, desperation in his eyes.

"She knew the risks," Cameron whispered. "We all did."

Nathan fought to suppress his grief, pushing it back down inside him, remembering Jessica's last words.

Never give up.

He gently placed her head and torso back down on the deck and then struggled back to his feet. "Helm, report," he finally managed to say.

"We're dead stick," Josh replied. "No maneuvering, no mains."

"Something has pushed us off course, as well," Loki added. "We're going down."

"Naralena is dead, too."

Nathan took a breath. "How long?"

"It's kind of hard to tell," Loki replied. "My best guess is that we'll hit atmo in a few minutes, at most."

Nathan tapped his comm-set. "Vlad, you still with us?"

"*Yes, I am here,*" Vladimir replied, "*surprisingly.*"

"How bad?"

"*Very, and yourself?*"

"Very," Nathan replied. "Jessica is dead, along with Kaylah and Naralena."

"*Bozhe moi,*" Vladimir exclaimed. "*I am so sorry, Nathan.*"

"We're going down, Vlad," Nathan told him, barely holding his grief at bay. "I need a miracle."

After a moment of silence, Vladimir responded. "*I don't think that is possible,*" he admitted, "*but I will try. I might be able to restore maneuvering, but it will not be much.*"

"I *need* the mains so I can accelerate to a higher orbit," Nathan told him.

"*That is impossible,*" Vladimir told him. "*We took a direct hit aft. Both inboards are destroyed, and the starboard outboard is leaking propellant all over its bay. If I try a restart, it will explode and take out the entire stern.*"

"Understood," Nathan replied, tapping his comm-set to end the call. He looked to Cameron.

"It worked," Cameron told him. "We saved SilTek."

Nathan looked down at Jessica's lifeless body. "But at what price?"

"What are your orders, Captain?" Cameron asked.

Nathan looked at Cameron, then over at Josh and Loki. Finally, he made his way back to his command chair, stepping over the fallen beam, yet again.

Josh and Loki watched their captain as he pressed the ship-wide button on the comm-panel of his chair and then tapped his comm-set. "Attention all hands, this is the captain. Abandon ship...... abandon ship......abandon ship."

"Nathan..." Cameron began.

"There's no other option, and you know it," Nathan insisted. "All of you get into the escape pods," he instructed, pointing aft.

"What about you?" Cameron asked, already knowing the answer. "Don't even try to pull that '*the captain goes down with the ship*' crap."

"Someone has to try and find a way to steer the ship toward an unpopulated area," Nathan explained. "It might as well be me."

"No offense, Captain, but I'm a much better pilot than you," Josh insisted.

"This isn't a debate, Josh," Nathan replied.

"Nathan, the alliance *needs* its leader. It *needs* Na-Tan."

Nathan smiled. "*You* are their leader now. You and General Telles. Get SilTek to build you another ship, a *new* Aurora. Use it to defeat the Dusahn once and for all. Just promise me one thing; once you defeat them, return to Earth and avenge my family. Take *down* that bastard Galiardi."

"I'm not promising any such thing," Cameron argued. "You're being stupid..."

"I'm already on my second life, Cam," Nathan interrupted, "one that I didn't *deserve*. I cannot ask any of *you* to sacrifice yourselves. I just can't."

"What about the AI?" Josh suggested.

"I can't take that risk," Nathan insisted.

"I'm not going anywhere," Cameron stated firmly.

In one smooth, fluid motion, Nathan pulled the stunner they had taken from one of the SilTek Security officers, raised it, and fired at Cameron, dropping her to the floor.

"What the fuck are you doing?" Josh blurted out in surprise.

"She's only stunned," Nathan replied. "Now, both of you grab her and carry her into an escape pod, and get the hell off this ship, or I'll stun the both of you and drag you there myself."

Loki said nothing, moving aft to follow his captain's orders.

Nathan nodded respectfully to Loki as he passed, conveying his thanks. "Josh?"

"You can't ask me to do this," Josh pleaded.

"I'm sorry, Josh, I must. You were right, you *are* a better pilot than me, and the new Aurora is going to need the best pilot around."

"She's gonna need the best *captain* around, as well," Josh insisted.

"And she'll have her," Nathan replied. "Now go, while there's still time."

Josh looked down at the deck for a moment, then back up again, a tear in his eye. "I'll never forget you, Nathan," he said, raising his right hand to his forehead and saluting his captain... *his friend.*

Nathan, saying nothing, returned Josh's salute. He stood fast, watching the image of the planet rising up toward them on the main view screen as Josh joined Loki in carrying Cameron to an escape pod.

Nathan sat down at the Aurora's helm, pausing to orient himself to the console. It had been years since he had first piloted this ship, and much had changed. "Aurora?" he called, hoping for some help, but got no response.

His console was covered with flashing red lights, warning him of a multitude of failed systems. He began trying to address the failed maneuvering systems but got nowhere. "Great," he muttered just as the plot display began working, and Nathan realized that his ship was heading into a heavily populated area, just as he had feared.

"*I apologize for the delay,*" the Aurora's AI said over Nathan's comm-set.

"Why are you on comm-sets?" Nathan wondered as he continued to try rerouting systems to regain flight control of his ship.

"*This ship is heavily damaged,*" the Aurora explained. "*I was unable to reroute around all of the failed intercom circuits, but I did manage to create a bridge between my ship's communications system and yours.*"

Nathan looked concerned. "Did my entire crew hear the order to abandon ship?"

"*The ship-wide circuit uses a protocol that confirms that every intercom speaker has successfully replayed the order. Eighty-four percent of the intercom stations confirmed replay of the order and those that did not were in non-critical areas. I believe it is safe to assume that everyone heard your order.*"

"Are you able to tell if everyone has made it off the ship?" Nathan wondered.

"*I can try, but again, many of the ship's systems have failed. So far, twelve escape pods have launched. Current crew compliment requires eighteen pods for complete evacuation. Four pods are in active boarding, and I have no connection with the other eleven pods on board.*"

"Understood," Nathan replied.

"*I should warn you, Captain, that on our current trajectory, we will crash-land in the middle of the Wellsley district. I estimate casualties to be in the tens of thousands.*"

"Yeah, I already figured that out," Nathan replied. "Anything you can do to get maneuvering back?"

"*Negative,*" the Aurora replied. "*However, running one of the ship's zero-point energy devices at one hundred and fifty percent would create a gravity well. My calculations show that, if the device is ejected while at this power level, it should alter our trajectory enough to move our point of impact to an unpopulated area.*"

"Should?"

"*There is a sixty-three percent probability of success,*" the Aurora replied.

"Risks?" Nathan wondered.

"*An implosion event that could tear the ship apart, increasing the size of the impact area.*"

"Will that increase the number of casualties?"

"*If the ship breaks up into smaller pieces, the mass of those individual pieces will be less than the whole, therefore those who are properly sheltered have a much better chance of survival,*" the Aurora explained. "*However, the casualty rate will still be in the thousands.*"

"Then, let's do it," Nathan decided.

"*I cannot comply,*" the Aurora replied. "*I do not have access to those systems.*"

"I grant you access," Nathan insisted.

"*I meant, I do not have physical access to those systems,*" the Aurora explained.

"Then, why the hell did you even bring it up?" Nathan wondered, becoming frustrated.

"*Because I believe someone is already attempting to make this happen,*" the Aurora explained.

"How do you know? I thought you said you don't have access to those systems."

"*I do not,*" the Aurora replied. "*However, I do have access to the status of power generation on this ship, and the port reactor has increased its output to one hundred and fifty percent. It is incapable of doing this without human intervention, as there are multiple safety protocols in place to prevent this from happening. Someone must have overridden those protocols.*"

Nathan tapped his comm-set. "Vlad, where are you?"

"*Power generation,*" Vladimir replied.

"Why aren't you in an escape pod?"

"*I cannot do this from an escape pod, Nathan. Even you should know this.*"

"I gave you a direct order to abandon ship," Nathan stated sternly.

"*I did not hear such an order,*" Vladimir replied.

"*The intercoms in engineering confirmed replay of your order to abandon ship,*" the Aurora reported.

"*She's lying,*" Vladimir insisted, fighting back a laugh.

The ship began to vibrate, only slightly, at first, but increasing in intensity with each passing second.

"*We are entering the planet's upper atmosphere,*" the Aurora reported. "*Hull temperature is at one thousand degrees Kelvin and rising.*"

"Vlad, get to an escape pod...*now!*" Nathan instructed. "That's an *order!*"

"*Do you want to waste time giving orders that we both know I will not follow, or do you want to try to save tens of thousands of people?*" Vladimir asked. "*This cannot be done from the bridge, Nathan.*"

"Aurora?"

"*The commander is correct,*" the Aurora confirmed. "*Manual overrides of safety protocols can only be done at the directly connected control console.*"

"Damn it, Vlad!" Nathan exclaimed.

"*Nathan, this is my job,*" Vladimir told him. "*This is how it should be. If we must go down, we go down together.*"

"*Starboard reactor output is also increasing,*" the Aurora reported. "*Passing one hundred and thirty percent.*"

"What are you doing, Vlad?"

"*Giving us a second shot, in case the first one isn't enough,*" Vladimir replied.

"Remind me to bust you back down to ensign, *if* we survive this," Nathan said as the shaking became more violent.

Vladimir laughed. "*We are not going to survive this, my friend.*"

"*Hull temperature at two thousand degrees Kelvin,*" the Aurora reported. "*Four minutes to impact. If you intend to attempt a course correction using the zero-point device, you must do so within the next ninety-seven seconds.*"

"Vlad, are you ready?" Nathan asked over comm-sets.

"*I am ready,*" Vladimir confirmed.

Nathan paused for a moment, closing his eyes, holding onto the sides of his console as his ship shook violently. "How do we do this?"

"*You must eject the port reactor from the ops panel,*" Vladimir explained. "*The ejection controls are located outside of the compartment, and I must remain here to prevent the reactor from automatically shutting down upon ejection.*"

Nathan quickly got out of Josh's seat on the right side of the helm and stumbled over to Loki's seat to the left. "Okay, I'm ready."

"*Eject the port reactor,*" Vladimir instructed.

Nathan took a deep breath and pressed the button. A warning light flashed, requiring him to push the button a second time, which he did.

"*The reactor is ejecting!*" Vladimir reported.

Nathan glanced at the plot display at the center of the helm, looking for a change. At first, nothing happened, but then the dotted line shifted slightly, indicating a minor change in their trajectory. "Did it work?"

"*Our trajectory has changed. However, the effect was insufficient. Impact point is still in a populated area,*" the Aurora reported.

"We have to try again!" Nathan shouted, the shaking becoming louder and more violent.

"*Based on the results of the first attempt, I recommend that you increase the output of the second reactor to one hundred and eighty percent of maximum before ejection,*" the Aurora suggested.

"*The reactor will not hold at that level,*" Vladimir warned.

"So, we die two minutes sooner!" Nathan replied.

"*Thirty seconds to trajectory threshold,*" the Aurora reported.

"Do it!" Nathan ordered.

"*Increasing output on starboard reactor,*" Vladimir replied.

"*Starboard reactor at one hundred and sixty percent, and rising,*" the Aurora reported.

Nathan studied the flickering main view screen, catching glimpses of the surface of SilTek rushing toward him.

"*Starboard reactor at one hundred and seventy percent, and rising.*"

"*Stand by to eject starboard reactor!*" Vladimir warned.

"*Starboard reactor at one hundred and seventy-five percent,*" the Aurora reported. "*Core containment is failing.*"

"*Eject, eject, eject!*" Vladimir yelled.

Nathan pressed the ejection button again, then pressed it a second time to confirm. The ship lurched, jumping upward sharply as it continued to fall toward the surface.

"*Starboard reactor breached during ejection,*" the Aurora reported.

"VLAD!" Nathan cried out.

"*Reactor compartment has been destroyed.*"

The plot display shifted again, catching Nathan's attention. "Our trajectory changed!" he exclaimed. "Did we do it?"

"*Affirmative,*" the Aurora confirmed. "*Impact point is now at the edge of the Wellsley district, in a predominantly unpopulated area. Casualties should be minimal.*"

"We did it, my friend," Nathan said to himself, hoping that somehow Vlad heard him.

"*One minute to impact,*" the Aurora reported.

"How many escape pods have launched?" Nathan asked somberly.

"*All sixteen escape pods that I am able to monitor have launched safely. Whether or not they made it to the surface, I am unable to determine due to the amount of damage to the ship's sensors.*"

"Let's just assume they all made it," Nathan said.

"*As you wish, Captain,*" the Aurora replied. "*My ship's communications systems are able to get a message out, if need be.*"

Nathan sighed. "That will not be necessary."

"*Thirty seconds to impact,*" the Aurora announced. "*It has been an honor serving you, Captain Scott.*"

Nathan laughed to himself. "Thank you, Aurora... for *everything.*"

Nathan stared at the flickering view screen, now able to make out some of the buildings on the surface as the planet slid past. Suddenly, his mind was filled with memories: his childhood, his parents, his sisters, and his brother, whose life he was forced to take.

Of Jessica.

At least, he would not have to deal with the pain of losing her for long.

Nathan closed his eyes, preparing himself for his

final demise. There would be no resurrection this time.

There was a sudden, deafening, unidentifiable sound; a combination of twisting and tearing of metal. Nathan's hands flew up to protect his face as debris came flying toward him from all directions. He was thrown forward into the helm console, causing a sharp, overwhelming pain in his back. He felt his left arm being broken and his left leg being twisted off. At the same time, something tore free and fell on him as something else slammed into his face, bending his head backward, snapping his neck, and ending his suffering.

* * *

There was darkness. Complete, all-consuming darkness. No light, no sound, no smell, no sensations whatsoever. Yet, there was awareness.

But of what?

Who am I? Where am I? What am I?

The darkness faded, a flicker of light cutting through it, pushing it aside. With it came sight, then sound, then touch and smell, and finally...

I am Nathan Scott, and I am alive.

Nathan opened his eyes, uncertain of both surroundings and events. Then, it all came back to him.

I should be dead.

"Nathan?"

A woman's voice; distant; familiar...

Nathan turned his head in the direction of the voice, forcing his eyes to open.

"*It takes a moment to come back to reality,*" the female voice told him.

"Jessica?" Nathan asked in disbelief. "You're alive?"

"Yes, I'm alive," she replied, her voice becoming clear. "We *both* are."

Nathan's eyes finally focused. He smiled, willing his hand to raise and touch her cheek. "You're alive," he said again, this time as a statement of fact, rather than a question in disbelief, and tears began streaming down his cheeks. "How is it possible?"

"It wasn't real," she explained, putting her hand on his. "It was all a simulation."

"I apologize for putting you through the simulation, Captain," a man's voice stated.

Nathan struggled to sit up; Jessica immediately gave him a hand. He looked around, realizing that he was back in the quarantine suite, still wearing the clothing they had been provided when he and Jessica had arrived. He noticed the man standing at the foot of his bed. He looked to be in his late thirties and was wearing the uniform of the SilTek security services. To his right was Caitrin Bindi, Ariana Batista's assistant, and to his left was Orana, the android nurse. "Who are you?"

"I am General Pellot, chief of SilTek Security and advisor to Missus Batista. Again, I apologize for putting you through such a grueling simulation. For the record, Missus Batista was against this, but I insisted."

Nathan stood, moving toward the foot of the bed. "This was all *your* idea?"

"It was," the general replied. "We had to be certain of your intentions, as well as your honor."

Nathan stepped up to the general, looking him in the eyes. "I assume I passed?"

"Indeed," the general replied. "Your honor is now without question."

"You son of a bitch," Nathan exclaimed as he

punched the general in the mouth, sending him to the floor. "*Now* my honor is without question!" he added, pointing to the general as he lay on the floor, holding his jaw.

CHAPTER ELEVEN

After a day in quarantine, two days in the simulation from hell, a day of apologies, and a week of negotiations, Nathan and Jessica were more than ready to return home.

"*Captain Scott!*" a woman called from behind them as they headed across the bay to their shuttle.

Nathan turned around, spotting Miss Bindi at the entrance. "I'll catch up to you," he told Jessica.

"I'll get the ship fired up, but don't be long," she insisted. "I've had more than enough of this place."

"You and me both," Nathan chuckled, turning back to speak with Miss Bindi.

"I won't delay you," Miss Bindi assured him as he approached. "I just wanted to convey our thanks, once again. You have given our leaders, and likely our entire world, *hope.*"

"*Hope?*" Nathan wondered.

"Indeed," she replied. "Missus Batista would never admit to this, of course, but it is true, nonetheless. The people of SilTek *believe* in peace."

"Yet, you *make* weapons of war," Nathan pointed out. "Quite formidable ones, at that."

"We understand the nature of humanity. We are a violent species. Without the *threat* of great suffering, there is no *incentive* to avoid it. This is both the curse and the blessing of humanity. The curse is our ability to wage war, and the blessing is having people, such as yourself, who understand this duality, accept it, and try to use it for the good of all."

"One man is not enough," Nathan told her.

"But one man *is* a start," she replied. "Safe travels,

Captain Scott. If there is anything I can ever do for you, you but need ask."

Nathan nodded, then turned to continue to his shuttle, but stopped and turned back around. "There is one thing," Nathan said. "I meant to ask this before but forgot. I know that Lieutenant Commander Nash shared the same simulation with me, but were we the *only* two people in that simulation?"

"If you are asking about Dylan, then the answer is yes, he was a real person, and he took part in the simulation with you. It was necessary to maintain the level of realism."

"I see," Nathan nodded. "Is he really a wannabe hacker?"

Miss Bindi smiled. "He is my son, and yes, he is."

Nathan smiled, nodding again. "I'd like to meet him someday...for *real.*"

"I'm sure he'd like that."

Nathan spoke nothing further as he walked across the bay to his shuttle and climbed aboard.

"What did she want?" Jessica asked as Nathan climbed into the pilot's seat next to her.

"Just to wish us a safe flight," Nathan said, taking his seat. "You were right, by the way," he added as he set the auto-flight for remote operation.

"About what?" Jessica wondered.

"Dylan *is* a real person, and he *was* in the sim with us."

"I told you."

"Bayside Departure, Karuzari Shuttle, ready for departure," he called over comms.

"*Karuzari Shuttle, Bayside. Auto-flight link confirmed. We'll take you out to your departure jump point and then hand control back to you, Captain.*"

"Understood," Nathan replied.

The shuttle rose gently off the deck, rotated ninety degrees to starboard, and then began to climb as the roof slid open.

"It counted," Nathan said as their shuttle pitched up and accelerated toward the sky.

"No, it didn't," Jessica argued.

"We were both in the sim *together*."

"There was no *actual* physical contact, so the sex did *not* happen."

"Oh, it happened," Nathan insisted, smiling.

Thank you for reading this story.
(*A review would be greatly appreciated!*)

COMING SOON

**Episode 13
of
The Frontiers Saga:
Rogue Castes**

Visit us online at
frontierssaga.com
or on Facebook

Want to be notified when
new episodes are published?
Want access to additional scenes and more?
Join our mailing list!

frontierssaga.com/mailinglist/

Made in the USA
Las Vegas, NV
11 August 2022

53090443R00217